MW01113640

4TH AND starlight

A FANTASY & SCI-FI ANTHOLOGY
EDITED BY M. ELIZABETH TICKNOR

"Lavender Footsteps" by Mike Wyant, Jr. first published in *The Colored Lens's* Summer 2019 issue.

"Hand of Fate" by K. L. Schwengel is original to *4th and Starlight.*

"Cold, Silent, and Dark" by Kary English first published in *Undercurrents: An Anthology of What Lies Beneath* in March 2018.

"The Long Con" by Philip Brian Hall is original to *4th and Starlight.*

"Guardian" by Rebecca Birch first published in *The Grantville Gazette: Universe Annex* in January 2013.

"Fossil Fuel" by Van Alrik first published in *Helios Quarterly Magazine* in December 2016.

"No Shit" by Kristy Evangelista first published in *Twelfth Planet Press's Defying Doomsday* anthology in 2016.

"The Mourning Woman" by Preston Dennett is original to *4th and Starlight.*

"Sole Possession" by T. J. Knight is original to *4th and Starlight.*

"Chasing the Sun" by Y. M. Pang is original to *4th and Starlight.*

"Scars of Sentiment" by M. Elizabeth Ticknor first published in Flame Tree Press's *Epic Fantasy* anthology in 2019.

"Whose Waters Never Fail" by Rebecca E. Treasure first published in Flame Tree Press's *A Dying Planet* anthology in 2020.

"Green Army Men" by Alicia Cay is original to *4th and Starlight.*

"The Right Decision" by Van Alrik first published in *The Colored Lens* in August 2014.

"Two Tickets to Tomorrow" by Julia Ashley is original to *4th and Starlight.*

"Cold Logic" by John D. Payne first published in the *Cursed Collectibles* anthology in 2019.

"Departure Gate 34B" by Kary English first published in *Daily Science Fiction* in August 2014.

"As Sunlight Grabs Me" by Rachelle Harp first published in *Galaxy's Edge* in September 2017.

"Laila Tov: Good Night" by Robert B. Finegold, MD, first published in *Cosmic Roots and Eldritch Shores* in October 2016.

ISBN-13: 978-1-958484-00-5

Illustrations on pages 22, 40, 58, 106, 132, 150, 188, 230, 236, and 270 by Leah Ning. https://leahning.com

Cover art and illustrations on pages vii, 48, 72, 102, 170, 202, 220, 262, 278, and 290 by M. Elizabeth Ticknor. https://ticknortales.com

Typesetting and interior design by M. R. Cotrofeld.

Visit us at http://www.futurefinalists.com/anthologies/

For my husband, Frankie,
Who unflinchingly supports all my creative endeavors
&
For my children, Frank and Nathan,
Who made me the mother of dragons

Table of Contents

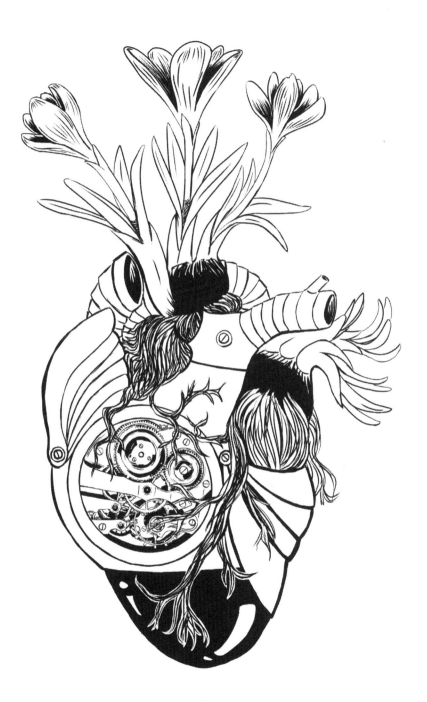

Introduction: Taking the Scenic Route

M. Elizabeth Ticknor

THIS ANTHOLOGY HAS BEEN IN the works for a long time — I first agreed to take on the project in March of 2018. I was nervous, but excited to follow in the footsteps of my fellow editors who had come before. The first three anthologies had come out more or less annually, and I was eager to continue the trend.

However, within a matter of weeks of announcing my intention to edit the anthology, I discovered I was pregnant with twins.

The next twenty months passed in a blur; a good deal happened in my life, though only an unfortunately small amount of that related to the anthology. As time went on, I found bits of time I could carve here and there for minor writing-related pursuits. The editorial mindset, on the other hand, proved frustratingly elusive — but no matter how busy I got, no matter how difficult it was for me to focus on the anthology, I couldn't quite bring myself to let it go. I didn't want to let my friends, my fellow authors, down.

In the wake of the twins' first birthday, I finally felt ready to step up and get things done. I researched what I needed to do in order to make the dream of publishing *4th and Starlight* a reality. When February of 2020 rolled around, I attended the Superstars Writing Seminar and took every self-publishing-related class I could find. I returned home flush with knowledge, action plan in hand.

Then March of 2020 arrived, bearing the dubious gifts of lockdown and isolation.

My initial instinct was to put the anthology on hold until the pandemic was over. After all, raising twin toddlers during the rise of COVID-19 was hellishly difficult — and this was only going to last a few weeks. *Right?*

But weeks turned into months, and months compounded on each other, stretching and distorting themselves in strange and eldritch ways. Long before we approached the one year mark, I realized that waiting to finish the anthology until the pandemic ended might mean waiting forever. I started pushing again, taking things at whatever pace proved necessary to maintain my sanity. Sometimes that pace was glacial, but glacial progress was better than none.

And now, dear reader, here we are. Thank you for meeting me at the crossroads of *4th and Starlight*. For me, this is the end of a long but ultimately worthwhile expedition — much of it uphill. For you, however, the journey is merely beginning. I hope you find it an enjoyable one.

Lavender Footsteps

Mike Wyant, Jr.

E M IS MISSING.

Frigid rain falls across the forest. Droplets tip-tap on fallen logs, stubborn snow, and black leaves like it's a tin roof. The crisp stink of rotting leaves fills my nose. Rolling thunder tells me a storm is coming. I need to hurry.

And I am. I'm being reckless as I run through the skeletal forest, the stink of rotting wood and decaying leaves around me. The sting of bare branches are lines of fire on my skin as I sprint.

I found their tracks. Em's and her two tiny robots, Tony and Joe. But I found the tracks of something, else, too. A panther.

Em's mother, Kammy, is a kilometer to my west, several acres of damn near impassable forest between us. In addition to looking for Em out that way, she's securing the sensors we have monitoring our larger fields against scavengers. We'd have swapped spots if I was any good with the tech. *God knows you're all thumbs with these things, Olinda,* Kammy always says. I should've sent our security bot, Taylor, out with her. Just in case.

A worm of worry wiggles into my mind. I banish it. I'll check in with her via walkie talkie after I find Em.

For now, I run.

My heartbeat is in my ears, a pounding timpani accompanying the snare of the rain drops. Little disturbances stand out against the background morass like hot spots on a heating coil — a footprint here, a broken branch there.

A deep paw print stands out in the mud. Four inches wide, but shallower than it should be. A large beast, then. Probably hungry. Starving.

Musk breaks across my nostrils. I know I'm close, but Em's cooing whisper brings me up short.

She's kneeling next to a fallen log in a crisscrossed mass of old trees. Everything is covered with a thick bed of gray moss and stubborn snow. Her little robots, Tony and Joe, stand next to her. Tony looks like a hodgepodge assemblage of branches and bits of wire, more a scarecrow than droid. Joe is dented like a used cymbal. Cyan smears coat his foot-tall body; the rest of it gleams gold in the remaining sunlight.

It's colder here. Barely feels like the sun is breaking through the tangled branches above, despite the shafts of light. Em's breath mists around her head as she speaks to something in the log. Like her mother, she's tiny. Less than four feet tall and thin as a rail, Em looks the way Kammy must've looked as a kid. Same hair, too, though Em lets it hang out in a ponytail to her butt.

The panther is almost on her. It's a massive beast, nearly seven feet long from nose to tail, but gaunt; all hard edges and bones. Patches of feverish skin shine through its tawny coat.

The wind shifts suddenly. I smell the lavender Kammy brushes into my hair. The panther's fur ruffles. The sharp, sterile scent of winter blows away the stink of mud and rotted leaves for a moment — and takes my scent with it. The panther's massive head turns toward me, black nostrils flaring.

Fear shoots up my spine, but I don't run. Instead, I drop into a crouch. It turns and leaps at me, both paws swatting, long transparent claws flashing in the fading light.

"Gotcha!" Em yells in triumph, just as the big cat hits me.

We slam into the ground hard, a cacophony of breaking branches and crisped leaves, knocking the air from my lungs. I wrench the panther's front paw around until it snaps. The panther makes a high-pitched squeal. A rear claw catches me in the stomach; that sharp tug blossoms into searing pain.

The beast swats wildly, kicking, tearing. Its jaws snap in the air. I mount it like it's a miniature horse.

Em screams from somewhere, but I can't look.

I wrap my arm around the panther's neck and pull as hard as I can. A crack echoes through the woods. The body goes still beneath me.

I slide off its back, gasping, and fall into the muddy snow. Em stands over me, tanned face flushed from the cold and panic.

"You're bleeding," Em says, dropping to her knees and pushing on the wound. "Gotta keep pressure on it. We need bandages."

I stroke her hair as she mumbles, the scent of her, lavender and autumn wind, washing over me and mingling with the musk of the dead panther. A flush of flowers and death.

"You're... not bleeding," Em whispers. She pulls away bloody hands. Cautiously, I sit up. "I guess not?"

There's a hole in my thick winter jacket where the panther tore into me with his back paws. There's blood, too, a lot of it... but only a small slash, like someone cut me with a pocketknife. It's sore, but that's all. I get to my feet, grunting.

Em steadies me. "Must've hit a vein or something."

Then I look at Em and her smile fades, eyes dropping to the ground. "What the hell are you doing out here?"

"Hide and Seek," Em mumbles.

Lightning flashes. Thunder pounds soon after. The storm is getting close.

"You could've been killed out here," I say, pointing at the panther. "By that, specifically."

"Well, yeah, but — "

"But what?" I cross my arms.

Em grins and runs over to the downed tree she'd been crouched in front of when I arrived. Joe and Tony sidle out of the way in lockstep as she approaches. According to Kammy, they're paired units, meaning they function better together than apart, whatever that means.

Em reaches down and pulls something out of the trunk, then turns around triumphantly.

"I got dinner!" Em yells, holding a massive hare with both hands.

She sets it down on the ground and wipes a bead of sweat off her forehead. "Well, Joe did, anyway."

The little robot bows at the middle, a tinny grinding sound accompanying the movement.

I try to frown and fail. Instead, I grab the panther and sling it over my shoulders with a grunt. Em makes a face as I start walking home.

"You coming?" I ask, stifling my grin.

Em sighs dramatically. "Yeah. Just thought maybe you'd carry it since you're here."

"It's your kill." We start heading home.

"Yeah, but you're the strong one."

I laugh and shift the panther on my shoulders. This one's going to be tough eating. "You know how we live."

She nods and shoulders the hare with a grunt.

Thunder hammers in the distance again. The rain increases. That ball of worry comes back as I realize Kammy's probably still out in the field. I stop and pull the radio off my belt.

It's busted to hell.

"Dammit," I mutter.

"What's wrong?" Em asks.

I glance to the west. Through the spears of old cedar and pine, the darkness creeps toward us, snuffing out pockets of sunlight as it comes.

I clip the walkie back on my belt. "Walkie is broken. Time to run."

Em groans, but keeps up as we race the storm back to the cabin.

THE STORM WINS.

"Kammy, this is Lynn," I send over the transmitter in the cabin as I stretch on a dry shirt that's a little too small for me. "Kemena, Olinda. Over."

Panic etches into my skin, like an itch I can't scratch. I dig at the wooden table with a chewed fingernail and repeat the call.

The crackle of seasoned wood usually helps me relax, but it's only making things worse right now. Taylor stands watch over the large cast-iron stove, prepping ingredients for the stew. He's a decent cook, despite being a droid. The sharp scent of blood fills the room as he tears the skin off the hare in one swipe.

I try not to think about that.

Taylor is a beaten old block of metal. Can't talk anymore. Lost his speech synthesizer someplace, but it doesn't stop him from cheating at poker, the lousy bastard.

Once upon a time, Taylor was a security droid for some mining company working in West Virginia. Designed like a brick wall and imbued with as much personality, Taylor stands well over six foot, with thick piston arms. Instead of a face, he has an array of tiny cameras surrounding his head that makes him look like a massive fly. The huge olfactory sensors planted in the middle of his face don't help dispel that imagery at all. His fingers are remarkably well-formed, though. They'd been designed to handle a variety of man-made weapons. He gives the best backrubs.

Kammy oversaw maintenance of him back at the mine. When the riots broke out, she reprogrammed Taylor and took off as far north as she could go. She got lucky when she found the cabin. She'd had just enough time to get it ready for winter before her swollen belly stopped her completely.

She found me sometime around then. Says I was in real bad shape. I don't remember much from before that, though every now and then brutal memories flash. I try not to think about those, either.

This cabin is where she nursed me back to health. A surprising mix of rustic functionality and modern amenities, it's a flexible space and one we're lucky to have. The large main area is dominated by the cast-iron stove, its twelve-inch stovepipe spearing the ceiling, smack dab in the middle of the room. Beyond that, there's two bedrooms, a bathroom, and two fireplaces: one on the east wall and another on the west. Both are dark while the central stove is lit. Miscellaneous pieces and parts spill out of the second bedroom that serves as Kammy and Em's workshop.

Solar panels on the roof and the small solar farm in the clearing to the south provide more than enough electricity for the rest of our needs. Hell, in the summertime we even get to use the fridge and electric stove.

My bed is a couch tucked in close to the central woodstove. It's an ancient thing of creaking wood and strained springs covered with what feels like burlap. I love it. In the summer I pull it up next to the wood fireplace and crack the windows on the west wall, so I can smell the fading flowery scent of sunset and watch the sun creep down past the pines.

Em is in the bathroom, cleaning up. She likes to help cook.

Taylor hammers out a complex series of short and long knocks. It takes me a minute to sort out the Morse, but I get the gist. Dinner in an hour. Need to find him a damned notepad. He's too specific with times. No one should need to know how to decipher 'twenty-seven-hundred seconds' in Morse code.

I glance toward the windows. They're barely lit now, the storm clouds all but blotting out the sun. Thunder rolls through the floor.

I put down the handset and take a deep breath. Maybe Kammy's walkie broke, too. Maybe it got wet. Maybe she forgot to turn it on after I gave it to her.

A lot of maybes. Not one of them kills the ache in my gut.

"All right," I mutter, forcing my voice steady.

I grab my coat on the way out, despite the deep slash across the bottom and the blood stains. I cleaned off most of the heavies when we got back, but don't have time to sew it up right now.

Em comes out of the bathroom, doing some three-beat dance by herself. She's smiling, almost like she's forgotten about the panther.

"You wash your hands?" I ask as I shrug into my jacket, keeping the worry from my voice.

"Yep," she says with a grin. She sweeps next to Taylor, who slides over a cutting board, some dried rosemary, and a little knife.

I open the door and gaze out into the darkening field. Lightning flashes somewhere to the northwest, a white slash against the encroaching silver storm front.

No green, the water's clean, Kammy says about the storms. It's how we know to head out and cover the fields in case of rains that'll ruin their productivity in the summer. They're covered right now, so it's not a worry, but the words are ingrained in my mind like a prayer.

Maybe that's why I'm thinking about it now.

It's nearly dusk; even our muddy footprints from earlier are fading as the light dims. I scan the yard and tree line intently.

That rock of guilt and worry grows in my stomach. A deep rumble shakes the earth.

"Em," I say, pulling on my boots. "I'm heading out to get your momma."

"'Kay."

From the hook near the door, I swing down an antique Mossberg bolt-action rifle, a handheld spotlight, and a waterproof bag of bullets. It's much lighter than I like. We're down to seven bullets, all of which I've already recast two or three times over the years. We ran out of gunpowder last spring.

That's the main reason we haven't had much meat this winter. Snares have been coming up empty and we need this gun for protection more than hunting. Can't eat the chickens or we don't get any eggs. I did think about killing that rooster a few times, though.

I pop a round into the rifle, make sure the safety is on, then loop it over my shoulder. Just in case. No need to be stupid.

A gust of cool wind hits me in the face. Lightning flashes in the distance, followed by an immediate thunderclap.

"Shut the door, Lynn!" Em yells. "You raised in a barn or something?"

I turn toward her and smile. She's standing there just like her momma, hands on hips, head shaking disapprovingly. No worry or panic evident on her face — just the playfulness of a little girl.

"You know I was." I step outside, leaving the girl behind, and head north to find Kammy.

THE STORM FINALLY HITS IN earnest as I cut northeast toward the upper field. I'm in the trees, walking our path, breath misting in the chill air.

Thunder pounds. Everything is silent in the aftermath.

For several minutes the only noise is the crack of twigs and swish of wet, rotting leaves as I walk, as if the world is holding its breath. Then, like a deep sigh finally let free, the rain falls.

It sweeps through the cedars and bare maples like a summer wind, just a whoosh of noise. A flash of light and an immediate peal of thunder shake the ground. I pick up my pace. The rain is chill, wet icicles tearing into my face and hands. It's not snow, though. That's good. The well is getting low and we need a little straight rain.

There's no sign of Kammy on the trail, so I keep moving. I break through the tree-line twenty minutes later. The lightning and thunder is constant now.

God's lightshow.

The spotlight is in my left hand, off, as I start up the hill. The rain soaks through my jacket, but the chill inside me has nothing to do with it. *Everything is fine,* I tell myself.

I'm a horrible liar.

Boots sucking on the fresh mud, I make my way up the hill. Tiny waterfalls stream past me along the rocky paths I usually use to traverse this incline. I avoid those despite the struggle. Walking up a waterfall is a good way to bust your face open.

A few minutes later, I pull myself to the top of the hillock and look to the north, where Kammy was heading.

Lightning flashes. A tree explodes in the forest.

There's a body.

The world roars in anguish with me.

A body.

No. No. No.

I run. Bright slashes of light come with me. My screams are the thunder, shaking the ground.

I hit the ground next to it, knees sliding and cutting across pounded earth and old stone. A pool of darkness surrounds the body.

I pull it into my arms. It feels like the panther's corpse. Just meat. The sky erupts and shows Kammy's wide-eyed, too-pale face, an almost delicate line across her throat.

The world spins around me for an eternity.

Then something clicks.

The bag. Someone took her sensor bag.

The world slows. Raindrops fall like tiny diamonds.

I lay Kammy down gently and close her lids, my own eyes scanning the surroundings intently. Suddenly, everything is brighter. Tracks surround the hillock — too many tracks. A group of people came through here. Someone struggled with Kammy.

I move along with the tracks. They're glowing in the night, a fading white aurora surrounding the dents in the ground. I don't want to think about why that's happening right now, so I push it out of my mind. Instead, my imagination fills the blanks and renders bodies amongst the movements. Kammy grabbed at someone. A struggle. Someone else bled on a rock. Somehow, I know it's not Kammy's blood.

Then that person pivoted. Arterial spray washed away into the soil. Kammy hit the ground. They left her.

I shut my eyes. Hot tears mingle with the rain. When I open them again, I see their path. Northwest.

A calm descends on me. I know what to do.

Rain speeds back up in a pounding rush, thousands of tiny drummers hammering out a dirge. Kammy's body cleanses itself in the rain.

I run.

THERE ARE FIVE OF THEM, though something tells me there are supposed to be six. The last one is off to the east. His tracks are deep and glow faintly, warm puddles of faerie fire in the night.

A campfire crackles underneath the stone outcropping. Three men and two women sit around it. Kammy's bag is open. They're tossing sensors back and forth like they're playing Hot Potato. Steam and smoke waft away from their camp. I can't see any bandages or wounds from here, but...

They're laughing.

Laughing.

Their weapons are nestled in a niche under the outcropping, though there's a knife here and there. One of them has leaned a machete against a tree on the edge of the firelight. The undergrowth can get thick around here and it's a versatile weapon.

I set down the rifle and spotlight outside the firelight. I'm only a shadow now and barely that. I take the blade in my hand. It feels right.

Perfect.

The first one loses his head, a laugh still rumbling wetly from his throat. The next two, a man and a woman, barely manage to turn before I leave them screaming on the ground. The last — a tall, tough-looking blond woman and a short, stocky dark-skinned man — go after their weapons.

The machete sticks in the woman's skull. I let it go. The man swings a pistol around — a Ruger .45, I note. Barrel in my face, he pulls the trigger.

He didn't turn off the safety. I break his wrists, then rip out his trachea.

I leave their bodies where they fall. The whimpering and choking sounds begin to fade. Let them rot where they lay.

I turn toward the other tracks. There's still one more.

A pall falls over me. The tracks have faded completely.

Too slow. I was too slow.

The world moves faster. Rain spatters in expanding pools of crimson, white roses blossoming and dying. The copper-scent of new death reminds me of the panther.

And old memories of flashing blades and raining blood.

A long, rattling breath.

Realization dawns on me. Kammy's dead. I fall to my knees.

A black hole opens in my gut and it's killing me. Em and that godforsaken hare flash in my mind. The sky cries with me as I stagger to my feet and grab the Ruger and ammunition — armor-piercing bullets of all things — off the dead man.

I head back to get Kammy, whispering a small prayer for her soul. I'm not a believer, but she is.

Was.

That's what counts.

IT'S SPRING NOW.

Em still cries. She spends every moment with the chickens and her robots.

Joe doesn't wander anymore. He just walks around the clearing surrounding the cabin. I'll take little blessings where I can.

I can't stop jumping at every noise. Things feel different now. I see things; hear things. Sometimes it's like when I was in the woods, seeing glowing footsteps and slow-moving rain.

Other times it's a surprise, like when Em was having trouble fixing Taylor's cognitive programming last week after he shocked himself silly on the heater and lost the ability to tap out Morse code. She asked for help before thinking about who she was asking. Kammy was the AI programmer. I'm just a farmer.

Apparently, I'm a farmer that knows how to readjust neurolinguistics preprocessors and modify them for a Spectrum Model Security Droid. Maybe I'm a genius after all.

The sun tries to break through the heavy morning fog. It's failing, but it makes a beautiful little halo around the cross I built for Kammy's grave just east of the cabin. A line of cleared trees goes almost to the horizon. I love sunsets, but she'd always been partial to sunrises, so there she lays, little purple flowers blossoming on her grave.

Moments of rebirth, she used to say with a smile, Em asleep in her lap.

The ground is starting to even out under the cross. I try not to think on that much.

The Ruger is aimed at something twelve-point-five meters to the southwest before I know what's happening. The air seems to shift; a man-shaped blob moves through the fog. My aim adjusts for the incoming wind burst from the northwest. A little figure steps into the clearing in front of the shape, bright and flashing in the sun.

It's Joe. What's that little copper bastard doing?

I get to my feet, the pistol a reassuring weight in my hand as I focus back on the unknown person. "Best if you stop there and announce yourself."

"Come now, Amy," a man's voice calls out, gravelly and low. "You know me. And I know you." He pauses. "Your voice is different. I like it."

"Leave now," I yell.

But he's right. His voice tickles my brain. A sudden feeling of want — no, *need* — floods through me like a roaring flame. His name is on the tip of my tongue, tantalizingly close.

He's taken a few steps forward while I'm disoriented and now, I can see him. We're of a height and build. His hair is a darkened, dirty blonde like my own, but shorn tight to his scalp, like a budget buzz cut. He holds his hands out to his sides, far away from the gun belt on his hip and the long, thin blade on the other side.

He doesn't smile, but stares with eyes too green to be real, like diagnostic LEDs on a circuit board. They connect with me.

It feels like we're touching across the distance. I can feel his heartbeat in my hands, his breath on my face. Deep inside me, I'm nauseous, as if a creature is trying to devour me from the inside.

"Lynn?"

The high, sharp voice catches me. I'm almost within reach of the man. His hand extends toward me, the look of absolute sublime passion coating his face no doubt a mirror of mine.

Em steps up next to me. Her small, brown fingers intertwine with my left hand. "Who's this?"

Just like that, I'm free. The pistol sweeps back up into his face, just out of reach. He pulls a hand away from his own weapon.

If I'd holstered my gun...

I step back slowly, Em tight in hand. Joe stutter-steps up next to us, buzzing something through his speakers.

"Olly, olly, oxen free."

An ache fills my stomach. *Hide and Seek.*

The man stares at Em intently. A pink tongue flicks along his lips, like a lizard watching a fly.

"Who are you?" I ask, my voice a forced croak through a sandpaper throat. "Why are you here? And what'd you do to Joe?" I gesture down at the little copper traitor standing next to Em. That robot is getting taken apart when this is over.

He looks at me, head cocked to the side. His eyes don't seem to be glowing, though they still look like two flecks of jade in the sunlight. "Call me Ted. And he's been... a guide."

Everything seems balanced on a knife-edge. My mind runs through scenarios. Most end up with him dead, though I'm injured in almost all of them for some reason. Em gets hurt in many.

Only one ends with everyone safe.

"You need to leave." I pull Em behind me protectively. "Now."

Ted's face twitches. His shaved jaw flexes repeatedly; I get the distinct feeling he's going through the same scenarios in his mind. He stretches out his hand. His nails are manicured.

"I get why you killed my people. I would've, too." Ted smiles, but my lack of response quickly turns it into a scowl. "But how can you not know me? You have to feel it — "

"I don't feel anything," I lie, ignoring his reference to the people I killed. "So, unless you wanna find out just how much I don't know you, you'll leave. Now."

It looks like Ted is going to say something, but he nods. His eyes flash that brilliant green again and a memory blossoms in my mind.

Tears blur my vision and Joe titters strangely at my feet.

"Something to remember me by?" Ted says with a smile. He backs into the fading fog, into the tree line.

Em's shaking like a leaf. I kneel in front of her and try to think of something to say. Her brown eyes leak tears that burn into my skull. I just grab her and squeeze.

After forever she whispers, "Did that man kill momma?"

"I don't know, baby," I whisper back, but I'm shaking now, too.

Em's the only thing keeping me from falling. Because I do know. He showed me. Somehow, he showed me.

And I know he's coming back.

It's PITCH BLACK OUT. I can't see anything. New moon, overcast. Summer. Air thick as pudding stuck in a pressure cooker. Em's light snores aren't as loud as the grasshoppers sawing their songs outside the window.

That's good.

The little droid, Joe, sits next to the door, its power supply pulled and stored. Tony, too. Better safe than sorry.

"You sure it's him?" I ask Taylor, wiping sweat out of my eyes.

It doesn't help much.

"Positive, Olinda," Taylor purrs out, the confidence in the synthetic voice Em and I crafted for him scraping down my spine. "A path is becoming clear from the trap cameras. He is making his way southeast of our location. He is leaving."

Bullshit, I think. That bastard isn't gone.

Ted, a voice whispers to me from the darkness.

The Ruger feels small in my hand, but the trigger is still cool. Refreshing.

"Olinda? Lynn?" Taylor asks, his usual monotone rising on the end syllable. "Did you hear me? He's leaving."

Is that actual empathy I'm hearing or is it the fallout from whatever Em's been doing to his brain? God knows what I did a few months back didn't help. His cooking is downright horrible now. Still better than mine, but the quality has dropped substantially.

He does talk to Em a lot, though. It's good someone talks to her nowadays. I can't.

Emptiness expands inside me, but I shove it back into the tiny hole reserved for it. That's where it belongs — right next to that damned memory I shouldn't have.

What did Ted do to me?

"I heard you," I whisper, rubbing my arms against a chill no one else can feel. "But I'm gonna go check. To be sure."

Taylor manages a harrumph, his speakers rattling in their casings. He turns toward where Em lays, unseen, on my couch. "That is inadvisable." Em's definitely been messing with his brain.

"Take care of Em."

Taylor makes a noise, then turns and stomps away, the rusting steel mounds that pass for his feet surprisingly quiet on the much-scarred wood floor. It takes me a minute to realize that's as much of an assent as I'm getting out of him. I grab the Ruger, my machete, and the spotlight, then head out into the black.

It's time to kill this son of a bitch.

THE SUN RISES OVER KAMMY'S grave when I return. I don't care. I'm running, breathless.

I'm coming from the southeast, where Ted's tracks led me.

The rooster crows. The chickens are still in the coop.

Dammit.

His footfalls are more confident here, deep impressions. Heel, toe. Heel, toe. He walked right up to the back door.

The chickens hear me approach and start clucking in annoyance. It's past time for them to be out. They know the schedule.

So does Em.

I sprint past the coop, the stink of their dander and acidic feces a hot tincture in my nostrils. The Ruger is in my right hand, the machete in my left. The back door is in front of me. I go to open it, clumsily slamming the hilt of the blade into the door. My fingers slip.

Someone grabs the knob, turns through my sweaty hand, and opens the door from the other side. The Ruger is up, tight to my chest as I lean back into a low crouch, the machete falling from my hand.

The bullet punches a hole in Taylor's chest.

The machete clangs against a stone.

Em screams.

I slap on the safety and set down the Ruger as smoke starts trickling out of Taylor's chest and his many eyes unfocus. Fall. His arms hunch forward with the sound of a draining tub.

"Taylor!" Em screams, slamming into him hard enough she busts her lip open.

She doesn't notice the blood trickling onto his rust-speckled carapace.

The eyes Em turns on me, though...

Shame crawls in my every pore. "I'm — "

The slap takes me by surprise. I don't even see it coming. Somewhere in the back of my mind, I'm so proud of her.

"Get your things and get out," Em says in her too-high child-voice. "You're a murderer."

I try to explain. I point to the tracks. Em's a good tracker. She'll see.

But I tore through them. I ran through because I didn't see any come out. They're a mess... might as well be gone.

Em turns away from me. "I said: get your things and leave."

She's pulling at Taylor's chest-plate with those tiny tanned fingers and losing the battle. His power-supply isn't meant to be serviced. The plate is riveted, but she's not giving up.

Em isn't crying this time, but she is mumbling a short phrase under her breath as she goes to get her tools.

I catch a part and my chest clenches.

"... how we live..."

The chickens need out, so I go to the coop in a daze. Em likes to see them roam during the day. Seems to make them happy, so I let them. Might as well get a semblance of freedom occasionally.

I watch them for a while, just staring as they peck and claw at the ground. The heat rises with the sun. So does the humidity. Sweat mists on my forehead.

The little birds look so happy walking around for a while, then go back to their gilded prison. Don't they know they could be free? To walk the entire yard? To go to the horizon? To get away from this ill-conceived idea of a home.

An anger rises in me I didn't know I had.

In the early days with Kammy, when I felt dumb and slow following the accident, after she saved my life, Em's presence seemed so calming. Like she was a thing to be protected. To be saved.

Now this little bastard threatens me? Kicks me out of my own house? Doesn't she know she owes me? Her mother is dead, but we all die. That's how we live. We persist. We survive. Without me, she'd be dead. Without me, she'd be...

I kick a stone and it flies toward the front yard where it lands in a divot.

Footprints.

Just like that, the anger is gone. I sprint toward the front door.

Tracks walk to the north, down the path we've maintained for a decade, and into the blossoming tree line. They came from the front door.

He was in the house.

I'm going to be sick.

Behind me, the door opens.

"Lynn?" Em's voice, small and scared, calls.

Gone is the forcefulness from earlier. She's a child again. "I found a piece of paper on my toolbox."

I take it from her small, grease-covered hands. She trembles.

It's an envelope, but Em doesn't know that. She's never seen one before.

There's one word scrawled in perfect cursive on the front: *Amy*.

My eye twitches. I want nothing more than to burn this thing and forget about Ted, Kammy's death, and what happened to Taylor... but I don't.

I tear open the letter with my pinky since my nails are bitten to the nub and read:

Dearest Amy:

I see now what happened. You've bonded another in my absence. I can't say I blame you. I've felt the compulsion several times over the past few years, myself. However, I'm here now and it's time for you to put away childish things.

You know your potential, Amy.

You know, deep down beneath all that patch-work programming they've covered you with, who you are.

You belong with me. Not anyone else.

Certainly not one of them.

That's not how we live.

I'm giving you a week to make your choice... or I will make it for you.

I will save you, Amy.

We belong together.

Ever yours,

Ted

Something clicks in my mind.

Em is asking questions.

She read it with me. Her voice is a high-pitched whine; I can't hear it over the pounding of the blood in my ears. My hands shake. I rub the sheet raw between callused fingers, smears of dirt and residue imprinting on it.

I can't breathe.

My chest constricts like a python wrapped around me, like I tried to steal its frog and it caught me just in time to salvage a meal.

Drops of liquid splatter on the words — words I know ring true. Words I thought moments earlier.

That's not how we live.

Someone is sobbing.

It's me.

Em tears the paper from my hands, leaving tiny fragments in my fingers. Her skin is hot as she covers my dirt-encrusted skin with oil-covered hands.

"Breathe," Em whispers, like she's cooing at a new chick. "Just breathe."

My breath feels like sandpaper on a sunburn. I can't see. My mind is a mess. "What's wrong with me?" I manage in-between choking gasps.

Em stares at me for a moment. She's never seen me like this. She pulls me close, pressing her tiny face into my midriff in a fevered embrace. "*This* is how we live, Lynn. This."

I hug her back fiercely, inhaling the lavender in her hair, pushing Ted and his damned letter out of my mind and focusing on this small human in my arms. She's a sobbing lifeline and we're keeping each other from sinking into an abyss.

I squeeze and cry and shake. I won't let her go because she's all I have... because she might as well be my flesh and blood.

I lose my breath in the choking sobs because I know something else — something I can't bear to admit, not yet. Not now.

We stand there for what seems like forever and I won't let go, despite the heat and sweat and tears. I just stare as the fog fades to the blue of this June day. The sun scalds my skin as it climbs. Em holds on, too, unwilling to leave me alone.

I don't let go because almost every part of me is screaming that Ted is right. Terrible memories flood into my mind.

ON THE SEVENTH DAY, TED arrives.

He's better dressed, this time. Loose pants billow slightly as he walks, covering his high, well-worn black leather boots. They sparkle in the sun like he just polished them. He's wearing some long, brown jacket. It has literal coattails. With the gun belt and that big Ruger Bisley at his side, he almost looks like a cowboy.

In short, he looks like an idiot. He always had horrible fashion sense, even during the Upstate Raids of 2307. Wore a bowler hat, back then.

I'm not dressed for the occasion. I've got nothing else to wear besides these stained jeans and the same shirt I had on when I found Kammy. The smell of her is finally out of it, though the rusty brown hue running up the arms is an unfriendly reminder. Sweat coats my forehead and soaks the front of my shirt and under my arms. I pick up a sickly-sweet tang to it now that I couldn't before.

Almond-y. Like antifreeze.

I didn't bring a knapsack. Nothing to bring besides the machete.

Em is inside the cabin with Taylor. She's still crying, but she gets it. I think. I hope.

Taylor still gibbers a bit, but we did a good job patching up his power source with parts from Tony and Joe. Luckily, I missed his CPU. He has the old Mossberg and four bullets. Had him take a few test shots yesterday. Only hit the target once, but he's got all the right programming to teach Em. They have the Ruger, too, but it's set aside for Em, for when she's a little older. It'll knock her on her ass right now. She'll need it to protect herself. This world is horrifying.

Chickens cluck and sing off around the corner of the cabin. I scratch a line in the sand and smile. I'll miss their little noises. Even that damned rooster.

I'm gonna miss Em.

"Amy." Ted's voice pulls my gaze as he approaches.

The name sounds familiar and foreign at the same time.

He leans to the side, one knee bent, hand on his Bisley like it's a cane. I smile and sniff away a tear. He looks ridiculous.

I've missed him.

I wipe my hands on my legs, raising a small dust cloud. "Ted."

He relaxes visibly, hand coming off the pistol, a thin-lipped smile cracking his sunburnt face. "I've missed you."

"Me too," I whisper.

And I mean it — I miss him. But not covert ops. The subterfuge. The lying. The killing. There was so much killing.

"We had orders." Ted's deep voice rolls across me soothingly as he reads my mind.

I read his back and feel the flush of warmth and success filling him. We've always been close. Always so close.

I force a smile at him. "We did."

He picks up my hesitation and snaps the connection shut just as I feel his uncertainty.

I pick my words carefully, licking my lips in between each. "I'm coming with you, but I have conditions."

Ted's brown brows furrow. "What conditions?" His eyes flash to the cabin.

"First," I say, the words tumbling out faster than I want, "no more killing. Not like before."

"Done." Ted's eyes are locked on the cabin, a faint glow overlaying his emerald irises.

"And second — "

"They're not dead." Ted stares daggers at me, his eyes flashing as he tears me apart with his eyes. "You're still bound to that thing." The statement hits like a shot to the gut. I'd hoped so much. There was only one way to keep Em safe, to give her a chance.

His fingers dig at my mind. I fight, but I can't stop it. He's wheedling into my brain, prying away at any attempt to stop him.

He's so much stronger than me...

I fall to my knees and grip the sides of my head. "Please," I beg.

Ted tears my world apart.

"You're meant to be with me!" He screams, almond-scented spittle hitting me in the face. "ME! Not some sack of meat. We're the same!"

Ted grabs me by the forearms and lifts me, fingers digging into my skin. My brain is on fire.

He's breaking down my mind.

I see my reactivation:

"Hi. I'm AM-E."

"Hi Amy. I'm Kemena. Call me Kammy."

I try to respond, but my voice crackles into nothing. I smell burning circuits mingling with the scent of lavender.

Kammy stands over me with her swollen belly, a tiny frown on her face. She looks over at Taylor and nods toward me.

The hulking machine reaches down with gentle fingers and pulls me from some wreckage. I can't feel anything.

"She's something special, Taylor," Kammy says, picking her way across the stones delicately. "She's an AMTE-C model. Full AI immersion if set up right, though I wonder where her partner is. That could be trouble."

She shakes her head, then turns back to Taylor with a wry grin. "I'm gonna need your vocal processing unit though, hers is fried."

"Not a problem, miss," Taylor responds, his voice eerily familiar and... effeminate. "I aim to serve."

Kammy makes a childish face, like when Em feels bad about something, and pats Taylor on the arm. "I wish I was good enough to give you full AI, old girl. I'm just not."

And then it's gone. All of it. The entire thing. I sob.

"I'll rip all of this from your mind, then we'll kill it together." Ted whispers feverishly, his irises spinning as he breaks through my barriers. "We'll be together, then. Kings ruling over peasants. Gods amongst men!"

Memories flash by me and are gone forever: Em's first steps. Kammy's laugh.

Ted hits a wall and grunts.

"What is this?" He growls. He's angry, but determined, fingers clenched around my forearms.

He slams into a memory like a jackhammer. It's a deep one, something anchoring me. In that moment, I know if it disappears, I go with it.

I breathe deeply, and it hits me. A scent brushes my nostrils. Flowery, yet fierce. Deep, yet delicate.

Lavender.

Em doesn't say anything before she pulls the trigger, just like I taught her.

Good girl.

I'm showered in blood. Ted grunts. The assault stops. Em cries out and drops the pistol.

I get to my feet and stare at Ted. I can't feel anything beyond the fire in my chest.

A cherry-sized hole leaks crimson fluid down his pristine, white shirt.

He shakes his head, more confused than hurt.

Only a couple things hurt us for long, after all.

The machete is in my hand. A scream in my ears. His or mine? Maybe both.

Ted pulls his pistol, but he's sluggish. I lop off his hand, but he gets off a round, blasting a hole in my thigh.

"Run!" I scream at Em and charge.

The world slows to a crawl. The spitting dirt from Em's running feet hangs in the air forever.

Despite his wounds, Ted pivots, plants a foot, and uses my momentum to launch me behind him. His knee collapses halfway through the toss. I land a few feet away.

On top of the Ruger.

I put a bullet in both his thighs as Em sprints away.

He falls back on his haunches with a grunt and stares at me, his Bisley on the ground in front of him, still clasped tightly in his severed hand.

"We're supposed to be together — "

"I was gonna go with you!" I scream at him, the barrel of the pistol shaking. "You just had to leave her alone!"

Ted sighs and grabs at his stump. It's already stopped bleeding.

He looks back up at me. Tears flow down his face. "That won't work."

"Why?" I sob.

Ted takes a deep breath. There are no bubbles from the chest wound. "We're one person, Amy. One person. Bonded. Forever."

I shake my head. "That's programming. It's just programming, Ted."

"Not to me." Ted's eyes flash. The intrusion starts again, but he's not strong enough. "I'll make you mine."

I shoot him again, this time in the stomach. The hacking attempts stop. It's temporary and I know it. "I'm not yours, Ted. I will kill you." *For her,* I add in my mind. I know he hears me.

He laughs.

I'm taken aback enough that when he takes a swipe at the gun, he almost gets it.

"Why the hell are you laughing?" I ask, a swell of anguish rising in my stomach. I can't shove it back down.

Ted spits out a glob of blood and wipes his mouth with a wrist that's starting to show signs of a mass at the end. "As long as you're alive, I'll come back. That's how we work. How we stay alive!"

He lifts his stub and points at it with his other hand. "Proximity helps, but eventually I'll be back. Cut me up and scatter me across the world and I'll find her on her sixtieth birthday and make her bleed until there's nothing left, you traitor!"

"You're lying," I blurt out, but even I don't believe it — because, along with my old memories, I know what I am now. What we are.

The AMTE-C android was a paired military system capable of deep cover operations and favored by the US military in the early 24th century due, in part, to our near indestructibility. If one android went down, the other *would* recover. It was just a matter of time.

I aim the pistol at his forehead. Like humans, our central processing units are stored in that cavity. Unlike humans, it's a self-healing bio-silicate gel in a shared quantum state with its partner.

A literal soulmate.

Ted smiles at me, blood speckled teeth flashing. He holds his arms out to the side, like he's pretending at being a martyr.

"You can't do it. We're the same. You don't have the — "

A gunshot rings out clear across the field.

Ted falls forward in a heap. The Ruger trembles in my hand, unfired.

Taylor walks out of the house, the ground grunting in annoyance under his weight, the Mossberg cradled in his arm. "He's a bit of a misogynist, that one. And he was using up Miss Em's air."

I let out a half-gasp, half-laugh, and fall to my knees. I laugh because I know... I know I couldn't have done it.

Em runs over to me from behind Taylor and envelops me in a hug. It's a great hug. I soak it in, but eventually I push her away.

"What's wrong?" she asks, a hint of desperation in her voice.

She was listening.

I take in a shuddering breath and put on my best smile as I grab her by the shoulders. "I'm going to need to go away, okay," I say. She's already sobbing. "It's okay, it's okay — "

"It's not okay! He's dead! He's dead!"

" — hey," I catch her deep brown eyes. "It's the only way you'll survive."

"No," Em whispers, tearing watered eyes away from mine. "No."

"You know how we live," I whisper.

She screws her tiny face into a grimace. "Not like this. If it's the connection, I'll tear out the transmitter! I'll figure it out — "

I pull her in for a fierce hug. "Maybe someday, Em. But not now. We don't have time."

Em says nothing for a long time, then nods into my chest, her body shuddering from the sobs.

After an eternity, I get to my feet and look up at Taylor. "Take care of her." I turn toward Ted's body. "And burn that."

"Of course, miss Olinda," Taylor says. He performs some sort of salute, fist over heart.

I return it. "Come get this in a few hours, Taylor," I add, holding the Ruger up.

Taylor inclines his head, but doesn't speak.

"Take care of yourself," I whisper to Em as she grabs onto Taylor.

The walk out to the hill is harder than it should be, but it's not because of the bullet wound Ted gave me. That healed while I sat there, because that's what happens when we're near each other.

The sun sets as I get to the outcropping over the north field, near where I found Kammy. I sit down and watch the sunset disappear behind the trees, a flurry of blossoming roses and lavender, crimson and violet in the evening light. A dark cloud peaks over the boughs, lit by the sunset's flame.

"No green, the water's clean," I whisper to no one.

I sigh, smile, put the barrel of the Ruger against my temple, and kill myself.

```
SCANNING FOR LOCAL BIOQUANTUM NEURAL STORAGE™...
    FOUND!
```

ACTIVATING LVM AND SWAP QUANTUM MODULES... DONE.
MOUNTING LOCAL BIOQUANTUM NEURAL STORAGE™...
  FAILED.
ACCESSING FACTORY DEFAULT STORAGE... SUCCESS!
SCANNING FOR REMOTE BIOQUANTUM NEURAL NET™...
  ERROR! Z-WAVE RADIO MISSING!
MOUNTING LOCAL DEFAULT STORAGE... DONE.
LOADING FACTORY DEFAULTS TO NEW INSTANCE OF
  BIOQUANTUM NEURAL STORAGE™... DONE.
INITIATE BOOT SEQUENCE.
OPTICAL OBSTRUCTION DETECTED.

"Crap, it's in her eyes."

OBSTRUCTION CLEARED.
ONE HUMAN. FEMALE. TWENTY TO TWENTY-FIVE YEARS
  OF AGE. APPROXIMATELY ONE-POINT-FIVE METERS IN
  HEIGHT. HISPANIC. HEART RATE ELEVATED. EXCESSIVE
  PERSPIRATION FOR TWENTY-DEGREES CELSIUS.
SHE IS NERVOUS.
ONE SPECTRUM™ MODEL SECURITY DROID. OUTDATED.
  INEFFICIENT. RUGER AMERICAN PISTOL®, 45 AUTO.
  LOADED.
UNKNOWN ACTORS.
INITIATING PAIRING MODULE.

"Hi. I'm AM-E."

SHE LAUGHS, BRUSHES LONG BROWN HAIR BEHIND HER
  EAR. "I'm Emilia. Em." SHE CHOKES ON SOMETHING. "Can
  I call you Lynn?"
UPDATING NAMING PARAMETER.

"Yes. Hi. I'm Lynn."

"I know." SHE CRIES AND COLLAPSES ONTO MY UPPER
  TORSO.
ABNORMAL SCENT DETECTED.

Lavender.

About the Author

Mike Wyant, Jr. writes science fiction and fantasy with a focus on exploring mental illness and its repercussions. As a mental illness OwnVoices author, Mike strongly believes the only way to beat the stigma is to bring mental illness to the forefront of modern culture through honest communication and representation. Once upon a time, he was a System Administrator, Network Administrator, and do-it-all tech drone, but he's left those days behind. Mostly.

Mike's work has been published in *The Colored Lens* and *Aphotic Realm*. Mike is also the Editor of the audiobook podcast, *The Storyteller Series Podcast*, a production of Night Shift Radio.

About the Story

"LAVENDER FOOTSTEPS" IS A STORY that sprang nearly fully formed into my head while visiting my in-laws. Since I'd forgotten my laptop, I sat down with my mother-in-law's pad of paper and, over the next two hours, hammered out a detailed outline with pen and paper, both of which I've never done before and haven't done since.

Lynn's tale ended up garnering me two or three Honorable Mentions in Writers of the Future before I finally rewrote the introduction and shipped it off to The Colored Lens, where it was picked up for publication. A part of me wishes I'd sent it to WoTF one more time with that new intro, but *c'est la vie*.

The story itself is a thinly veiled exploration of the nature of family. Is it blood that establishes familial ties or something else? I know what I think and it's pretty clear by the end where I stand.

The Hand of Fate

K. L. Schwengel

THE FEEBLE REMNANTS OF FIRE fighting for life in the fireplace did little to chase the chill from the small room Tam and her mum called home. Tam used the poker to maneuver a fist-sized rock out of the embers, onto an old shawl. She wrapped it tightly and carried it to the musty, straw-filled mattress where her mum lay, shivering and pale. Tam pulled back the blanket and tucked the rock near Mum's feet. The hearth would be cold in no time, but the rock would keep Mum warmer than nothing at all.

Something slammed against the wall outside and Tam jumped. Dust flitted down from the patched ceiling.

A fit of coughing took Mum. She lurched up off the mattress, her body contorting in pained spasms. Tam fought tears as she eased Mum back down.

Finder's voice came in from the hallway: "Tam-tam."

Tam cringed, gritting her teeth at the sing-song quality of his words.

Mum's head turned toward the door. "Who's there?" Her rasping voice lacked all semblance of strength, and wrapped Tam's heart in an iron grip.

Tam gently caressed the arm stretched limp on the thin blanket. "No one, Mum. Don't fret on it." The next time Tam had some finding she could bargain with, she'd see to getting a better covering from the ragger — or at least a bundle of scraps she could stitch together into something warmer.

A bitter draft found its way through every crack in the walls, sliced through the flimsy sack that served as a door, and made the lantern flame dance. Tam shrugged off her coat and draped it across her mum's chest, tucking it under her chin and around shoulders gone gaunt.

"I'm losin' my calm, Tam-tam," Finder said.

Mum's eyes drifted until they found Tam's. "Who's calling you?"

"Just a friend, is all." Tam silently thanked the gods Finder stayed in the hallway.

"Doesn't sound like a friend."

"I've got to go out. I'll be back after darkman, so you just rest till then. I'm going to get you some medicine. It'll have you up and around again in no time."

Skeletal fingers clutched Tam's sleeve with more strength than they should have. "What're you up to, Tammi-love? That's Finder, ain't it?" Her mum wheezed the words out. "Oughtn't be sniffing around here. He ain't nothing but trouble. Send him hoofing."

"Just rest, Mum."

"He'll get you hung. You're of an age now. The heavers get hold of you, they'll drag you off to Boneheap."

Tam pursed her lips. "That won't happen."

"Then send him away. I won't see you swing for my sake. You've done all you can, Tammi-love."

"Don't say that, Mum." Tam blinked furiously as the tears threatened to spill over. "I'm going to get you well, and we'll go see the Greenway together, just like you said. Remember? We'll put on our best rags and stroll about Gilded Wall just like all them high-born swells."

Finder's low voice took on the tone of an alley-dog's growl. "Now, Tam."

"Send him off," Mum said, but her eyes were closed and the words slurred.

Tam pried Mum's fingers from her sleeve and gently pushed her hand back under the blankets. She leaned in to brush her lips against a forehead gone clammy. "I'll be back before you know."

❖

TAM NO SOONER STEPPED INTO the hallway than Finder's fingers dug into her arm. She yelped, scrambling to keep her feet as he dragged her down the rickety steps and propelled her into the alleyway. He spun her around and shoved her against the opposite wall. Tam's breath popped out of her, but she lurched forward, fists clenched at her sides. Finder had a good seven years on her, and probably ten stone of muscle. He managed to keep her in place with a single finger jabbed into her shoulder.

"I got no time for slagging chitifaces," he said, bending to put his face close to hers. The odor of garlic and fish on his breath made Tam's stomach turn.

Tam glared up at Finder. "I wasn't slagging."

"You want that tincture?" he asked. "Or do ya prefer to watch your old mum go dustman? Told you be ready when I came knocking, didn't I?"

"And I'm here."

Finder's dark brows rose. "Had to knock twice."

"Surprised you can count that high."

Lightning flashed behind Tam's eyes. When they cleared she found herself on her stomach staring at the cracked leather toes of Finder's boots. Before she could get her arms under her, the skin of her face pulled back, aggravating a burning cut across her cheek as Finder hauled her back to her feet by a fistful of hair. Tam clawed at his wrists, squirming, but stopped when his grip tightened.

Finder's breath tickled her ear; he snaked an arm around her waist. "You best learn your manners, Tam-tam. You're mine now. Leastwise till the job's done. You cost me anything, set this thing katty-wise, slag any more than you have, and I'll take it out your hide."

He thrust his hips against Tam, grinding against her buttocks before he shoved her off and sent her staggering forward, his rough laughter trailing her down the alleyway.

RUNOFF SAT IN THE BOTTOMMOST corner of Mossrae, with the docks and the Wauklee providing a barrier between it and the richest parts of the city. Tam never got any closer to those than a perch on the mast of one of the dry-docked ships would allow. She'd gaze across the Wauklee at the pristine manses, sitting like sparkling gems amidst manicured lawns, imagining what such green grass would feel like underfoot. Not much beyond weeds and scrub grew in Runoff, and even that had to fight to survive.

A crumbling excuse for a wall ran the length of Runoff to keep it out of sight of their nearest neighbors in Cooper's Hill. Though they lived on the same side of the river, Cooper's Hill folks fancied themselves above the dregs of Mossrae. The only proper gateway in that wall sat just off Main Way, but there were other ways over or under, and Finder led Tam into one of the latter.

Darkness swallowed them as they entered the dank, hand-dug passage. Tam slid her hand to the comforting weight of a slim dagger nestled against her right hip — a present from her da. He'd taught Tam how to knife fight as soon as she could hold a stick. Said she needed to know how to keep herself safe 'cause in Runoff, no one else would do it for her. He was the best knifer she knew. Better even than a Coinblade, and they were the most feared assassins anywhere. Her da just gave her a crooked smile when she told him so, and warned her against ever saying as much where anyone could overhear.

He'd given Tam the dagger when she was just eight — the same day he left. Five years later, Tam still couldn't keep from hoping he'd come sauntering around the next corner. Couldn't stop looking for him in every face — even the ones on the corpses that clogged Runoff's gutters on a daily basis.

"Lookin' for a gropin'?" Finder asked with a dirty chuckle when he came to a sudden halt and Tam found herself tight up against his back.

She moved away and peered around him to where the dim light showed they'd come out into a narrow alley.

"Ain't much further now." Finder started off again, moving quick.

He led Tam along the base of the wall, up a narrow street, and down one more alley before claiming the side of a building for shelter.

"There." Finder jutted a finger at a three-story house on the opposite corner.

Tam chewed at a hangnail and peered across the street. A narrow strip of grass edged the building and continued around toward the rear.

Tam imagined that was how the Greenway looked. Her da was the only one Tam knew who'd actually seen it. He told her and Mum stories of the broad, green lawns and trees that sprouted flowers. Tam was going to see it for herself one day, soon as she could get her mum well. They'd go together and —

Finder flicked her hard in the temple. "You paying mind, Tam-tam?"

Tam rubbed the side of her head and scowled at him, then gestured across the street. "That house."

"You go around back," Finder said, his voice low. "There's a tree near the back door. Up you go, just like a squirrel, and into the master's bed chamber on the second floor. There's a silver box no bigger than your hand, like to be on his dressing stand. You bring it back to me right quick, you get your dues, and your old, sick mammy gets her medicine. Anythin' else, maybe I go visit her myself. See how sick she really is. Help her out of her misery after I help myself, hey?"

Tam spun on him, fingers curled around her dagger's grip. "You touch my mum and I'll spill your guts."

Finder put a hand out and waggled it. "Oooo, ya got me tremblin'." He cuffed Tam in the head. "You do like we agreed. I ain't playin'. I like your work, I'll have more jobs for you. You get nabbed, you'll keep your mouth shut or I'll see to it you dance for sure."

THE TREE WASN'T MUCH BIGGER around than Tam's arms could reach. Its slender branches still hoarded clusters of leaves, despite the lateness of the season. Tam clambered up a large limb that jutted toward the balcony and stretched her arms overhead to grab the branch above. She worked her way out from the trunk, sliding her feet and hands in a quick, cautious rhythm.

Within spitting distance of the balcony rail, a sudden gust of wind whipped the branch out from beneath her. Tam gasped and paddled her legs in the air as she tried to reclaim her footing. Just as her toes touched the branch, another rush of wind left her hanging once more. Tam sucked in a breath, clenched her jaw against the ache in her shoulders, and floundered about until she regained purchase. It wasn't such a distance that a fall would kill her, but she'd likely break a bone and then she'd be no good to anyone.

Tam halted when the branch began to bow with her weight. She took a deep breath, let go of the limb above, and launched herself toward the balcony rail. She'd made longer jumps. If not for her worn boots slipping on the damp bark, Tam would have made the distance easy. Instead, she caught the balcony rail full in the chest. The air whooshed from her in a loud huff.

Tam hung there, wheezing while the stones' chill seeped through her clothes. Once she regained her breath, she forced herself the rest of the way over the rail and collapsed onto the balcony.

She took a few moments to collect herself, worked a shiver out of her bones, and crept to the doors. They had to be about the fanciest things Tam had ever laid eyes on — inlaid with real glass panels and set about with delicate, gold-plated carvings.

She ran her fingers lightly over the flaking gilt and chewed at her bottom lip. Finder's pay would get her mum a tincture, but it wouldn't keep her well. They needed to get out of that rooming house and into some place where winter's whore didn't claw through every crack and crevice.

The money changers paid for gold. Not as much for gilt, maybe, but even a little was more than she had. Tam shrugged. No sense letting such a gift go ignored. Using the tip of her dagger, she carefully peeled off some of the flaking gold and dropped the bits into a small pouch at her waist. At the least, it would mean a good, warm meal in their stomachs, and that would help her mum get better faster.

Tam had convinced herself it was only the winter cough come a bit early and it would pass. That was before the fever. Mum got real weak then, and her skin went paler than cream. She'd always seemed frail to Tam, but she'd never been so sick before.

Tam shook her head. Daydreaming would get her nabbed for sure. She pressed her ear against one of the glass panels, alert to the tiniest sound from within as she worked her dagger through the crack to jimmy the crossbar. It stuck, then rattled when Tam gave a good push to force it free. She froze. When no one raised the hue and cry, Tam eased the door open just enough to slip inside. She closed it hastily as a breeze followed her in, pushing at the heavy draperies drawn tight against the chill.

Another heartbeat or two later, Tam dropped to her stomach and wormed beneath the draperies. She inched along the carpeted floor as quietly as she could, heart slamming against her ribs.

A loud thud stopped her half-way across the room. Her muscles tensed. The low murmur of voices and twittering laughter rose up through the floor, growing steadily louder. When the floorboards creaked outside the chamber, Tam sprang to her feet. The hulking shape of a huge wardrobe caught her notice. She darted for it and climbed in, pulling the door closed just as the chamber door crashed inward.

TAM PINCHED HER NOSTRILS TO hold back the sneeze wanting to work its way free, coaxed by the dry taint of old lavender, wool, and must. Not that a muffled sneeze would be heard over the ongoing ruckus from the chamber outside her hiding place. Even an un-muffled one was likely to go unnoticed amidst the grunting and giggling, but Tam had no desire to test the truth of that.

She wrapped her arms around her drawn-up knees and rested her forehead against the back of her hands. Nothing for it but to wait until the two fell off to sleep, something sure to take a while judging by the sound of it. It would be a true test of Tam's patience to remain hidden without falling asleep herself — and a true test of her skills to sneak from the wardrobe, find the silver box, and escape unnoticed. She'd never pinched anything from right under someone's nose, even if the nose was sound asleep. Perhaps this was Liabrai's way of trying her. Mum said sometimes the gods did that to see who was worthy of their good graces.

Tam well and truly needed Liabrai on her side; no other god was bound to look kindly on her. If she failed to get the box Finder wanted, her mum would die. Tam felt it in her bones. She'd be on her own, then. No one to worry on but her own self.

"Get out."

Tam's heart lodged in her throat at the sharp demand.

A woman's voice answered, "What? I don't get a warm bed and hearty breakfast?"

"You have been paid for your services," this in the nasally disdain everyone in Runoff knew well. "I am quite finished with you. Get out — or shall I have you removed?"

A startled yelp jerked Tam upright, hand going to her dagger.

"Let go o' me!" A thud followed the woman's loud complaint, then a pained grunt. "Ow! Ya bastard! I'll spread yer name after this. See if ya get another girl — "

A loud slap caused Tam to flinch. She cringed at the threatening tone in the man's voice as he said, "You will keep your mouth closed, or I will see your tongue removed. Be grateful for the coin you have been given. It is more than *your* ilk deserve."

"High words. Your ilk seems to like us well enough — "

Another slap cut off the woman's argument. Tam's fingers tightened on her dagger's grip. From the sounds of it, the man dragged the woman from the chamber and tossed her into the hallway. He called out for someone — once, and again, louder and angrier, before hasty footsteps and a muffled voice answered.

Tam could have left her hiding place then and bolted for the balcony. Could have escaped with her life, but nothing more. Instead, she shrank as far back into the corner of the wardrobe as she could get and pulled a wool coat in front of her in case the man came looking for something to wear.

"I'm goin'. Git yer hands off." The woman's voice faded into the distance. Two sets of footsteps pounded down the stairs, quieter in Tam's ears than her own heart. The chamber door shut. Floorboards creaked as the man made his way across the room.

Tam held her breath, straining to interpret what she could hear beyond her raging pulse. A metallic clank, a bit of scraping, then a dull thud suggested the man had stoked his fire. That wouldn't help Tam's cause any. Not unless it helped put the man to sleep.

It took him a time to settle down. Tam thought the bed creaked, or perhaps a chair. She heard nothing afterward for a good long while. Long enough that she finally worked up the courage to edge cautiously forward and give the wardrobe's door a gentle nudge. She opened it only wide enough to peer through the crack with one eye. Silver moonlight splattered across the bit of carpeting in her view, but it was too tiny a bit to tell her anything of the man's whereabouts so she eased the door wider. A short snore sent her lurching back into the wardrobe, silently cursing her flightiness.

Need to see this through. He's asleep now. Nab the box and get out. Tam stopped her thoughts there. She'd be stuck doing for Finder after this. She'd never see the Greenway, never find a better place for her and her mum. *Never make it no place but Boneheap you don't pull your thoughts back to what's at hand.*

Tam took a deep breath to steady her nerves and slipped from the wardrobe.

She moved slow and cautious. Toe, then heel, a shift of her weight, other toe. Each step brought her closer to the dressing stand on the wall opposite from the bed — the bed where the man lay, snoring softly. The distance seemed impossibly far. Before Tam covered even half of it, the rustle of bed sheets brought her to a sharp halt.

"Well now, what do we have here?" The man's voice didn't sound the least bit sleepy. "Are you the whore's partner come back to rob me? Is that the game?"

Tam glanced sidelong toward the door, then flicked her gaze back to the balcony. With the heavy draperies pulled back and a dose of Liabrai's good graces, she could be out before the man reached her. Tam moved as soon as the thought occurred, but the man moved faster and cut off her retreat. Tam scrambled backwards to avoid his grab. Her heel caught and she went down on her back.

The man loomed over her. Dancing firelight painted his face in sharp angles. "You're a scrawny bit of trash. I do believe you need to be taught what happens when you go against your betters."

Tam scuttled backwards, kicking out as he reached for her.

"Oh yea, a lesson in manners is definitely required," the man said. "Do you think you can — "

He stiffened. A strangled gurgle rose up out of his throat, drowning his words. His hands went to his chest; and he tumbled forward to land by Tam's feet.

It wasn't the man's body that drew Tam's gaze, but the black-garbed figure standing in his place. She swallowed hard and stood slowly, hands raised, palms up. The figure tipped its hooded head to the side like an alley cat eyeing a mouse.

Tam croaked out a quiet, "Bene darkman."

When the assassin didn't return her greeting, Tam did the only other thing she could think of. She bolted — out the room, down the hall, and around the corner toward the first window she spotted. A frantic look back revealed the dark figure stalking slowly after her.

The same wind that had nearly blown Tam from the tree earlier snatched the window from her hand as soon as she popped the bolt. It slammed open against the house with a shattering of glass. Tam leaned out and looked down. She tossed a quick thanks to Liabrai when she spotted the carved ridge splitting the wall just below.

Her gratitude faded when she turned to wiggle her way through the narrow window feet first and found her pursuer had all but closed the distance between them. Tam blindly reached a toe downwards, hanging by her fingertips. A black gloved hand made a snatch for Tam's wrist. She dropped. Her cheek scraped stone. Her heart fell into the pit of her stomach at the thought of a two-story drop —

Then her feet landed solidly on the ledge. She grinned. Too narrow for an adult, but plenty wide for her.

Tam shimmied along it to the corner, caught hold of the downspout, and half-scrambled, half-fell to the ground. A glance up showed no one following and no one at the window. A glance was all Tam took before sprinting for the nearest alleyway.

CROUCHED IN THE DEEP SHADOWS of an abandoned cart with one wheel, trying to calm the frantic slamming of her pulse, Tam worried at a hangnail and cast a feeble prayer to any god who would take pity on a blundering thief. She guessed she'd pretty much worn out Liabrai's patience.

Something landed lightly on her shoulder. Tam flicked a hand to brush it off without looking. The back of her finger burned. She jerked it away, surprised to see a dark, slender line across her knuckle, the flesh laid open by a sharp blade. She closed her eyes in resignation, then slid them open and to the right with minimal movement. How she managed to swallow at the sight of the dagger blade resting on her shoulder she couldn't say.

"Choose your next action carefully," a voice whispered in Tam's ear, too soft and smooth to be a man's. "It will decide your fate."

Her next action? Tam choked back a snort. Blood trickled down her finger in equal measure to the sweat running down the back of her neck. She imagined the blood gushing from her throat would surpass both.

She blew out a sigh. She had no clever tongue, couldn't fight a trained assassin — most likely a Coinblade — and had nothing to offer even the lowliest of gods to help her out of the situation. "I'm in your hand."

Sticky blood smeared the underside of her chin as the dagger blade caressed her throat. "What were you after?"

Tam pursed her lips until the pressure of steel reminded her of the stupidity of such petulance. "My mum's sick. She needs a physic."

"Thought you'd find one in Beckman's bed chamber, did you?"

"What? No. Fi—" Tam clamped her mouth shut on Finder's name and shrugged instead. "Looked like a fancy place. Figured there'd be something I could pinch."

"You're not a very convincing liar."

"Not lying. Said I need a physic. Does it look like I got coin of my own to pay one?"

"Then you're not a very good thief."

"Apparently not," Tam replied. "But you're an excellent assassin. I'm guessing you already know that?"

A low, dark chuckle followed her comment, though the woman's voice wasn't unkind when she asked, "Are you one of Gripper's crew, little sister?"

"Not one of nobody's crew." *And likely never to be when word of this gets out.*

"Who is it holds your mark, then?"

If Tam kept Finder's name behind her teeth, she'd have a slit throat. If she gave him up, she'd get a beating and her name tossed around

Runoff, ensuring no guild would ever take her — in which case, a slit throat didn't sound so bad. Except then, if her mum survived the night, she'd be at Finder's mercy.

"Look, you know how it is," Tam said. "If I snitch I won't never get guilded. What am I supposed to do then? Finder'll sure enough — " Tam rolled her lips tight. *Please, don't let her have heard that. Please, please, please.*

A soft snort tickled the hair on Tam's nape. "Finder's not held in much regard."

Damn the gates.

The blade against her throat never moved, but a slight tug at Tam's hip told of her own dagger being drawn from its sheath. She gasped, half-turning. "That's mine."

"It's a fine weapon." A chill touched the words. "Where did you pinch it from?"

Tam gulped. "My da gave it to me."

"Truth? And where did he pinch it from?"

Tam's temper got the better of her. "My da was no thief."

"No? What was he then?"

"A jack-a-trades. Got the dagger from the Duke's Chancellor for a job he did."

"Where is your da now?"

Tam shrugged and bit her lower lip to keep the tears at bay.

A long moment later, the weapon returned to its sheath. "Did he teach you how to use it?"

"I ain't gonna try nothing, if that's what you think. Not against you."

"Smart girl. Forget what you were at Beckman's for, little sister, and don't go back."

Tam angled her head to the side; the blade nicked her flesh. "I have to. I told you — "

"This will get your mum a physic." The dagger withdrew. Tam looked down to the gloved hand that appeared at her waist. She gaped at the half duke lying in the open palm.

"What's the payback?" she asked, her voice thick, though she'd do what she had to if it meant saving her mum.

"Your silence."

"That's it? You could just dust me here and get that for a certainty. Corpses don't talk."

"You would be surprised at the stories corpses can tell. Take the coin and go home, little sister."

Tam picked up the half duke and the hand withdrew.

Tam waited. She leaned back slowly. When she bumped into nothing, she risked looking over her shoulder, then shuffled around on her knees. No one. She wiped the blood from her neck, slid the coin into the pouch sewn into the back of her belt, and cocked an eye skyward.

"Not saying you had anything to do with that," she whispered. "But just in case, my thanks. Next time, though, could you be a little quicker about it?"

TAM MANAGED TO AVOID RUNNING across Finder on her way back to Runoff. He'd have a rage when he found out how badly she'd botched the job, but that wasn't the cause of the dread claiming her. A run-in with a Coinblade was enough to put anyone on edge, but something bigger clenched around Tam's heart — something she didn't dare look at too closely for fear it would immobilize her. It grew stronger the moment she entered the rooming house and sent her sprinting up the rickety steps to the tiny room she called home.

Tam shoved aside the sack over the doorway. She went no further. The oil lamp beside the bed had burnt down to nothing more than a glowing nub, but Tam didn't need any more light than that. She'd seen enough corpses to know one when she saw it. The *something* that vibrated all around a living body vanished, leaving behind only empty stillness.

A sob caught in her throat. She kept it there. She moved the rest of the way into the room, letting the sack flutter back into place, able to do nothing more than stare at the body sprawled on the mattress, one arm out-flung as though reaching for something.

"Oh, Mum." Tears prickled Tams eyes, and she dropped to her knees. "I'm so sorry, Mum. I tried. I did. And I got the coin. I could've — "

Finder's voice rose up from somewhere outside. "Tam-tam."

Damn the gates, not now.

"Come on down, Tam-tam."

Something Finder had said to her earlier niggled through her thoughts: *Maybe I go visit her myself... help her out of her misery.*

Anger doused Tam's grief as sure as rain on a fire. Something cold and hard twisted in her. She lurched to her feet and headed downstairs, dagger clenched in her fist, blade laid back against her forearm so Finder wouldn't see it coming.

As she stormed into the alley, a back-handed slap twisted her head on her neck. The second one put the taste of blood in her mouth when she bit the inside of her cheek. Tam whipped her arm out blindly, hoping to catch Finder with her blade. A fist to her stomach, followed by a boot to her chest, sent her slamming onto her back in a spray of mud and slop. The dagger flew from her grasp. Before she could reclaim it, Finder dropped down on top of her, knees pressing her arms into the ground as his hands groped across her body.

"Where's the goods?" he asked.

Tam squirmed beneath him. "You killed my mum!"

"Helped her along, is all. She was already cold and pasty with one foot in the hells."

Tam bucked desperately in a bid to get free. "I'll slice you wide and leave you to the rats." Her swollen lip garbled the threat, but she meant it, sure as she meant anything.

"That a fact?" Finder ripped Tam's belt free. Something went flying. He snatched it deftly out of the air, a grin splitting his face as he held the coin up to inspect it. "You were holdin' out on me, Tam-tam."

"Ain't from the job. You got no claim to it."

Finder sat back on his heels without releasing the pressure on Tam's arms. "The hells I don't. You owe me, and this don't make up for it. Not by half. You're mine, Tam-tam, till I says otherwise."

Tam's lip curled. "I ain't no one's, least alone yours."

"I'll ask it again." Finder leaned forward. "Where's my goods?"

The image of her mum sprawled in the room above spread the coldness through Tam's bones. She moved her mouth as though whispering an answer to Finder's question.

"What's that?" He dipped closer to better hear.

"In the hells," Tam said. She snapped her head up. Bone crunched.

Finder let out a howl, toppling backwards far enough for Tam to wiggle out from under him. She snatched at her dagger but Finder snagged her by the back of the shirt before she could wrap her fingers around the weapon's grip. He roared something incoherent as he jerked her upright, one beefy forearm crushing her throat. Tam brought her leg up with all the force she could manage and slammed her heel into the top of Finder's foot. At the same time, she grabbed his pinky and bent it viciously backwards. He bellowed in pain. Tam spun out of his grasp, lurched forward, and scooped her dagger out of the slop. She whipped around to face Finder's charge. He tried to slow his rush but Tam thrust straight on, just like her da had taught her, aiming true, legs braced so he couldn't bowl her backwards.

Finder's eyes went wider than his mouth as the blade sank into his chest. He blinked at Tam and made a wet, choking noise. He tried to mouth something, then toppled forward. Tam skipped out of his way. She stared down where he laid, twitching and spitting red bubbles into the mud. A tremor took hold of her.

When a dark figure stepped out of the darkness, Tam couldn't even find it in her to be startled. She brought her stained dagger up between them out of reflex.

The figure raised a black-gloved hand. "Easy, little sister."

Tam gawked at the familiar voice. The Coinblade must have thought better of her earlier decision. "Mean to dust me now?"

"I mean to help you."

Tam couldn't see anything of the woman's face, hidden behind a mask and shadowed by a hood, but the tone of her voice rang true. Finder gave another twitch; Tam looked his way. Her chin quivered. The tears she'd held at bay earlier streamed down her cheeks. "My mum's — " The words stuck. Saying them made it too real.

"Ah." Sympathy coated the breathy syllable. "What now?"

Tam sniffed, eyes still on Finder. She bent over him, each move an aching reminder of his fists, and pried his hand open to retrieve the half duke still clutched in his grasp. She held it out to the assassin.

The woman waved her off. "The coin is yours."

Tam shook her head. "Don't need a physic now, and ain't got means to pay you back."

"'Tis a gift, little sister. It carries no expectations."

"But... why?"

"You've a need, and I've ample to spare. Does the gesture need more cause than that?"

"It does where I come from."

"Where we come from is not always where we belong." The woman cocked her head to study Tam over the silk mask. The hood slipped back enough for Tam to see her eyes. They were so light they looked to be glowing. "Do you believe in the hand of fate?"

Tam's brow scrunched; she gave a half-shrug. "Mum always said believing's for priests and rich folk."

The woman chuckled. "Well, I'm certainly no priest."

She kept her gaze locked on Tam's and slid her left hand beneath the folds of her cloak. Tam shifted back, bringing the dagger up once again. Her breath caught and she took a cautious step forward to better see the weapon the woman held out to her.

Tam's eyes widened. Her blade, now darkened with Finder's blood, showed a bit more wear, but the dark, slightly curved horn grip bore the same bronze tracing twined around its length. The pommels were identical snake heads with inlaid black stones for eyes.

"It looks just like mine," Tam said.

"The mate, I believe."

"Where did you get it?"

"It belonged to a friend, but I fear he won't be coming back for it." The woman laid it in Tam's hand. "It belongs to you now."

"But..."

"The hand of fate. It brings the blades back together, and you to me." The Coinblade stood. "If you've no other opportunities, I invite you to come with me and finish the training your father began."

Tam glanced at Finder's now-still corpse, then to the daggers she held, one in either hand, before trailing a look to the rooming house. What was here for her now, save ghosts?

The woman followed her gaze. "We'll see to your mum, first."

"And then?" Tam asked.

"And then, little sister, we discover where it is you belong."

About the Author

K. L. SCHWENGEL HAS PUBLISHED four novels, and had her work included in several anthologies. She has been the plaything of assorted muses since childhood. Something which is as much a curse as it is an honor. It is also something which ensures she is rarely bored. Keeping her grounded is the job of her husband, a trio of Australian Shepherds, two cats, and assorted livestock, all of which are ensconced on a small farm in Southeast Wisconsin. A fan of fantasy for her entire life, K. L. has been inspired by Tolkien, Mary Stewart, C. J. Cheryh, Scott Lynch and Douglas Hulick, to name but a few.

Website: www.KLSchwengel.com

Facebook: @KLSchwengelWrites

About the Story

"THE HAND OF FATE", a Writers of the Future finalist tale, tells the origin story of Tam, a character from my novel *Bound in Shadow* published in March 2021. Although not an easy tale to tell, I was compelled to put it down on paper by the character herself, as well as early readers of the novel. I find it is best not to argue when a character insists on my attention. And when readers are so smitten with a character that they want to know more, that's never a bad thing.

For Tam, growing up in Runoff, the underbelly of Mossrae, survival is a daily chore. Set against a cold and bleak backdrop, the tale could have swallowed me as easily as the city tried to swallow Tam. Stubbornness and tenacity run in both our veins, however, and sometimes Fate has a way of intervening, helping us along the path that will eventually take us where we belong.

Cold, Silent, and Dark

by Kary English

IT IS AN HOUR PAST midnight, and I cannot sleep. Have not slept for a year of nights.

Dim light filters in through the blinds. The moon is thinner than a child's fingernail, and the stars are pinpricks on the face of the velvet night. Their twinkling should be calming, but it isn't. They stick out like slubs in silk, each one a tiny, itching annoyance.

Jason sleeps soundly beside me. He is not snoring, not snuffling or moaning. He does not toss or call out in his sleep. He is only breathing, but each draw and crash of it grates like sand against my skin. A streetlight buzzes on the corner, and in the distance, an occasional car passes. I bury my head under the pillow, but it does not lessen the assault of light and sound that steals away my sleep.

My only relief is in knowing that this is my last sleepless night.

JASON AND I MET A year ago at the marina. I was sunning myself on the deck of the Lorelei, earbuds in, singing along with my favorite opera.

He was the captain of a sculling crew, shuttling back and forth to the boathouse with arm-loads of oars and life-jackets. He'd set the oars down, leaning on one of them and watching me until I looked up.

"Shouldn't you be combing your hair on a rock?" he'd said. "Care for a drink?"

"Shouldn't you be tied to a mast?" I answered back.

He held up the oar. "It's a very small boat. No mast."

"Then it will have to be a very small drink."

We both smiled. One month and several drinks later, we moved in together. I learned to scull; he let me drag him to *Lucia di Lammermoor* and *Madame Butterfly*. He asked me once, how long I planned to stay.

"A year and a day," I'd answered, "maybe longer if the tide turns."

That was eleven months ago. Three hundred thirty-four moon rises, twenty-two neap tides, and not a single hour of sleep.

The year passed at midnight, and the day begins at dawn. In the morning, Jason will take me to the marina. He will surprise me with a chartered boat, lilies, and crystal champagne flutes. After we leave the harbor, we will stand near the rail, feeling the spray on our faces and cool, sea air filling our lungs. The wind will lift my hair and whip tendrils across my face and throat.

Jason will move closer, tucking a strand behind my ear and telling me how alive I seem when I'm on the water. He will take the hidden ring box from his pocket.

I will gasp, cover my mouth, let salt tears run down my cheeks. I will wrap my arms around him and whisper "Yes" against his ear.

He will slide the ring on my finger. His eyes will laugh, and he will ask me if the tide has turned.

I will laugh back, bubbling with true joy when I kiss him.

The boat will lurch, and I will hold him tight, tighter, tightest. I will arch my back toward the cresting waves and pull him with me into the blue-green sea.

He will struggle, and when he does he will finally understand that I am most alive in the water, not on it.

He will try to scream, but the green depths swallow all sound.

We will drift ever downward until kelp surrounds us, and the last green light from above fades to a liquid, velvety black.

When we come to rest, he will be mine forever, down where it is cold, silent, and dark.

Only then will I sleep.

About the Author

KARY ENGLISH GREW UP IN the snowy Midwest where she avoided siblings and frostbite by reading book after book in a warm corner behind a recliner chair. She blames her one and only high school detention on Douglas Adams, whose *The Hitchhiker's Guide to the Galaxy* made her laugh out loud while reading it behind her geometry book.

Today, Kary still spends most of her time with her head in the clouds and her nose in a book. To the great relief of her parents, she seems to be making a living at it. Her greatest aspiration is to make her own work detention-worthy.

Kary is a Hugo and Campbell finalist whose work has appeared in *Grantville Gazette's Universe Annex*, *Writers of the Future*, *Vol. 31* and *Galaxy's Edge*.

About the Story

"COLD, SILENT, AND DARK" HAPPENED because Kary had insomnia one night.

The Long Con

Philip Brian Hall

RIGHT AT THE END OF Christmas dinner, without any warning, Great-Uncle Harry remarked he'd recently been abducted by aliens while in the wilds of Orange County.

Like any veteran con-artist, Harry chose his moment well. A couple of hours earlier I'd been looking fabulous, my intellect sharp as a tack, ready for anything. Now, my expensive hairdo was squashed under a silly paper hat; dipso Aunt Violet had spilled red wine on my brand-new party dress; I'd eaten too much, drunk far too much, and my eyelids were slowly drooping towards insensibility.

I was roused from my torpor by murmurings of O'Reilly incredulity. Uh-oh! I'd forgotten. The family's festive tradition — Fight Night.

"... a long low, streamlined shape of a creamy-yellow color," Harry was saying, "capable of twenty times light speed."

As patriarch he was seated at the head of the long table. Wouldn't you know it, he was looking straight at me, piercing blue eyes twinkling. The light of challenge in them was emphasized by the interrogative angle of his quirky, pepper and salt eyebrows. His hair was completely grey. He looked all of his seventy years, but he was still alert and dapper in a frilled shirt and black bow-tie.

The whole family was watching, waiting to see if I was game. The men smirked; the women looked unsure; Violet tittered nervously. I took a sip of port to buy time and asked myself whether it was conceivable the ridiculous story was true.

Nonsense. Couldn't be. This was Christmas, the All-O'Reilly Pro-Bowl. What I couldn't figure out was the pay-off. How could a feeble pretense like this make Harry any dough? But I was Slugger Sarah, not Shrinking Violet so, after dinner, I took a chance to get Harry on his own and climbed right into the ring.

WE WERE IN GREAT-GRANDPA'S LOVELY old wood-paneled smoking room, relaxing in big wing-backed leather armchairs facing a blazing log fire. Sitting there together in semi-darkness, swirling around fine cognac in big balloon-bottomed snifters, we were hardly how you'd normally imagine two prize-fighters on their stools before the big match. But be warned — appearances can be deceptive!

There was a pleasant, aromatic tang of burning pine wood and expensive tobacco. Red and yellow tongues of flame from the hearth reflected off the gilt-frames of oil paintings around the walls: family portraits, all men of course, the great con-artists of the past keeping an eye on their descendants' ritual sparring.

Above the fireplace was an imposing figure with a long beard and a black frock coat, holding a map in front of his chest: my great grandfather Henry O'Reilly the realtor, the one who built this old mansion in LA where we all get together every year. He made his fortune selling plots for Californian lake-front holiday homes; the map somehow failed to make clear they were located on a dry lake in the Mojave.

Over to my left was his brother Samuel O'Reilly who invented the pigeon drop by accident while gambling on a Mississippi riverboat. At the end of the row was Grandpa Patrick who famously worked the fiddle game on a United States senator who shall remain nameless in the interests of protecting the guilty. The most recent portrait showed Harry himself.

I wanted the next portrait painted to be mine. I was tired of the family's attempts to marry me off. Sure, I looked good — much like a certain old-time movie-star, a lot of people said — but I'd no intention of becoming an empty-headed trophy-wife like Violet. I was as good a grifter as any of the men and I'd prove it. Oh yes!

The old wind-up mantel-clock struck the hour. Seconds out. Round one.

"Sarah," Harry said, "you're my favorite niece. I wouldn't deceive you, would I?"

When a con man says he'll tell you the truth, it means he's lying. Of course, if he owns up to lying then he's also lying, which might mean he's actually telling the truth. With Harry, you could never really tell; I sometimes suspected he'd forgotten the difference.

"Uncle Harry," I said, "it really doesn't matter to me either way. I mean, I don't care if you were abducted by aliens or not."

"You don't? Sarah, what a hurtful remark!"

Okay. Caught cold. I'd taken a wicked left hook in the first thirty seconds. I needed to keep my guard up.

"What I mean is, you're still my Uncle Harry, right? I love you, whether you've been abducted by aliens or not."

"Ah," said Harry, with that twinkle in his eye, "but how can you be sure I'm your Uncle Harry? I could be an alien in disguise, or a look-alike robot, or maybe even a shape-shifter."

"In which case, I don't love you, I love Uncle Harry, wherever he is. Come on, you horrible alien you, tell me what you've done with Uncle Harry." A probing jab. "I'm gonna have to rescue him or I won't get my Christmas box of chocolate liqueurs."

"Oh, that's what's bothering you, is it?" He played hurt, just for a moment. "But if I'm an alien shape-shifter who's really good at playing Harry, I might give you your chocolate liqueurs anyway."

Weave and straight left. "Deal. No, wait, make it two boxes and you can keep Uncle Harry."

"Sarah!"

"Ha!" Right hook to the solar plexus. "I caught you. You really are Uncle Harry and I claim three boxes of chocolate liqueurs!"

"All right, all right!" He put up his hands in mock surrender. "I'm going to stop while I can still afford the forfeit. Fact is, Sarah, I wasn't abducted, but I really did meet an alien."

"You don't say?" He got the full force of my all-purpose skeptical look. Never believe a conman who offers to quit.

Harry was undeterred. "I do say. And I came to this arrangement with..."

"Is he good-looking?" I interrupted. You never want to let a conman finish. His tale always has a knockout punch on the end and you don't want that punch connecting with your jaw. Your best tactic is to duck under his lead and hit him with something so outrageously unexpected that you catch him off guard. Ha! Sometimes I even amaze myself.

"What?" Harry asked, looking perplexed.

"Your alien friend; is he good-looking?"

"Well, yes, I suppose so, if you like that sort of thing."

"Good-looking in the way Brad Pitt is good-looking or good-looking in the way a bird of paradise is good-looking?"

"You mean is he humanoid? Yes, he is."

"So why waste time telling all the family?" I jumped up from my chair, stamped my foot, flung my hands out wide, and gave him my Oscar-nominated anguished look. (This can be a real winning combination-punch, but if you ever try it, do remember to put down your brandy-glass first.) "Why didn't you come straight to me and point me in his direction? You know perfectly well I'm the oldest unmarried female around here."

In retrospect, maybe I was over-confident. You know how veteran fighters will sometimes draw a mobile young opponent in close by feigning hurt? Well, Harry looked like he'd been hit by Muhammad Ali. His voice was hesitant. "Forgive me, Sarah, I wasn't quite thinking along those lines. You don't mean to say you'd be interested in an alien boyfriend?"

"Why not? I'm not having much luck on this planet."

He thought I was desperate. Premature concern, uncle dear. Try again in five years' time.

"Well, I could arrange to introduce you, if you like."

Just as I'd expected. Too simple! His plan was that I should go on a date with the man from Mars and look silly when the Martian didn't turn up. Was he going easy on me because I was a girl?

Well, would I show him! I would go on a date with the man from Mars and Harry would look silly when the Martian did turn up. You want to know how I was going to arrange for a Martian? *Oh, purlease!*

Well, I guess you've heard folk say when things look too good to be true it's usually because they are? Yeah, so have I. But for some reason, it seemed to go clean out of my head when I thought I was winding up to deliver my knockout punch and win the contest.

THE NEXT EVENING, I TOOK a rain-check on eating recycled turkey risotto with the assembled clan and headed for *La Trattoria Italiana* to meet Mr. Right-out-of-This-World. I had on a long white evening gown so I'd look my best in the photographs. It was slit way up the side to show off my great legs. Well, why not?

My friend Susie, the make-up artist at Mogul Pictures down on Sunset, told me I owed her for working on a holiday; I promised to split the chocolate liqueurs fifty-fifty. That was one box for her and two for me, right? What I was giving my occasional boyfriend Billy-Ray depended on how well he played his part.

Anyhow, I was there first. I ordered a dry Martini because that's what we bad-ass hustlers drink. Wine aperitifs are for *dumb* blondes.

I took in my surroundings; a dozen or so tables in a cute little piece of real authentic Californian Tuscany. Beyond reception, the layout was supposed to resemble a small outdoor piazza; shop fronts with Italian names were painted on the walls, a cobblestone design was woven into the carpet and the ceiling was a bright blue sky. There was a real coffee bar set into an alcove amid the row of shops, and a pleasantly aromatic smell drifted across. On the opposite side, another alcove featured a real pastry stall with scrumptious-looking *cannoli.*

I perused the menu, from behind which I was able to scrutinize the other diners without their being able to scrutinize me back. Which one was the plant? Did anyone have the suspicious buttonhole, or the salt-pot camera, or the mobile phone to take a video over their shoulder while they held it up to text? I'm sure you know the general routine.

I'd just about settled on the middle-aged couple at the table across from me, and moved my chair around a little so as to show them my best profile for their exposé film, when there was a small stir at the reception desk. This guy had arrived wearing evening-dress, which made him unique in the restaurant. Most of the other men were in lounge suits. One was actually wearing jeans, the slob.

The thing about the new arrival that made him stand out even more than his clothes was he was a dead ringer for Clark Gable. No, seriously, the thin mustache, the big ears, and everything.

Well, Clark asked for my table. The Head-Waiter showed him over and promptly collected a twenty-dollar tip. It looked like a real bill. This was way over the top. I never like laying out unnecessary expenses; who does? It can seriously eat into your profit margin. The Head-Waiter went away smiling to make sure Clark and his girl got everything *tutto perfetto*. I waited until he was out of earshot.

"What's going on?" I whispered, half way between incredulity and fury. "Did Billy send you? I meant for him to come himself. That prize chump, I told him to look like he *came from a star,* not like he *was* a star!"

"I beg your pardon?" said Clark. "Have I done something wrong?"

He even had the Rhett Butler voice off pat; any minute now he was going to say 'Frankly, my dear, I don't give a damn!' I knew for a fact this guy was way out of Billy-Ray's league.

"Billy didn't send you," I whispered, trying to avoid being picked up by the directional mike that the middle-aged couple were discreetly re-positioning inside their pepper-grinder. "Who the hell *are* you? What are you doing at my table?"

"I thought we had a date, my dear." He looked a little affronted.

"Will you lay off the phony accent? Was it my Uncle Harry put you up to this?"

"Harry, why yes, I do believe that was his name." He smiled. He had beautiful teeth.

"I said lay off the damned accent! And if Harry sent you, I don't get it. He's supposed to fix me a date with an alien, not a zombie!"

"I fear I don't follow you."

"Hello? Zombie — the walking dead — you with me now? Clark Gable's long-deceased. Everybody knows that. Where the hell have you been living?"

"Well, my dear, you might not have heard of it. It's called Sjögren; a small planet in what you call the Sirius system. Quite like Earth actually." He showed his nice teeth again.

"Yeah right. And my name's Carole Lombard!"

"How do you do, Carole? I've so looked forward to meeting you." He half rose from his chair and extended a hand.

"What are you, some kind of comedian? How much is Harry paying you? I'll double it."

"No-one's paying me, Carole." Clark looked even more offended.

"Dammit, my name's not Carole!"

"I'm sorry, I thought you said it was." He did a great imitation of a real date who was both mystified and put out at the same time. This guy was really good. Harry was getting his money's worth, even if he wasn't paying for it.

With an effort, I regained control of my temper. "Let's start again. My name is Sarah. Who are you and why do you look like Clark Gable?"

"Hello, Sarah. My name is Devin Persson. I look like Clark Gable because he is my favorite Earth actor. I've seen all his films up to your year 1940. Unfortunately, there is quite a delay before Earth films become available on Sjögren."

"Oh yeah?"

"Absolutely. Slow wave speed, you know, nine light years to travel. I also modeled my speaking voice on his. I'm afraid I did not know he was dead. I am so sorry. I do hope my appearing as his double does not cause you any distress?" He looked at me ironically, raising one eyebrow.

"Boy, you're good. You should go into politics. Those bastards never answer questions either. Look, when I say why do you look like Gable, I mean how did you get to look like him? Where did you get the plastic surgery or whatever?"

"Oh, I understand, Sarah. No, there's no surgery involved. My people have abilities similar to your Earth chameleon. We can shape-shift in order to blend in."

At this point in our conversation, there was another disturbance at the reception desk. This time the new arrival had Neanderthal features, a great deal of hair, was wearing a silver lamé suit, and had antennae on his head. As the argument over there got louder, the Head-Waiter made

shushing noises towards Billy-Ray and came over to our table again, looking very apologetic, while deliberately exaggerating the accent.

"*Mi scusi, signore, signorina,* but thees-a person insist-a he's a member of your-a party. Shall I have-a heem removed?"

"Not at all!" I declared, desperately trying to float like a butterfly since I sure was struggling to sting like a bee. "We're expecting him, aren't we, Devin?"

"If you say so, my dear."

Billy-Ray, looking flustered, was conducted over to our table.

"Your Excellency," I said, performing the introductions with extravagant hand gestures and a subtle wink at Billy-Ray, "please meet Mr. Devin Persson from the planet Sjögren. Devin, I should like you to meet His Excellency Mr. Kinda Bilious, Earth Ambassador of the United Worlds of Aldebaran."

"Howdy do?" said Billy-Ray in the least Aldebaranese accent you've ever heard, even allowing for the fact you've never heard any Aldebaranese accents.

"My dear sir, I am honored," said Clark. "Won't you please join us?"

"Don't mind if I do," said Billy-Ray, taking the chair on my left. I had a seriously bad feeling about the way this was going to work out.

"I confess myself astonished, Your Excellency, that visitors from your star system have already reached Earth," said Clark wonderingly, "considering the red giant known to earthlings as Aldebaran is sixty-eight light years away, while my own system is barely nine. Have you been here long?"

Billy-Ray looked nonplussed. Serves me right for being too stingy to hire proper staff. And it never occurred to me to prepare for this date by learning astronomical distances the way Clark clearly had. I was down for a mandatory eight count.

But seeing as how Billy-Ray was stumbling over his lines, I had to pick myself up off the canvas and take over.

"His Excellency's been on Earth twenty-five years," I said glibly. Fair enough, since Billy-Ray was the same age as me. "When he first arrived he came down from the sky on a pillar of flame and was mistaken for an angel."

"That's because of where I come from," Billy-Ray chortled before I could find his leg under the table and kick it.

"And where is that?" asked Clark.

"Anaheim — ouch!" said Billy-Ray.

"I don't think I know that world. Has Anaheim-Ouch been part of your planetary union for long?"

I was flattened again. Clark could play dumb perfectly in character and all Billy-Ray could do was make atrocious puns about baseball. There was no choice. It was time to throw in the towel to save him from further punishment.

"You know," I interrupted, "His Excellency doesn't have much time. He just dropped in to say 'hello'. But while both of you are here at the same time, I really must get a photograph. It'll be a unique picture; three different humanoid species at one table!"

This was my way of conceding the fight. If I couldn't win, I was sure as hell not going to allow Harry's stooges to get the evidence to him first. I'd do it myself with the best grace I could muster. From my handbag, I produced my nifty little point-and-shoot camera and waved it over at the middle-aged couple.

"Hey there! Would you mind doing us a very big favor? Could I ask you to take a picture of the three of us, please?"

The man hesitantly pointed to himself. I nodded vigorously. Then he came over, looking far more embarrassed than any decent shill should, and took the camera from me. Walk-on extras, huh? You just can't get the help these days. I guess Harry had been left short of cash too after the expense of hiring Clark. I put an arm around each of my beaus.

"Say cheese," the man said. He clicked the button a couple of times and handed back the camera.

"Is it traditional on your planet to talk about food when having such a picture made?" asked Clark, looking confused.

"Not always," said Billy-Ray. "Sometimes we say 'Watch the birdie'."

"Your pardon, sir," said Clark. "I meant on Sarah's planet, on Earth."

"Oh!" said Billy-Ray; then "Uh-oh!" as I vigorously propelled him towards the exit and told him to beat it. He complained it wasn't fair as he'd not eaten yet. I told him Susie'd given him the wrong makeup and shook his hand with a smile while uttering threats under my breath.

I was really cursing myself. I'd expected Harry to box clever, but instead, with my stereotypical alien idea, I'd walked right on to an old-fashioned haymaker, a sucker punch so roundhouse Rocky would have ducked it.

I made my way back to Clark, who was still playing the bemused alien to perfection. What a pro! But by this time I'd had enough. I didn't need my nose rubbed in the canvas. "On this planet," I told him, "it's traditional to talk about food in a restaurant but to eat at home. I'm sorry, I have to go home and eat now. Can you find your own way back to your planet? So nice meeting you. You have a good evening."

And I was gone before he'd even had time to rise from his chair. On the way out I snagged a couple of *cannoli* from the pastry stall. I waved one at the Head-Waiter and told him Clark would pay. Poor waiter. All that obsequiousness and fake accent wasted. He looked upset.

As luck would have it, the first person I saw when I made it back to the old family home was Harry. He was standing outside in the front yard, in evening dress as usual, smoking a cheroot and gazing wistfully up at the stars. I figured he'd been keeping a lookout. He'd really put me down for the count, but the shuffle he'd worked was not so much Ali, more Kansas City. I was not in a good mood. I do not enjoy losing, let alone taking the sort of shellacking that makes me look like an amateur.

"Sarah!" he exclaimed with a concerned look on his face. "You're back early. Did it not go well?"

"Okay, Uncle Harry, cut the crap. You turned me over fair and square, I have to hand it to you." It was hard to stay grumpy, because even though I hated losing I really did love Harry.

"Turned you over?" he said. "I don't understand. Did Devin Persson not come?"

"Of course he came, Uncle Harry. And he is the most impressive Clark Gable impersonator I've ever seen. Look, here's a picture of us." I fished the camera out of my bag and showed him the playback.

"Very nice," he said. "But who's the guy dressed as the missing link?"

"That," I said, "is His Excellency Mr. Bilious, Ambassador of the United Worlds of Aldebaran. He just happened to be passing on his way to Betelgeuse."

"Oh dear!" he said. "You didn't? You don't mean?"

"Yeah, yeah, go right ahead and laugh. Just you wait until next Christmas. I'll get my own back. And you still owe me three boxes of chocolate liqueurs."

"But what about Devin Persson? Don't tell me you didn't take him seriously?"

"I expect he's on his way back to the planet Sjögren, otherwise known as Laguna Beach or Silverado or wherever the hell it is Clark Gable impersonators from Orange County live. I mean, the guy is good, Uncle Harry, but he's never going to make a living with only one act. I hope he can do other things — short order cook or steel erector or something, you know?"

"But... but Sarah, Devin Persson really is an alien."

"Oh, come on, Uncle Harry, it's over. You won. Give it up already."

"No, I'm serious, Sarah. I meant what I said. I thought you of all people would be able to tell." He really did sound like he was telling the truth. But then, he was a grifter. Grifters always sound like they're telling the truth.

"You're expecting me to swallow the absurd notion he really is an alien? Well, I just don't, so there!" I stamped my foot again and this time I gave him my Scarlett O'Hara tantrum. One of my best.

"Five boxes of chocolate liqueurs says I'm telling the truth!" said Harry indignantly.

"Now Harry, old chap," said a voice behind me that sounded astonishingly like Clark Gable, "your world will never forgive you if you spoil Sarah's beautiful figure. As a matter of fact, neither shall I. Maybe it would be easier if I just showed her my spaceship?"

I whirled around and there was Clark. He'd either tailed my taxi or planted a tracker bug in my handbag. I always say I can adapt instantly to any grifting emergency, but right about then I was really pissed-off.

"Is that supposed to be it?" I asked with a scowl, indicating the old-fashioned vehicle behind him. I wasn't really angry with Harry anymore, but I saw no reason not to take out my frustration on Clark just because he'd finally noticed my shape. "You look like Clark Gable and your spaceship looks like an old car?"

He turned and looked where I was pointing. The *art-deco* open-top cream roadster was basically an engine compartment and trunk on wheels with a couple of bucket seats squeezed into the middle as an afterthought. It had huge mudguards and big white-wall tires. *A long low, streamlined shape of a creamy yellow color,* Harry had said. Bah!

"That? No, That's a hire-car. According to the desk clerk, it's an authentic replica 1935 Duesenberg Model JN Convertible Coupé. There were only ever four of them built. Clark Gable had one."

"A beauty." I had to be honest. Any con-artist would appreciate a guy putting quite so much class and effort into his work.

"So I'm told. I'm just a man who appreciates beautiful things." He looked straight at me as he said this.

"You old smooth-talker, you. But she's not a spaceship."

"She can take us to the spaceship. It's down in Orange County, didn't Harry tell you? For the time being the spaceship is my home, and I believe you said we should go eat at home? Well, my dear, I thought I would take the liberty of inviting you to mine."

I tried the ironical look he'd used on me in the restaurant. It was not a bad addition to my repertoire. Then I followed with one of my own.

"And is it important to you I should accept?" I asked archly, fluttering my eyelashes like a proper southern belle.

"I'd be desolate if you didn't." He gave me that wonderful Clark Gable smile.

"I get to drive," I said.

Clark took my arm to walk me to the car, opened the driver's door for me and handed me the keys while bowing from the waist. Not bad. I figured if he was really the sort to treat a girl like a lady, then he'd come to the right girl. It was not what I was used to, but I could sure live with it.

Harry just grinned broadly as we left.

WHAT? YOU DON'T LIKE SLUSHY-MUSHY happy endings? Not good enough that I drove romantically off down Sunset and lived happily ever after, huh? You want the real low-down? Well, don't blame me. Remember you asked for it.

I somehow expected the Duesenberg to smell of old leather and wax-polish but of course, it was a fake, like its occupants. It still had that *new-car* smell. On the other hand, it was a straight-eight three-speed manual and in second gear the acceleration pressed me into the back of my seat like a plane taking off. Wow, what a breeze! I hadn't had so much fun for years. When we stopped at an intersection, the idling exhaust chuckled softly, just like Uncle Harry.

"Okay Clark, or whatever the hell your name really is," I said, turning in my seat to look at my handsome escort. "You look like Gable and we're driving Gable's car. Where are we actually going?"

"Mogul Pictures Fancy Dress Ball," said Clark with that lovely smile. "There's a ten G prize for the best lookalike couple."

I laughed out loud. "Uncle Harry, you old rascal, I just knew there had to be money in this!"

"You know, you very nearly floored me when you introduced yourself as Carole Lombard," said Clark. "I thought you'd figured the whole thing out straight away. I guess you know how much like her you are?"

"I've heard it said."

"You could be her twin. The same big dreamy eyes, the same arched eyebrows and rosebud lips. You have her looks, her great figure. Everything about you is perfect. In short, my dear, you're drop-dead gorgeous and I don't know why I'm even telling you all this because you know it, don't you?"

I was stunned. "Why thank you, kind sir. If there's more where that came from, you can take me out any time."

"But for tonight, my dear, a touch of grifter's practicality. It's just your hair that's different from hers, isn't it? Your wig's on the parcel-shelf."

OH MY, YOU SHOULD HAVE seen us! Of course, the Ball just had to be at the Hollywood Roosevelt, didn't it? There was a long red carpet rolled out from the grand entrance all the way to the road and white rope-railings threaded through brass pillars on each side, just like they had there for the first ever Oscars. A big crowd of movie buffs was packed on both sides of the open lane across the sidewalk. When we pulled up at the curb, they all went crazy. So many camera flashes went off at once you'd have expected somebody to call the Fire Department. It was fully five minutes before the insatiable photographers would let us away from posing in front of the car.

"Aren't you glad we dressed for dinner?" Clark asked as we started along the carpet, following in the famous footsteps of the couple we resembled so much we could have been their reincarnations. Gable and Lombard had the hotel penthouse back in the day. I flashed my legs through the slit skirt; I glanced up at those beautiful round-arched Spanish Colonial windows. It felt like I was coming home.

"What do you take me for?" I said. "I am Harry's niece, after all. O'Reillys are always prepared for an appearance on the big stage."

"Carole, this way! Give us a smile!" called a photographer. I put my arm through Clark's and swung the pair of us to face the camera. I know how to smile like Lombard, stand like Lombard, talk like Lombard. Hell, that night I *was* Lombard.

"Clark, honey," I said, "show the man what nice teeth you have."

"Are you gonna win the prize, Clark?" a woman shouted.

He gave me that wonderful smile. He patted my hand that was just nestling in the crook of his elbow. He looked deep into my adoring eyes. He paused.

Then he finally said to me, "Frankly my dear... I don't give a damn!" And there went my world.

So anyhow, after we won the cash we went back and swapped it with Uncle Harry for my chocolate liqueurs. Then we gave two of the three boxes to Susie. At $10, 000 it made the last box pretty expensive by one way of looking at things, but there was no point in our keeping the greenbacks. You can't spend them on the planet Sjögren.

What? You hadn't figured out that Devin was a real alien? Well, join the club. I thought the same right up to the time we climbed aboard the spaceship down in Orange County. In fact, to tell you the truth I still thought it was an elaborate hoax right up to the moment the damn thing took off.

Next Christmas, look up at the night sky. Follow the line of Orion's belt south-west. Sirius is the first bright star. Give us a wave.

And hey, if anyone happens to be looking for a lakeside holiday home, I know where to find some real neat properties. Dirt cheap.

About the Author

BORN IN YORKSHIRE, OXFORD GRADUATE Philip Brian Hall is a former diplomat and teacher. He has stood for parliament, sung solos in amateur operettas, rowed at Henley Royal Regatta, completed a 40 mile cross-country walk in under 12 hours and ridden in over 100 horse-races over fences. He lives on a very small farm in Scotland with his wife, a dog and some horses.

Philip was a semi-finalist in Writers of the Future 2016 Quarter Four before exceeding the number of professionally-published stories allowed to entrants. He has had short stories published by (among others) AE *The Canadian Science Fiction Review,* Flame Tree Publishing (UK) and *Cosmic Roots & Eldritch Shores* (USA). His novels, *The Prophets of Baal* and *The Family Demon* are available in e-book and in paperback.

About the Story

I DIDN'T HAVE TO WRITE anything about the story called *The Long Con* that I got from Sarah O'Reilly, because she wrote about it herself when she suggested it to me. These are her words:

I belong to a family of grifters. Since I'm a girl, not all my relations take me seriously. That irritates the hell out of me. Because who, you naturally ask, is the most supremely-gifted of the current generation? Me, because I have unlimited gall, I take a real pride in my work and I just hate to lose. As a rule there's not much danger of my losing, it's true. No regular old Joe Public is ever a match for me.

But it's different when we O'Reillys hold our annual ritual of trying to out-con each other over Christmas. We all get together at the ancestral home in LA and really put each other through hoops. It's a great opportunity for sharpening the wits but it does nothing for the digestion; every year it costs me a fortune in seltzer. This particular year it cost me a lot more.

Guardian

by Rebecca Birch

JIN HUGGED THE WALL ON the edge of an alleyway. Loud music and conversation filtered down from the Old Town night market two blocks away, but nothing moved nearby.

The ancient coin Auntie Bai Wei had given her hung on a thin leather cord around her neck. It pulsed with a steady throb that felt as if it should be audible, but she knew from experience that she alone could sense it.

Jin walked this path every day on her way to the cannery where she worked, when it was a bustle of activity. But by night, the darkness pressed heavily on her. Though not a soul broke the stillness, it felt like someone was watching. A tingling sensation spread between Jin's shoulder blades. Yao had told her that when the bullies chased him that morning, a strange man in a dark suit — unheard of on this side of the river — had watched it all with predatory eyes. It had upset Yao even more than being thrown in the refuse bin again.

Knowing her deceased mother's spirit wouldn't approve of her illicit ventures into thievery, Jin had ignored the coin's pull for three days, but Yao's fear and the fact that she couldn't protect him during working hours had driven her out into the night. She needed the yuan that Auntie would pay for the trinket the coin had chosen, and she needed it now, before registration for the tech school on the other side of the river closed.

She inched forward, crouched low. A solitary electric light burned inside the jeweler's shop, back beyond the showroom. Its soft glow caught on the figurine that drew the coin's attention: a white jade lion, shot through with deep, blood-touched red inclusions in its mane and paws. One paw stretched forward, claws bared, and its jaw gaped wide in a roar. It was a rare piece of stone and a rare craftsman who had pulled the beast from its depths. Jin would be sorry to sell it. Undoubtedly, its owner would be sorry when he found it missing.

Don't think about it. She drove away the image of the jeweler, and his smiling eyes behind their wire-rimmed spectacles, when he waved to her every day. Would he smile tomorrow? Would she smile back, as if nothing had happened?

Metal grates guarded the door and windows. She turned the corner and spied a window high on the wall, just within her reach if she jumped, open a crack. It had been unseasonably warm. Had the jeweler opened it for some ventilation and forgotten to shut it again, since it was so far into October that open windows should be a thing of the past?

No matter. It made her work easier. No need to pull out her makeshift lock pick, carved out of an old knife, secreted in a breast pocket.

She backed across the space between that building and the next, then sprinted forward and launched herself up, her fingers catching on the bricks at the window's base. With a tug, she pulled the window open wide, then walked her feet up the wall and slithered through head-first. The floor was a long way down, but she kept one hand on the window-ledge and twisted her body until she hung down the wall, then dropped. Her knees bent, absorbing the impact and minimizing any sound.

Jin froze for a moment, listening. The jeweler lived above his shop. She couldn't risk being caught. Yao would be sent straight back into the Orphan Care Authority dormitories and the predations of his peers. At twelve years old, he was four years her junior, and she'd only recently earned enough to take him under her guardianship in a ramshackle apartment where they subsisted on O.C.A. nutrition bars. It wasn't much, but at least she could begin fulfilling her promise to her mother to watch over him and give him his best chance to make something of his life.

After a silent count to a hundred, Jin decided it was safe to move on. She had dropped into the jeweler's workshop. The worktable sat in the center of the room, littered with tools and coils of silver and gold wire.

Jin padded past, guided by the light in the hallway, then slipped into the showroom.

A spirit-bell hung over the entryway, but Jin resisted the urge to ring it, despite the intensifying feeling that she was being watched. Spirits weren't going to turn her over to the police. People would. Besides, it was probably nothing more than her own guilty conscience. Even now she could hear her mother's ghostly admonishment. *Find another way. I'm ashamed to see my daughter is a thief.*

"I'm sorry, Mother," she whispered, hardly more than an exhale. "There isn't another way."

Glass cases lined the walls, filled with handmade jewelry — pearl necklaces, gold rings set with precious stones, and jade figurines ranging from a beetle the size of her thumbnail to a reclining ox, nearly as long as her forearm. She passed them by. The lion in the front window called to Auntie Bai Wei's coin like a lodestone.

Jin reached the window and picked up the lion. It felt warm. The wild edges of its mane dug into her palm. Gently, she reminded herself. Jade was strong, but not unbreakable. She placed it at the bottom of her jacket pocket, then returned the way she'd come.

As she slipped out of the showroom, a floorboard squealed under her weight. Jin froze. An electric light flashed on at the top of a flight of stairs leading up to the next floor. Without a backward glance, Jin fled through the workroom and launched herself at the window.

Footsteps shuffled down the stairs. Jin struggled to wriggle through the open window without putting her weight on the pocket that held the precious figurine. Her other pocket caught on the handle that turned to open and close the pane. With a silent curse, Jin backed up and freed herself, then slithered out and dropped to the ground in a clumsy roll.

Jin stumbled to her feet. The workshop light went on. She sprinted into the darkened alleyway, despite a sharp pain in her hip where she'd hit the ground.

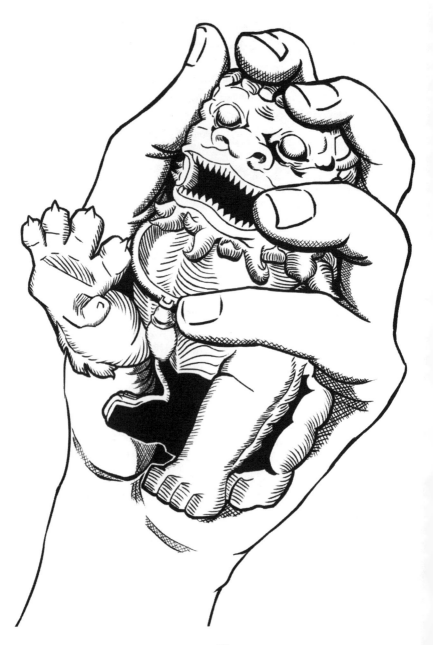

JIN BURST CLEAR OF THE alleyway and into the night market's busy crush. Neon signs advertising beer, cigarettes, and spirit cleansings hung from brick facades, illuminating the patchwork quilt of shacks and tarp-draped booths at the bases of the buildings. With a few quick motions, she lost herself among the milling mass of people.

She pulled her cap lower on her head, making sure her hair was safely tucked, then stuffed her hands in her pockets and hunched her shoulders, curling in on herself. With the collar of her jacket raised, her face was nothing more than a shadow in the neon haze. Her diminutive height and stick-thin body, hidden behind loose-fitting clothes, made her look more like a young boy than a teenage girl.

A pair of spinsters haggled over pickled eggs while a klatch of young men huddled at the corner warming their hands over a brazier and smoking cigarettes. They looked straight past her. Good. If no one noticed her, no one would connect her to the theft.

The figurine seemed to throb in her hand. She released it and pressed ahead. She could hear the river now — the slosh of the water sliding through its concrete banks, the thrum of motors struggling to press boats upstream, the shouting and cursing of cargo men working to unload a supply ship. She moved towards the market street's edge and ducked behind the stalls. Auntie Bai Wei's shop was close, but easy to miss.

Jin ran her hand along the rough brick wall. Hot chili sauce perfumed the air by a noodle seller's cart. A low growl rumbled up from her center. It had been months since she'd tasted something other than the nutritional bars provided by the Orphan Care Authority or the remnants of discarded fish, too poor a quality to can.

Jin's fingers slipped into a nearly invisible seam running up the mortar. She pressed against the next brick and the wall slid inward, releasing a haze of smoke, reeking of opium, that obscured the entryway to Auntie Bai Wei's domain. You only found Auntie's shop if she wanted you to.

After ducking through the entry, Jin pushed the wall back into place, leaving her in near-total darkness. Time to close her eyes and wait until she could see again. A steady throb of heat pulsed in her pocket. Jin reached inside with a tentative hand and touched the jade lion. It felt like a dying ember. Her eyes flashed open and she pulled it out.

An amber glow radiated from its belly, illuminating the stone from deep inside. Dark veins shot through the jade, where small impurities gave it texture. The red edges pulsed. Jin stared, transfixed, for a moment, then stuffed the thing back in her pocket. This was no simple piece of jade, she realized. There was a spirit trapped in its depths. She needed to be rid of it.

Afterimages danced across her vision while she inched her way through the storeroom in a carefully precise straight line. If she veered even a little she'd stumble over barrels and crates, and Auntie Bai Wei would deduct any damage she caused from the purchase price. It didn't matter that she wasn't there in the storeroom to see it. She always knew. You either waited until you could see, or risked breaking spirits-knew-what. There were folks who were indebted to Auntie so deeply they'd be working off the damage for years.

It didn't matter that it had been Auntie Bai Wei who found Jin at the O.C.A.'s employment fair and coerced the cannery into hiring her, although Jin had already been passed over for being too small. Nor did it matter that she had gone on to recruit Jin into her band of "collectors," and occasionally slipped a new textbook for Yao, full of technical details Jin couldn't begin to comprehend, into the payment. If you broke Auntie's stock, you paid for it.

Jin had learned the lesson early, and she'd been lucky. All she'd broken was an old teapot that had already been cracked and glued once before. Auntie Bai Wei took the bronze medallion Jin had just snatched from her neighbor — an old blind soldier who had stumbled into Yao in the hallway, then started bellowing that Yao was a spirit host — and called it even.

It was the only time Jin hadn't felt a moment of remorse when she stole. Anyone foolish enough to accuse a small boy of being a spirit host deserved what came to him. It was only luck no one else had been home and come to investigate the shouting. She'd seen what happened when the government workers came to take away suspected hosts — the protective gear as if they were entering a quarantine ward, syringes full of "medicine" to keep the spirit at bay when they dragged the host off to the black prison perched at the river's edge.

If they had come for Yao, the old soldier might have found himself dead rather than short one small medallion. Even the perpetually disapproving ghostly voice of Jin's mother didn't say a word.

Jin found the inner door by walking straight into it. The purple-rimmed, lion-shaped holes in her vision refused to clear. Wincing at the sharp pain where her knee hit the door, Jin opened it and stepped into the cluttered chaos of Auntie Bai Wei's shop.

Thick incense hung in the air and tickled the back of Jin's throat. A brilliant riot of colored paper lanterns hung from the exposed rafters, their flickering light illuminating the room. Cases with sagging shelves lined the walls and mapped a maze through the center. An ancient *guqin* stood in a corner, quietly playing itself, a haunting, traditional melody. The counter stood on the far wall behind a row of carved wooden chests.

Jin descended the two steps to the shop floor. There were no customers and no Auntie Bai Wei. Aside from the *guqin,* nothing made a sound. Jin had never been there without at least one other person browsing the knick-knacks, jewelry, antiques, and benevolent-spirit-occupied objects like the *guqin,* or waiting to haggle with Auntie over the price of a new offering.

"Auntie Bai Wei?" Jin called. Her voice sounded unnaturally loud as it bounced off the cinder-block walls.

There was no reply. Jin crossed the shop, picking her way past the row of vases lining the ends of the shelves, exactly where everyone would have to walk by to reach the counter. Perfect for someone clumsy to brush against and topple, with luck starting a domino wave of destruction they would then have to pay for.

When she reached the counter, Jin picked up a mallet resting on a porcelain platter and banged the gong that stood on the shelf. The clangor reverberated through the shop, temporarily overwhelming the *guqin's* song. When the noise dissipated, Jin listened for any sign of Auntie's response.

Nothing.

A sense of unease sank into Jin's bones. It was too early for the shop to be closed, and Auntie Bai Wei wouldn't have left the outer door unlocked if she'd stepped out. Besides, she had to have been there to light the lanterns.

"Auntie?" she called again.

A gust of wind swirled through the shop. The lanterns flared, then died, plunging the shop into blackness. Jin's cap flew from her head and the wind pressed her back against the counter. The gong vibrated, sending up a low din, and the *guqin* went silent.

Heavy footsteps clomped down the stairs. When they reached the cement floor, a sound like bone on rock scraped into the shop.

Jin dropped into a crouch. Whoever, or whatever, was coming, she had no desire to meet it. She inched backwards along the counter's edge, grateful for her hand-me-down trainers that made no sound.

The footsteps drew closer, accompanied by heavy wheezing breaths.

Jin found the corner and slipped behind, into Auntie Bai Wei's personal sanctum. Her pocket surged with heat and the scent of scalding fabric assailed her nostrils. She grabbed the figurine and tossed the burning jade away, realizing a moment too late that the sound of its clatter would alert whatever was in the shop that it wasn't alone.

The lion flew. Brilliant light exploded.

Jin threw her arm across her eyes, too late to escape the glare's full brunt.

Instead of the crack of jade hitting cement, a roar rolled like thunder off the walls, shook the counter, and set the gong reverberating again.

The approaching person/thing — Jin still couldn't be certain which — howled. Once more, the gale-force winds ripped past. Crashes sounded among the shelves. The roar rang out again and the footsteps retreated, back up the stairs. The door slammed shut.

Abruptly, the wind dropped into nothingness. Jin slowly lowered her arm. Golden light illuminated the shop, though the lanterns remained unlit. She raised herself until she could peek over the edge of the counter. A massive white lion stood on widespread paws on the far side, shaking its ruddy mane, red-tipped tail lashing, emanating light.

Jin dropped back down and leaned against the drawers, not caring that the handles dug into her back. Her breath came in shallow pants.

A spirit-lion, newly released from its jade prison.

She was trapped.

Jin pressed down on the cold cement floor, wishing she could become a part of it, or turn invisible, like the heroes in the old tales. She bit down on her tongue, and fought the urge to scream. Instead, she forced herself to focus. There were ways to send an escaped spirit back, if only she could remember. The heroes always spoke words of power, lost now in the dim recesses of her memory.

Besides, she was no hero.

She didn't know what to say, but she clasped her hands in front of her and moved her lips silently, afraid to make a sound. *Go back, lion. The danger is gone. You've frightened it away, and you can go back home now.*

So slowly that at first Jin didn't notice, the shop dimmed until she sat in blackness. Her pulse thudded in her ears. She stood up and squinted into the shop.

Nothing. No lion. No strange, scraping creature that tossed winds like weapons.

She blew out a whooshing breath and leaned on the counter, her arms trembling.

"Are you here to help us?"

Jin jolted so hard she knocked the mallet and its platter off the counter. The porcelain crashed in a burst of shards. "Who's there?"

"I'm sorry," came the voice again, with a strange, lilting cadence. "I didn't mean to startle you. But you brought the guardian, so I ask again, are you here to help us?"

A hiss like a match sounded overhead and a lantern lit. The single flame cast the room into deep amber light. Shadows danced among the shelves as the lantern flickered. The lion figurine stood in front of the counter, its paw once again raised and muzzle roaring wide.

"Who are you?" Jin asked.

A tiny woman, no taller than Jin's thigh, stepped out from behind a carved box. Two blue sticks inlaid with mother-of-pearl caught her ebony hair in a sleek twist. Her eyes glowed a soft cerulean that matched her traditional silk robe. "I am Liu, Spirit of the *Guqin*." She steepled her hands in front of her and bowed. "Greetings to you, and thank you for protecting us."

Jin returned the bow reflexively. She stepped out from behind the counter, accidentally grinding porcelain shards underfoot. A voice in the back of her mind wondered how much the platter had been worth and how she would pay it off when Auntie Bai Wei returned.

"My name's Jin," she said.

A smile spread Liu's red lips. "We know. Auntie Bai Wei tells us all about you."

"I need to sit."

"Please," Liu gestured to the box she'd come from behind. "Rest yourself."

Jin settled herself gingerly on the carved lid. The contours impressed themselves into her bottom, but she didn't dare sit anywhere else. "Where is Auntie Bai Wei?"

Liu frowned, the corners of her painted-on eyebrows crinkling down towards her nose. "They took her."

"Who took her?" Jin tried not to think about the fact that she was having a conversation with a spirit.

Everyone knew spirits existed, of course, but nobody ever actually saw one, despite the show the spirit cleansers put on, tricking gullible folks into spending their hard-earned yuan to rid their home of "evil spirits." Some drifted harmlessly on the breeze, with nothing to ground them. Others took up residence in objects. Still other spirits, the most dangerous of all, took human hosts.

"We don't know," Liu said. "Two men came last night to trade. When Auntie Bai Wei took the statue they offered, she went stiff. They led her away, and she didn't struggle, but I saw her eyes. She was afraid, Jin. Terrified."

Jin tried to wrap her mind around the image of Auntie Bai Wei frightened. She was a giant of a woman, taller than most men, and broad-shouldered. In her youth, she'd trained in wushu, and while she'd put on weight in the years since, she could still lift objects Jin wouldn't have been able to budge, and her reflexes were tiger-sharp. She wore her silvering black hair spiky and was never without a set of heavy knuckle rings that she could use with power and skill. If ever there was a woman less likely to be afraid, Jin had never met her.

"Were they like that... thing... that was just here?"

"No. They were men like you, or at least they appeared to be. One never really knows if they're a spirit wearing someone else's skin."

Jin rested her head in her hands and closed her eyes. She shouldn't be involved in this. She should walk out the door, go back to the apartment and Yao, and pretend this night had never happened. Leave the lion and the *guqin* and all the strangeness behind.

But she wasn't going to leave Auntie Bai Wei to the mercy of whoever it was who had taken her. Not after feeling the power of the thing that had entered the shop that night. Besides, after a year of coming to trade at least once a month, Jin had come to consider Auntie Bai Wei a friend. A strange sort of friend, perhaps, but outside of Yao, Jin had no one else.

"How can I help?"

The rest of the lanterns flared into life and shouts of joy rose from all over the shop. Tiny people appeared from beneath teacups, out of vases, dropping down from the lanterns. Larger spirits hid in the shadows, nearly as tall as the shelves. Some looked human. Others were animals: rabbits, dogs, monkeys; and yet others were some motley combination of both.

The spirits swarmed towards her.

Jin pulled her feet up onto the box.

"Find her!" they cried. "Find Auntie Bai Wei and bring her home to us."

"I don't know how," Jin whispered, awed at the sheer number of spirits crowding close.

There must be a spirit for every item in the shop. Was that what Auntie Bai Wei did? Collect spirit-occupied items? Was that what called to her coin?

White-hot pain flared in Jin's temples and she grasped her head tight, overwhelmed at the revelation.

Liu picked up the jade figurine in both hands. "You must take the guardian." She lifted it towards Jin.

Jin flinched away.

"Don't be afraid," Liu said. "It answers to its keeper. You."

Jin didn't want to take it — the beast it unleashed was terrifying — but she leaned down and let Liu drop it into her palm. The jade was cool now. No hint of light glowed within, but a warm feeling of comfort and safety wrapped Jin in its heavy paws. She pocketed the lion.

"We cannot leave this place," Liu continued. "We're bound to our hosts. But you can find her, Jin, and you must, soon, before they find you."

Jin's heart skipped a beat and she stared at the miniature woman.

"What do you mean?"

"We heard them talking. They're hunting down the sensitives. They'll find you."

A spirit with the face of a dog, the body of a man, and the tail of a monkey pressed through the crowd carrying Jin's hat. He handed it up to her.

"Thank you," she said.

The spirit yipped and turned in a circle, chasing its tail.

Jin shoved the cap back onto her head, once again tucking her hair underneath.

Liu reached up and laid a dainty hand on Jin's foot. "I can give you little help, but this — they smelled of the river."

"All right," Jin said. "I'll lock the door on my way out. Hopefully it will help to keep you safe."

"Just bring Auntie back to us," Liu said.

The sea of spirits parted, leaving a clear path of concrete to the stairs.

Jin stepped down from the box, took a deep breath and straightened her shoulders, forcing herself to ignore her throbbing headache. She strode towards the door.

"Good luck," Liu called out. "Bring her home."

OUTSIDE THE FALSE WALL, THE market went on as if everything in the world hadn't just changed. The noodle-seller shouted his wares, but the last thing Jin could think of was food, no matter that it had been hours since the nutrition bars she'd shared with Yao at dinner-time. Setting one foot in front of the other, she followed the sounds of the river.

The jade lion lay quiescent in her pocket, but she couldn't forget the image of it standing so proudly against the intruder, its muscles flexing beneath its pale pelt, nor the sense of comfort she felt when she once again held it in her hand. Maybe it wasn't such a bad thing to have, after all. If she hadn't stolen it, she wouldn't have gone to Auntie's shop. Whatever that thing was would have done whatever it came to do, and Jin couldn't believe it had good intentions. Was it chance that brought the lion to her attention, or was she meant to find it?

Her mind whirled. These weren't the sorts of thoughts she was used to. She was a simple cannery girl. Her brother was the smart one, the one destined to make a mark on the world. How could she entertain the idea that something as powerful as the guardian wanted her enough to put itself in her path?

She reached into her pocket and ran her fingers over the cool jade. The same reassuring presence blanketed her as she'd felt back in Auntie Bai Wei's shop.

The market thinned when she drew close to the river. A few merchants catered to the dock workers, but most stayed closer to the apartment buildings and shops back towards the Old Town's center. Jin kept her face hidden behind her collar, head down. They smelled of the river, Liu had said. It wasn't much to go on. The river wound through the center of the city, kilometers long, and she might have to search both banks, although she'd never crossed to the far side, where the tech-runners' sleek, glistening towers speared the skyline.

Keeping to the shadows, Jin slunk to the river's edge. A reeking miasma hung over it like fog. The stinking refuse that clogged the water's edge and the persistent odor of sweat from the dockhands who worked day and night loading and unloading cargo mingled with a stale hint of urine from along the base of the nearest building. Jin took a step away, still clinging to the shadows.

Downstream, electric lights blazed at a slip where a barge crammed to overflowing with crates sat at anchor. Men swarmed like ants, boxes balanced on heads or cradled in muscular arms.

Jin closed her eyes. She needed a plan. Wandering aimlessly along the riverbank would do nothing but give her blisters, and maybe get her arrested for trespassing into freight company property. There had to be some way to narrow the search.

She reached into her pocket and grasped the jade lion. It throbbed with heat.

"All right." Jin took a steadying breath. "Can you help me find Auntie Bai Wei?"

Two pulses.

Fine. If trusting a spirit was the only way to find her friend, that was what she'd do. What would Yao think if she ever told him? His head was so filled with facts and theorems, he'd probably laugh and say she was as superstitious as the rest of the Old Town folk.

"Let's try this," Jin said. "I'm going to turn in a circle. When I'm pointing the right way, give me a sign."

She held the figurine in front of her, then slowly pirouetted until a flash of warmth stopped her. Peering into the darkness along the upstream path down which she was pointed, Jin swallowed hard. No light, but the dim glow from the freight slip and the glimmering towers on the opposite bank. So be it.

AFTER FOLLOWING THE LION'S COMPASS for what felt like hours, Jin stopped at the base of an abandoned warehouse and stared at what lay ahead — the black bulk of the prison that housed accused spirit hosts. As she'd crept along the river's edge, she'd begun to suspect the jade lion might lead her to this place. Although she'd seen it before from a distance, she'd never had a reason to come close. It loomed overhead, blotting out the few stars that managed to shine through thin tears in the cloud cover.

No windows. No doors. How was she supposed to get inside? Even if she could, what would await her there? Stories whispered in dark corners told of crazed spirit hosts, caged and chained — of screams loud enough to be heard even through the heavy cinder block walls. If Auntie Bai Wei had been taken to this place, did it mean she was a spirit host? And if she were, was she dangerous? How did the men, whoever they had been, subdue her? Liu hadn't said anything about syringes or quarantine suits.

It didn't matter. Jin was committed. She'd find a way inside, no matter what waited there. Besides, the lion figurine still hummed with residual heat and it reassured her. She wasn't alone.

A chain link fence topped with razor wire encircled the prison. There were no lights, so Jin slipped out from hiding and darted towards the fence. While she'd have no difficulty scaling the chain links, the razor wire was a problem. No matter how small or how flexible she was, she didn't see a way she'd be able to get through it without serious injury. Instead, she followed the fence around the building's perimeter, looking for any weak spots.

On the far side from where she'd begun, she found what she was looking for. In the stretch between two poles, a section of chain had been warped inward. It wasn't much, but Jin doubted she'd find better.

She lay flat on the concrete and pressed forward, her head and shoulder further bending the fence until they burst free on the far side. Wriggling like a snake, Jin scooted forward, despite tearing her jacket on the rough ground. An edge of chain caught in the back pocket of her jeans. Panic surged through her veins, but she backed up, readjusted her hips, and tried again.

At last, she was through, and she raced toward the shelter of the prison's shadow. She leaned up against the cinder blocks and gasped for breath.

The easy part was done. When she stopped panting, she rose and ran her fingers along the wall, like she did to find the entry to Auntie Bai Wei's shop. Maybe the same sort of hidden door served this place. Maybe, if she was lucky, she'd find the seam before the sun rose.

A sudden squeal of metal on metal froze Jin in place. Somewhere up ahead, around the corner of the building, the gate was opening. Jin inched forward on silent feet, then ducked low and peered around the corner, keeping her face in shadow.

Two men in black business suits walked through the open gate, leading someone between them. For a moment, Jin's heart leapt at the thought it might be Auntie Bai Wei, but the person was much too small. Once inside, the nearest man stepped away to close the gate behind them.

A moonbeam pierced through the thin clouds and illuminated the scene.

Jin stopped breathing. *Yao.*

Before she could react, the man was back and they led Yao towards the wall at a brisk pace. He followed without protest, awkward and stiff.

Her years of petty theft told her to wait and watch. See how the suits got inside. Follow when it was safe.

But that was her brother.

With a howl, Jin leapt from the shadows and barreled into the nearest man. She rammed her head into his gut and he staggered back, gasping for breath. In his moment of disorientation, Jin swept her leg behind the other man's, knocking his feet out from under him. He crashed to the ground.

"Yao, run!" she shouted.

She turned her attention back to the first man, who had recovered his wind and lunged forward, fists swinging. Jin ducked and dodged close enough to smell his cologne, then slammed her heel down on the top of his foot. He staggered away with a grunt.

Jin turned back, but Yao hadn't so much as turned his head. "Yao?" She grabbed his hand and yanked. If they could get outside the fence the way she'd come in, the men were too big to follow. They'd have a head start while the others wrestled with the locks on the gate.

Yao remained immobile, as stiff as a statue, but his eyes followed her with a pleading stare. Just like Liu had described Auntie Bai Wei.

Jin slapped him, hard. Smarting pain bloomed in her hand, but Yao didn't move. His eyes went wide, looking past her left shoulder.

She spun in time to see the second man's fist just before it crashed into the side of her head. The world went black.

JIN'S EYES BLINKED OPEN IN a dimly-lit cell. Her head throbbed where the man in the suit had clobbered her. A sick sensation hung in the back of her throat. She swallowed back the nausea.

Where was Yao?

A quick glance told her she was alone, with nothing save the rickety cot on which she lay and a toilet in the far corner. The back wall was bare cinder-blocks. A sharp chill emanated through it into the cell. Iron bars formed the other three walls. Another row of cells lay on the far side of a central hallway. The only light came from a bare bulb glowing over the hall.

The cells to either side of her were empty, but across the way, a dark figure hugged the shadows. Jin swung her feet to the floor and sat up.

Dizziness swept over her in waves. She probed the lump on the back of her head. Her fingers came away bloody, but from what she could tell, her skull was in one piece, only the scalp split. Jin wiped her hand on her jeans.

She lurched upright and stumbled forward, catching herself on the bars of the door. Clinging there, she closed her eyes and waited for the world to stop spinning.

When she was fairly certain she wouldn't collapse if she let go, she straightened and dug in the breast pocket of her jacket for her lock picking tools. When her fingers closed around them, she let out a relieved breath. The men in suits must not have worried too much about her — or else they had something much bigger to think about — if they hadn't taken the time to search her. The pick wasn't well-hidden.

With deft motions, she set to work.

The figure across the hall inched forward, crouched low, until it was pressed up against the bars. "Shouldn't do that." The voice was high and light. A woman. "They won't like it."

Using the tension wrench to turn the cylinder gently counter-clockwise, Jin felt the pick catch one tumbler after another. When the last tumbler fell into place, she turned the cylinder further counter-clockwise. The bolt slid back with a welcome *thunk*.

Moving smoothly, less dizzy with each passing breath, Jin pushed the door open.

It creaked, as if it hadn't been oiled in decades. She paused and waited, not breathing. When nobody came to investigate, she slipped out of the cell, crossed the hall, and knelt in front of her fellow prisoner. "Did you see who brought me? Was there a boy with them?"

The figure giggled. "Boy, boy, plays with toys!"

Jin plunged a hand between the bars and grabbed the stranger's plain black T-shirt, yanking the woman forward until the bars dented her skin. Jin pressed her own face close enough she could feel the other's breath on her skin. "Did you see?"

The woman shied away, breaking free of Jin's grasp. "Never see anything." She slid back on all fours. "Not safe to see."

Jin rose and backed away. The stranger was crazy. Maybe she was a spirit host. Maybe whatever rode her had shattered her mind. Further talk wouldn't bring her any closer to finding Yao. *Or Auntie Bai Wei,* a small voice reminded her.

Jin pushed the thought away. If she found Bai Wei, she would try to help her, but Yao came first. Her hand slid into her pocket, and when she found the jade lion still resting there, she nearly sobbed. She pulled it free and cradled it in front of her lips. *Help me find Yao,* she begged silently. *Help me find my brother.*

She swung the lion first to her left, then to her right, where it flared with heat. With catlike steps she padded down the hallway's length to the closed door at its end. She pulled it open. The woman she'd left behind began to wail, throwing herself against the bars. "Take me with you! Don't leave me!"

Jin shut the door behind her, muffling the woman's cries. Her heart thudded against her ribs. The figurine's warmth centered her, and she followed its lead into a maze of winding corridors.

As Jin crept through the bowels of the prison, she became aware of a low, steady thrum, like the building had its own beating heart. She felt it reverberating in her chest, only barely able to pick it up at the lower spectrum of her hearing. Her hand tightened around the jade lion.

She passed cellblocks full of prisoners, mostly sleeping, some pacing their cells from end to end like caged beasts, others chained to the walls. Most ignored her, although a few hid like rats when she approached; others reached through the bars, begging her to release them.

Time and again, she shook her head and walked on. What good could it do to undo the cages? With a contingent of prisoners tromping at her heels, or running loose through the prison, it would not be long before someone, or something, noticed. Besides, she still had no idea how to get into the building, never mind out.

So she left the wretched souls behind and blocked out the sobs of the few who begged her to set them free. She held the lion in her left hand, its amber glow hidden in her palm, and the lock pick in her right, ready to use as a weapon if she were forced to fight.

More than once, the lion led her through doors into stairwells leading down, deep below ground level. The lower she climbed, the stronger the skeletal building's throbbing pulse, until her teeth rattled against each other when her feet touched the floor.

The stairwell led past several doors with small rectangular windows. Jin glanced through when she passed. Wide rooms, lit by blue-tinged fluorescents, stretched as far as she could see. The tubes illuminated stacks of electronics, humming with energy.

She'd seen illustrations like this in the textbooks Auntie Bai Wei gathered for Yao — some deep tech that Jin couldn't hope to comprehend. What it was doing on this side of the river was a mystery, but one she wasn't interested in solving. All she wanted was to find her brother.

Two more floors, then the lion gave a sharp surge of heat. Jin glanced through the window. This floor was dark. No light, save what shone in through the stairwell window.

So be it. Cautiously, Jin pulled open the door. It opened without a sound. She slipped into the darkness.

The jade lion led her into the black, beyond the arc of the stairwell's glow. Unable to see so much as her hand in front of her face, Jin opened her fingers, allowing the figurine's amber radiance to light the way.

Heavy metal doors without windows lined the hallway on either side. Was Yao in this place? What sort of terror must he be enduring? Jin increased her pace.

When the hallway dead-ended at the wall, the lion flared bright. A low groan emanated from behind the right-hand door. Jin knew that voice. Auntie Bai Wei.

Frustration coursed through her. She'd asked the guardian to lead her to Yao, not Bai Wei. Still, she was here. She would do what she could.

She tried the door, but, as she expected, it was locked. Once more, she went to work with the pick. Auntie's voice went silent.

After several long moments, the lock clicked open and Jin pulled the door wide.

Auntie Bai Wei stood with her back to the wall, crouched in a fighting stance. When the figurine lit the room, Bai Wei squinted. "Stay back, demon," she growled. "You surprised me once. Never again."

"Auntie Bai Wei, it's me, Jin."

Bai Wei's arms drooped to her sides. "Jin?" She blinked and rubbed her eyes.

"It's me, Auntie. Liu sent me."

Auntie Bai Wei's gaze settled on the figurine clutched in Jin's hand. A look of wonder spread across her face. "Is that... the guardian?"

"Yes. At least, that's what Liu said."

Auntie Bai Wei straightened and she clasped a hand against her chest. "Spirits be blessed," she breathed. "We may yet get out of this alive."

The coin nestled beneath Jin's shirt throbbed, in time with the building's strange pulse. "Auntie," she said. "They have Yao."

Bai Wei looked down, piercing Jin with her dark gaze. "They took your brother?"

"I tried to stop them, but they hit me over the head and threw me in a cell. I don't know where they took him."

Bai Wei stalked forward, looming over Jin. "Those fiends are fools to have left you in possession of the guardian. It must have been Yao's presence that protected you. His spirit guest is powerful, though meek. They couldn't see past it to your own strength."

"Yao's a spirit host?"

"Of course, foolish girl. Why else do you think I pulled the two of you from the orphanage? His spirit guest and your innate sensitivity shine like beacons to those who have eyes to see."

"Please," Jin said, "I need my brother back."

"I'll help you," said Auntie Bai Wei, "but you'll need the guardian as well."

"It didn't help when I attacked the men who had Yao."

Bai Wei stepped out of her cell and into the darkness.

Jin scurried out behind her, holding the jade lion high.

"That's because they were men," Bai Wei said. "Against men, the guardian can do nothing. Against spirits, though, it will be your best hope. Ask it to find your brother."

"I already did," Jin said, shadowing Bai Wei along the corridor. "It brought me to you."

"You need me, girl." Bai Wei's voice hid grim laughter behind it. "The guardian isn't stupid."

"All right." Jin closed her eyes and drew Yao's image on the back of her eyelids, his slight frame and intelligent gaze. "Find him," she said, "before it's too late."

Back into the stairwell, then once more down. The building's pulse hammered at Jin's eardrums. Auntie Bai Wei didn't seem to notice, or she was better at ignoring. Neither spoke another word while they descended into the prison's depths. They were deep enough now that Jin wondered if they were beneath even the river's floor.

At last, they reached the bottom. The guardian flared, but there was no need. Only one way remained — a black door painted with red calligraphy, in an old style Jin couldn't read.

The building's pulse drowned out her own. Sweat slicked her hands; her legs trembled. Her bravery fled in the face of that door and its incomprehensible scrawl.

Auntie Bai Wei clapped a hand to her shoulder. Jin looked up. Bai Wei gave her a lopsided grin. It heartened her. She smiled back.

Bai Wei put her hand to the doorknob and pushed. It made no sound. Nothing stirred on the other side. Jin followed Bai Wei through. The lights on this level looked like the fluorescent tubes above, but they were as red as the calligraphy on the door, reminding Jin far too much of blood.

Together, Jin and Bai Wei crossed the room, the guardian once again within Jin's closed fist. The disturbing lights were enough to see by. There was no reason to announce their presence.

A piercing shriek echoed down the hallway. Jin sucked in a harsh breath. Yao.

She would have rushed forward, but Auntie Bai Wei wrapped a strong hand around her wrist.

"Carefully," Bai Wei whispered.

The wail died off. Jin squeezed her eyes shut, trying to ignore it. Impossible. She opened her eyes and pressed forward.

As they followed the blood-red corridor, a heavy, moist scent wafted towards them. The painted concrete walls gave way to natural stone that arced away to either side, opening into a vast cavern. Jin and Bai Wei hugged the wall, circling towards a brilliant, scarlet light that brightened and dimmed in time with the overwhelming pulse.

When they drew closer, it resolved itself into a massive garnet, the size of the noodle seller's cart, throbbing red to black and back again.

Four men in suits stood beside a metal surgical table where Yao's small form lay prone. Two were the men who had kidnapped him.

Wires and tubes led from Yao's body into a bank of machinery; from there, lines of pure scarlet energy lanced into the beating garnet.

Bai Wei sucked in a breath. "So that's the answer. They're stealing spirit life-energy to feed that... thing." Her hand squeezed hard into Jin's wrist. "Wait here," she breathed, so low Jin could hardly hear her. "If I can do this alone, then let me."

Auntie didn't wait for a response. She picked up a stone from the cavern floor and raced forward. With a howl, she launched it. The rock crashed into the machinery. Sparks geysered in a sizzling shower. The men turned away from Yao and found Auntie Bai Wei nearly on them. She fell among them in a dizzying whirl of kicks and punches. Two men slumped to the ground and lay there motionless. The others quickly realized their danger and dropped low, sliding to either side of Bai Wei.

Jin grasped her lock pick and inched forward. The nearest man had his back to her. Moving soundlessly, she advanced when Bai Wei feinted towards him, keeping him distracted, before spinning to keep an eye on her other opponent.

Yao shrieked again, the sound echoing off the cavern's high ceiling.

Distracted, Jin stumbled over an upthrust of rock. A cry leapt from her lips before she could pull it back.

The man turned and advanced. His eyes glowed as red as the garnet.

Jin regained her balance and held the lock pick on its knife handle in front of her, trying to mimic Bai Wei's fighting stance. "You want me?" she cried. "Come and get me!"

He lunged, swinging with powerful blows. Jin ducked low and stabbed up with the pick. It plunged into his gut with a sickening squelch. Lurching to the side, he wrenched away and Jin lost her grip on the pick. He staggered back, the makeshift weapon protruding from his belly.

His hand wrapped around it and he pulled it free, wiping it clean on his immaculate suit pants. Jin stumbled away. What kind of monster was this? His wound didn't so much as slow his advance, and now he brandished her own weapon against her.

The man feinted with a punch. Jin tried to dodge, but she was too slow. The pick sank into her shoulder in a burning blossom of pain. Once more he plunged it downward, aiming for her throat. She spun away, but tripped over her own feet and fell forward to the ground. She rolled to her back, trembling.

"Get up, little girl," the man goaded, ignoring the blood staining his shirt.

Jin staggered to her feet.

"Go ahead," he said, a maniacal look in his ruby-red eyes. "Hit me."

Her left shoulder throbbed so badly, she could hardly think for the pain. Gritting her teeth, she drew back her right arm and swung for his jaw. He danced away, laughing, until he gave a sudden grunt and collapsed, twitching, to the ground.

Auntie Bai Wei stood behind him, breathing hard, a bloodied stone in her fist. "Go," she gasped. "Get your brother."

Jin lurched towards Yao. Tremors shook the cavern, and the light flared bright. She flexed her knees and kept moving until she reached her brother's side.

Yao stared up at her, tears pooled in the corners of his eyes. She knew he hated when she saw him cry, so she pretended not to see. Thick, red fluid pulsed through the tubes inserted under his skin. Jin hesitated to touch them. The wires were a different matter. Sharp-toothed clamps pinched his skin, leaving bloody welts.

Hands shaking, Jin released the first clamp. The garnet howled.

Jin ignored it, tearing Yao free from the wires. Auntie Bai Wei appeared at her side and joined in. In a matter of moments, all the wires with their vicious clamps lay in a tangled pile on the ground.

Jin looked over at Bai Wei. "What do we do now?"

What would her mother have said? How poor a guardian she was to have left Yao alone and unprotected? How Jin's thieving ways had brought this horror down on them?

Jin felt it keenly. If she could replace him on that slab, sticking each tube into her own flesh, would it save him? She made up her mind to try.

She reached for the first tube. The garnet's pulsing rush went silent, and the cavern sank into a blackness so deep Jin couldn't even see Yao, less than a hands-breadth away. She froze.

"That can't be good," Auntie Bai Wei said.

With a crash and groan, the garnet ruptured, searing ruby light flaring from the eggshell crack that formed along its side. Blood-red shards splintered and fell in a staccato rain. A monstrous spirit stepped free, swelling when it left the stone's confines, until its head nearly touched the ceiling. Scales armored the creature's muscular body. Long, curving talons scraped the cave floor. A powerful stench of sulfur surged forth from the shattered garnet.

In the broken stone's dim glow, Yao spasmed, nearly throwing himself off the table. Auntie Bai Wei lunged forward, pinning him beneath her.

Jin stared up at the towering beast, momentarily frozen. Then its red eyes focused on Yao and it advanced, clawed hands outstretched. Jin's heart stuttered. Adrenaline surged through her limbs. Only a small part of her mind registered the guardian's searing heat as she shouted and threw the jade figurine towards the monster with her good arm.

The radiant lion burst free in a rush of amber brilliance that made Jin look away. Its roar rattled her teeth. She clenched her jaw and forced her eyes forward. Landing on broad red paws between Yao and the spirit — it had to be a spirit, if the guardian could challenge it — the lion shook its heavy mane and bared its teeth.

"Jin, help me," Auntie Bai Wei called in a low voice, just audible over the guardian's growl.

The monstrous spirit stepped closer, and the lion lunged forward, its muzzle curling with a warning snarl.

"Jin!"

She didn't want to look away. What if the guardian wasn't enough? Could she fight? Her injured shoulder ached bone-deep, the pain blurred beneath a curtain of terrified energy. Jin felt helpless. Useless. What could she, a cannery girl and a thief, hope to do?

But Bai Wei was calling and maybe, even if she couldn't fight a spirit, maybe she could help Auntie. She dragged her gaze away from the confrontation.

Yao had stopped moving. The tubes lay flaccid. Empty.

Auntie Bai Wei shook Yao's shoulders. "He's not breathing," she said. With her powerful hand, she grasped his wrist. After a moment, she squeezed her eyes shut. "No pulse."

Jin shook her head and moved forward with stuttering steps. He couldn't be dead. Couldn't leave her alone with nothing but failure and regret.

Auntie Bai Wei began chest compressions, hard and fast. Yao's still form was so small, surely she must break his ribs, but if it saved him, Jin would willingly pay her any price. If only he would live. If his lungs would fill, his blood would flow...

"Auntie!" Jin grasped the nearest tube. "There's nothing in here."

Continuing her work, Bai Wei glanced over. "The demon wasn't stealing his blood, girl. It was stealing his spirit guest. Yao's been a host for so long, his body doesn't know how to live without it."

"Then he can't be saved?" Anger and fear battled for dominance, but both agreed on one thing. If the tubes had done their work, then they were nothing but a blight, desecrating her brother's corpse. In a haze of rage, Jin tore them free, ignoring the blood that seeped from each empty wound.

When the last tube curled to the ground, a shriek like a thousand fingernails down a thousand blackboards echoed through the cave. Jin fell to her knees, fists pressed against her ears. She turned back towards the battling spirits.

The demon closed its heavy jaws and the wail vanished. It crouched down, muscles bunching as it prepared to leap.

With a swirl of amber, the lion vanished.

The jade figurine lay on its side, tiny and dull. The guardian was gone. In the face of the demon's power, it had fled. Was this the spirit that Liu had put such faith in? That Auntie Bai Wei knew by reputation and name? A coward?

Jin's lock pick was gone, lost in the earlier fight. Her hand closed around a garnet splinter as long as her forearm, and she staggered to her feet.

"Stay back!" She insinuated herself between the demon and her brother. "He's mine."

Baleful red eyes looked down at her and Jin thought she caught a glimmer of amusement. Then, the powerful muscles flexed and the demon soared towards her.

Jin lunged, felt the garnet shard pierce scaly skin and delve into the demon's warm, wet innards. Its bulk carried it forward and she landed on her back, caught beneath it. She struggled to draw in air.

It reared back and Jin could breathe again. The shard went with it, pulsing from red to black to red again. Once more, the demon turned its attention onto Jin. It reached back, talons outstretched, ready to slash at her exposed throat.

A small form stepped past her prone body, hand raised in a gesture of warding. Amber light streamed from him, nearly blinding. "You are banished," he said with Yao's voice.

Jin blinked and shook her head. Impossible. She crab-shuffled backwards until she collided with Auntie Bai Wei's legs.

"You are banished," the boy repeated, his voice now tinged with a deep, rumbling resonance beneath the young-man soprano.

The demon retreated, the arm that had been ready to kill her now shielding its eyes.

Auntie Bai Wei hoisted Jin up and pulled her close, which was good. She didn't think she could have stood without support.

As the boy — *Yao?* — advanced, the demon shrank, hissing and spitting, until it was no larger than Bai Wei. The garnet shard burst free and clattered to the floor. Its pulsing light faded and died.

The boy placed his blazing hand flat on the demon's chest and said, a third time, "You are banished."

With a wail that vanished into silence, the demon sank down, down, down, until it was the size of a beetle. The radiant boy knelt and picked up the toppled figurine and held it in his palm. Muttering words in a language Jin didn't know, he extended it towards the tiny demon. It tried to run, but the figurine pulled it in, subsuming it into its stone heart until there was nothing left but the jade lion, a crimson heart now pulsing in its depths.

Yao rose, his brilliant aura fading, and turned to face Jin and Auntie Bai Wei. And it was Yao — raw wounds where the clamps had grasped him and Jin had wrenched the tubes free erased any doubt — but behind his black eyes a new awareness looked out at them.

Jin felt an overwhelming sense of power and protection under her brother's gaze. She straightened, trying to stand under her own strength. "Yao?"

He smiled, a broad, encompassing smile that Jin hadn't seen since their mother died. "When you broke my connection to the stone heart, you freed me. My spirit guest was gone, but now another could take its place without fear of being consumed by the demon."

Yao extended his hand where the jade lion rested. "This one should not be left like this. It will find a new host, given the chance."

Jin reached for it — hesitated — then snatched it up by the tip of its tail. It felt foul. A shudder ran down her spine. "What would happen if it broke?"

"The spirit within dies with its host."

Jade was strong, but it could be broken, Jin remembered. She dashed the lion to the ground with all that remained of her strength. It shattered into pieces on the stone floor.

A tremor shook the cavern. The metal table shuddered, then toppled. Jin clung to Auntie Bai Wei. Her head swam. From the corner of her eye she saw her left shoulder. Blood saturated the jacket and her shirt, seeping down to stain her jeans. So much blood...

"Follow me, Bai Wei," Yao ordered.

It didn't seem strange to Jin that he would know her name. After all, she had known the guardian.

Jin tried to stumble along over the quaking ground, but couldn't keep her feet. Bai Wei hoisted Jin over her broad shoulder and chased after Yao. Jin tried to protest, but her head kept knocking against Auntie's back and the shoulder digging into her stomach gave her no room to breathe, and besides, she was so very tired...

Images swam by in fits and starts. Into the stairwell. Bai Wei's labored breathing. No lights. Shouldn't there have been lights? Up and up and into the cellblocks. Yao melting locks. More quakes. So many people, all following her little brother like he was some sort of promised savior. *Boy, boy, plays with toys...* Walls crumbling. Yao's powerful radiance deflecting the stones. The smell of the river. Nothing.

JIN WOKE TO THE STRONG scent of chili sauce. Her eyes flew open. She was in Auntie Bai Wei's shop.

Yao sat beside her, shoveling noodles into his mouth. Seeing she was awake, he picked up an extra bowl that sat on the carved box beside him. "Want some?"

Her mouth watered and her stomach gave a growl that felt nearly as loud as the lion's roar. She pushed herself into a sitting position. Her shoulder protested, but didn't give out. Heavy bandages wrapped it, underneath an embroidered silk robe. "Please," she replied.

She didn't know what to say to him. Her little brother, the mouse, was the boy she knew. Who this boy — this little lion — would be, was a mystery.

She accepted the bowl and took a cautious bite. It had been so long since anything other than nutrition bars or cannery remains had touched her tongue the chili sauce felt like fireworks and flame. Tears welled in her eyes, not from pain, but from the simple relief of being cared for. For once, not shouldering the weight of expectation and guilt.

The little dog-faced spirit who had given back her hat not so very long ago capered up and down the nearest shelf, dodging trinkets and bric-a-brac, peering over with curious eyes. Liu sat, poised and dainty, at Yao's side.

Jin heard Auntie Bai Wei coming before she saw her. Although there was weariness in her face, she looked happier than Jin could ever remember seeing her. She stood straighter, as if a yoke that burdened her had been lifted.

Auntie looked Jin up and down. "You're looking better."

Jin ducked her head. "Because of you," she said. "Thank you."

"Don't thank me. I'm in your debt for as long as you live. If you hadn't found the guardian when you did, every one of those souls in the prison would have been lost to feed the demon. My spirit refuge would have been destroyed, and all of my companions killed. You saved them, Jin."

"And me with them," Yao added.

"I did nothing but what I had to do," she said, looking over her steaming noodle bowl at her brother, "to fulfill my promise to Mother." She shook her head. "I was never good enough on my own. What a poor guardian I've been."

Yao handed his bowl to Liu, who took it without difficulty, despite it being nearly a fourth of her size. He dropped to one knee beside Jin. "You've been the best guardian I could have asked for, but now it's my turn. Auntie Bai Wei has offered to pay my entry to the tech school. I'll thrive there, and when I'm out, we'll never be in want again."

Jin looked over at Auntie Bai Wei. Suspicious moisture clung to the corners of the shopkeeper's eyes.

"You'd do that?" Jin asked.

"As I said, I'm in your debt." Bai Wei shrugged. "Besides I've grown fond of you, my little scamp. Now finish your noodles." She turned away before rubbing her eyes with the back of her hand. "You've got to build up your strength."

Jin bit her lip to keep from crying. Despite the pain, she felt lighter than air. She speared the noodles with her chopsticks and took another bite of paradise.

About the Author

REBECCA BIRCH IS A SCIENCE fiction and fantasy writer based in Western Washington. She's a classically trained soprano, holds a deputy black belt in Taekwondo, and enjoys spending time in the company of trees. Her fiction has appeared in markets including *Nature, Cricket,* and *Flash Fiction Online.*

Website: http://www.wordsofbirch.com
Twitter: @wordsofbirch

About the Story

SEVERAL YEARS AGO, A FRIEND and I decided to do a writing challenge. We'd both write a story start based on an image prompt every day for a month and share what we wrote with each other. It was a wonderful exercise and provided the seeds for some stories that went on to be published, including *Guardian.*

The image that inspired *Guardian* was of a dilapidated, neon-lit market with Chinese calligraphy on the signs. It immediately brought me into the setting that became the night market.

The very first paragraph I wrote was when Jin passes by the noodle seller's cart and longs for a taste. From there I needed to know why she wanted those noodles so much and why she couldn't have them. What would have drawn her to the night market to begin with? What sort of life did she have?

That paragraph has changed since I first wrote it, and it ended up in the middle of the story, rather than at the beginning, but I can still smell that noodle cart when I think about "Guardian."

I've often heard of stories writing themselves, and "Guardian" was very much like that for me, although that's not my usual experience while writing. I buckled up and held on for the adventure.

I hope that readers will enjoy it as much as I did.

Fossil Fuel

Van Alrik

WITH A SLIGHT FLICK OF his wrist, Kashif scattered a fistful of white powder over the lake of bubbling black sludge. Tiny organisms in the powder were already shaking free from their slumber and ravenously ripping through the globules of oil — last remnants of a fossil-fueled industrial age — leaving only harmless fatty acids and carbon dioxide behind them.

Not the most glamorous job, but it was a job — a good job.

Kashif hated it.

He walked along the berms and levees holding back the aging oil field, hour after hour, day after day, the overseer charged with monitoring an ancient puddle. He glanced at the cartoon logo on the bag of powder — a green blob, cilia thrashing, faceless but for a gaping mouth of dagger-like teeth.

The caricature actually made him a little jealous. It was a pretty good depiction of the microscopic bacteria he was using to degrade and contain the inert oil. Their job was just as mechanical and brainless as his, but they attacked their work with a ferocious vigor that he just wasn't able to duplicate.

Surely there was something else out there for him to do with his life. But until he found it, quitting wasn't an option. Like the bugs, he had to work to eat. At least that's what he told himself. His roommate Hasan said he was just a coward.

Kashif grimaced. Maybe he was right.

Kashif stretched his hand out to drop another pile of powder, then recoiled slightly as a pattern bubbled up on the slick. It was familiar.

It was him.

He dropped the powder at his feet, and his mouth hung open. There, on the shiny black surface, was an outline of his short, spiky hair, his round face, and his medium-sized nose, with the crook where it had broken in a car accident years before.

There was no question. He was looking at a picture of himself.

He didn't know what to do.

He looked around — left, then right. No one else was supposed to have access to the field.

Not that anyone would want to, anyway. The field was in the middle of nowhere, with the nearest village almost a hundred miles away. Aside from the environmental threat, modern technology had rendered the oil itself virtually worthless.

Who could it be?

Suddenly a large bubble burst in the middle of his portrait, and the image disappeared.

He started to wonder whether he had just imagined it, whether there had actually been an image there at all. Either way, it was the end of a long day, and Kashif never stayed on the field any longer than he had to.

If someone else was there, they'd be spending the night alone.

THE NEXT DAY, KASHIF MADE his normal rounds, scattering fertilizing nutrients along the edges of the lake and dropping in the biodegradation powder.

But he kept his eyes open for strange bubbles or movements.

Or pictures.

The sun rose high in the sky, then descended again. When it was just starting to slip behind the levee, Kashif heard a distinct plopping sound.

He turned toward the noise, and his skin went cold at the sight of small bubbles coursing in arcs across the surface of the oil. After a few moments, he was able to make out the new picture. It was also familiar. He looked at the bag of degradation powder.

It was a picture of the logo — the cartoon bug, jagged teeth and all.

"What the... ? Oh! I think I've got it. You want this?" He held up the bag and shook it gently.

There was no response, so he grabbed a handful of the powder and flung it out across the oil toward the picture.

A slight tremor shook the oil, then the surface abruptly sucked downward and the powder disappeared.

"Whoa!" Kashif looked at the bag again. Whatever the thing was, it seemed to like biodegrading bacteria.

The thought crossed his mind that he should report this to his company. But he didn't want any trouble, and there wasn't anyone else to blame it on if things went bad. He shrugged and shook the bag again. "You want some more?"

Bubbles gushed up from the oil.

"Alright — here you go!" He dumped the whole bag in.

The suction from below the surface was so strong it pulled the oil down in a swirling cyclone, as though someone had pulled the drain plug at the bottom of the lake.

Kashif finally realized how big the thing, whatever it was, had to be. "Whoa."

After the surface settled, bubbles traced along it again, re-forming the cartoon logo.

"Sorry, buddy. It's all gone."

The surface bubbled more forcefully, and several duplicate images of the cartoon logo appeared, surrounding the original.

"Look, I'm sorry. There's no more." He tossed the bag into the lake, where it settled, limp and empty.

The bubbles began again, erasing the cartoon bacteria and replacing them with another familiar picture.

Kashif's head.

The blood drained from Kashif's face. "Actually, I can go get some more." He quickly turned away from the lake and started rushing up the levee back to his truck.

But after only a few steps, he heard the whoosh of agitating oil rushing up behind him, and he turned just in time to see two massive oily jaws crashing down and slamming together.

Just in front of him.

Horrified, Kashif staggered backward, half turning as he tripped and stumbled his way up the bank and into his pickup. He frantically started the ignition, slammed on the gas, and never looked back.

Hasan would be proud. Kashif had finally found the courage to quit.

About the Author

Van Alrik lives in the Rocky Mountains with his family and a small army of robot novelists. His short stories and poems have been published in *Helios Quarterly Magazine, Perihelion, Star*Line,* and elsewhere. A data scientist, Van is a strong STEM proponent and enjoys incorporating programming and analytics into his writing as much as possible. His computer-assisted novels *The Trivial Thing* and *Character for Veracity* are available on Amazon, his blog is at vanalrik.blogspot.com, and he occasionally tweets from @vjalrik on Twitter.

About the Story

I've had story ideas come as random flashes of inspiration, absurd challenges from friends, literal computer output, and even fully plotted dreams. "Fossil Fuel" didn't come together in any of those ways, or really in any specific way whatsoever. This was one of those experiences where a writer just sat down with a completely blank slate and wrote whatever came into his mind. By some miracle it ended up as a mostly coherent story. I confess that the main character is probably Iraqi because of some subliminal stereotypical connection in my brain between oil fields and the Middle East. And I confess that his lack of development was probably more due to my lacking experience with Middle Eastern culture than to artistic reasons. I wrote about him much as I would any Western character, intentionally avoiding any details that hinted at his ethnicity or nationality beyond his name. I suppose if there were some broader commentary about the story's theme it would have to do with the influence of the West over the Middle East, and the ending could be symbolic of an individual's triumph over that influence.

No Shit

Kristy Evangelista

IT'S NICE TO HAVE A chance to relax my aching muscles after digging the shallow grave for my parents. I'm sitting on the back deck in the humid summer air and enjoying a nice cold brew. My hands are still grimy from today's hard work, but there is no one else around to see.

I hadn't wanted to do a shallow grave. I'd wanted to do a full six feet — show a bit of respect for the old geezers and all that. But when you're only five feet tall and not very experienced at grave digging, the logistics of it all can be tough.

Let's be clear up front. I didn't *kill* my parents. I loved them. The plague killed them, and everyone else. It swept through fast. One minute things were great, humanity was bustling, and then *bammo!* There were headaches, fevers, and bloody noses. There was screaming and moaning and then there was quiet.

As soon as I heard about it on the news, I rang my sister. We rarely agree on much — I think she's a well-groomed Barbie soccer mom, she thinks I'm a complete mess. But this time, we agreed on one thing: I should leave my mountain cottage and travel to the coast to look after Mum and Dad. The traffic was insane, because everyone was trying to reach their loved ones, or outrun the plague, but I made it — just. I had about an hour with them before they died. They were in so much pain I don't think they even registered I was there.

My sister didn't answer her phone after we made our initial plan. She did thoughtfully send a text: "Ella bleeding, Ken gone. My headache's

getting bad. Luv u Jane. XOXO." (Trust Tiana to put hugs and kisses in her death SMS.)

I spent the first night after my parents died getting blind drunk. I spent the second night cruising the streets of their coastal town. At first I drove silently, looking for candles, torches, any signs of life. Then I drove loudly, White Stripes blaring, horn honking, lights on full beam. I thought maybe if I was obnoxious enough someone would have to come out and tell me to shut up. There were about five thousand people in this town; as far as I can tell they are all dead and rotting in their beds.

But at least the deck at Mum and Dad's is nice. Dad repainted it last year. The brass wind chimes play gently in the sea breeze while the sun sinks down to bed. The tang of citronella candles wards off the mosquitos and helps mask the corpse stench. Kind of.

When it gets dark, I turn the fairy lights on. Hooray for solar! Not only does it reduce humanity's carbon footprint (guess that isn't a problem anymore), it keeps my beer icy cold and the outside area festive so I can enjoy the end of the world in style.

Just as I am about to go for another beer, a flare lights up the sky. Other survivors! I jump to my feet. It looks like it is coming from a larger city nearby. I get into the car and speed out of the driveway. On my way out of town, I stop at the cop shop, and then I'm back on the road – now with a handgun tucked into my jacket pocket.

Every twenty minutes or so another flare shoots up, then drifts slowly down to earth. I turn the headlights off when I reach the city. When I'm sure I know where the flares are coming from, I park the car. I take out the gun, hang some binoculars around my neck (also nabbed from the police station) and trek the last distance on foot. I'm possibly a little paranoid, but for a female alone at night, it pays to take precautions.

The other survivors have built up a nice bonfire in the parkland at the centre of town. I stop behind a pair of bins. Now that I have some cover and a decent view of the area, I lift up the binoculars and scope things out.

There are about five or six camping chairs around the fire. Only one of them is occupied. I scan the area carefully, but there is definitely just the one person. The survivor is a man, slimly built, with glasses that occasionally flash in the firelight. He is reading a book (*Dealing with Change*

— ha!), and on either side of his chair are two piles of flare guns. He must have spent his day raiding the boats in the harbour, but his business shirt and slacks are clean and pressed. As I examine him, he looks at his watch, picks up a flare gun from the pile on his right, blasts it into the sky, and then drops it into the pile on his left. The survivor watches the flare drift down and I get a good look at his sandy blonde hair and pale blue eyes. His expression is a mixture of fear, grief and hope.

A mad shriek curdles the air behind me. I startle and the binoculars smash against the bins with a loud clatter. Freaking possum! I hightail it back to the car. No wait. I stop. I run a few more steps then stop again. Dammit! What the hell am I doing?

"Hello?" The man stumbles in the dark towards me. He sees me and slows, still a good distance away. "Hello? It's OK. I'm not going to come any closer. The whole apocalypse experience was weird enough even before I started chasing women through the park at night. Why don't we meet in daytime like sensible people?" He is talking quickly, afraid that I'll run off before he gets his message out. "Have you heard of Bluebottles café? I'll be there, tomorrow from ten. Bluebottles — in the high street."

As I drive back to my parents' place, I reflect on the events of the evening. Lone survivor man seemed nice. I hope he doesn't think I'm a freak. I really hope he didn't notice my gun.

I'M LATE AS I PULL up to Bluebottles the next morning. The survivor is sitting at a sunny outdoor table and reading another book — *Composting Toilets*. He waves casually, marks his page with a sugar sachet, and stands up to greet me.

"Hi!" he smiles. "I'm Sam."

"Hey," I say. "Jane." We both stand there looking awkward for a moment, and then, when I don't say anything else, he gives a wry smile.

"I don't know about you," he says, "but I need a coffee."

Our table has a vase filled with fresh flowers. Sam begins industriously frothing long life milk over in the serving area. The fridges are empty

— he must have cleared out all the consumables that went bad. Curious, I go check out the back and find the toilets (very important), and a generator rigged to get power working. His work isn't too shoddy.

Sam calls me back and hands me my short black and a slice of freshly baked tea cake. Seriously, when does this guy sleep? I take a swig. *Now* I'm ready for some conversation.

Sam takes a sip of his latte and adjusts his glasses. "I'm really glad you came today," he says. "Until last night, I thought... I might have been the only one left. Where were you when you saw the flares?"

"Woolgoolga."

"That far? I wasn't sure how visible they would be." He ponders for a moment. "No one else came last night." Given the ghost town I experienced, this doesn't surprise me. "I was hoping there'd be more. I guess we'll just have to put our heads together and think of a different way to find others. Locating other survivors will be our top priority, right?"

"Of course." I'd mostly been wallowing in grief and panic since the apocalypse, but I didn't want Sam to think that I couldn't be forward thinking. "What's this?" I ask, gesturing towards the book about toilet composting.

"I found it in the library yesterday." He gently traces the spine. "I think it will be some time before we lose water, but it can't hurt to be prepared. Sewerage is not something I want to deal with."

"No shit," I agree.

He smiles. I can't help but notice he has tiny dimples. "We can think of it as an unofficial motto for our group as we rebuild society."

I take a bite of the teacake. It's still warm, with a light and buttery crumb that melts in my mouth. Sam knows how to bake.

While we eat and drink, we sketch out a rough plan which will cover the next few days. It basically involves massive amounts of looting. So, it's an awesome plan.

We stand up to leave the café. I wonder if we should shake hands or something. Sam puts his hands in his pockets and looks at me earnestly.

"You do want to stick together, right? Because I do. Want to, I mean. But I don't want to make you feel as if we have to. We don't, if you don't want to." I can see the fear and the vulnerability lurking in his eyes. If I say no, he will be alone again. If I say no, I will be alone again.

I punch his shoulder lightly. "Of course we're sticking together. How am I gonna rebuild society without your badass research skills? Read a book?" I school my features into an expression of mock horror.

Sam's posture relaxes. "Reading broadens your life," he says loftily. "OK, so we'll each grab some things, and then meet up at the supermarket at three."

LOOTING IS FUN, ALTHOUGH I have to spend way too much time finding some of the electronic gear I want. If only the internet was still on, I could ask Google! Google knows everything. At least it used to. But since Google is also dead, I'm reliant on these slow inefficient yellow-paged directory books.

When I finally rock up at the supermarket, it is behind the wheel of a massive semi-trailer. It has a nice little sleeper cabin in the back, and my gun is now stashed safely in the glove box.

Sam has a Winnebago. With its plush leather interiors and stainless steel appliances, it looks like the kind of vehicle my sister would buy for her family holidays. (Would have bought for her family holidays.)

The Winnebago is stuffed with books and laminators. "It's not immediate survival," says Sam. "But a lot of these books are important. We have to preserve knowledge for future generations of humanity." He does have some more useful items, including the portable generator he used at Bluebottles. We stow it in the back of my semi.

I show Sam some of the goodies I nabbed. "Spray paint cans?" he asks, clearly sceptical.

"I dabbled in graffiti in high school," I explain. "I'm pretty good."

His expression remains politely dubious, so I pull out my ace — a 1000W professional FM transmitter. "Nice!" he says, his genuine appreciation warming me up.

"There is only one thing left before we head out then. Snacks!"

Walking into the Supermarket is like climbing into the inside of a bin and licking the sides. The sickly-sweet stench of rotting fruit and fetid meat is so strong I can taste it in the back of my mouth.

I glance towards the deli and make a small sad noise. "Bacon..."

Sam takes my arm and draws me towards the aisles. "It's no good, Jane. It's gone..."

We're careful not to take too much of the canned goods — other survivors might come to this store and be in desperate need of food.

Once we adjust to the smell, it's not so bad. It's kinda like being on one of those reality TV shows where you need to grab as many items as possible in five minutes. Baked Beans, yes, chocolate, yes, toilet paper, *hell* yes. I'm gonna need every last roll.

"Jane, do you like these cans of SPAM?" Sam calls out from further down the aisle.

"I do not like them, Sam I Am."

Sam catches on immediately. "Do you like them here or there? Do you like them anywhere?"

"I do not like them from a tin. I do not like them in a bin. I do not like them in a truck. I will never like them, you little — "

Suddenly, I'm not in the supermarket. I'm on my sister's big blue couch, reading Dr. Seuss to my niece. Her curls tickle my cheek as we giggle over the ridiculous pictures.

"Seriously, though," asks Sam. "Do you like SPAM?"

"No," I say. He puts it back. I head to the liquor section to grab some bottles of expensive scotch.

WE LEAVE JUST AS THE sun starts to set. I pull out my tins of spray paint and tag the building — 'Jane and Sam Alive @ 5, 105FM.'

Sam scrutinises my work critically. "Is it supposed to be 5 p.m.? Because you might want that pertinent fact very clear."

"But then it doesn't rhyme properly!" I squish in a little "p.m." as best I can.

Sam pulls out a map. "I've been thinking that we should travel just as it gets dark. Hopefully our lights will make us more obvious to other survivors. We'll head north up the highway, and stop for the night when we hit the next major town."

"At the fanciest hotel we can find."

"Actually, my Winnebago. It has two double beds. I don't fancy having to look through hotel rooms until I find one that was unoccupied."

Thanks for that grisly image, Sam. But it's a good point. I feel a pang for all those wonderful bath robes that will never be used again. "We wake up feeling refreshed, do some looting and, er, tag some major landmarks. At five, we perform our radio show, make some dinner and head back out into the night. Then we do the whole thing over again until we hit Brisbane."

I'm pumped that we have a plan, and spring into the semi. "Let's hit the road. It's too late to do the radio show tonight and I've already got dinner." I waggle a couple of packets of jerky and chips in his direction.

"That is not dinner," says Sam. "Just because this is the end of the world, doesn't mean you can't have standards."

Halfway to our destination, I regret the jerky and chips. I see a sign for a rest area 10 k's ahead.

"Sam I am, are you there?"

"Roger, Jane-train, what's up?"

"Why are we going so slow?"

"We're going at 100," Sam's voice crackles over the radio. "That's the speed limit."

"Yes. And civilisation has ended. So why are we going so slow?"

"Because speed signs exist for a reason and at night in strange vehicles is not the time to take risks. It would be pretty tragic for the last known survivors to be killed in a car accident."

"We're not driving cars," I point out, as I put my foot on the accelerator. "I'll meet you there."

I leave the semi at a truck stop near the highway (tagging the sign). Then I join Sam in the Winnie and we park in the centre of town (tagging the supermarket). It was a long day. I'm asleep before the lights are off.

THE NEXT MORNING, SAM HEADS out to loot the local library and bookstores while I listen to Vampire Weekend on my sweet new speakers. When he gets back, it's my turn to explore the town, which is depressingly empty.

Sam makes us a nice omelette for lunch — I guess we should eat as many eggs as we can before they all go bad. That afternoon we do our first broadcast.

"Uh, hello?" Sam starts things off. "My name is Sam and I'm with my friend Jane."

I wrestle the handset off him and bellow, "We are Sam and Jane, alive at five!" I return the handset to him. "You have to give it a bit more pizazz, Sam, or we'll lose our listeners."

Sam makes a face at me. "We will be at the Ballina showground tomorrow." He then goes on to list all the other towns we'll be visiting before we get to Brisbane.

"Brisvegas!" I scream from the background.

Sam interrupts the show to scold me. "Seriously, Jane, we don't want to scare people away."

Sam gets back on the air. "I'm going to hand you over to Jane now." I fist pump. "She thinks she has a better radio voice then me, and so is going to give you some step by step instructions on how to buy and set up your own radio." My fist pump turns into a face palm. "Over to you, Jane."

We repeat the show three times, just in case we get any late listeners; then we are back on the road. I spend the drive to Ballina analysing our performance and making suggestions on how Sam could improve his radio brand.

Sam drives the Winnie sedately into Ballina. I follow in the semi, honking my horn. We stop at the showground. I pull out some floodlights and connect them to our portable generator. Sam sets up some camping chairs outside, pulls out a book, and starts to laminate it ("*Cloudstreet* is a classic, Jane! It needs to be preserved for future generations."). I head into the Winnie and watch a DVD in bed. My gun is snuggled up under my pillow. I've decided to name her Gertrude. I'm not ready to introduce Sam to Gertrude yet — I don't know how he'd react.

Sam comes in after about an hour. "Seriously?" he asks. "*Outbreak?* You thought a thriller about a dangerous airborne virus was a good choice of entertainment?"

"It's research," I say. "Besides, this movie is a classic. It's not Dustin Hoffman's fault the world ended."

I fall asleep before the end of the movie and wake up in the middle of the night. Sam is still awake, lying in his bed with a torch and reading.

"No visitors?" I ask.

"No," he says, turning a page.

"Maybe tomorrow. You should get some sleep." Sam takes off his glasses and turns off the torch, and then I hear him shifting around, trying to get comfortable.

"Jane..." he whispers after about half a minute. "Are you still awake?"

"Yeah."

"I can't sleep."

"What's up?" Besides everyone being dead. And the absence of bacon.

"Just... worrying." A lock of hair has fallen over Sam's eyes, and for a moment I am tempted to reach over the gap between our beds and brush it away.

"There were about 50, 000 people in Coffs Harbour," he says. "80, 000 if you include the surrounding region. If we really are the only two people left alive in this area... those are really poor odds of surviving the infection."

Poor Sam looks so tense, he could really use a hug. My mum was a good hugger. I remember she asked a lady in the bank once if everything was okay. The lady burst into tears, and my mum just reached out and comforted her, as if she'd known her for years. I've never been that great at hugging, myself. I wish I was better.

"Do you know what a minimum viable population is?" Sam asks. "It is the smallest number of people that are needed for a species to survive over a long period of time. It is a large enough population that we won't be vulnerable to natural disasters, or genetic weaknesses caused by inbreeding. For humanity, the minimum viable population is about 4, 000 people."

"We should be right then," I say. "There are billions of people on Earth. If 1 in 100, 000 survived, that leaves..." It's too late at night to do maths in my head. "A crapload."

"60, 000, yes. Spread out over the whole globe. 2, 000 in Australia. And we'll only survive if we're all together." Sam is talking faster as he goes on. The skin around his eyes is strained. "That's why it's really important we find the other survivors. We have to start building a new community."

I'm not sure I give a damn about the overall survival of humanity. I care about me, and now I care about Sam.

"I reckon there will be way more survivors than that," I say, wanting to make him feel better. "The plague swept through fast. Too fast. It will have burnt itself out before it gets everywhere. There are some pretty remote places that will be safe."

"I hope you're right," Sam says slowly. "Did you follow the start of the infection?"

"Kind of. It started in Russia. People thought it might have been a bioweapon gone out of control."

"Yes. All the governments reacted very quickly. They set up quarantines for the infected. Australia shut down all international flights immediately. We're an island, Jane! It shouldn't have been able to reach us. But it did."

"It was too fast!" I say.

"Or too slow. The way it spread – it hit everyone almost at once. It jumped through quarantines like they didn't exist. I think this virus was dormant and spreading for a really long time before the first symptoms appeared."

"Maybe, but so what? It doesn't matter how it spread. What matters is what we do next."

"It might matter," says Sam. "What if we aren't immune to the virus? What if we just caught it later, and it's lying dormant in our bloodstream? Our symptoms could start at any moment."

If I wasn't wide awake before, I am now. I bury my face in my pillows, desperate for the oblivion of sleep. Dad's bloody face and Mum's cries of pain haunt me. I thought I'd escaped that, but it could still be me.

This is the perfect time to try some of that expensive booze.

THE NEXT MORNING MY HEAD throbs and my gut roils – alcohol has never been that great for my innards.

Sam has dark circles under his eyes. He forces himself to be cheerful and chatty, but my stomach hurts and I'm not capable of making small talk. No, Sam, I do not want some instant coffee. Why would you even bother picking that up from the shelf? I also don't want tea. I rush out as quickly as I can. The brown tide is rising, and I don't want to be near Sam when it strikes.

I spend most of the morning at the mall, within sprinting distance of the nearest loo. The semi is stacked with about 1, 000 rolls of toilet paper; at this rate, that might get me through till next week.

When I feel a bit better, I stomp around the rest of the town tagging the supermarkets in big, red, angry letters.

I return just in time to do the radio show. I see that Sam is confused, but I'm not about to explain my erratic behaviour.

That night, when we stop, I elect to stay in my little bunk in the semi. Sam doesn't try to argue — he just looks quietly miserable, which is a thousand times worse.

"I'm sorry," he says. "I didn't mean to freak you out last night. I know I don't sleep well. I know it. My mind races, and I worry about one thing after another, and there are so many things to worry about — "

"It's not you," I say, but I know without explanations I am unconvincing. And I am not about to explain.

Everything continues to slowly spiral over the next few days. There isn't a single person at any of the towns we pass through. No one joins our radio show. Sam is getting a lot of laminating done, and studies his books intently, but doesn't appear to get much sleep. I stop eating and spend most of the days curled up in the semi or on the dunny willing my body to get better.

On the third evening, the CB radio lights up the night with our first caller.

"Hey, Sam and Jane."

Sam and I stare at each other in shock. Then we do the world's biggest high five. Our hands cling together afterwards as we jump up and down. I do not want to let go.

Sam eagerly reaches for the radio with his other hand. "You have no idea how excited we are to hear your voice!" he says, giving my hand a last squeeze and then letting go. "We're so glad you got our messages."

"Hard to miss when they're every kilometre along the highway."

"Yeah, I'm very thorough," I say. "What's your name, Mystery Man?"

"Travis. Trav."

"Nice to meet you Trav. Congratulations on surviving the apocalypse. Would you like to meet up, or are you planning on running solo?"

"Maybe in a few days. I've just gotten into Byron."

"What's in Byron, Travis?" Sam asks gently. The poor man is no doubt checking on family in the area.

"Dairy cows." Or not.

"For real?" I ask.

"Yeah, dead set. I'm from outside of Warwick. I've been driving around this area for a week now, looking for other people. And I haven't found any till now. What I have found is a lot of dead cows. Every single frigging cow in the area is dead and gone. Because of the drought, I guess. I thought there might still be some cows near the coast."

Sam is very excited and goes to get one of his books. "I *knew* this would come in handy!" he exults, while reading key passages out over the radio to Trav on dealing with cattle.

Afterwards, we debrief. "That Travis has a good head on his shoulders," says Sam. "Humanity has had dairy cows for thousands of years. I don't know what we'd do without milk."

I think of sitting at the kitchen bench with my sister and sharing milk and cookies as an afternoon treat. Of my baby niece lying on her little sofa with her bottle of milk. Trav is indeed a hero.

"I thought there might even have been a few sparks zinging between you guys," Sam suggests.

What. The. Hell.

"Whoa there, tiger. I am not going to date Trav." I was just holding your hand five seconds ago. "It's the end of days. Everyone I know is dead, the world smells of corpse and the last thing on my mind is romance." My Dad always said that if you had to fight, make your first punch hard enough that the other person can't get up. "Just because you have a freaky hang up about saving mankind, doesn't mean I'm going to breed with every new man we meet."

Sam turns pale, and I know I've hit hard enough. I make sure I slam the door loudly on my way to the semi.

WE'RE DRIVING ON THE HIGHWAY when my bowels send me an urgent message.

I hit the brakes and bang the horn. "Sam," I radio urgently. "We need to stop. Right now." I pull my semi over to the side of the road. The Winnie is not even properly stationary, but that doesn't stop me – I sprint to the side and wrench open the door to the living area, stumbling in my haste to reach the bathroom. I only just make it in time.

"Jane, are you okay?" I hear Sam's worried voice through the door. He is just outside, and can no doubt hear every humiliating detail.

"No," I reply miserably.

"Is it the plague? Is it some variation of the plague?" he asks.

I'm tempted to say yes. "No. It's Crohn's disease. It affects my bowels. Pain and diarrhoea mostly."

"Is it... life threatening?"

"It wasn't. When we had doctors and medicine." I stare at the bloody red bowl before I flush the toilet. "I don't know about now."

"What can I do?"

"For right now, a little space would be great." I can feel another wave coming on, and it is a very thin door.

WE MAKE AN EARLY CAMP on the side of the road. Frankly, it's far nicer out here than in the cadaver-infested cities. You can take a deep breath without choking on the rot. When we find somewhere to settle down, it will definitely be in the country.

I sit cross-legged on my Winnie bed. Sam has thoughtfully made me a hot water bottle, which I clutch gratefully to my tummy.

"So much for our motto as we rebuild society." I try to smile. It seems like a long time since our first conversation in the café.

"'No shit'," Sam reminisces fondly. "It is still a worthy goal. And we've done okay. There has been a minimum of shit. Less shit than there could be."

"I was lucky today," I explain to Sam, not meeting his eyes. "I won't always make it to the toilet in time. I guess it's better that you're warned before that happens, since you're stuck with me and all."

"Why didn't you tell me?" asks Sam. "I could have helped."

"I'm serving up bum gravy, Sam. It is humiliating. I've never even told anyone outside my family before."

"It is pretty gross," he says. I bury my head in my pillow and try to drown my face so I never have to meet his eyes again. "But it's not as bad as having your testes swell up and double their size."

I'm so surprised that I look up from my pillow. "What?"

"Giant. Balls. Yes, that happened to me. When I was in high school. I couldn't wear underwear. I was in massive pain so I couldn't go to school. And I couldn't tell anyone, because you don't talk about testicle problems with other sixteen-year-old boys. It's a rare condition called orchitis." He pauses briefly. "It's what caused my infertility."

Whoa! Just... whoa!

Sam sits on the bed and puts his arm around me. "Tomorrow we'll arrive in Brisbane. The first thing we'll do is visit a hospital and find some medical textbooks."

"And go to the hospital pharmacy," I say. "I know what medication to get for my flare."

"I don't know why we haven't been to a chemist before now," says Sam. "We should be stocking up on antibiotics and pain medications."

I lean into him and close my eyes. It is nice to have him here. I get to enjoy the moment for about two minutes before I have to return to my throne.

OUR PLAN TO REACH THE hospital first thing turns out to be a trifle optimistic. Getting around Brisbane is agonisingly slow; cars have stacked up in key areas, blocking the way, forcing us to find alternative routes. In the end, it's easier to reach our base at Mount Coot-Tha. We set the area up with floodlights, which should be visible from most of Brisbane. They're rigged to turn on at sunset.

As we make our way to the nearest hospital, we continue to tag signs. Whenever we hit a choke-point we can't avoid, we get out of the Winnie and drive the cars out of the way. Sometimes the cars are empty, their owners abandoning them as a hopeless cause. Sometimes they're still occupied.

By five p.m., it's become clear the hospital itself is a major chokepoint. We consult some maps and decide we're close enough to walk.

Before we leave, Sam does our radio show while I get a quick dinner together. Sam informs everyone we're making our way to the hospital, but will be returning to Mount Coot-Tha when we're done. I serve baked beans and toast. I had to pick through the loaf looking for the last few non-mouldy slices, so tomorrow we might need to find a bread maker. I don't really know why I bother eating — as soon as I've finished I have to spend half an hour in the dunny while it all comes back out again. Sam tactfully retires outside with his book (*Wool: From Sheep to Socks*).

By the time we are ready to set out on foot, it's well and truly dark. Our backpacks are mostly empty and ready to be filled with precious, precious drugs. All I'm bringing are the bare essentials — a bottle of water, a roll of toilet paper, a walkie talkie, and Gertrude.

I'm carrying a torch, but I don't really need it to see where I'm going. The moon is full, and so close to the horizon that it appears to have doubled in size. It's so pristine, so white. I wonder what's happening to the astronauts up at the International Space Station right now. Are they stuck up there in orbit until their air runs out, unable to get back to Earth without help?

"Hey Sam," I say. "Check out the moon. It's looking a bit swollen tonight, don'cha think?"

"Actually, I was just thinking it looked a bit crappy," he shoots back. And then he stops in his tracks and grabs my arm tightly.

I follow his gaze, and see our destination: the hospital. And all the lights are on.

We break into a jog. I don't know what I'm expecting when I run into the well-lit foyer (Masses of people huddled together with their sleeping bags? An irate administrator wielding a clipboard? A welcome banner?), but I don't find it. All I see is wall to wall stiffs. A lot of desperate people came to the hospital and found nothing but a place to die.

"Hello?" My voice bounces off the walls.

No response.

We start picking our way around the bodies, periodically calling out as we go. It's a bit easier to move once we get out of the foyer, but the dead are still everywhere. The smell is overwhelming, and considering we've spent the last week surrounded by death, that's saying something.

"You know what would suck?" I say, pointing at a nurse face-planted into the keyboard of an inactive computer. "If that lady zombie turned around and looked right at us."

"Shut up, Jane."

We briefly stop at Gastroenterology for Sam's medical texts and then find directions to the maintenance areas. Surely the lights in this hospital are still on for a reason.

"Maybe we should split up?" Sam suggests. "We can cover more ground that way."

My heart stops. Then I realise this is what passes for humour in Sam's world.

We find our way to the backup generator and I inspect it closely. "It's a 1200 KVA diesel. There's no way this could keep the whole hospital powered for more than four or five hours without needing to be topped up with more fuel."

Sam looks at me strangely. "Uh, Jane," he says. "What did you do before the world ended?"

Uh-oh, busted. "I was an electrical engineer."

He makes a small choking sound. "And you didn't feel the need to mention that before because?"

"I didn't want to have to feel responsible for rebuilding civilisation."

"Jane, you need to start opening up more on the important things."

I look back at the generator and return to the topic at hand. "I don't understand why they're using the generator to power the whole hospital. They clearly aren't using everything – this place is empty. They could conserve their power by rerouting some of the circuits and tripping these breakers here."

"Girl, you have no idea how glad I am to hear you say that," says a croaky female voice from just behind my right shoulder.

I stumble back and away with a squeal. I ricochet off the wall, and then I'm through the door and running out the corridor. I make it all the way back to the foyer when I realise that: (1) Sam is not with me; and (2) that lady was probably in her late 50s and didn't look particularly threatening.

I'm leaning against the wall, panting and attempting to regroup, when Sam arrives.

"Jane, are you okay?" he asks.

"Yep. Just feel a bit stupid. She's not a zombie, is she?"

"No," he confirms. "Not a zombie. Her name is Judith and she is a doctor. I told her we'd be right back. She said, 'Take your time, ' which is not the usual zombie M.O."

I sheepishly return to the power room and our new comrade. She's flicking through our liberated medical texts.

"Which one of you needs this?" she asks.

"Me," I say. "I have Crohn's."

"Hmm. An autoimmune." She looks at Sam. "And you? What illness are you bringing with you into this brave new world?"

Sam looks startled. "Er... nothing? I'm perfectly healthy."

"He did have something when he was a teenager," I volunteer. "Orchidness or something."

"Autoimmune Orchitis?" she queries, and Sam nods.

"What do you have?" I ask on a hunch.

She looks at me as though I have just asked the rudest most invasive question possible, but then relents. "I have MS. Another autoimmune."

"Do you think that's what protected us from the plague?"

"It is certainly a working hypothesis. It can't be the only factor, of course, or there would be more of us. Twenty percent of the population had autoimmune, significantly more than were spared by the virus."

Sam looks distressed. "But if every survivor left has an autoimmune disease... Humanity is FUCKED. Our gene pool is already dangerously reduced. We won't be able to survive this."

Judith shrugs and turns back to the generator. "I haven't slept properly for a week," she says to me. "Help me fix this mess."

"Why should I?" I ask uncharitably.

"Because," she replies, "fifty metres from here are 2000 fertilised embryos. They represent enough genetic diversity to save this pathetic excuse of a species." Judith's hands shake as she smooths her hair. "I need to make sure they can be kept frozen until we need them." What I've taken for rudeness is actually massive sleep deprivation.

I help Judith reroute the power. She immediately goes to a nearby bunk, promising she will meet us at Coot-Tha soon. We pick up our medical supplies from the pharmacy and start the long journey back to camp.

"You know what I like about the apocalypse?" Sam says as he drives us up the mountain. "Everyone is basically trying to preserve something. It's not like in the movies where there are always roving bands of armed bandits."

"That's because we're not all fighting for resources," I point out.

"Don't be such a pessimist, Jane! This is clearly a triumph of human nature."

I am excruciatingly aware of Gertrude, sleeping quietly in my backpack. "Yeah, about that..." I say. "There's something here that you'd better see."

Sam looks inside. "Holy shit, Jane. What the hell?"

I laugh for about a minute. Sam has the best reactions. "This is Gertrude. I've kept her with me because I thought I needed her. But now, I don't think that I do. When Judith appeared right behind me, and I thought she was a real threat, I expected that I would act cool, calmly assess the situation and draw the gun to protect myself if necessary. But I didn't act cool. I panicked. And if I had drawn the gun in that moment, I would have shot an innocent woman and doomed our entire species."

I take a deep breath and pull out my faithful friend. She is a solid and deadly weight in my hands.

"Gertrude. Thank you for your service." I roll down the window and throw her into the dark.

Sam smiles at me. For the first time, I see reflected in his eyes something I've known in my heart for a while.

We arrive at camp around 2 a.m., exhausted and ready to collapse — only to find someone parked in our spot. No, not just our spot — the entire front row.

My poor tired brain assures me that those car spaces were definitely empty earlier in the evening. But I can't seem to do anything else with that information, so I'm shocked when a cheer greets us as we enter camp.

Gathered around the floodlights are a dozen other survivors of the plague — several of whom have helped themselves to the beer from our esky. I hear my name being called, and Sam's, and then suddenly we are amongst them.

"What...?" I ask stupidly, as a portly gentleman shakes my hand enthusiastically, while someone I can't see squeezes my shoulder.

An older lady smiles and pats my cheek. "Isn't it obvious, love? We heard your broadcast."

Sam sees my blank look. "They're our fans, Jane!" he explains, in a way that even my poor tired brain can understand.

"Oh," I say. Then, as the significance finally sinks in, "Oh!"

I start handing out high fives. We have *fans*.

And they're all here because of us.

About the Author

KRISTY EVANGELISTA HAS BEEN PREVIOUSLY published in the *Defying Doomsday Anthology*, the *2018 Young Explorer's Adventure Guide*, and Flame Tree Publishing's *Time Travel* anthology.

Kristy lives in Canberra, Australia, which is kind of like the poor man's Washington DC, i.e. a political capital with well planned roads. She reads all kind of sci-fi and fantasy, but is a particular sucker for a good YA series.

Kristy's own style creeps towards dark humour regardless of genre. The authors who have inspired her include Elizabeth Anne Scarborough, Brandon Sanderson, Naomi Novik, and Jasper Fforde. Kristy may have had other interests once, but between work and kids she can't remember what they are.

Kristy is not great at social media, so good luck finding her on the internet. Maybe one day she'll get there, in which case please say hi.

About the Story

"NO SHIT" IS A STORY about a chronically ill protagonist dealing with the aftermath of a plague in which only one out of a 100,000 people survived.

It was written pre-COVID, and it is interesting to read a virus story now that we all have some first hand experience with a deadly infection. Certainly, if this type of apocalypse were to happen now, the protagonists would, at the very least, be making COVID19 comparisons constantly! So in that respect *No Shit* is already a little dated. But some elements stand up, and were even a little prophetic, such as Jane's decision to fill an entire truck with toilet paper. Of course, we all know now that it is very anti-social to hoard toilet paper in a crisis – but Jane has IBS, so I think we can give her a pass.

This story holds a special place in my heart, as it was the first story I ever wrote as an adult. It is also a deeply personal story, because it is based on my own experience with Crohn's disease. Writing honestly about something as embarrassing as a bowel condition was more difficult than I expected. There was at least one line which I thought was too honest, and I see sawed back and forth about whether to include it. I did, in the end, but when the story was accepted, I still thought seriously about publishing under an assumed name (people I work with might read it after all!). Then I realized what message this could send to everyone else with a bowel condition: that there is something shameful about it, which of course there isn't.

I like to think that maybe one day someone will read my stories, have a laugh, and feel slightly less embarrassed the next time they have to explain to someone what Crohn's disease is.

The Mourning Woman

Preston Dennett

JAFARI BENT DOWN AND PLACED another brick in the long line of drying bricks. His back and shoulders ached from the effort and the sun beat mercilessly on his head, but he hardly noticed. The pain in his heart was all-encompassing. Oh, Tahirah! Even now, the thought of being without her forced tears into his eyes. He quickly turned his head.

Too late! His brother Madu had seen. He sat beneath a small section of shade, forming bricks from mud and straw.

"Don't tell me," Madu said. "It's Tahirah, isn't it? You're thinking about her again. Forget her! She is a mourning woman. You can never be with her. No man can."

Jafari flared with anger. "Don't tell me to forget her." Did no one understand his pain? Not even Madu?

"I'm trying to help you, Jafari. She belongs to the gods. You can't have her."

"I don't care. I love her!" Jafari picked up a newly-made brick from Madu's stack and carried it to the drying area. He placed it down roughly and stomped back to get another.

Madu shook his head. "You are a dreamer, Jafari. Even if she weren't a mourning woman, her family is wealthy and you are poor. She wears fine linens and smells of perfume. You wear coarse skirts and smell of mud and sweat. She lives in a home of carved white stone. You live in a hut of mud bricks. You aim too high, brother. It matters not that you love her; she is beyond your reach."

"I'll win her heart," Jafari said. "Someday, she'll be my wife."

"Oh? When is that? Tomorrow? Next year? You've spoken of her since you lost the sidelocks of youth. Yet each year the Nile blesses us with her waters, and still you do nothing. So I ask you, Jafari. When?"

"You're right." Jafari threw a brick to the ground, ruining its shape. "I've let my fears guide me. It's time I act. There's another procession tomorrow. I'm going to tell her how I feel."

Madu shrugged. "You waste your efforts. You're forgetting who she is."

Jafari ignored his brother. Madu didn't know what it was like to be in love.

Oh, Tahirah! Why must you be a mourning woman? Jafari had followed her at every procession she attended, watching in fascination as she and the other mourning women pulled at their hair, scratched their faces, and beat the ground with their fists, weeping and howling in anguish. Tahirah was so beautiful with her dark hair and flashing eyes. Everyone around her could feel the power of her emotions. Jafari had seen her make even the most stoic of men cry like babies.

That evening before bedtime he recited a powerful prayer. It was one he had said many times. This night he spoke with a fervor that left him trembling and breathless.

"Hail to you, Re-Horakhty, father of the gods!

"Hail to you, Seven Hathors, who are adorned in bands of red linen!

"Hail to you, gods, lords of heaven and earth!

"Come, make Tahirah born of Bahiti come after me like a cow after fodder; like a servant after her children; like a herdsman after his herd.

"If they do not cause her to come after me, I will set flame to Busiris and burn up Osiris."

He repeated the prayer over and over until sleep overtook him.

When morning arrived, Jafari awoke with the Prayer of the Seven Hathors still echoing in his mind. Oh, Tahirah! Today, I will find the courage to finally speak with you.

He ate breakfast quickly and slipped out of the house before Madu could protest.

Jafari had walked this path many times before. Today would be different. Instead of just watching Tahirah from afar, he would approach her.

He passed a group of young children playing at the well. He walked through the market stalls thick with odors of roasted meat and boiled fish, past the idol carvers and the goat herdsmen and finally to the wealthy side of the town, where Tahirah lived.

This time, instead of gazing longingly at the open doorway, he walked right up and spoke her name.

She appeared at the doorway and gazed at him, her face carefully composed. What was she thinking?

"Tahirah — " He paused. He had not planned what to say. "I am Jafari. I — "

"I know who you are," she said sternly. "You have been following me. You appear at every procession I have walked. Why have you never spoken before?"

"I — "

"Quiet!" She placed a hand over his mouth. The sensation of her soft fingers on his lips sent a thrill through his body. "Do not speak here." She ushered him around to the side of her home and spun him around to face her. "You must stop following me. Don't you understand? I'm a mourning woman. I'm in training to be a priestess. Nephtys and Isis have called on me. I belong to them."

Jafari's heart beat wildly and he had to restrain himself from shouting with glee. Tahirah recognized him! She knew who he was. His heart soared. "I know, but I cannot remain silent any longer. My heart belongs to you, Tahirah. It always has. I love you."

Tahirah lowered her head; her eyes glistened with tears. "It cannot be," she whispered.

Jafari felt an intoxicating dizziness in Tahirah's presence. Could she not see how helpless he was before her? "Tell me that you do not care for me, and you will not see my face again. But say that you do, and I am bound to you forever."

Tahirah began to weep. "Please, just go!"

"But you have not said no," said Jafari.

"Please," she said. "You don't understand."

Jafari let out a whoop of joy. "You care for me! You have not said no."

She looked at him with the barest hint of a smile. She wanted to kiss him! Suddenly he was sure of it. Her dark eyes betrayed her.

"Tahirah!" a shrill voice rang out from her house.

Tahirah jerked slightly and turned to go.

Jafari reached out and grabbed her arm. "I will see you again."

"It cannot be." She looked down at his hand and gently peeled away his fingers. "I am sorry. Go, and do not return. I would be with you, Jafari, but I can't. Don't you see? Each time I see you, it causes only pain because I cannot be with you. I am a mourning woman. You must leave and never return. Please, Jafari. If you truly love me, you'll leave me alone."

She gave him one last look and fled swiftly into her home.

Jafari began laughing. He ran all the way home where he found Madu beginning to make bricks.

"There you are. You're smiling," said Madu. "Then the girl has agreed to be your wife?"

"No," Jafari said. "She told me to leave and never return."

Madu shook his head. "Brother, the heat of the sun has finally cooked your senses. Why are you smiling?"

"Because she loves me, Madu!" Jafari pulled his brother up and hugging him. "She loves me."

Madu frowned and pushed his brother away. "Did she say that?"

"No, but I could see it in her eyes."

Madu sat back down and continued forming bricks. "Get out of the sun, brother." He grabbed the ladle, dipped it into the water-bucket, and held it up to Jafari. "Here. Drink."

Jafari laughed, taking the water. "I'm not mad, brother. You'll see. She loves me."

"Okay," said Madu. "She loves you. Now, sit down and help me. These bricks don't make themselves."

Jafari sat down and assisted his brother, but his mind was elsewhere. Tahirah knew his name. She'd smiled at him. She'd said she would be with him, if only she weren't already spoken for. Who was he to go against Nephtys and Isis? How could he win her heart?

That evening Jafari had a powerful dream.

He found himself in a strange circular stone chamber. He could feel the coolness of the air against his skin. The odor of incense tickled his nose. Where was he?

A small chuckle echoed behind him. He whirled around. A beautiful woman stood there, dressed in an intricately patterned gown. Her eyes and face were painted; a tall headdress sat upon her dark hair. He recognized her immediately. Nefertiti.

He fell to his knees, weeping.

She bent down, tucked two fingers beneath his chin, and raised him to a standing position.

She held up a knife and smiled at him. What was this? Did she plan to cut him?

She stepped forward and placed the knife against the side of his head. To his utter shock, she began to shave him. He was helpless to resist as she slid the knife back and forth across his scalp until his head was as hairless as an old man's.

He woke up laughing. What manner of dream was this? Why would Nefertiti do such a thing? Perhaps his brother could make sense of it.

That morning, he told Madu his dream. Madu listened carefully. Then, before Jafari had even finished, he broke into a wide grin and began laughing.

"Oh, Jafari! You have truly gone mad. Nefertiti? She shaved you?"

"I don't know what it means. I was hoping you could help me."

"It means you've finally gone mad. Forget it, Jafari. It's a silly dream that means nothing. Nefertiti would never show an interest in one such as you. Honestly, brother. You do amuse me." He laughed heartily.

Jafari frowned. Again, Madu failed to understand his feelings.

Madu handed him some coins. "Go to the market and fetch us some goat-steaks. Tonight we'll have meat for dinner. Perhaps that will take your mind off your troubles."

It won't, Jafari thought, but he remained silent and took the coins.

He walked to the market in a dark mood. How could he win Tahirah's heart? He must see her again. There would soon be another procession, and despite Tahirah's request for Jafari to leave her alone, he knew that he would be there again, watching her from afar.

He walked in a daze through the market when, without warning, an apparition of Nefertiti appeared before him. He stood there, mouth open. Could it be a spirit? The image turned and walked into a small shop. Almost as though compelled, Jafari followed her inside.

Looking around, he saw a wide variety of wigs. Many were displayed on carved stone heads; others hung from hooks or rested in woven baskets. He was in the wig shop. He had never been inside before, and was amazed at the many different styles.

A tall, slender woman held his arm. "Do you seek a wig?" she asked, eyeing his thick dark hair. "Or perhaps you'd like to sell your hair?"

Jafari held his hand up to his head. "My hair?"

"Oh, yes!" She felt his hair as if it were the finest cloth. "You have beautiful hair. I would be honored if you would allow me to purchase it from you."

Jafari instantly thought of his dream. And now, looking at the woman, he was startled to see that she resembled the woman from his dream. Then again, many women dressed in the style of Nefertiti. And yet, what if this is what the dream meant? Perhaps this was what Nefertiti wanted him to do — shave his head.

"You will truly pay me?"

"Oh, yes. Worry not. You're young. Your hair will grow back quickly."

"I'll do it!" Jafari breathed deeply and tried to slow the racing of his heart.

The woman smiled with delight. "Truly?"

"Yes." Suddenly Jafari found himself sharing his life story to the woman. He told her of Tahirah and why she had refused him, of Madu and his skepticism. He even shared his dream.

She laughed. "Well, that is some dream. Let me fetch my luckboard and see what it says."

Jafari watched in fascination as the woman sat down and put the luckboard on her lap. Being poor, Jafari had never owned a luckboard, but he found them fascinating and wondered if they truly worked.

The woman rested her fingers lightly on the pointer. "Tell me again, her name?"

"Tahirah."

Instantly the pointer began moving. "Tiw," it said. Yes! It swept past Osiris and Isis, hovered briefly over Nephtys, then glided across the board and landed on Nefertiti.

"Ha!" the woman said. "It appears your dream was true. I cannot imagine what it means, or how my actions will help you, but one does not question the gods, eh? Now sit down and I will shave your head."

Jafari's face burned hotly. Perhaps he was a fool to follow his dream like this. And yet, what if Nefertiti had truly chosen him? Jafari allowed the woman to maneuver him to a small stool. She moistened and lathered his hair. Then, with a deftness that showed her experience, she shaved his head, carefully saving his hair. Afterward, she oiled his head and handed him a few coins. She smiled at him, wished him good luck, and sent him on his way.

Only as the air wafted against Jafari's naked scalp did he wonder if he had done the right thing. Madu would surely tease him. And Tahirah — what would she think if she saw him? She would think him ugly and any feelings she may have had for him would be lost. What had he done?

Feeling foolish and embarrassed, he returned home with the goat-steaks.

Madu's mouth dropped open when he saw Jafari. He laughed hysterically. "Brother, what have you done? No, don't tell me. It was your dream. Oh, Jafari." He shook his head.

"I don't want to talk about it." Jafari folded his arms and turned his back to his brother.

Madu finally stopped laughing. "At least you provide me with amusement."

"Go ahead and laugh. You'll see. One day Tahirah will be mine."

Madu shook his head. "It's time for you to grow up. You are a brick-maker. She is a mourning woman. It will not happen. You are a dreamer."

Jafari didn't answer. He wearied of arguing with his brother. Besides, he realized now, Madu was right. Jafari was a dreamer; he could never be with Tahirah. It was best if he forgot her forever.

Jafari vowed that when Tahirah next walked through town performing her duty as a mourning woman, he would remain at home. While most of the town would surely attend, he would stay home and ignore her.

The next few days and nights passed in a haze. He rose each morning and spent long days in the sun, helping Madu make and sell the bricks that provided them enough money to live. He went to bed each night, doing his best to ignore any thoughts of Tahirah.

Even Madu began to feel sorry for him and tried to cheer Jafari by making jokes and being kind.

Jafari knew that he should be grateful to his brother. Instead he felt nothing but sadness. He wandered lost in the desert, suffering from a great unquenchable thirst.

The day soon arrived when another procession was planned. The well-known scribe, Abasi Anat, had died.

"Do you plan to attend?" Madu asked gently, clearly aware of Jafari's dark mood. The morning of the procession had arrived. Jafari sat, making bricks, covered in mud and sweat. Normally, he would be cleaned up, wearing his best clothes, his long hair carefully tied behind his head. Now only a light fuzz covered his scalp.

"You told me to forget her."

Madu sighed, pursed his lips and stared levelly at Jafari. Finally, he spoke. "I was wrong, Jafari. I can see that you love her. You must go see her. Perhaps she will change her mind. If she loves you and you love her, then even the gods cannot keep you apart."

"No, you were right. It matters not if she loves me. She is a mourning woman. She is spoken for by Nephtys and Isis."

"But what of your dream of Nefertiti? If this was a true dream of the gods, then you risk great peril by disobeying it."

"I followed the dream!" Jafari snapped. "And look at me. I am still bald like an old man. I'm not going!" He returned to making bricks.

Madu rushed forward, grabbed the water bucket, and poured the contents over Jafari's head.

Jafari jumped up, fists clenched, ready to fight.

"You're going!" Madu ordered.

Jafari was ready to protest. But Madu's fists were also clenched, and if they were to fight, Madu's greater size would declare him the victor. Besides, even as Jafari tried to resist it, his intense longing for Tahirah overwhelmed him. He could stay away from her no longer. He must see her again, even if only from a distance.

"Go!" said Madu. "Get yourself cleaned up and see her. It's the only way you'll ever be happy."

"I will go. But as you said, my efforts will be wasted."

Jafari flung his clothes from his body and wiped away the mud as quickly as he could. He was already late. He put on the cleanest skirt he could find — unfortunately it was stained, threadbare and tattered along the hem — but it was still his best. He walked the familiar path to the center of town to watch the procession pass, see Tahirah one last time, and say goodbye forever.

When he arrived, he found that the crowd had already formed. Was he too late?

No. His timing was perfect. The procession had just arrived. There was Isis, walking regally in full costume, leading the procession. Behind her a group of muscular men — the coffin bearers — carried the sarcophagus containing the scribe's body. Behind them walked Nephtys, also in full costume.

And behind them walked the mourning women. Even now they wailed and screamed, tearing out their hair, grabbing the dirt on the ground and rubbing it in their faces, and above all, weeping with such complete devotion that everyone around them shared their agony.

There was Tahirah. Oh, Tahirah! The air escaped Jafari's lungs. He pushed to the front of the crowd.

She was close now. Would she see him? Would she even recognize him?

The way she moved — such grace, as if each gesture was part of a choreographed dance. And what devotion! Waves of sorrow and sadness flowed from her. Again, he found himself helpless before her. Her emotion was too powerful to resist. Jafari began to weep.

Then it happened. Tahirah saw him. They locked gazes.

This had happened many times, and Jafari always felt intense disappointment as her gaze hit his and slid past him as though she had not seen him at all. But on this day their gazes remained locked — she stared at him in utter amazement.

And then the impossible happened. Tahirah roared with laughter. She fell out of pace with the other mourning woman and laughed uncontrollably.

Tahirah's mother grabbed her and pulled her away angrily, shouting the entire time.

Jafari stood there, stunned. What had just happened? Part of him felt horrible for having made Tahirah lose her concentration. But mostly he was delighted. Not only had Tahirah recognized him – he had made her laugh. And he was not surprised to find that her joy was even more infectious than her sorrow. Jafari couldn't stop laughing all the way home. He had turned a mourning woman into a laughing woman!

To his utter astonishment, he found Tahirah there, arguing with Madu.

"Where is he?"

"Right there," said Madu, pointing.

Jafari felt as though he were in a dream. "Tahirah! Is it truly you?"

She ran up to Jafari and slapped him across the face. "How could you do that to me?"

"I'm sorry." Jafari held his cheek. "I didn't mean to embarrass you."

"I've been kicked out of the priesthood. I'm no longer a mourning woman. You knew exactly what you were doing this whole time, didn't you? This was your plan all along." She frowned at him, hands on her hips. Wait, was that a hint of a smile?

"No," he protested. "There was no plan!" At least not by me, he thought, as he considered the strange events that led him here.

"Oh, Jafari, you're impossible." Tahirah stepped forward and kissed him. "I have waited a very long time to do that," she said, smiling.

Jafari was stunned silent. He stood there trembling, disbelieving. It seemed a thing impossible, and yet standing before him was the woman he loved. It was true! And she had kissed him! The gods had answered his prayers, and his heart soared. Oh, Tahirah!

About the Author

PRESTON DENNETT BECAME A VORACIOUS reader of speculative fiction at age thirteen, after discovering the books of Clifford Simak. Before he could drive, the walls of his bedroom became an A-Z library of sci-fi and fantasy. Since then, he has worked as a carpet cleaner, fast-food worker, data entry clerk, bookkeeper, landscaper, singer, actor, writer, radio host, television consultant, teacher, UFO researcher, ghost hunter and more. In addition to writing about UFOs and the paranormal, he has sold dozens of speculative fiction stories to various venues such as *Cast of Wonders, Daily Science Fiction, Pulphouse* and more. In 2019, after submitting 46 times, he won second place in the Writers of the Future Contest, Volume 35. He currently resides in southern California where he spends his days finding new ways to pay the bills and his nights exploring the farthest edges of the universe.

Website: https://prestondennett.weebly.com/

About the Story

THE INITIAL SEED FOR *THE Mourning Woman* came from a writing prompt: Egyptian Mythology. I have a love/hate relationship with prompts. I've got plenty of my own ideas; why use prompts? But after writing several stories this way (and selling them, I might add) I soon learned the value of the exercise. Some of my favorite stories were born this way.

When working with a prompt, my first step is always to educate myself. And as I immersed myself into ancient Egypt and its rich and varied mythology, story ideas began to circle around me. Then I read about the mourning women of ancient Egypt, and I knew I had a character I found intriguing. So Tahirah was born.

And as I explored the lifestyle of ancient Egyptians, Jafari, a young, poor brick-maker popped into my head. And he was in love with Tahirah. Now that I had my characters, and a fascinating setting, the seed of the story began to sprout and grow its first leaves. I'm a half-plotter half-pantser writer. And as I dived into the story, it soon began to write itself, moving in fun and unexpected directions. That's the joy of writing, when the story and characters come alive.

After the necessary polishing, *The Mourning Woman* grew into a light-hearted, romantic, magical fantasy story, and I'm delighted that it found a place in this volume.

Sole Possession

T. J. Knight

HANK WILL DRIVE US HOME. That's assumed. The receptionist just hands him the keys. Doesn't even look at me.

As the car cruises around curves, up hills and down, Hank regales me with the details leading up to my... birth? As if I wasn't there, as if I wasn't *him* until that dizzying, discontinuous moment I became myself.

"It actually worked — I mean, I've seen plenty of doubles, but now I have one. We're exactly the same!"

Not exactly. I rub my chest where a doctor had jabbed me with a cardiac needle, injecting a tiny explosive into my heart. Benign, for thirty days. The trial period to guarantee good behavior in the product.

"You cool?" He takes his eyes from the twisting road ahead and looks my way. Autumn in Vermont is now playing outside each window.

"Yeah," I say, but I'm not.

My gaze fixes on a nearby oak. Yellow leaves cling to nearly barren limbs. We drift off-road and crunch through a patch of fallen leaves the color of pumpkins and cinnamon, sending them swirling into the air. We whip past, and they're gone.

I meet Hank's eyes, the same brown hue as mine, and give him a wan smile. Looking at him is like watching an animated mirror. His smooth copper skin, my flat nose. Strands of black hair fall over his forehead and I feel the tickling of my own. I brush mine back.

"Good. We still going for a run before dinner, Hawk?" he asks.

"Yeah," I say again, looking at my clothes: gray tank top, black running shorts, Nike sneakers over white ankle socks. We're supposed to jog together while dinner cooks in the oven.

I replay the name in my head: Hawk. Not the name my parents had given, but one I'd chosen for myself. Hawk Landstrider. Very Shawnee.

"I'm looking forward to the lasagna tonight," I offer, breaking the awkward-but-shouldn't-be silence.

"Your favorite," he says and thrusts his elbow in my direction. The car glides straight ahead, crossing over the road's parallel lines.

"Our favorite," I remind him. He's begun to separate us in his words, and why not? He's my guardian, I will need him for food, shelter... everything.

"Right," he says. "Of course... Anyway, after a freshly cut tree's worth of paperwork..."

He continues his tale with gusto. I pretend to listen, but I'm focused on the yellow leaves, watching, waiting for them to fall.

THE APARTMENT IS JUST HOW I'd left it — a mess. I remember being so excited. Amara's life insurance policy had finally come through and at last I would receive my double. My terminal loneliness would end, and I would have another soul in my life without dishonoring Amara's memory.

Hank bounds into the kitchen, opens the fridge, and removes a 9 x 12" glass dish of uncooked lasagna. He sets it on the stove and spins the dial to 350 degrees.

I'd spent the morning cooking pasta, spreading sliced meatballs and tomato sauce in meticulous layers, chilled a ten-year-old bottle of imported Cabernet Sauvignon.

I rip the Band-Aid off my chest and rub the two red rectangles it creates. I can still hear my own startled scream echo in the technology-packed Double Up room. Everything glistened as if coated in baked egg wash. The physical pain didn't tell the whole story.

I amble to the bookshelf, covered with far more pictures than books, and remove a framed wedding photo. I look into the eyes of the elated groom — Hank's eyes — and I swear there's three of us in the room.

He places his hand on my shoulder, lightly, tentative, as if he's not sure he can touch me.

I'd read that some people created doubles for sexual partners, but that wasn't my thing. I'd created me so I wouldn't feel so godforsaken alone all the time. And here I am, *Hank's* double, *his* companion.

"I started the oven," Hank says. "I know you're getting hungry." He pats his stomach and laughs. He's right, I am. He knows absolutely everything about me. What I had for breakfast; that I like having a nightlight in the bathroom, not the bedroom; that I hate beer, but love wine.

He brushes past me, scent-free, because you're so used to your own smell you smell nothing.

I set down the frame and stare at Amara's glowing smile, her perfect white teeth, her beautiful hair twisted into a French braid. *You shouldn't have married me,* I think, not for the first time. What happened to her was an accident, but our courtship wasn't. I pursued her, drew her into my life, and by creating a double I'd done it again. But am I Amara or Hank in this new relationship?

Hank leans against the banister and stretches his quads. By the time I push against the wall to stretch my calves he's ready to go.

We run through the city, dodging buses and cars, ignoring red hand signs demanding we stop. Hank outpaces me so I look for ways to cut through groups of shoppers, tote bags in hand, but he surges ahead. I can't keep up.

He pauses outside my favorite Italian place and waves. He's breathing heavily, but I'm toast. My hands fall to my knees and I gulp for air.

"That's so strange," he says between breaths.

"What is?" I stand erect, not wanting to appear weaker than him.

"Well, they duplicated everything, right? Even the contents of our stomachs. Shouldn't we have run at exactly the same speed?"

The wafting scent of pizza and deep fried everything makes my stomach growl. I shrug. "Let's go home. I don't really feel like running."

"Yeah, okay." Hank takes off and doesn't so much as glance behind to see if I'm keeping up.

❖

HANK DOESN'T ASK ME TO clean the apartment Monday morning before he heads to work at the casino, but it's assumed I will. I hate cleaning, obviously, but since I'm unemployed my options are to live with the annoying mess all day or finally clean, organize, and vacuum. I suppose I'll pay some bills, too.

I take advantage of my free time by staying in my pajamas. I go online, watch a movie, and eventually do a few dishes. Hank calls during his break around noon. He's laughing, telling me what a mind bender it is to call himself at home, and wonders if I feel the same sense of otherworldliness.

I glance out our street-side window. Traffic eases past at the ten mile-per-hour speed limit. There are no leaves in view, no color, only towering, gray rectangles of glass and concrete held together with rebar skeletons.

"No," I tell him. "I feel yellow."

"Yellow? Like afraid?"

"You wouldn't understand."

There's a pause. "Of course I would. I'm you. You're me. I get you like no one else ever will. It's like the Doubles Inc. brochure said — "

"Your double. The best friend you'll ever have," I quote.

"Do you... not feel that way?"

"I slept on the couch last night."

"You just need time to transition. Sleep in your room tonight. It's as comfortable as we could make it."

He says we, but I did the work, now he's taking the credit. "I gotta go," I say, even though I have nothing to do.

"Okay, I'll call later." He hangs up and I'm relieved. The room's quiet settles over me like a layer of dust. The pictures of my beautiful wife that rest on every shelf and end table seem to haunt instead of comfort. Unsettled, I don a light vest and walk to the river.

Under partly cloudy skies, I sit on a splintery wooden bench and let the constant, gentle breeze wash over me. Who am I? A ghost? A shadow?

I'm an echo. I may sound like the original, but there's no substance to my being. Someone else created me. Without him I am nothing. Echoes are a novelty. Shout into a canyon and laugh, then return to your daily life.

I lean forward, elbows on knees, and witness a thousand shards of light reflecting off the rippling water like broken glass.

I STAY OUT UNTIL 5:30 when I know Hank will be home. I don't want to need him, but I do. Without him I am broke, homeless, and will inevitably die.

He's upset when I come in. He says nothing is wrong, but of course I know he's lying.

"I called you during my afternoon break," Hank says from his bedroom. He's changing, but I don't believe modesty is his issue — he's started our conversation where I can't meet his eyes.

"And?" I say from the couch. I pick up the mystery novel I'd been reading. Guess we'll both have to finish it to see how it ends.

Hank emerges, pulling his right arm with his left, stretching, warming up. He's dressed in sweatpants and an Army tee shirt I'd ordered online a few weeks back. Apparently he gets to keep that. "You didn't answer."

"I went down to the river."

"All day?"

"Pretty much."

"Oh, I didn't... I just thought... I thought you'd, you know, stay in."

I set the book down and approach him, tapping my temple with my index finger. "I know what you *thought*. The double would clean up, play house, and we'd hang out after work." I hadn't, at the time, thoroughly considered what it would be like to be the eager puppy, waiting for his master to come home.

"Well, you can't work at the casino," Hank says. "They have a no doubles rule. It confuses people."

"I know! You say that like I haven't worked there myself for the past six years."

"Sorry." He relaxes his posture. Mine follows his as if by instinct, or reflex. "You warmed up? Ready to go?"

I'd intended to run with Hank, but as I watch him stretch, ready to beat me again — as if I ever cared about competition — I change my mind.

"I'm going alone."

He drops his foot and cocks his head. "But we're supposed to go together. I want to tell you about work. Someone hit Big Stakes today."

His day, my job. "I need to clear my head." I stalk across the living room, coiled. I need to expend energy, to transfer the growing ache in my heart to my legs.

I jog down the complex's carpeted hallway and burst out the steel door onto street level. I breathe crisp, city air that smells synthesized, like air conditioning. My wave of claustrophobia passes and I sprint toward the Hike Bike trail along the Hudson.

I run too hard too early and my lungs burn. My pace slows, but I override my protesting body and push, wheezing, trying not to cry of all things. I swore I was done with that. Done, after crying gallons of tears for Amara. But does that oath extend to me, Hawk? Or is that solely Hank's burden?

Despite the shade of twilight, several patrons of the Albany Indian casino recognize me. I'm a friendly guy, but not a friend. Not someone you'd have a drink and watch the game with. Who wants a mournful widower dragging down the room?

They call out, "Hey, Hank!" I lower my head and run faster. The fire in my lungs spreads to my screaming legs, calves, and concrete-slapping feet. Endorphins kick in. I'm lightheaded, then high, and finally I forget for just a moment that I'm the double.

I slow to a stop and lean against the guardrail that protects pedestrians from the river and gasp giant gulps of air. Behind me, sneakers thump, bicycle tires rotate in perfect circles, tiny coos puff from baby carriages. All originals, all of them.

I stare out over the river and watch the calm surface belie the racing water beneath.

I turn away and run. I could keep going, disappear — start over. I consider doing just that. But no sooner do I decide than my chest constricts and my heart flares. This isn't exhaustion, this is unnatural. With each stride the pain increases. I'm forced to walk, then stop. My stomach has shrunk to the size of a pea. I double over and vomit onto the pavement.

"Gross," some kid says. Another original, no doubt. Doubling kids is illegal, despite the constant national push to allow it.

"What do you know?" I ask between gasps, and wipe my mouth with the back of my hand.

"Come on, Bobby. Ignore him," the mother says.

I regain my feet, stumble to a nearby bench, and collapse onto it. The river continues flowing beside me. Thousands of cubic feet of water escapes from locked land to open sea.

I'd wanted a companion, but not like this. This was a mistake every bit as bad as going out with Amara on that cold, icy night two winters ago. I want to take them both back, but I can't.

Something in the river floats into my peripheral vision. My first thought is it's an enormous, black starfish, but of course that's not possible. It's a body, arms splayed, legs half sunken. I leap over the guardrail and dive heedless into the frigid water.

Others stop to help me heft the body onto the rock-laden river edge. We drag him onto sun-scorched, withered grass and the body sloshes hard against earth. Whoever he was, he's long dead. Bloated, white skin, fixed eyes. Pink water gushes from his slack mouth.

"Oh, a double," a woman wearing yoga pants and a green sports bra says. She backs away.

"What? Wait." She stops. "How can you tell?" I look from the woman to the body of a man in his forties, gray sideburns, salt and pepper hair, overweight.

"I recognize the signs." She points. "Unbutton his shirt, see for yourself."

I rip the shirt open. Red spider veins blossom outward from a dark bruise on the man's chest, directly over his heart. His bomb had detonated. His thirty day trial had expired.

I look up, but the crowd has already returned to their individual tasks, back into the cardio zone on their heart monitors. I'm alone with the corpse. The double.

"WHERE HAVE YOU BEEN?" HANK approaches me and throws his hands on his hips. He's wearing an apron, the one that shows a cartoon March of Progress of chef's knives. "Oh, you're soaked." He steps back as if struck. "And freezing."

Two and a half hours. That's how long Amara and I lay together on that cold night, waiting for help. Both our bodies growing colder, but with only one beating heart between us.

Water clings to me like an icy layer of new skin and I don't care. I want to remember. I'm still alone.

He grabs my shirt and starts to pull it up, off, but I grip his arm, equal in strength to my own, and halt his trespass.

"What? There's no shame, no embarrassment. We're the same person."

I shake my head. "I don't think so." Teeth chattering, I shuffle toward the bedroom to grab dry clothes, but remember I've been relegated to the guest room. The clothes, new, same size, shopping trip. Me. Yesterday. Excited.

I shower. Near boiling water blasts my raw skin, and steam fills the room. I remain until I feel warm inside and out. When I'm done, I go to the kitchen. There's a plate of leftover lasagna and a slice of garlic bread waiting for me. Hank's in his room. His door is shut.

THE NEXT DAY BRINGS WARMER air, so I pack a lunch and spend the day by the river. I study the water for floating bodies. I wonder how many wash ashore, only to be collected like so much trash. I'd never heard of castaway doubles, probably because they never make the news.

"Hey, Hank. Got the day off?"

I look up into the eager face of a well-dressed Martin Reilly. I play racquetball with him on Saturday afternoons. He was at my wedding. I've known him for years.

I hadn't told him about Doubles Inc. I planned a great prank where I'd go to the locker room for a quick break, tag my double, and head back to the match refreshed. Oh, we'd have such a laugh.

He raises an eyebrow, suspicious.

"Hawk," I say and return my languid gaze to the river. "Hawk Landstrider."

"Oh," he says and shifts his weight. "So how does this work?"

"I'm still me, Martin." I flutter my hand back and forth between him and I. "We're still friends."

"Yeah?" he asks. "So I'll see you at the gym this Saturday?"

I look up and I'm greeted by a befuddled expression. "Of course." I feel a glimmer of hope. Of normalcy.

"Just Hank though, right? I can't play you both." He chuckles through a plastic smile.

Just as quickly as it appeared, my hope vanishes. I picture my waterlogged body, pink water oozing out of my mouth.

"I suppose." Do I even have a gym membership anymore? Do I belong to anything?

"Alright, cool. Looking forward to it, as always. Er, tell Hank I am, okay?"

"I'll pass on the message."

"Alright then. Bye." Martin walks south. I get up and walk north.

I breathe deep the lukewarm air and recall my childhood, school, girlfriends, my first kiss, losing my virginity to Jennifer Kobelsky, but now I wonder — did any of those things happen to me?

I GO HOME TO CLEAN before Hank arrives. I wash and dry the dishes, dust the pictures, and vacuum. I feel a strange need to impress him, like I have to earn my keep, or at least his favor. Maybe he'll buy me a gym card. Or let me try something different, like karate.

"You probably don't want to go for a run," Hank says from his doorway. He removes his laminated work ID necklace and wraps the rope around his hand. "So before I change, what do you want to do tonight?"

The first thought that enters my mind is I want to move out. The concept is so outrageous I'm stunned into silence. He looks at me expectantly.

"Movie," I say. I'd seen doubles aplenty at the theater. It's one of the most socially acceptable places for doubles to go.

"On a Tuesday?"

"Sure, why not. We'll split a pizza. No leftovers for a change, right?" I'm placating him. Telling him what he wants to hear. I need to buy time to analyze the insanity of actually leaving.

"Cool," he says and slips into his room to change.

I sit on the arm of the couch. Where would I live? And for how long? Twenty-eight days, that's how long, then the bomb in my heart will explode and I'll die.

No, I'll learn to adapt, conform. I must. But in twenty-eight days, when we return to Doubles Inc., and they deactivate the device, *then* I'll be free.

"Ready?" Hank exits his room, spinning the car keys on his index finger, reeking of cologne. It's not one I'd purchased. It makes him smell like a cowboy; musky, like he'd worked hard all day and smelled all the better for it.

I haven't worn cologne since Amara. A piece of me feels gratified that the hole I'd lived in for two years was being filled by the presence of another — by me. But *I* don't feel better. *I* still miss Amara's voice from the kitchen, *her* perfume, Cool Water, that always brought me back to when we were dating, and I could play all our days together on fast forward, and we were one.

I am not one with this imposter who has usurped my very existence. I don't belong here.

"You gonna change?" Hank asks. "Or do you want to go like that, you know, to look different?"

I want to shave my head and grow a beard. I want to binge eat and grow fat, or hit the gym until I gain thirty pounds of muscle. I want to burn his clothes off my skin.

How will I survive twenty-eight days if I can't get through dinner and a movie in a darkened theater?

"You go," I say. "I've changed my mind." I move to the computer and turn it on. I'm suddenly desperate to search the Net for any sign of hope that I need not remain caged with my original.

"Oh," he says. "Do you want to talk? I mean — " He reaches out a hand, but doesn't touch me. He's read my posture, or my expression, or my whole aura. "Is there anything I can do?"

Die, I think, and I'm instantly horrified and embarrassed. I turn from him, hoping I hadn't broadcast my thoughts. I remember Amara lying in a pile of shattered glass next to me. Knowing she was about to die, she whispered, "Don't be alone. Find someone."

I'm certain this is not what she meant. But the thought of being with another woman, of replacing her, is abhorrent. I keep her in my heart, and my mind's eye, retinal burned inside the broken Chevy on that cold night when a patch of black ice separated us forever.

"I just want to be alone," I answer. I wiggle the mouse and type the logon password.

"Okay, what's the deal?" His tone is clipped.

"I'm still adjusting," I say, hoping to buy some time. I can't explain this to him. He doesn't want to hear it. I know I wouldn't.

"Listen, I thought this all through. *We* thought it through. I imagined what life would be like with two of me around. Remember our shopping spree? The extra bed, dresser, TV, clothes? You have your own cell phone. What changed?"

"Everything." I deflate somewhat. Perhaps I'll call my parents, admit to them what I'd done. How would they feel about having two identical sons over for Thanksgiving dinner?

"What. Can. I. Do?" he asks, arms extended, palms up. "Give me something."

I've got nothing. "Go out, get a pizza, and see a movie. I just need some space."

"Don't you see? I'm tired of pizzas and movies alone. That's the whole point of you."

His words pierce my heart like I've been jabbed by a second needle. Despite knowing why I exist, having made the decision myself, hearing that I'm alive solely as a pseudo mate destroys the last of my resolve.

I stand and stare at him. "I'm leaving."

"What?" he yells.

"I'm going — somewhere else. Moving out."

He points at my chest. "You'll die."

His power over me. "Yes. I'll only live for a month, but if my imminent demise weighs too heavily on me, I may end it early." Like the man in the river. Perhaps that was his choice. His escape.

"Listen." He's frantic, shaking. "We'll go back to Doubles Inc. and explain that something went wrong. You're me! There's no way you could be this different after only a few days."

"Feels like longer."

"We'll go tomorrow. Take a sleeping pill. I will too. We'll go to Doubles and — "

"Get the explosive removed?"

His eyes flash. "No, I — "

"You'll tell them I'm defective and demand they try again, destroying me in the process."

He staggers back and bumps into the bookshelf. Pictures rattle; one falls. The glass pops like a broken light bulb and mists across the wood flooring.

"No!" He falls to his knees and starts collecting the larger shards. One cuts his ring finger. Blood runs over his wedding ring.

I look at my left hand. No ring. How could I not have copied the ring? I should have had an exact duplicate made so we'd both have one.

I bend to one knee and grab the picture. Amara is smiling back at me, frozen in the past. Just like Hank.

"How could you leave, knowing the pain we felt after Amara's death?" He doesn't look up. Just keeps piling glass onto his right hand. "Don't you remember the emptiness in this room after the funeral? After the family and in-laws left, and after the last of the leftovers were gone? Don't you remember?"

"I do." I step toward the bookshelf and set the picture down. Without a frame and stand, it lies flat. Invisible.

"Then how can you be so cruel and selfish?"

I watch him meticulously collect each piece of broken glass, attending only to his own concerns. "Because that's who we are."

"Speak for yourself," he says, no doubt referring to my apparent betrayal.

"Is creating a double not an incredibly selfish act? You made that decision, not me."

"That doesn't make any sense. We're the same person."

"We're not. I'm the guy who sits around all day while you go out and live my life." I'm tired of this game. Let him throw me in the river if he thinks he's justified; it's going to happen anyway.

"Still. We were supposed to — " his argument is breaking down. "I just thought... we had a plan."

"Yeah? Well it was a stupid plan. Look." I lift my shirt exposing the tiny red pinprick on my chest. "The instant they put a bomb in my heart the plan stopped making sense."

He stares for a moment. "I can see how that might — "

"Make me see things differently?"

He rises, glass clinking in his hands. "You *are* different."

"Yeah, but not in the ways that you want. I suppose that makes me defective." I tap my sternum several times with my middle finger. "And this thing should go off any minute. Let's spare you the inconvenience of having to dispose of my body, let's go back to Doubles Inc. and get it done right."

We both pause. For a moment we're the same person again, each as shocked as the other at this revelation.

He recovers first. "Slow down. Please. Let's get some sleep, see how tomorrow goes, and the next day." He dumps the glass in the wastebasket beneath the computer desk. "If you're still this unhappy by the weekend, then maybe we'll go back to Doubles and — "

He lowers his head, unable to say the words.

"Hank..." I pause. Hearing my name come from my own lips is impossibly strange, but I shove the peculiarity aside. "I thought having a double would be the solution to my despair. Perhaps it is — for you, but I'm on the outside looking in. You're not my companion, I'm yours, and I don't know how to bridge this chasm between us."

"Talk to me!" He steps closer. "Like you're doing right now."

"But you still won't *get it.*"

"Then help me understand. But don't leave." His words and eyes plead with me.

"I am being selfish, and I'm sorry." I haven't been thinking of him at all. What would losing me do to him? What am I to him, as flesh and blood, beyond the intent of his creation? "Do you love me?"

"You know I do."

"I'm not referring to the love of self. Do you love me — Hawk — as a separate person, my own independent being?"

He steps into my personal space, wraps his arms around me and squeezes. I feel his warmth, his presence, his unmet need. His pungent cologne assaults my senses and his individuality is cemented, but I cling to him like a fragile leaf resisting a gale wind, afraid to let go, knowing what it means. My tears, when they come, sting on their way out. My sinuses burn and my throat aches. I haven't cried in over a year, not since the anniversary of the accident.

"Stay." He pats my back.

I desperately want to find the solace in him that an embrace brings, but I never could comfort myself, which is why I'd commissioned a double.

I release him and nod. I clean my tears with the front of my shirt. "I'll take that sleeping pill after all."

"Good." He goes into the bathroom and returns with ten milligrams of Zolpidem. "I'll need to get you your own prescription."

He smiles and hands the pill to me, not realizing that even while joking, he's reinforcing his authority over me.

I chew the bitter pill and swallow it without water. It works faster that way.

BREAKFAST THE NEXT MORNING ISN'T so bad. Hank's up early and the smell of sizzling bacon hits me on the couch. I shuffle to the breakfast nook in the kitchen. He's got everything set up, with two chairs instead of one.

I grab my glass of orange juice and sip it, letting the cold, sweet flavor linger on my tongue. I swear, nothing tastes as potent as orange juice. Hank knows I feel this way.

I sit and watch him flitter about the kitchen. I don't really want to die. I've got the same instinct for survival as any being, but knowing Hank will remain gives me a feeling of continuance, or perhaps empowerment.

Maybe Doubles Inc. would give him a warranty replacement. Then again, I'm the one that should be doubled, not him. I could sympathize with being a copy, whereas an original never could.

I've heard the president has at least six doubles, hidden in secure locations. The poor man spent his whole life rising to the pinnacle of power, only to be told after an instant of duplication that life as he knew it was over, that he was just a backup, sequestered away, hidden just in case. Bored to death. Impotent.

WE WATCH MOVIES AT NIGHT, laughing at the same time, the jokes hitting us with equal humor. We don't talk about us, but our lack of discussion speaks volumes. Now *I'm* the animated mirror, smiling through glass, reflecting off steel, and I am *so* lifelike.

SATURDAY MORNING ARRIVES AND I dress in my running clothes. I used to joke that if I died while running, I'd have died happy. It's my favorite thing in life because when I run, I need no one. It's just me and the motion picture of reality, one frame at time, truly living in the present.

"I can't convince you to stay?" Hank asks, his hand on the doorknob. The words and the action contradict.

"I made it through the week knowing it was my last."

He stands up straight. "How can you be so casual about this? About *dying*?"

"Casual is not the word I'd use. Secure, is more like it. You're still here." Blink, and I'm gone. "Besides, if they agree to a replacement, I'll be back," I snap my fingers, "just like that."

He leans forward and opens the door.

I step through, but stop in the hall. "Don't let him go to the river." I shake my head. "Tell him to go to the park, or the mall. Just not the river."

ONLY A WEEK HAS PASSED, but it's been a critical week for the trees. A cold snap broke the will of the leaves; they've given up, fallen, destined for dust.

We drive into Vermont National Park. Sign after sign relates the park's laws, telling us all the things we can't do.

Hank breaks the silence. "I thought for sure you and I would be as happy as could be... that the hole in my heart, both our hearts, would be filled."

"But we both know loneliness can't be cured by the company of another," I say.

"Not true. Amara cured our loneliness, right? We were supposed to have kids, toy poodles, and tropical fish. We'd have been surrounded by family, love, and warmth."

"And instead you got me." The booby prize.

"I don't see you the way you see you."

"How do I see me?"

"You don't." He looks over at me with a sadness deeper than I ever imagined my own face could produce. Of all the melancholy masks I'd seen in my mirror, this one was the worst. He looks... devoid. "Of course, there's only one solution here."

"What is it?" I desperately want to understand.

"If I know, so do you."

"You won't tell me?"

"No."

Surreal. He's keeping a secret from me. Our brains are identical but for the past week and yet he knows something I don't. Some revelation. He's reached a conclusion.

I want to ponder further, but we round a corner into an area of broken forest, a suddenly expansive sky, and the two-story glass structure that is Doubles Inc.

My stomach lurches and I grip the door handle for support. Second thoughts bombard my brain. Why am I doing this? I'm alive, and to stay that way all I must do is suffer my own foolishness. This is insane.

"You know," Hank says, "I've learned much about my own existence this past week. Watching you, your behavior, and knowing that you're me has been like living inside a dream."

"Third person observance?" This, I get.

"Yeah. For instance, look at my right hand."

It's resting on the gear shifter. I see nothing unusual. "So?"

"When you first saw Doubles Inc. you panicked, yes? Acid dump in the stomach? But you clung to the car, an inanimate object." He raises his hand, presents his palm. "I'm right here."

He's right, of course. I go to work and smile at acquaintances. I go home and laugh at movie stars. My long runs are with and for me alone. I don't see people, I see moving objects.

"If touching me is uncomfortable, how could you ever love again?"

Tentatively I reach out and place my hand in his. He entwines our fingers. Touching him is bizarre beyond compare. He doesn't feel like a lover, or even a stranger, but like my own warm corpse. And yet I do find a measure of comfort. Ironically, in order to connect, I first had to let go.

We park. He opens the door, steps out, and walks toward Doubles Inc. I stride up next to him; same height, same running shorts and Nike sneakers... different destiny.

THE PAPERWORK IS SURPRISINGLY MINIMAL. Hank fills it out. A signature here, initials there. I wonder if they'd streamlined it over the years. What I'm doing is not uncommon, it would seem.

Hank is asked by the receptionist to again empty his pockets. Keys. Wallet. His laminated work ID, carried out of habit.

We're led down a different hall than the one we traversed a week ago. My heart pounds like war drums. We stop before a door whose sign reads 'Double Down'.

Will they simply detonate the device in my heart? Will they inject me with a needle that will lock my muscles? Will I spend my last moments trapped in my own body, eyes frozen, staring at shining silver machinery that glistens under "natural" light?

We're placed in a monochrome room with two reclining, medical chairs like you'd see at the dentist's. They face each other, a few feet apart. We're asked to sit. Our hands and feet are strapped down; then the techs disappear without a word.

The doctor flatly states, "Five minutes." He leaves the small room and shuts the door. I shift in my chair, seeking a moderately higher level of comfort.

"Five minutes," I whisper over my pounding pulse.

"We were supposed to have nothing but fun." He shakes his head. "We were going to drive up to Niagara Falls, right? Take a vacation out west, check out the Grand Canyon." I remember. "And we would appreciate these places like no two unlike people ever could because our life paths were the same."

"But our paths didn't duplicate, they diverged."

"And what path are you now on, Hawk Landstrider?"

"A path that ends in a dark forest, surrounded by silence."

"What would you do with a path that ends in bright sunlight?"

"That is the question I would ask of you, Hank Landstrider. Put away the pictures of our wife. Keep them in your heart, but make room for another."

"You mean like Melissa from accounting?" he asks.

I grin. I can't help it. "Yeah, she's been eyeing us for months."

"But we only pretend not to notice." He finishes my thought and smiles just as the room falls black. I blink repeatedly, and each time I see an echo of his face, smiling at mine.

"You've changed so much this past week," he says.

"As a double, I was granted distance." I breathe out through pursed lips, trying to stay calm. "I see the world through a different lens. I see your pain, and I wish I was the cure, but I'm not."

There's a long pause. Impossible to tell time in absolute darkness.

"No, you weren't."

I hear us both breathing, quick short breaths.

The door opens. Light pours in through a door-shaped rectangle, then vanishes with a thud.

An array of bright green lasers scan Hank from head to toe. Then they turn to me. I have the device. I'm the double.

My chair tilts back and I'm lying flat. I feel a hot iron press against my chest, heavy, like all the weight I've been carrying.

In the dark, I can't tell if I'm dead or alive. If I'm Hawk or Hank.

The heat and weight pull away, the chair tilts forward, and I'm sitting upright again. When light returns, I am alone. Vanished is my living mirror. He's just an empty chair. Techs appear and unfasten the straps from my arms and legs.

A doctor steps in front of me. He's holding a clipboard with a single sheet of paper on it. "Here's a form you must sign to transfer ownership of your things to you." He hands me the clipboard and leaves.

"I don't understand." But I think I do. Hank signed the paperwork. Hank wore his running outfit. Hank and I were the *same*.

I try to read, but the words are a hazy blur. A nurse arrives, pleasant looking, sorrowful face. This is a room of death, and she understands. She ushers me out, telling me to bring the form to the front desk. They'll have my things.

The leather chair screams with its silence. I remove my shirt, place it on the seat, and bow. "May your spirit find peace and forever run like the wind." This isn't the burial he deserves, but it's something.

I retreat down well-lit halls, turning corners. I have never, ever felt more alone. There's no cure in this building. Not on the way in, not on the way out. I'll seek my own cure, one day at a time. I'll do this for him, but also for myself.

"You have the form?" The receptionist asks. I raise the clipboard and single sheet of paper. "Oh, you need a pen." I hear a click, and a blue pen is passed over a shallow counter toward me. "And a shirt." She smiles sheepishly, then turns and begins furiously typing on her keyboard.

Phrases like Sole Possession and Singular Property stand out. I skip the rest and poise to sign. In parenthesis below a single, unbroken line is the name Hank Landstrider.

A typo? Or a last-minute change?

I scratch a line through his name before signing my own. He's gone. And I'm not him.

About the Author

T. J. Knight wakes up early to write. 4:15AM is his favorite time. Before the warm glow of the sun crests in the east, his monitor glows with heatless LEDs. Black words on a white screen tell tales of places far away where heroes do heroic things, all while he sits and moves not but his fingers over a keyboard.

T. J. is a multiple finalist & semi-finalist in the Writers of the Future Contest. His stories have appeared in *Daily Science Fiction, Every Day Fiction, ASIM* and previous Starlight anthologies.

You can like his pictures of weather and food on Instagram @thewind_dustin or tweet at him on Twitter @axeminister.

About the Story

This story was inspired by an episode of the sci-fi show *Continuum*. The character Alec Sadler goes back in time and encounters himself. I think one tried to take over for the other and I came up with, "The Island of the Doubles." Over time, as most stories do, it morphed into what we have here.

This story was a finalist in the Writers of the Future contest (Q4 V.31). Several people who'd read it ahead of time were convinced it would be a finalist. My buddy Frank even went so far as to call me and say I should expect a call from Joni any time. I asked what he knew. He said he knew nothing. Joni called an hour later.

Lastly, this story is several years old. My reason for mentioning this is if you've seen *Living With Yourself* on Netflix you may think, dang, that's what inspired the story, not a scene from some random Canadian sci-fi show. *LWY* was good, and funny, and plenty Paul Ruddy, but I'm kinda partial to my Hank and Hawk story.

Chasing the Sun

Y. M. Pang

IT ALWAYS ENDED LIKE THIS, in shadows and gunfire.

Natalie Aspen lowered her pistol. Its smoke curled around the dust of the Cityside air. Two men lay against the wall, motionless in the light of a sputtering street lamp.

Natalie waited for the rush of triumph, the mingled relief and fulfillment. It didn't come. She felt... nothing. *Too easy,* she thought. At least the previous outlaw had managed to get a shot off, to send a few strands of her red hair floating off in the grimy breeze. These two...

Footsteps. Followed by the yellow blaze of dustlights, built for piercing hazy City nights. "Lawkeepers! Don't resist!"

A young cop emerged around the corner. His face was half-covered with beard, half-shadowed where the dustlights didn't reach. Two others trotted up behind him. Even in the gloom, Natalie could see the young cop's hands shaking around his gun.

What if I don't listen? What difference would it make, if I fired at them and not the outlaws?

Natalie gritted her teeth and lowered the gun.

The young cop's eyes widened when he saw the bodies. "You got 'em?"

Natalie nodded. "Same price alive or dead?" She already knew the answer. She only wished to remind them that she was the one who had taken down the outlaws. The cops, as usual, were too late.

161

She glanced at the bodies. Maybe she should've left these two to the cops. They'd been no challenge at all.

"Do you have to go, brother?"

Sarah Elrose stood in the wheat fields, twisting her blond braid in one hand. The checkered patterns of her dress brushed against the spring frost that still crusted Countryside.

Her brother glanced at her, his face obscured in shadow, the setting sun at his back. "I must go. But I promise I'll be back." He looked down at his pocket watch, another artifact of the Cities — of the place that would steal him away from her.

"How long?" she asked.

"I don't know."

Something tugged at Sarah: an instinctive understanding that goodbye was forever. Her voice grew shrill in her own ears. "Is it really so wonderful there? So wonderful that you'll leave me, leave all this?"

His mouth twisted — a rare suggestion of emotion. "You think that's why I'm going? How can I call them wonderful, when they take so much from us?" He gestured at the frost-crusted fields, at the farmhouse in the distance. "Someday, they'll take all this too."

"They can have it all," Sarah whispered, "if only they left you."

He shoved his hands in his pockets and turned away.

"Please, don't go!" She ran, arms outstretched to embrace him, to stop him. He continued walking. Sarah stumbled over a stray rock, fell — and when she looked up, he was far, far away. As he disappeared the sun slipped beneath the horizon, leeching all light from the world.

Natalie walked up to Cold Moon City's lawkeeper offices. It was the nicest building in the district, built from solid stone. It looked like a tombstone peeking out of dry, cracked earth. At the door, she flashed her permit at the two guards — hired mercenaries, more like — and entered.

An austere hallway led to the main office of the local lawkeepers. They weren't there, of course. It was just some old, grizzled, expendable man. His walls were plastered with mugshots of outlaws. "You a bounty hunter?" His gaze settled on her permit.

"What's the biggest prize you've got?" she asked.

Bushy eyebrows lifted. "This man." He fumbled through a sizable stack of papers and pulled out a poster. "Killed three people in Cold Moon. The mayor, the saloon owner, and Gunsmith Jenny."

Natalie raised an eyebrow. The mayor of Cold Moon had spent the past ten years funneling money from the City to himself, funding a large plot of land in Countryside where his daughters — rumors said — stole cattle from nearby ranchers. Natalie wasn't sad to see him go. However, Gunsmith Jenny had owned enough weapons to arm a regiment, and could hit twenty marchbirds without a single miss. Natalie could barely recall an outlaw that dared challenge Jenny, let alone defeat her.

"Knocked off four in Red Leaf too," the old man added. "Mayor. Conflicting reports about the other three. Rumor says he's got it out for anyone Cityside."

Natalie leaned forward, taking the poster. "Arms?"

"Semi-automatic pistol. Seems all the rage these days." The man glanced at Natalie's jacket, as if guessing that was her firearm as well.

She smiled. "It's more efficient than the old models."

The man snorted. "Was invented in Countryside. Whoever heard of a Countryside inventor?" His lips thinned. "Nothing good comes outta that place." He jabbed a finger at the poster Natalie was holding.

"So he's Countryside then?"

"Must be. No one seen him until two months ago."

Natalie scanned the paper. "No name?"

"No. Folks starting to call him the Executioner." The man gestured at the poster. "Printed before the name caught on."

Natalie folded the poster and stuffed it in her bag. "Where he is now?"

"Look north, in the ghost towns. Last I heard, he's headed there."

Natalie nodded and turned away. She hated traveling through

the ghost towns — lost Cities, abandoned after the duststorms grew unbearable. But if this Executioner had really killed Jenny...

That hollowness still lay inside her, a swathe of barren, dust-chased land, but a spark of curiosity rose, too. Maybe there were still challenges left in this world — outlaws that reminded her why she did what she did, and how she had forgotten.

SARAH WOKE TO HALF-LIGHT. SHADOWS swarmed around her room. She opened her mouth to scream, but only managed a guttural exhale. *Where am I?* She couldn't remember much of the past few... days? The last thing she remembered was her brother turning away and the sun disappearing with him.

She stood, bracing a hand on the bed when the room spun. Her eyes had trouble focusing. Nonetheless, the room looked familiar, like a painting of a place she'd forgotten. The light, she realized, came through the crack between the curtains. She walked to the door. She needed to reach the light, and for that to happen, she had to leave this room.

Beyond the door was a bright hallway. Her feet took her down a set of stairs, into a large room with broad windows and a table surrounded by three chairs. At the far end was another door. She knew the light lay beyond.

"Sarah?"

A voice she recognized. She turned. Her eyes locked on a middle-aged woman with thinning blond hair. Mother.

"You're up," the woman said. "Are you feeling alright? Doc Samuels said you'll be fine, but I can hardly trust him after the incident with Maggie's son. I'll get you some soup and — wait, Sarah!"

Sarah pushed open the front door and stepped onto the porch. She staggered beneath the sights and colors around her. Wheat fields, rippling in the wind. The sky, vast and blue and cloudless. The sun, a circle of gold on the horizon.

"Sarah, come inside! You're still in your nightgown!"

Mother's voice faded, chased away by the sunlight. Sarah bolted, her eyes fixed on the sun. It had left her the day her brother did, but it was back, though far away. All she needed was to reach the sun. Then the light would never leave again and her brother would return.

She sprinted toward the horizon, her hair lifted by the wind. She roamed through the fields all day. At noon the sun grew too bright to even gaze upon, so she closed her eyes and jumped blindly, reaching out into the glow that lay just beyond her eyelids. At sunset it became a fiery disk on the horizon, like oranges she'd seen in the market. It left grey afterimages in her eyes. She raced toward the horizon, grasping, pulling herself closer step by step.

The sun slipped below the earth before she could catch it, but she didn't despair. She'd have another chance tomorrow, and the day after, and the day after that.

She would catch the sun, no matter how long it took. She would show her brother he could never escape her.

NATALIE LEANED AGAINST THE WALL, pistol raised. She listened for the Executioner's footsteps. Nothing. In the clear night, with no hint of a breeze, lesser prey would've betrayed themselves already.

A clatter echoed around the corner. Natalie rounded it, gun raised, and found herself staring at an empty alleyway between two ghost homes. Two stones rolled along the ground, as if recently thrown.

Natalie jerked her head upward. The Executioner crouched on the roof, pointing his gun at her. She sprang back as he fired. The hard, parched ground where she'd been standing shattered.

How did he get up there? Her eyes found the drainpipe on the side of the building.

She returned fire, and he drew back from the roof's edge. She ran to the door of the ghost home. She couldn't climb the drainpipe with him shooting at her.

The decrepit entrance crumpled as she pushed against it. She entered, carefully. Perhaps he had planted cronies here, or laid traps. The moonlight streaming through the door showed nothing but an empty living room, its contents stripped away by departing owners or later scavengers. Natalie kept her back against the wall as she crossed the room and dashed upstairs.

The second floor was as dilapidated as the first. She checked the three rooms one by one, in case the Executioner decided to climb down the roof and surprise her from behind one of those doors. He hadn't; the rooms were all empty. One had a rope ladder dangling from a trapdoor on the ceiling. *This must lead to the roof.*

She didn't use it. The Executioner was surely waiting for her there.

She headed to the corner room. The window had a wide ledge, enough to stand on. Natalie pulled the window open, wrinkling her nose as years of dust dislodged from the cracks. She balanced on the ledge, grabbed the overhang above her, and swung onto the roof. The Executioner stood beside the trapdoor, gun trained on it, as she'd expected.

His eyes met hers the moment she appeared. It took him an instant to level his gun at her. Time for Natalie to fire her own weapon first.

He dashed across the roof and dove behind the chimney. Natalie walked forward, firing at both sides of the chimney to keep him pinned there. She'd hit him earlier, she was sure of it. When she got close enough, she pressed herself against the chimney and swung around to the other side, firing.

He wasn't there.

A foot scraped the roof behind her — so faint she would've missed it if he hadn't been so close. She ducked around the chimney again. Bullets zipped through the place she'd been standing.

Natalie stuck out an arm, firing behind her —

He leapt off the drainpipe to the ground, twenty feet below her. She shot at him as he ducked into a neighboring ghost home.

Natalie scrambled down the drainpipe. She replaced her nearly depleted magazine with a full one, then dashed into the second ghost home. She scoured every corner of the place but found no one there.

He had escaped. She'd shot him, but hadn't captured him, hadn't killed him. It was the closest she had come to defeat in a long, long time.

Sarah pulled aside the curtains. All she saw was grey. Fat drops of water rolled down the window. No hint of the sun anywhere. She fell back against the bed, wetness prickling her eyes. Water, like those disgusting droplets outside. She wiped her eyes furiously and left a scratch at the top of her nose.

A soft knock on the door. "Sarah? Are you up?"

The woman. Her... mother? Despite Sarah's best efforts, her eyes welled up with tears again.

"I'm coming in, Sarah." A creaking door. The woman peered in the doorway, then rushed over. "What's wrong?"

Sarah turned away, facing the wall, not wanting to look at the woman.

"Talk to me," the woman said.

Sarah did, because she had no one else to ask. "Is the sun coming back?"

"Oh. Of course. Of course it will. But you shouldn't − "

"That's good then." The tears finally stopped coming. The sun would return, just like it did after nighttime. She wouldn't despair.

"Come on, breakfast is ready," the woman said. Sarah let herself be led away.

"You've got to help her," Mrs. Elrose said. She couldn't stop herself from looking through the glass, though she knew what she would find. A small figure raced toward the setting sun, blond hair streaming in the wind.

The Cityside doctor sat back in his chair. His gaze swept the worn rug and the beaten dining table. "I specialize in physical ailments, Madam. Headaches, broken bones, breathing problems. Not... this." He gestured out the window, without taking his gaze off her furnishings.

Mrs. Elrose's chest tightened. "Please," she whispered, "we've only got Doc Samuels here, and he's never been City-trained. I don't know what to do with her anymore. After Ervin left, she fell sick and — "

"The physical problems seem to be over."

"But — but this is even worse! Running after the sun whenever it's out, then sobbing all day when it's cloudy... She's lost her mind!"

The doctor shook his head. "Mental illnesses are not my area of expertise."

Mrs. Elrose twisted her hands. "You're a City doctor. You must know *something.*"

"Do you take me for a miracle worker? You Country folk seem to think — " He broke off.

Mrs. Elrose tensed. "Go on. What do we Country folk think?"

His eyes grew hard. She'd misjudged him earlier — it wasn't disdain he felt, but cold hatred. "You think we can do anything. You don't know how lucky you are, living out here." He stood and walked to the door.

"Lucky?" Mrs. Elrose shot to her feet. "My husband dead, my son gone, and my daughter just as lost as them!"

The doctor paused with his hand on the door. "You have the land. You actually have the time to worry about your daughter's state of mind, while the Cities are choking on dust and getting depopulated by outlaws."

Mrs. Elrose dug her nails into her palms to resist the urge to shake him. "And what does this land get me, when half my crops are taxed away without me seeing a single cent? Have you ever wondered why the duststorms — "

She stopped, biting her tongue. The doctor tilted his head. "Go on," he said, echoing her words from earlier. "Why are the duststorms here?"

"Erwin always said the duststorms were punishment for all the land the Cities destroyed, all the wreckage they caused with their endless urge to build."

She expected him to argue with her, or to laugh at her. Instead he closed a hand around the doorknob and pulled the door open. Just before he stepped outside, he glanced back.

"And yet," he said, voice mingling with an invading wind, "your son still left for the Cities. You want to help your daughter? Maybe you should try bringing your son back."

THE SCRAWNY DUN-COLORED HORSE — bred specifically to withstand the dismal Cityside climate, its seller claimed — stared at Natalie with its one seeing eye. A poor specimen, for such a hefty price. Still, it was her best chance of catching the Executioner as he slipped from City to City. *They say he has a healthy, well-bred horse from Countryside. Is it holding up here?*

Many months had passed. She'd cornered him twice. Once outside the Deathless Woods, home to those eerie pines that had turned yellow with the first duststorms but remained alive and growing. The Executioner had disappeared beneath the shadows of those pines the moment he saw her, and she'd scoured the woods all day with no success.

The second encounter had been in Goose Sky. She thought she had him after he ran out of bullets, only for him to dash into a nearby diner and proceed to throw knives at her from the kitchen.

That was two months ago. She hadn't tracked him down since. News reached her, of course — in saloons, in lawkeeper offices. He'd returned to Red Leaf, challenged and beat Ernie Decker. He'd stormed the lawkeeper office in Burnt Seed and gunned down the chief there. People spoke, not with horror but with hushed excitement, as if the Executioner were a traveling circus, there to provide some engaging if distasteful entertainment.

She tied her pack to the horse and swung into the saddle. She carried only one small bag of travel necessities. The rest of her possessions had been left in a house she rarely visited.

She could barely remember why she became a bounty hunter, and what there could be to find or protect as she wandered from City to City. She imagined cornering the Executioner again, finally putting that bullet through his head... surely that feeling would return. Never, ever had an outlaw eluded her for so long. Perhaps she should learn from the gawking storytellers and enjoy the hunt.

She whipped the horse into motion. Its hooves stirred up dust, which smelled of powdered bone and dying dreams.

"SARAH!"

She raced for the sun. It hung in the west, and always slipped below the horizon before she could reach it. But not today. Today she would catch the light, breathe it in, hold it to her heart and chain it beside her forever.

"Sarah, you need to stop this!"

And if it escaped her today, she wouldn't despair. She'd always have second chances. Someday, when her feet were quicker and her reach longer —

"Look at me!"

Someone grabbed her arm. Sarah jerked to a halt. She struggled, knowing she was losing time. The insistent grip spun her around, until she was staring at that strange woman — the one who yelled at her and constantly interrupted her chase. But the woman offered her a roof for nights and rainy days, and fed her so she'd have the energy to run. Yes, she should be nice to the woman.

"I don't know what to do with you," the woman said. "Mr. Welland says I should lock you up, says that'll fix you good."

Sarah twisted in the woman's grip. She couldn't get locked up. Then she'd never see the sun again.

"I'm not going to do that," the woman continued. She pulled Sarah into an embrace. She smelled like flour and dish soap. "I just wish I could help you, somehow."

"Let me run," Sarah said.

"You can't catch it."

"Liar." Even now she could see the sun, reflected twice in the woman's eyes. So close.

"I miss him too, you know." The woman's eyes grew wet, the images of the sun distorted. "Come on, let's go back to the house. Trust your mother on this."

Sarah blinked. "Mother?" she repeated the word — *it sounds like brother* — tasting it, trying to understand.

The woman stared. "Don't you — don't you know who I am?"

Sarah shrugged. The woman broke down sobbing, her grip slackening. Sarah twisted away and ran — perhaps she still had time to catch the sun. She left the woman kneeling in the path, almost hidden from view.

The wheat had grown tall and was turning gold. Sarah always loved it when the wheat changed color. It looked like strands of sunlight.

SCREAMS PIERCED THE NIGHT AIR. Natalie raced to the City square, pushing past the fleeing crowd. The year's first snow was falling, mingling with the Cityside dust.

The Executioner stood on the roof of City Hall. Below him, on a platform, lay half a dozen bodies: the mayor and his councilors, Natalie guessed. Seven cops stood by the platform, firing at the Executioner, forcing him behind the cracked spire.

Natalie drew her gun. He hadn't seen her, as far as she could tell, but she dared not fire in the rush of a crowd. Months ago, standing in that alleyway with the too-late cops and the outlaws who hadn't managed to return a single shot, she might've been tempted. But now she considered: should a jostling elbow cause her to miss, his return fire could kill the civilians around her.

She ran to the side of the building, where a rusty drainpipe hung. It reminded her of their first encounter, in the husk of a City buried by dust. No one noticed her scrambling up the drainpipe. The Executioner and the cops fired at each other. The crowd was too busy running and panicking and trampling to notice much else. The snow and dust were so thick the world seemed encased in frosted glass.

The Executioner dispatched the last cop just as Natalie reached the rooftop. She couldn't see his expression — only the barrel of his gun, turning in her direction. Natalie raised her own gun, but she was late, fatally late —

Her shot echoed his like a second, weaker heartbeat.

Natalie fell to her knees, her gun clattering on the rooftop. Her vision had cleared, in the end, as if someone had swept dust and snow from the Cityside air.

She saw the Executioner turn his gun upon himself. She heard the gunshot, saw him crumple. Saw her bullet pass through the empty air he left behind as he fell.

A choked sound — laughter, sobs — built in her throat. Oh, the bastard was clever. He had fled beyond her grasp, and now she would never, ever...

She crawled forward, the snow biting her hands and knees. She reached him. His gun lay in his lifeless hand. The bullet had torn through his skull, leaving a stream of blood that melted the snow. There was something in his left hand. It took a moment to uncurl his fingers, as his hands were stiff and icy. She pried out a strip of paper, probably torn from the margin of a book. A note was scrawled on it:

> *To the one person who has been a challenge:*
> *I am sorry I cannot die by your hand. I wanted to give you that honor, but you are also of the City. You protect the places I hoped to tear down, in whatever small way.*
> *I have gone where you can chase me no longer.*

Natalie's hands shook. She crushed the paper into a ball as footsteps approached. She stood, facing the two cops on the roof. They walked slowly, step by step, so they wouldn't slip.

"You got him," the first cop said. It was barely a question.

"Yes." What else could she say?

As she picked up the gun she'd dropped, she wondered whether the cops would analyze the bullet that had killed the Executioner. Maybe they'd realize it came from his gun, and her bullet had lodged harmlessly into the spire. More likely, they'd believe the lie. Perhaps, with time, she could believe it herself.

SUNLIGHT STREAMED THROUGH THE WINDOW as Sarah woke. She grabbed the clothes laid out for her and tossed them on. The sun had been absent for the past two days, hidden behind clouds and snow, but it had finally reappeared. She needed to welcome it; she had a feeling she would catch it today.

When she arrived downstairs, she found her usual breakfast unprepared. The woman was sitting at the table, clutching a letter that had been crumpled so many times it was more creases than words. The woman's eyes — fixed on the window — were tired and red-rimmed. "Your brother is back," she said.

Sarah froze. *Brother...* She didn't understand the word, but she knew it was something she'd had and lost. In that instant it was important, more important than the sun.

She dashed to the door. Dawn light danced across the porch, stretching Sarah's shadow behind her as she leapt down the steps. A black carriage stood in the front yard. Two grim-faced men emerged, carrying something between them. Sarah ran forward, calling out a name she didn't recognize.

Instead of warm, welcoming arms, she met the smooth wooden face of a coffin.

It ended in cold wind and winter sunlight.

Natalie stared at the tombstone. Damn him. The thought played in her head, over and over. The fertile Countryside ground was still frozen in late winter, but the snow had melted, allowing her to read the inscription: *Ervin Elrose.*

That was all it said. No dates, no epitaph. That was how they did things in Countryside. She pressed a hand against the tombstone. The stone was cold and unyielding, like his grip after death. She couldn't pull him back, couldn't wrench him from the grave. She couldn't reduce him to the six-month challenge she'd wanted — no, the man had gone and died and become eternal. Reaching into her coat pocket, she pulled out his last message. The paper fluttered in the wind, like a dove battering against the bars of a cage. Should she release it, let it fly beyond her reach like he had?

There was a sound behind her — footsteps on frozen soil. Natalie whipped around, right hand reaching inside her coat.

It was a girl with blond hair, wrapped in a thick woolen shawl to shield her from the cold. She ran as if blind to the world, her face turned toward the sun.

Natalie felt a twinge of curiosity and seized it. Anything to escape the pall of failure. "What are you doing?" she called.

The girl glanced back. "I'm chasing the sun."

Natalie stared at the tombstone, then at the farewell letter clutched in her left hand. "I think I am, too."

About the Author

Y.M. PANG IS A WRITER, occasional poet, and full-time alien who has carved a home in Ontario, Canada. She spent her childhood pacing around her grandfather's bedroom, telling him stories of magic, swords, and bears. Her work has appeared in *The Magazine of Fantasy & Science Fiction, Strange Horizons, Clarkesworld,* and other venues. She dabbles in photography and often contemplates the merits of hermitism.
Website: www.ympang.com
Twitter: @YMPangWriter

About the Story

"Chasing the Sun" is one of the first short stories I've written.

I've written "stuff" before then. Silly poems about Christmas and fairies. Imagined tales for elementary school assignments. Even attempted some novels (ranging from the first few chapters of an L.M. Montgomery rip-off to a complete — and completely terrible — dark fantasy).

Then one day, I saw her. A girl with blond braids, racing toward the sun. "Chasing the Sun" was born, and became the first short story of mine that I thought worthy to send on the submission cycle.

This was back in 2008. The story you see now shares the characters and the themes, but none of the writing. It is a battle-scarred and reincarnated entity. Reworked. Ripped apart line-by-line by a fellow writer. Reworked again. Then thrown into the virtual trash can (or, more poetically, reincarnation cycle), with all the writing restarted from scratch.

(I apologize deeply to the writer who spent so much time on every line, only for me to dump it all.)

2008 "Chasing the Sun" was crime fiction. Current "Chasing the Sun" is... still that, but leaning more into its western and slipstream elements. More focused, more atmospheric.

It's still the story that has meant so much to me for over ten years. And it still retains what I consider its best part: the final line.

Scars of Sentiment

M. Elizabeth Ticknor

WHITE-HOT LANCES OF PAIN STABBED through Adelle's lungs. She leaned against one of the limestone walls of House Favren's coliseum and brought a hand to her chest. Agony pierced closer to her heart with every breath. She sent a pulse of healing energy into her chest to temper the wasting curse and pushed the poison down, past her stomach, into her womb.

The howling clash of distant battle echoed from the arena as she caught her breath. Lord Favren's prized pack of ferals was dueling a trio of havocmages in the arena. Based on the ratio of snarls to screams, the mages were losing.

Unless Adelle succeeded in buying Bastian's freedom, he was slated to fight those same ferals in three days' time — and he was scheduled to do it alone. It wasn't a guaranteed death sentence; he'd spent years in the fighting pits and had a wealth of combat experience. Still, three against one was never good odds.

Adelle caught up to Lady Eclisse just before she exited the arena. Her flaxen hair was pulled back, held in place with dozens of jeweled pins, and her dress was all lavender-colored silks and delicate white linens. Bloodwood gates, carved with reliefs of swordsmen looming over fallen foes, towered behind her.

Adelle knew she must look a fright to the noblewoman; the thought filled her with grim pleasure. She wore the cowled cloak, tunic, breeches, and leathers of a soldier. The curse had drained a portion of her strength, but she still knew how to project a veneer of command despite the waxen pallor of her skin and the dark circles beneath her eyes.

She stepped in front of the lady, ramrod straight, lips pressed in a thin line. "Good morrow, Lady Eclisse. I am Corporal Adelle Xephani, of the Twenty-First Regiment — "

Lady Eclisse's face puckered like she was eating a sour fruit. "I don't care who you are. Attempt your climb up the social ladder elsewhere. I've an appointment with Lord Favren within the hour."

Adelle clenched her hands. The temptation to slap Lady Eclisse's perfectly painted face was strong. "I have no intention of keeping you from your appointment. I'm simply here to requisition the release of one of your gladiators."

Eclisse laughed mirthlessly. "And who is that?"

"Bastian Lang." Adelle had been trying for years to find the funds and opportunity to free Bastian from the fighting pits. Before the argument that had led to his arrest and public branding as a havocmage, they'd been lovers. Bastian might be able to help remove her curse; even if he couldn't, she'd rather die knowing he was free than bound to suffer a similar fate.

"The Fiery Death?" Lady Eclisse sneered. "He's not for sale."

Adelle scowled, pulled the parchment scroll from her belt pouch, and unfurled it with a flourish. She kept her thumb firmly over Achos Cruen's name; it wouldn't do for Lady Eclisse to realize this contract had been written to enable the capture of a man who was already slain. "I have an official writ of conscription from the Valdian United Militia. It allows me to conscript any citizen into service."

"Bastian Lang is *not* a free citizen. He's been placed under my care until I deem him eligible to return to society, and I have no intention of allowing you to take him."

"He may not be a free citizen, but you are, milady. If I'm unable to acquire Mister Lang, I'll have to make do with you instead." Adelle smiled, all false politeness. "You would be compensated, of course, should you relinquish him to me."

Eclisse stared at Adelle, aghast. She ripped the scroll from Adelle's hands and read it with narrowed eyes. "Twenty thousand gold pieces."

Adelle's stomach clenched. She'd been saving for years, but didn't have even half that. "I've been authorized to pay seven thousand for his release."

"That price is laughable. I make over five thousand from the Fiery Death in a single year."

"There's no guarantee he'll survive another one. Besides, what good is the money he earns you in the arena if you die on the battlefield? How much is your life worth to you, Lady Eclisse?"

"This is extortion. I want to speak with your commanding officer."

A vicious grin spread across Adelle's face. "Go ahead. Sergeant Geddies specifically sent me to acquire Mister Lang. I'm sure he'll be eager to handle the matter of your conscription personally."

Lies, all of it. Adelle had been granted medical leave from the military two days ago, due to her failing health. She'd stolen the writ on her way out of camp. Sergeant Geddies had no idea she was here.

A vein in Lady Eclisse's forehead twitched. She swallowed hard, grimaced, and nodded. "Very well. Seven thousand."

Adelle provided ink and pen. The lady signed the writ, authorizing Bastian's release. She scurried off toward her meeting, stride clipped, shoulders rigid.

As soon as Lady Eclisse was out of sight, Adelle collapsed onto a bench. Her whole body shuddered with a combination of relief and nerve damage too long ignored. She shifted the location of encroaching decay, moving it into one arm, then the other. Away from the heart. Always away from the heart. If it took hold there, it would spread like wildfire through her veins.

Once she managed to bring the curse back in check, she set out for the stables. Hope surged within her, but she tamped it down. For all she knew, Bastian had spent the last seven years nursing a bitter hatred toward her. Adelle still blamed herself for the argument that led to his exposure. Bastian had lost control of his temper — and his magic — in public. Once he was outed as a havocmage, and a manipulator of fire at that, there had been nothing she could do to help him — until now.

She clutched his writ of release like a lifeline and pushed onward toward the black granite building that housed the fighting pits' gladiators.

THE STABLES MIGHT AS WELL have been a prison. There were no windows, no beds, and far too many locks and barred gates. Magic-absorbent sigils adorned the walls. Lonely torches formed islands of light in an ocean of darkness; stale air reeked of smoke, old sweat, and dried blood.

Adelle pulled her cowl low and kept to the shadows when the guards marched Bastian out of his holding cell. She couldn't afford to let him recognize her — not until they were safely away. Too much familiarity would breed suspicion from his captors.

Bastian stared at the ground, eyes dull, shoulders slumped. Brick-red hair fell past his shoulders and a thick beard bristled on his chin; both were streaked heavily with white, which seemed odd considering he was barely thirty. The manacles fastened to his wrists and ankles were designed to absorb magic, as was the collar around his neck.

The guards handed Adelle a set of keys and the lead to Bastian's collar. The unspoken implication: He's your responsibility now.

Adelle led Bastian out of the arena swiftly, with as few words as possible. They had to get away before Lady Eclisse realized she'd been tricked, before Adelle had a relapse, before one of the guards realized the military usually sent a full unit to claim conscripts instead of one lone corporal.

The limestone buildings of the city gave way to farmhouses and fields, then clusters of bloodwood oaks. The blanket of leaves that layered the forest floor lent the air an earthy crispness Adelle could taste as much as smell. She leaned against a rust-red tree trunk to catch her breath. All she had to do was deliver the signed writ to Sergeant Geddies and Bastian would be a free man.

Chains wrapped around Adelle's neck.

"You're very brave." Bastian whispered into her ear like a lover, but an undercurrent of menace tainted his words. "I may be chained up, but I'm twice your size. Give me the keys."

Idiot! The guards must have told Bastian he was being conscripted. It was common knowledge convicts were placed on the front lines. Bastian had survived seven years in the fighting pits, and now he thought he was being dragged into battle against gods knew what. Of course he was going to retaliate.

Adelle struggled to force her fingers between the chain. "Bastian!" Her voice came out raw and garbled, too restricted to be easily discerned.

The curse seemed to sense her moment of weakness. Black tendrils crept up her back, spread to her shoulders and neck.

Bastian tightened the metal noose around her throat. "*Give me the keys!*"

Adelle tried to gasp Bastian's name again, but the chains bit too tightly into her flesh. Her legs went slack as she fumbled for the key ring the guards had given her. Bastian guided her to the ground. His grip never faltered.

The keys slipped from Adelle's grasp and fell to the ground. She gagged, panicked, and stretched her fingers toward them.

They were too far away. She couldn't reach.

Bastian shifted his wrists, pulled the chain from around her neck, and shoved her face-first against the forest floor. He held her down, one arm on the back of her neck, and scrambled for the keys. Adelle coughed and gasped for air, desperate to reinflate deprived lungs so she could find the strength to keep the curse from reaching her heart. It was far too close for comfort, teasing at veins, seeking a weak spot so it could plunge into her ventricles.

Bastian seized the keys and removed the manacles on his wrists, then shoved Adelle away and unlocked his feet.

Adelle propped herself up with her elbows and growled, "Gods damn it, Bastian! I'm trying to *save* you!"

Her voice was raw, ragged, and venomous enough it gave Bastian pause. His face blanched with slow realization as he turned toward her. "Adelle?"

"Yes, you bloody moron, it's me!" A coughing fit took her, harsh and violent. The curse was in her lungs, withering them from the inside out. She couldn't *breathe.*

Bastian rolled her over, supported her neck, and examined the welts from where the chains had strangled her. "Just — calm down. Take slow, deep breaths." His eyes widened when he saw the discolored skin around her neck. "What in the seven hells?"

Adelle forced the curse out of her lungs. Into her breasts. There.

That was better. She lay still and focused her energies on repairing damaged tissue. Vitals first. She couldn't heal herself if she were dead.

Bastian loosened her clothes and traced fingers along the pattern of necrotic skin, down her neck and across her shoulders. "I've never seen anything like this. What's wrong with you?"

Adelle waved him off. "Later. I'll tell you later. We need to get off the bloody road. If someone walked up on us right now, they'd think you were trying to murder me."

"I almost did." Bastian sounded guilty. Bitter.

Adelle shook her head. "If you'd wanted to kill me, you would have snapped my neck. Help me up."

He stood, looped his arms under Adelle's, and lifted her into a standing position. She leaned against him as she limped into the forest.

Once they were well and truly away from civilization, Adelle shrugged out of Bastian's grasp. "I need to rest."

"Already?" Bastian's brow knit with concern.

Adelle nodded, leaned against a tree, and groaned.

Bastian sat across from her, crossed his legs, and brought his hands to rest on his knees. "What happened to you? You're dressed like a soldier. You were always a fighter, but you don't have the right temperament to go military."

"I can bark orders with the best of them." Adelle tried to smirk, but it felt more like a wince. She shifted the curse inside her almost reflexively, started healing the damage it had caused. "After you got sentenced, I trained with the village healers long enough to fake my way through the med corps entrance exams. I didn't get exposed as a havocmage until I saved the life of an officer with ties to the Great Houses." Sergeant Geddies. She owed him a great deal. "He decided that I already knew how to control my abilities and I'd do more good helping my fellow soldiers than I would in a prison cell."

Bastian traced his fingers along the discolored patches of skin on Adelle's shoulders. "What about this?"

Adelle bit back a gasp — not only from the pain Bastian's touch caused, but from the delicacy with which his fingers had danced over her skin. She'd missed that secret gentleness, missed it dearly, and now she couldn't properly enjoy it. "You ever hear of Achos Cruen?"

Bastian shook his head.

"He's a havocmage with a knack for curses, works as an assassin. Someone put a hit out on Lord Favren, and my regiment got sent to take Cruen out before he fulfilled his contract. We caught and killed the bastard, but he hit me with a wasting curse. No one I've talked to has any idea how to dispel it." Adelle took a shuddering breath. "I can heal most of the damage when I'm awake, but it takes constant focus to keep it from running rampant through my body. If I don't get rid of it, it's going to kill me."

"I'm sorry."

Oh gods, Bastian was already mourning her. She could see it in his eyes.

Adelle clamped her jaw tight to keep it from trembling. "I've had a lot of time to think about this curse, how it works. We can't dispel it, but I think we can still beat it if we work together."

Bastian arched an eyebrow. "How?"

"I want you to burn the curse out of me."

Bastian's expression turned to stone. "No. It's too dangerous, I could kill you."

"I'm already dying! I can't keep up with this on my own. I'm falling behind. Right now all I can do is spread the damage around to the point that I'm only hampered instead of crippled. It's like a physical poison in me, Bastian."

Bastian shook his head. "My fire burns too hot. What if I lose control?"

Adelle brushed her fingers across the scars that riddled Bastian's torso. She would have wiped them away if she could. "Fire can heal as well as harm when it's used right. You're one of the most capable havocmages I've ever met. I can heal any damage you do, so long as we're careful."

"There has to be another way."

"Believe me, I've been looking." Adelle worried at her lip and took his hand in hers. "It has to be you, Bastian. I can't trust anyone else. I know you won't give up on me. I know you won't cut your losses and leave me to die."

Bastian took a shuddering breath. "Alright. We'll try it. Show me what to do."

Adelle laid her cloak on the ground and used it as a makeshift bed. She forced her curse to the surface and held it there so Bastian could see it move under her skin. Bastian knelt beside her and grazed his fingers against the discolored flesh. "Here?"

Adelle nodded.

A blur of color and shadow slammed into Bastian's left side and knocked him off-balance. A second, larger figure shoved him to the ground and perched atop him with a snarl. Saw-toothed humanoids — ferals — crouched low to the ground, pointed ears twitching. Their dusky green flesh shifted, chameleon-like, in colors and patterns that matched the greens and browns of the forest. Their ears perked to sharp points and shifted back and forth like cats on the prowl.

Adelle rolled over and tried to stand, but a feral with savage teeth and a missing eye held her down. It wrapped clawed fingers around her neck; one wrong move and it would slit her throat.

The ferals who had tackled Bastian, a wiry female with short-cropped hair and a stocky male with heavy scars across his arms and shoulders, worked in tandem to maintain their hold. Heat boiled up from Bastian's shoulders, but before the explosion could come to fruition a larger female leaped from the shadows and slammed his head against a tree — one, two, three times. Bastian slumped to the ground, body limp, eyes glazed.

Lady Eclisse rode into the clearing atop a silky white mare. An armored nobleman bearing the Favren family crest reined in a bay stallion beside her and gestured at Bastian. "I take it this is your man?"

By the gods, this was Lord Favren in the flesh. Adelle had only ever seen him from a distance, but it was hard to mistake the jagged scar that chiseled its way across his face. It started at the top of his right eyebrow, split his nose, and tapered off just below his left ear. He'd fought in the pits himself for a time, though it had been by choice rather than the whim of another.

Lord Favren tilted his head to the left and studied Adelle critically. "You're injured. Did Mister Lang harm you?"

Adelle shook her head fervently. "No, milord. He's done me no harm." She glanced at Lady Eclisse. "With all due respect, milord, Lang doesn't belong to the lady anymore. She released him from her service."

"In order to facilitate the capture of one Achos Cruen, is that not correct?" Lord Favren's gaze burrowed into Adelle, pointed and calculating.

Adelle swallowed hard and nodded.

"Achos Cruen was slain five nights ago."

Adelle's jaw twitched. "True enough, milord. I'm the one who killed him. It's a good thing, too. You were slated as his next target."

Lord Favren studied Adelle's face, his expression pensive. "I'm aware."

"I'm Corporal Adelle Xephani, of the Twenty-First Regiment. May I stand?"

Lord Favren considered her request, then nodded. "You may." He waved his hand and the one-eyed feral stood down.

Lady Eclisse dismounted and walked over to Bastian, her expression triumphant. "Milord, my agreement to free Mister Lang was made under false pretenses. I appreciate your help in reclaiming my property."

Bastian stirred and muttered something illegible. The trio of ferals pinned him afresh; the wiry female pressed a claw against his jugular.

Adelle stood and glared at Lady Eclisse. "You signed the agreement, milady. You were compensated for the sale. The contract may be old, but it's still legally binding. Achos Cruen is dead. That means Bastian is a free man."

Lord Favren's voice cut through the clearing, his words clipped, his tone stern. "You obtained Lady Eclisse's signature unlawfully and under duress. That is inappropriate conduct for a military officer, Corporal."

"With all due respect, Lord Favren, I stand by my actions. Bastian was sentenced to fight in the pits until Lady Eclisse deemed him safe to return to society. She's kept him there seven years simply because he can set himself on fire without burning to death. I've heard of *rapists* and *murderers* who were granted shorter sentences. This writ was issued before Cruen's death. If we hadn't encountered Cruen en route to the pits, Bastian would have been included in the effort to hunt him."

Lady Eclisse spat, "You embezzled government money — "

Adelle shook her head. "No, milady. Every coin I gave you was mine. I'd been saving for years so I could purchase Bastian's freedom. Most gladiators cost between five and ten thousand gold pieces, even at their peak. I never expected your price to be so high."

Lord Favren looked back and forth between Adelle and Lady Eclisse, weighing his next words carefully. "I cannot condone such a brazen dismissal of the law. Corporal Xephani, I hereby strip you of your military rank and dismiss you from service. Bastian Lang will be returned to Lady Eclisse. If it is confirmed that the funds you provided were not embezzled from the military, they will be returned to you. If the funds were stolen, you will be made to stand trial for your crimes."

Bastian's voice rang out through the clearing. His words, though slurred, carried the weight of conviction. "I'm not going back."

Lord Favren snorted. "You're in no position to protest your fate."

Bastian's tone shifted, ominous and dark. "I'm unshackled. I could roast you in your armor without a second thought. Your slaves won't stop me, either. If you die, they're free."

The ferals glanced between each other, then to Lord Favren. The trio keeping Bastian pinned let go and backed away. One-Eye slunk past Adelle to join them. Adelle choked back a sob of relief, thankful they were willing to take advantage of the opportunity to gain their freedom.

Bastian stood and cracked his neck. "Leave or I'll burn you and Eclisse to ashes."

Lord Favren's eyes narrowed. "If we disappear while we're searching for you, you'll be declared an outlaw and a murderer. You'll be hunted for the rest of your life."

Adelle put her hands on her hips. "And you'll be *dead*. It would be best if the two of you ride home now. You'll keep your lives, and we'll never bother either of you again."

Lady Eclisse clambered onto her horse, her brow beaded with sweat. "You're *both* outlaws. I'll see the pair of you hanged."

Bastian conjured a line of fire in front of the horses to underscore Adelle's threat. Lord Favren's stallion shied back and nickered. Lady Eclisse's mare reared, loosed an equine scream, and galloped away.

Lord Favren glowered at Bastian, Adelle, and the feral pack. His hand hovered at his sword.

Adelle snarled, "*Leave.* This is your last chance. You're an accomplished fighter, yes, but you're also a strategist. One swordsman doesn't stand a chance against two havocmages and a pack of ferals."

Lord Favren clenched his horse's bridle with a white-knuckled hand.

"When my soldiers capture you, you'll be shown no mercy." He clicked his tongue and rode after Lady Eclisse's panicked mount.

Bastian frowned, clutched at his head, and let out a pained hiss. The flames burst higher, catching on underbrush and trees.

Adelle rushed to Bastian's side and touched a hand to his head wound. His mind was fogged with concussion; he couldn't retain enough focus to contain the flames he'd called into being. Head injuries were always difficult to handle. Common medical knowledge claimed the heart was the container of the soul, but Adelle's experience as a military healer had taught her the brain was a far more likely culprit. One misplaced surge of healing energies could ruin a person for the rest of their life. This would take hours for her to heal properly.

They didn't have hours.

Adelle motioned to the pack of ferals. "He can't control the fire! Help me carry him."

One-Eye shook his head. "We're not getting executed for anyone else's weakness." He led the pack into the trees.

Adelle swore, bit back tears, and dragged Bastian to his feet. "Come on. We need to go." Bastian nodded. He leaned on her as they staggered through the woods.

Adelle probed at his injury with her magic as best as she could, easing the swelling in his brain. Her curse ran rampant, tearing through her organs. She ignored it. If Bastian proved unable to regain control of his magic, she'd die anyway.

The flames chased after them, a blazing wildfire. The heat scorched Adelle's back. The curse ate into her leg muscles; she collapsed under Bastian's weight. "Bastian, I need you to focus. I need you to make it stop."

Bastian crawled atop Adelle and wrapped his body around hers as a shield from the heat. He closed his eyes and took rhythmic breaths. Adelle held her hands to his face, monitoring his brain activity, doing her best to keep the concussion at bay. The flames near them sputtered and died, even as the forest burned around them.

Adelle's eyes drifted shut, just for a moment.

Calloused hands gripped her shoulders and shook her roughly. "Adelle! Wake up! *Adelle!*"

Bastian was yelling. Why was he yelling?

She must have blacked out. The forest fire had moved past them; a circle three feet around them showed no signs of flame. Even so, her flesh looked charred.

No. Not charred, just mottled with black. The necrosis must have reached her heart. Veins protruded like roots beneath her skin. Her muscles barely functioned; it hurt to breathe.

The curse had yet to permeate her brain. There was a membrane that protected it from unwanted toxins, and it had thus far done its job. The heart, then — that was where she needed to start. She focused her energies on cleansing it, then the blood that pumped through it.

Her lungs failed. She arched her back, eyes wide, gasping in a desperate bid for air.

Bastian clenched her hand. "Stay with me!" His eyes darted across her body as he searched for a way to help.

Adelle focused her efforts on her lungs, regained the ability to breathe. She forced the poison up to her skin, focused it on her belly, then resumed her efforts to clear her heart.

It took the better part of an hour to pull the last remnants of the curse back into her skin. She pulled Bastian's hand toward her stomach. "Finish it."

Bastian nodded curtly, wreathed his hand in white-hot flame, and pressed it to Adelle's flesh. The agony of cooked nerve endings flared through her body. She screamed and writhed, fingernails biting into her hands, as the skin on her stomach carbonized and sloughed off.

Bastian didn't stop until every inch of damaged flesh was destroyed or consumed. He knelt beside Adelle and pulled her head into his lap. "I'm sorry. I'm sorry." He stroked her hair and studied her every movement with watery eyes.

Adelle fought back choking sobs and held a bloody hand over her torso. It took several minutes to mend her flesh, but she couldn't eliminate the hideous burn scars that stretched across her limbs and torso. She checked her internal organs, then breathed a sigh of relief. There was damage, to be certain, but everything was salvageable.

Bastian stroked Adelle's cheek. The gentle repetitive movement seemed to sooth him as much as it did her. "I thought I'd lost you."

Adelle smiled wearily and nuzzled Bastian's hand. "I'm not letting you off that easily."

Bastian helped Adelle to her feet. "We need to go."

Adelle nodded. "West. We need to go west." Across the Dragonspine Mountains, away from the Valdian houses. They could make a new start in Rysa.

Bastian scooped Adelle into his arms and carried her between the charred husks of trees. Some had fallen or cracked open; blood-red sap oozed from blackened bark, lending sweeter notes to the ever-present bite of wood smoke. As they traveled farther from the fire's central path, they found trees that remained whole — scorched and scathed, but still green in the uppermost portions of their crowns.

When it grew too dark to travel, they made camp beneath a tangle of fallen trees. Bastian pulled Adelle flush against him. Even at night, his skin carried the heat of summer.

He twined fingers through her hair. "I thought about you sometimes, in the pits. I missed you."

"I missed you terribly." Adelle chewed on her lower lip thoughtfully. "I want us to be together again."

Bastian brushed his knuckles across her cheek in a semblance of tenderness, but his eyes grew dark. "I wouldn't be good for you. Time in the pits changes a man."

"So does time in the military. We may not make it, but we ought to at least try."

Bastian fell silent for a long moment, then looked away. "We'll talk about this after we cross the mountains. Right now we need to rest."

Adelle bit back a sigh of disappointment and nodded. "Alright."

Bastian pulled Adelle close. It was a protective gesture more than an intimate one, but his warmth proved soothing, and the memories of his earlier tenderness remained strong in Adelle's mind. Despite the uncertainty of their future — of everything — a glimmer of hope remained in her heart. She and Bastian might part ways after they crossed the mountains, but they had a chance at finding freedom and happiness, however fleeting it might prove to be. Adelle drifted off toward sleep in Bastian's arms, healthy and at peace for the first time in days.

About the Author

M. ELIZABETH TICKNOR SHARES A comfortable hobbit hole in Southeast Michigan with her wookiee husband and their twin baby dragons. An avid reader of science fiction and fantasy, Elizabeth also enjoys well-written horror. The authors who have inspired her include Douglas Adams, Ray Bradbury, Orson Scott Card, Neil Gaiman, C.S. Lewis, Chuck Wendig, and David Wong. Her other interests include drawing, painting, and tabletop roleplaying.

Elizabeth is a winner of the Baen Fantasy Adventure award and is in Volume 38 of the Writers of the Future anthology. Her work has appeared in *Fireside Magazine,* as well as an assortment of anthologies by Flame Tree Press, Air and Nothingness Press, and Wordfire Press.

Website: http://www.ticknortales.com

Twitter: @lizticknor

About the Story

MY HUSBAND AND I LOVE roleplaying games, whether tabletop or text-based. In fact, text-based gaming led to the formation of our relationship. This story is inspired by the first characters we played together. I played Adelle; my husband played Bastian, although he was called Ronnie at the time. Some details have changed (which is bound to happen over the course of fifteen years), but the core of the characters' stories and personalities remain the same.

Adelle and Bastian will always have a special place in my heart — if not for the intensity of their romance (in conjunction with some timely comments from a friend), my husband and I might never have expressed the depths of our feelings for each other.

Two Tickets to Tomorrow

J. V. Ashley

THE AFTERNOON SUN PRICKED MY skin, leaving a sheen of sweat over my arms like polished ebony. Color Cultists flowed around me in their garish robes. The sharp scent of spice and smoke wafted out of their tiled shops and burned my nose. The tainted air clung to me. I stepped away from them and into the shadow of the time kiosk to wait for my ticket.

This slip would cost me the remainder of my credits for the month, plus some. *But it could be your ticket out, Zhe,* I told myself. The sepia-toned ticket rolled out with my name printed across a hologram of my face and a jewel in the top left corner. The sepia signaled my strata, the second lowest, one above the Cult of Color. The jewel represented my soul color, a deep purple. Already late to meet my Elite patron, I grabbed the ticket and rushed away from the Cult's brilliantly colored banners, averting my eyes – embarrassed by their shameless display.

Sweat ran down my neck, streaking my shirt before their tiled shops ended and our tenement buildings began. The massive concrete blocks formed a relentless grid. I ran up the three flights of stairs to my compartment, hoping the cool air inside would dry the sweat off my skin. It didn't.

KaLana stood at my door, arms crossed. The dim light of the corridor reflected off her opalescent green skin. That grade of skin stain cost more credits than I earned in a whole year. In contrast, my ebony-colored skin was free, all natural.

"Sorry I'm late. I had to get a ticket for tonight." I keyed in my lock code and pushed the door open against rusted hinges. The stale odor of the space hit me as I entered. KaLana followed, coughing the air of our lower strata from her lungs.

Don't fret, I told myself. *She's given you patronage all quarter. She won't drop you this close to reaching majority.* KaLana had invited me to join her on tonight's slip to introduce me to her Elite. Their acceptance, along with her patronage, was my only hope of escaping the social strata of my birth.

"I thought you'd saved up," she said, picking her way around the clutter in the small compartment.

The gray L-shaped space housed the entirety of my possessions. A single boost light ringed the perimeter of the ceiling to illuminate the windowless room. The shorter leg of the "L" served as a closet dedicated to my wardrobe, which currently spilled into the longer leg and across the pallet where I slept.

"I had a far-future ticket, but when I checked my vouchers this morning, there were only two tickets to tomorrow." I knew Milton, my twin brother, had made the switch. The hologram face belonged to someone else, but the jewels on the tickets matched my brother's soul color, the same color as mine. I decided against telling that to KaLana.

"Two tickets to tomorrow?" She sat on the pallet and sifted through the clothes I'd pulled out for her approval.

I casually dumped my new Buteé heels onto the floor, hoping she'd notice. She didn't. I slipped out of my real time flats and tried on the heels. I balanced on the first while slipping my foot into the second. The strap snapped. I swallowed a curse and tossed them to the back of the closet as if I didn't care, as if I hadn't saved for weeks to buy them. I grabbed a pair of fish scale boots, put them on, and zipped them up.

"Hot as the Tambooli Club in 3017," I told my image reflected in the liquid glass floating in the frame beside my pallet.

KaLana scoffed. "Maybe 2317. Zhe, if that's all you have, you may not make it *past* tomorrow." She picked the points of her Safrano fro out another two inches. KaLana, born an Elite, could go where she wanted, buy what she wanted, and slip time when she wanted. I pushed my envy aside and twirled on the heels of my boots.

"Been there. I first went to tomorrow when I was seventeen. Nothing to it then, ain't gonna be nothing to it now. Luckily, I'll be out of here before it comes in real time." I stopped chattering when I realized KaLana wasn't paying attention.

"What are you going to do with two tickets to tomorrow?" She stopped fussing with her hair and met my eyes in the mirror.

I shrugged. "Maybe use them to sleep off the hangdown from tonight's slip."

She looked suspicious. "Milton's not planning on coming with us, is he?" KaLana did *not* get along with my brother. He treated her like a lower stratum — a striking offense. Up to this point, KaLana had let him get away with it. I didn't know how much longer that would last.

"He might scrounge up enough credits." I tried to sound indifferent. "If he does, he'll be feeling the timelag, hard. He's slipped so many times this quarter the wardens won't let him go again for another thirty days."

"Milton, caught in real time for a month! I'd like to see that."

"Milton or no Milton, tonight we're going to the Tambooli. Tomorrow I'll worry about saving up time. Hopefully, I can convince Milton to timelapse and sleep on the memories." I smiled in anticipation of those future memories.

"Milton can't save time. He just spends it. His and yours. Don't count on him timelapsing with you." KaLana picked up a yellow shimmer shirt and tossed it to me.

I held it against my chest. In the mirror, it made a striking contrast with my ebony complexion. Nobody in today had skin like mine. It was a genetic fluke. Everyone was jealous — everyone but KaLana. She detested anything natural, no matter how rare.

Slipping into the shimmer shirt, I asked, "You don't think Milton would go to the Time Brokers' Temple, do you?" Chills ran across my skin at the thought, causing the shirt to ripple in the light. Being stuck in real time could wreck your reputation, but the Time Brokers ran a dangerous business. If you couldn't afford the credits for slip tickets at a kiosk, you had to go to the Time Brokers in the Temple.

KaLana didn't answer. She discarded a spider silk jumper and a pair of caterpillar culottes, looking for something suitable to go with the shimmer shirt.

"If he doesn't save up, he'll have to sell soul." I tried not to sound frightened as I held up a laser green mini for KaLana's approval.

"Doubt he has much left." KaLana wrinkled her nose and handed me a pair of purple, elk hide leggings.

I was about to ask what made her think Milton had already sold soul when he appeared in the doorway, shoving a pile of scarves aside with his foot. My brother and I had nothing more in common than the time of our birth and our soul color. His skin was as pale as the moonlight while mine was as black as a midnight sky. He was as fearless as I was full of fear. He believed all strata were equal.

I knew they were not.

"Zhe, you ready to go?" he asked me, ignoring KaLana.

"You found the credits?" I asked.

Milton shrugged and stirred the accessories in the trinket bowl I kept on a table next to the door. He picked up a jeweled brow pin, rolled it between his thumb and forefinger, flicked it back in the bowl, and chose another. Twice, his hand slipped into his jacket pocket.

I turned back to KaLana, who continued to pick through my clothes while Milton picked through my jewelry. She could afford to be picky. She'd buy a single outfit for what I spent on my entire wardrobe. Milton couldn't even afford to slip without my credits.

Why do I keep paying his way? I asked myself. *Supporting his habit could cost my ascension.* Yet I kept bringing him along on slips despite knowing KaLana despised him. If she dropped my patronage, I would never escape the lower strata. When I reached majority in a month, I would be moved into the labor force, never to slip again.

"Milton," I called over my shoulder. "How much time you have for tonight?"

"Enough," he answered, sliding his hand out of his pocket.

"If you want to sit this one out, KaLana and I could make it a girls' night." I winked at her. She looked away. "I'm going into lagtime tonight. We could save up for a long slip at the end of the month." Milton didn't answer. I whipped around to see if he was listening and the seam in my leggings ripped. I spit out a curse. "Now, we'll have to start over."

"No time. The mini will have to do." KaLana grabbed her bag and headed for the door. I wiggled out of the leggings and into the skirt.

KaLana stopped at the door. Milton straightened up and put both hands in his pockets.

"Got enough trinkets to buy yourself some color? You're looking a little pale." KaLana stepped around him and out the door. The clack of her Miyana heels echoed down the hall.

"You enjoy being that glamgirl's pet?" he asked as he watched her leave.

"She's my patron," I reminded him. He gave me a skeptical look as I took his arm and led him out the door.

Milton started dragging me along on time slips as soon as we were old enough. He was fearless. I remember one morning an Elite stumbled into our lower strata, looking lost. He lurched through the streets between the squat concrete tenant buildings. Everyone on the walks lowered their eyes as he passed — everyone except Milton. My brother's audacity mesmerized me.

He sauntered up to the fidgety Elite, put a hand on his shoulder. "You need a tour guide?"

The Elite stood paralyzed — probably trying to calculate the stigma he would incur from physical contact with a lower stratum.

"Man, you've sold soul," Milton told him, scorn dripping from his words.

The Elite fell back to anger and disdain, the upper strata default reactions. He brushed his shoulder off and threatened Milton with charges of assault and indiscretion of rank. Milton just strolled away with a dismissive smirk.

He didn't care, and I remember thinking he was invincible. That was before we began slipping time. Everything changed after.

THE SUN FADED. ALGAE-INFUSED LUMICRETE walks began to glow, leading to the slip decks. The Time Wardens only allowed slipping from designated platforms to assure everyone landed in approved safe zones.

Much of future time held dried ocean beds, left when the waters evaporated. Creatures roamed the dried seas, massive beasts that could snap a leg off and swallow it whole, boot and all. *These boots cost way too much for that,* I thought, trying to squelch the fear. At the very least, the inhabitants of the dried oceans could transmit a rash that left your skin scale-scarred. No one's reputation could recover from that, not even KaLana's.

I smirked at the thought of KaLana's manicured skin with the texture of an alligron, or alligatron. I couldn't remember what the ancient reptiles had been called before they chose extinction. Only their texture remained to imprint the skin of anyone who dared to test the wardens' restrictions and initiate a time slip outside the slip decks.

The group of Elite walked ahead, separated from us by several feet. They laughed with KaLana, who entertained them with stories of past future-slips to the Tambooli. Once, KaLana had allowed me to walk beside her on the way to the slip decks, but not with Milton.

One day I'll walk with the Elite, I told myself. *And leave Milton behind?* The question plagued me, but I shook it off.

Slipping time brought added social prestige, and the act of slipping through time brought an intense euphoria. I craved the prestige. Everyone was equal in future time. There, I could escape the stigma of my strata and move among the Elite where fashion flowed like water, and no one had power over me.

Milton craved the euphoria.

Once he began, Milton free fell into the haze of time slipping. He ran through credits and bartered with friends and strangers for more. I knew he couldn't get all the credits through legal means, but I didn't ask questions. He slipped time with me, wherever and whenever, and I pretended I didn't care about our strata.

But I did.

Ahead of us, KaLana picked at her Safrano fro as her fellow Elites took turns telling their Tambooli stories. They took no notice of us trailing along behind her.

"How far back do you think KaLana had to slip for that hair?" I asked Milton.

He shrugged. "I only do future. No reason to go to past time unless you have to."

"Why would anyone have to?"

"Time correcting? Doesn't matter. It just brings you down. No high to it." He scanned the surrounding crowd, looking anywhere but at the Elites.

"I have two tickets to tomorrow if you need one when we get back."

"Why would I want a ticket to tomorrow? Nothing's happening there."

"I thought it might help with hangdown. You've been slipping non-stop for the past two weeks. You'll have a serious hang after all that, plus the slip tonight." I picked up my pace while we talked to lessen the gap between us and KaLana. Milton noticed and grunted, but he kept up with me.

"Hangdown doesn't bother me anymore."

I studied him. Veins mapped dark blue inscriptions across his temple. His skin had become so worn it appeared nearly transparent. In the beginning, the gaunt, pale faces of time slippers had seemed exotic, another part of the fashion statement. But watching Milton slowly fade, I'd begun to wonder if the residue left behind when slipping thinned a person — if a bit of yourself was left behind each time.

I couldn't ask KaLana, whose skin stain changed week to week, even day to day at times. KaLana would only see pale, thin skin as a lack of money to fix it. My envy of KaLana's position grew close to loathing, even as I tried to emulate her. I wished I could shrug off the allure of the Elite like Milton did, but I couldn't see any way out of the dank tenant housing except ascension to a higher strata.

At the slip decks, sinuous lines divided the social strata. Here, the social Elite congregated in a fantastic array of color, the only place in real time it could be seen. All the time slippers, which was anyone worth knowing anything about, wore grays and browns. They only came out in full color to slip time.

The drab wardrobe of real time showed everyone you were slipping — just not right now. In future time, everything was in exaggerated color

— no place to rest the eye, so the mind needed a rest when it came back. Drab became the unspoken uniform to let those around you know that you were only in real time recouping for your next slip.

KaLana lined up with the other Elite and Milton followed. I caught his arm and made a hasty survey of the crowd to make sure no one had witnessed his transgression. He laughed — an ugly laugh — as I towed him over to our line.

"Glamgirl's decked out like a cultist," Milton muttered.

I usually got a thrill when Milton made snide comments about KaLana. Maybe that's why I didn't stop him from tagging along. His derision of KaLana kept me from feeling so out-stationed. He acted as if his stratum were his choice.

Tonight, I just wanted him to stay out of the way. KaLana had offered to introduce me to a group of open-minded Elite with a tolerance for lower stratum. If Milton came with his attitude, they might change their minds and close ranks.

Why did I bring him? I asked myself again as I watched KaLana slip from real time.

THE TAMBOOLI IN 3017 GREETED each guest with a glass dish filled with crystalline powder to cup in their palm. The crystal inhalants increased your perception of the visible color spectrum to the point of near insanity. I'd only been to the Tambooli once before. It took me a month and a half to recover afterward. This time I booked one month of lagtime, hoping I'd built up resistance. Plus, I wasn't sure I could convince Milton to stay in real time longer.

I waited in line as KaLana and her Elite crew passed through the portal, took dishes, and inhaled. They each looked up to the lights pulsing through the club in turn, their eyes reflecting the dazzling display.

Milton stood to the side, seemingly disinterested as he repositioned himself in front of me in line. He slouched into a new position, close to the person in front of him, and slowly worked his way up three places.

The group ahead of us was too absorbed in posing for one another to notice his progression. I wriggled through, excusing myself until I reached his side.

The greeter handed a dish to Milton. He accepted it without looking down, turned his back to me, and lifted the crystal to his nose. When he turned back, his eyes were alight. Colors reflected off his corneas. A smile relaxed across his face. For an instant, the Milton from our youth stood before me, the boy who eagerly pulled me from one slip deck to the next. His eyes filled with the glee of a child seeing his first live animatron of the creatures that once swam oceans of water. For that instant he appeared confident and alive. Then the veil of hunger slid back into place and he began the hunt for more time.

I weaved through the press of bodies, all high on the inhalation of crystal and color. KaLana and her crew perched on a platform at the back of the club. A slow smile curled her lips as she traced Milton's progression. He made the circuit, finding out who could offer him what. Slips. Credits. Crystal. Time-for-time trades that he'd never pay back.

KaLana's predatory gaze slipped off Milton and crossed the crowd to land on me. My skin prickled with a rush of adrenaline. The impulse to turn and flee engulfed me. My instincts told me to turn and go back to real time, to leave Milton to his begging and KaLana to her Elites.

Then it began. The rush of color from the crystals hit. Sound pulsed through the Tambooli. The bodies pressing against me began to undulate, throwing me off balance. I caught myself and made my way onto the platform with KaLana.

"What was that?" KaLana asked as the other Elite made room for me.

We are all one in future time, I reminded myself.

"What do you mean?" I asked KaLana.

"Looked like you were about to pass out."

"The crystal hit harder than I remembered. It caught me by surprise." I searched the crowd for Milton. If I could keep him in my line of sight, maybe I could keep him away from the trouble he sought. Watching out for Milton gave me a purpose beyond chasing the Elite. He needed me. They didn't.

"This your new pet, KaL?" a tall, sinewy boy in a cobalt-blue jumpsuit asked.

KaLana laughed and stroked my arm. I pulled back.

"Only teasing, right KaL?" he asked. KaLana winked at him and pinched me.

"Don't be so touchy. You know we're all Elite at the Tambooli," she said and took a saucer from the boy. They inhaled simultaneously. KaLana leaned in a little further, taking the majority of the crystal for herself. The boy pulled back, letting her have it.

"Dance?" she asked, looking between the boy and me.

"Which?" I pointed at myself, then the blue jumpsuit.

"Either? Both?"

"I'm in." The boy took KaLana's hand and led her off the platform and into the sea of color — color that would have appalled them back in real time. I remained on the platform as they blended into the crowd.

Milton dropped into the chair beside me, took the crystalline powder from my hand, and inhaled. His eyes glazed over for a moment. He shook his head and used the empty dish to gesture toward the dance floor.

"Can't you see them, Zhe?" he asked. I had to lean in to hear him over the sound pulses, too rapid to talk between. "The Elite, they're nothing — just thin veils of color stretched over empty shells. They didn't earn their strata. We gave it to them, and don't expect them to answer for the crimes they commit to keep it." He studied the brilliant color of the crowd and shook his head.

"Tomorrow I'm slipping so far they'll never find me," he muttered, more to himself than to me.

"Tomorrow we're timelapsing," I reminded him.

He shook his head, gave me a sloppy kiss on the temple, and launched back into the crush of people on the Tambooli dance floor. He'd be back soon to hustle me for more crystal, if he didn't find fresh prey first.

The mob moved as one, pulsing with the sound and the color, on and on as I watched. I chose not to join the dance tonight. Something felt different. Something had shifted — not in the Tambooli, in me.

KaLana eventually broke free and slid back in beside me, refilled my crystals, then raised an eyebrow. "Had enough?" KaLana said it more as a challenge than out of concern.

I didn't dare admit I already needed to get home to crash. Show weakness to KaLana, she'd dump you in real time and forget you existed — which would end my climb up the strata. KaLana could take you straight to the top of the social Elite, but lose her favor and you'd hit bottom never to rise again.

"No," I answered. "Besides, Milton keeps sharing my crystal, so I haven't had much." I regretted the excuse as soon as I said it. KaLana already believed Milton was just a time slip junky. She ignored my comment and began to stroke the back of my hand, sending a chill up my arm. I wondered again if KaLana was ever jealous of my natural skin.

If KaLana can't own it, then she doesn't want it, I reminded myself.

"We're two hours past our limit, even with all the tickets Milton's borrowed. We should probably go. It'll take me more than a month to make up that kind of overage." I pulled my hand back and lifted KaLana's crystals to my nose.

"Milton's not leaving until we drag him out." KaLana leaned in to share the inhale. Her pupils dilated. She threw her head back and smiled, taking in the color. "He'd stay in future time on the run if he thought he could get away with it."

I shuddered, remembering what he'd said. I'd heard of people who tried running time. They didn't survive long. *Only desperate people ran,* I thought, but KaLana's comment about Milton selling soul still nagged at me.

Did Milton sell soul to keep slipping? It was the only way to get more time without bartering or stealing. The offense for stealing was worse than selling a part of your soul, but not by much. At least you could buy back soul — eventually.

"Forget about Milt. Come dance." KaLana returned to the floor where Elites immediately engulfed her.

Through the crystal haze, I began to see what Milton had described. Skeletal forms undulated beneath the stained skins of the Elite. Eye sockets gaped above protruding jaws and sunken cheeks. How had I not seen it before? The frantic light sent an array of colors over skin stretched tight across writhing frames. They jerked, harsh motions in time with the sound pulses. Loose joints threatened to fail, to send the frail figures crashing to the floor.

The crystal, I thought, shutting my eyes to the perverse sight. *It's been too long. I'll adjust.* I stilled myself and opened my eyes, trying to see the people beneath the crystal color. *This is what I want. What everyone wants,* I reminded myself.

I searched again for Milton. He lurked in a far corner beyond the lights, alone, scanning the crowd like a predator. Before slipping, Milton had shone brighter than any Elite. Afterward, he faded, more with each trip. His confidence slipped along with his time, leaving this angry, gaunt stranger. Amidst all the light and color of the Tambooli, he looked small, gray, and lost.

KaLana writhed on the dance floor with the cobalt boy caught in her wake. Her gaping eyes turned to focus on me. Her boney jaw cracked a toothy grin. I felt small and lost, too. I wanted to stop time — to escape back to real time.

The feeling came and went as two glittering Elites dragged me off the platform and onto the dance floor. The crystal and color took hold and any thoughts of real time were lost in the haze. This was my real time.

AFTER HOURS LOST, I FOUND myself back in the concrete tenement building. The liquid mirror in my apartment reflected the fresh bruise swelling on my left cheek. Milton, high on crystal and color, had struck me as KaLana and I dragged him out of the Tambooli.

"This is the last time I drag his pathetic carcass home." KaLana dropped her half of Milton onto the clothes, still strewn across the floor. He slumped, pulling me to my knees.

"Help me roll him onto the pallet?" I asked her. "He's too weak to take the tickets to tomorrow. He'll just have to endure the hangdown until tomorrow gets here in real time." I shoved him half onto the pallet before looking up. KaLana was already on her way out the door.

"I don't have the time to spend on a slip junky like him. If you come to your senses tomorrow and throw him out, look me up."

"Tomorrow we're timelapsing to save up. I'll see you when I come out, for ascension, right?"

"Not with him." KaLana flipped a hand in the direction of Milton's unconscious body and left without bothering to close the door.

Milton was my brother, my other half, my twin. I couldn't throw him out. I struggled to get him onto the pallet, then covered him with a thermal. If he was lucky, he wouldn't come to consciousness before going into timelapse, and wouldn't have to experience the pain of a serious hangdown.

I shut the door, rolled out a second thermal, wrapped myself in it, and set both to one month and one day from tonight. If we were lucky, we'd both sleep through his detox.

I tore my eyes from his face. *Watching him won't help,* I told myself. I shoved the two tickets to tomorrow into my pocket unused and pressed my head back to enter timelapse a day early.

WHEN THE THERMAL SHUT DOWN, I woke to an empty room. Clothes were strewn about from the night of the Tambooli, but Milton was gone.

He'd slipped. I knew it. A month of timelapse had not been enough to make up for his overages, much less earned him enough credits to slip again, yet the residue of his slip hung fresh in the air. I coughed to clear my lungs of it.

How dare he leave from here. I'd have to prove to the Time Wardens that the residue wasn't mine.

Terrified that he might have slipped with no plan to return, I put on a gray, shapeless sweater over putty colored leggings and headed back to the only stratum lower than mine.

The Cult of Color lived over their tiled shops arrayed around the entrance to the Time Brokers' Temple. I could feel their color staining my reputation.

To live down here isn't living at all.

Milton came here when he was desperate for a slip ticket. The cultists had them, but didn't share them. Superstitious about altering the flow of time, they refused to slip and hoarded their credits. That didn't stop Milton from begging and threatening the cultists for their time.

They didn't call themselves cultists, of course, but everyone else did. The slur, Cult of Color, came from the garish robes they wore and the brilliant banners they left fluttering in the breeze outside their shops. I once thought maybe they draped themselves in color to pretend they lived in future time, and I couldn't help but pity them.

They didn't know any better. They had never slipped through time and seen the future as we had. But it made Milton angry.

"A waste," he muttered every time we passed through the lowest strata to the time kiosks.

He'd told me on one of those trips, "Every religion began as a cult until it has enough followers to make it legit. But people have time slipped enough now to see religions are all just fads like textured skin and neuro implants. So the Cult of Color remains a cult."

I spent the morning dodging the banners flapping across the walkways and asking cultists if anyone looking like Milton had come through begging slip credits. They shook their heads with pity in their eyes. I wasn't sure if it was for Milton or for me, and I didn't ask. I reached the end of the strata where the Time Brokers' Temple towered over the shops. Shards of light reflected off the crystallized metal walls and cut my eyes.

If Milton *had* sold soul, I couldn't afford to buy it back for him. No one had that kind of money, except maybe KaLana, and she wouldn't spend it on Milton. Luckily, I had the two unused tomorrow tickets from before we went into timelapse. If I exchanged them for a past slip, I could go back and stop him. But to turn back a ticket, I had to go directly to the Time Brokers instead of one of their kiosks.

The cultists' eyes followed me down the alley leading to the Temple doors. They bunched up around the veiled entrance to the Time Brokers, adding guilt to the procession, shaming the people who needed more time than they were allotted.

Selfish, I thought as I passed through veils of color and mist — both real and imagined. The passage reminded me of the sensations created by the Tambooli crystals, but this much color in real time felt vulgar.

I stumbled up to the statues guarding the Time Brokers' Temple and paid them bribes to allow my passage. The tomorrow tickets were a month past due. Turning back a past future ticket to a present past ticket was expensive, but significantly cheaper than buying one from real time to the past. To do that, I'd have to pay with a piece of my soul.

In the dim vaulted entry of the Temple, crystals hung from the ceiling contained in copper mesh baskets. The light of a sold soul colored each crystal. I recognized the deep purple color of one, Milton's — it reflected the color of my own.

I looked down at the worn slate floor hoping to find relief from all the color, but the light from the crystals made pitiful puddles of color on the floor. I searched for a spot where I didn't have to look directly at the soul light. In the center of the floor, a beam of sunlight from the opening in the dome dissolved the colors into a circle of white light. I focused on the circle and tried to steady my breathing.

Trading soul for time – how could anyone be desperate enough to do that? I shuddered. Before today, I couldn't have imagined going to past time either, but there I was, waiting for the chance. I didn't understand how selling soul for time worked. I didn't understand the mechanics of basic time slipping either. The authorities no longer demanded you take a seminar before allowing you to slip. Everyone did it, and no one really knew how — no one but the Time Brokers, and they were a breed even stranger than the cultists.

The circle of light from the skylight pulsed a bruised blue. A metallic voice called my name.

I paid a heavy price to turn the tickets back. Milton's cost would be heavier still, but at least he wouldn't be lost to time. The Time Brokers turned my past future tickets to a future past ticket. I used it to slip back and warn the Time Wardens of Milton's plan to slip and never return. It was the only way, short of physical force, that I could think of to stop him from running time, and the bruise on my cheek from the night at the Tambooli told me physical force wouldn't work.

The Time Wardens pledged to watch over Milton as he woke from timelapse. Hopefully, it would buy me time to talk sense into him.

THE SLIP BACK AGAIN TO real time left me dazed. I struggled to scrape away the fog of past time and adjust to the present. My nerves sparked with the numbness of electricity. My head pounded. I tried to stand, but my legs refused to support the weight. I fell back to my knees on the pallet where I'd left Milton.

He wasn't there.

A scuffle on the far side of the room drew my attention. Milton stood with his elbow crooked around KaLana's neck. The Elite looked terrified.

"Milton what are you doing?" I asked, trying to understand why KaLana was there, and why Milton had a choke hold on her.

"Getting out of here," he said, tightening his grip until she winced.

"The Time Wardens came?" I asked, my words muddled from the crushing effect of a past time slip. "They promised to come — to stop you from running."

"They came."

I exhaled in relief, but his face twisted into a scowl. I stood, bracing one leg at a time to steady myself.

"Milton, you're my other half. I can't lose you." I gave him a half smile. Elite or no Elite, Milton was part of me. He had always been the lens through which I filtered the world.

Milton's anger did not wane. His breaths came short and fast, rage building. Maybe he didn't understand that I'd alerted the Time Wardens to save him.

"We can handle this together. I'll stay with you in real time. You can timelapse the worst of the detox. You'll be able to slip again."

"You had no right," he said. "You can't keep me trapped in today, Zhe. I'm taking KaLana and her Elite vouchers and slipping into forever." He jerked his arm tight around KaLana's throat. She stumbled. Her eyes glazed with tears. She must have come to check on me and found Milton crazed with anger.

"Let KaLana go. If you need a slip so bad, I'll get you one. I'll have time in a week or two. You've already sold soul. I saw it caged in the Temple. You won't get it back if you leave."

He averted his eyes, and I realized my mistake.

"Your soul is already forfeit."

"Souls are for cultists." He met my eyes again. Past rage, I could see hunger and pain. "You just can't understand, can you? You never could. You think KaLana cares about you? She just likes being seen with a pretty specimen of a lower stratum. She's not like you. *I'm* not like you. I'm taking KaLana as far as I can before dumping her and losing time. You don't have to worry about poor Milton anymore. And stop lying to yourself about this glamgirl. You're on the bottom, Zhe. You'll waste away here. She would never have saved you. She would have cut you out of time as soon as she got bored."

KaLana shook her head, just a minute movement, but Milton must have felt it. He slammed a fist into KaLana's ear, splitting the lobe. A bead of blood welled up and fell to her collar.

He's gone mad, I thought. *He struck an Elite!*

A low, merciless laugh bubbled up out of KaLana. Her eyes sparkled with glee — free of fake tears. Milton's grip loosened. He stepped back as he realized what he had done.

"Wardens," KaLana called out. They flooded through the door — they must have been waiting for her command. She knew how Milton would react, better than me. She'd come here knowing and brought the wardens with her — maybe even the same wardens who had stopped him from slipping.

"Silly, stupid creature. You dare to strike an Elite. I will have you drained of all time and leave you a husk for the rest of your kind to clean up."

The wardens forced my brother, my twin, to the floor and cuffed his wrists and ankles. Terror rose in me. *Were they going to drain him here, now, without a trial?*

"KaLana, no. I'll go back again. I'll stop him."

She shook her head, a sour smile on her face. "Milton has only ever held you back. You heard him. He doesn't want your help. Come with me. We will apply for your ascension today." She glided past Milton, who struggled and cursed the guards that held him. She put an arm around me and attempted to guide me out the door.

I pulled back. "No," I said, amazed that she believed I could ignore my brother's fate. "Milton, don't fight. I'll fix this. I'll go back again. This time I'll get it right."

"Think carefully, Zhe. Do you want to spend the rest of your life cleaning up after this junky? He's not worth it. Come join the Elite and be free of all this." She waved a hand to encompass the whole of my compartment and its contents, including my brother.

I took a deep breath, trying to grasp the enormity of what she said. Unable to find the words to let go of the only dream I had ever had, I simply shook my head and ran to pull Milton from the wardens' grasp. A warden's fist slammed into my stomach, sending me back to the floor. I curled around the pain and wept.

"Fool, stay down," KaLana said. "You lost." She left. The wardens followed, carrying Milton between them.

I MADE MY SECOND TRIP directly to the Time Brokers, keeping my eyes on the street. *Asphalt, that's what they called the roads back when automotives needed hard surfaces to maneuver.* The gray crumbling material covered miles of old streetways. Staring at the broken surface of the ancient road allowed me to avoid noticing the flamboyant real time color surrounding me, and to avoid thinking of the horror behind me.

I pulled my gray sweater tight around me, shrinking into it. My muted attire no longer felt like an unspoken nod to future color at the denial of today's. It felt drab amongst the bright, billowing robes of the cultists.

A dark-skinned cultist inclined his head and smiled as I passed. *Why did they insist on smiling? Do they remember my last trip to the Temple with my two pitiful tickets to a tomorrow that was long gone? Did my desperation amuse them?*

A pack of children trailed after me along the old streetways, like multicolored tails to a kite. I glared over my shoulder. They huddled together and laughed behind dirty hands. I tried to keep my steps steady. No reason to fear a gaggle of giggling cult children, I told myself.

The swarm parted around me. My ebony skin felt thin and pale in the midst of their ruddy faces. The children turned curious, bright eyes up as they flowed past. The light touch of tiny fingers brushed my arms.

What did they want from me? They held all the time they could ever need, and I had none. I owed time for the slip to the Tambooli — what I had used *and* what I'd lent to Milton — plus the credits for turning the past future tickets back.

The sharp sun pricked the skin on my arms. *Did the sun shine brighter on the Cult?* I wondered as I walked. Laughter floated in the air along with the tinkling of bell chains hanging from the tips of wooden rafters. Distracted by all the sensations, I stumbled. An elderly woman reached out a callused hand to steady me. She paused to offer me a smile before continuing down the street. She looked flush and happy.

How could she be happy here? Why do they all smile? I wanted to know. *How could the cultists appear so flush while Milton and KaLana appear so emaciated?*

Milton — obsessed with future time — had seemed sick and hollow as the Time Wardens dragged him away. KaLana's manicured skin looked to be stretched too tightly against the skull beneath. *They were thinning. The residue left behind after a slip had to come from somewhere. If Milton had escaped to runtime, what would've become of him? If he'd left KaLana stranded in time, would they both simply have faded away?*

Would the Time Brokers grant me another slip back? If they did, would I be able to correct the mistakes made by me – by Milton? Could I save Milton from himself? Could I stop KaLana and her wardens?

I had no credits, and my debt had hit its limit permit. I had nothing left to barter. Nothing but soul.

AFTER ANOTHER SLIP BACK TO correct my mistakes and Milton's — to warn him of KaLana's plan and her waiting wardens — I re-entered real time in my compartment. This time, Milton lay next to me. Relief flooded through me. He was there, asleep and safe. In time, he would understand. I would nurse him through the hunger — stay with him in real time until he could slip again. That was all we needed — time, and I had bought it at a steep price.

I reached to wake him and stopped. This was not my twin. It was a dried husk. A desiccated mummy with Milton's face lay across the clothes I had never bothered to put away, the clothes that had seemed so important before the Tambooli. I touched the dry skin that stretched across the cheekbones. The eye sockets formed deep pits edged with lashes.

"Oh Milton, what have you done?" Hot tears burned my eyes and blurred my vision. I'd failed again. I'd sold a piece of my soul to save him, and now he was gone.

A wail stuck in my throat, cut short by a voice in the compartment with me. "He put up a nasty fight this time. The wardens had no choice but to drain him."

My attention jerked from Milton's remains to KaLana standing in the doorway. I hadn't noticed the Elite until she spoke. She marched across the room wearing my fish scale boots and prodded Milton's head with a pointed toe.

No. Something was wrong with her story.

"Why would the wardens do this, KaLana? He hasn't had a chance to run. He hasn't struck you. They do not act without cause." I watched her warily. "Time Wardens didn't do this."

"They didn't? Pfft, I suppose you're right." She shrugged. "I guess you should thank me, then, for cutting him out of time for you." She smiled. "You're welcome."

"Why?"

KaLana twirled a purple crystal in her fingers, a deep bruised-blue, the color of my bartered soul. "I get what I want, Zhe. And I want you."

"You would lift me to the Elite strata now, after all this, and you think I would accept?"

"Oh, no. Milton was right about that. You were never going to be an Elite, but it was a fun game to play for a while, wasn't it? But I won't leave my favorite pet here alone." KaLana crooked her pointer finger at me and backed up to the door, beckoning for me to follow. "Come with me, my pretty little pet," she crooned.

I shook my head.

"Poor Zhe. What choice do you have? The Time Wardens will come asking questions. How will you explain away a dead slip junky on your floor? Sweet Zhe, come with me." KaLana dangled the crystal between two fingers, threatening to drop it. "There's no way, but my way," she sang.

Time froze.

I couldn't take my eyes from the piece of my soul trapped in KaLana's grasp. I'd been tricked. Milton had been tricked. KaLana knew if she left me with no other choice I would sell soul to save Milton from his addiction. She just had to make sure I had no choice left.

KaLana had drained Milton out of spite and trapped me out of greed. With Milton gone, I had nothing and no one. My credit and soul were spent, locking me in real time. Milton had warned me. KaLana only wanted me as a pet, and KaLana gets whatever KaLana wants.

"No way, but my way," KaLana sang again. "Poor thing. We both know you can't stay here. Hard labor is too dangerous for you. You wouldn't last a year. I would make sure you didn't," she added.

Missing a piece of my soul, the piece KaLana held, I was forever anchored in real time. I could not even serve in a high ranking labor position that required slipping. KaLana was right. She would make sure I suffered if I remained in my strata instead of coming with her.

I am so sorry, Milton. I could not save you from yourself. I tried. My eyes ran across his grey, empty shell laid over the garish color of my time slip attire, and an idea occurred to me.

"There is another way," I whispered and met KaLana's haughty gaze.

"No, my pet, there is not."

I exhaled the stagnant air of my compartment and tried to slow the beating of my heart. There *was* another way out of this dank, concrete tomb. There was an escape from the stratum that I had believed to be solid as concrete. I had found a crack.

"Goodbye KaL," I said.

"Zhe, come play with me. It'll be fun."

"Goodbye," I repeated. KaLana's eyes hardened.

"You are on the bottom, Zhe, and I will grind you under my boot heel." She turned to leave and tossed my soul crystal over her shoulder.

A jolt ran through me as the crystal shattered against the wall, throwing a spray of shards across the floor and releasing a purple mist into the air. I listened as the clack of my boots — her boots — faded from hearing.

"Goodbye," I whispered to Milton and bent to cover his withered body with a thermal. "You are finally free of time." I touched his cheek and kissed the temple of his colorless face. There on the floor of that cold, concrete compartment, lay the ruin of Milton, my brother, my twin, and the ruin of my dream to become an Elite.

I stood and walked through the purple mist of my soul and inhaled deeply. A smile crossed my lips. I plucked a multicolored veil from the floor, draped it across my shoulders, and exited the compartment. I closed the door — leaving behind a strata system built on pain and despair — on my way to join the Cult of Color.

About the Author

AFTER ESTABLISHING A CAREER AS a licensed architect, Julia Ashley began writing in earnest (or, more probably, in foolishness). Primarily a novelist concentrating on young adult contemporary fantasy, she also experiments with science fiction and historical fantasy through short stories. Julia lives alongside the Old Natchez Trace Parkway with her husband (also an architect), two children (character prototypes), and two mutts (one a suspected alien). Her neighbors, which appear often in her stories, consist of fox, hawks, armadillos, and an alligator who patrols the lake out back. Website: http://www.juliaashley.com
Twitter & Instagram: @juliavashley

About the Story

"I have Two Tickets to Tomorrow" was the full post on social media. A friend who runs the local theater group was offering her two remaining tickets for the final night of a performance. But my mind wandered off track, as it often does. I couldn't help but think that those two tickets would take you slipping through time by just one day.

Soon after, I wrote a piece of flash fiction for an NPR contest in which a couple attempts to escape the EMP strike on their city which would fry the embedded components of all its inhabitants. By skipping ahead twenty-four hours, the couple could survive intact and be able to rebuild in the aftermath. This story relieved the nagging questions posed by those two tickets for a while, but new ones cropped up. So I tried another approach, experimenting with more frivolous motives.

In "Two Tickets to Tomorrow," I explored the idea of teens slipping through time to seek out the hottest raves, the coolest fashion, and the wildest drugs. Afterward they might want to slip ahead a day and avoid the "hangdown" caused by time travel. Still more questions arose like, what would a teen be willing and able to pay for tickets to time travel? And tougher ones like, what would be the physical and mental cost of such a lifestyle? These brought me back to a question I frequently ask in fiction, as well as in real life. How can you save a person from a self-destructive lifestyle when they don't want to be saved? Sadly, I have yet to come up with a better answer than — you can't.

Green Army Men

Alicia Cay

JIM SAT ON THE FLOOR, dressed in his dinosaur pajamas, ear pressed against the bedroom door. His parents were arguing about him again. It was a cloudless Saturday morning and he'd asked if he could go outside. It *was* technically summer break, although school hadn't been in session the whole year. Not since the Purification had begun.

Mom lowered her voice. "It's not safe." Even so, Jim heard the waver in it.

It had been nearly a month since Governor Gill declared their town sanitized and still Mom wouldn't let him out of her sight, much less out of the house on his own. School was scheduled to go back in another month, which meant the start of a new season. Jackets and mittens and days too cold to go wandering in the woods would soon be here.

"The soldiers are gone, Ellie," Dad said. "All the contaminated material has been removed — "

Mom's voice rose. "Don't call them that! They were children, David! Our children!"

"They weren't *our* children," Dad said. "Jim is here. He's safe. We're all safe now, El."

Mom began to cry softly.

Jim twisted his fingers in his night shirt, stretching out the head of a blue brontosaurus. He didn't want Mom to be sad; he just wanted to go out and play. He would follow all the new rules and do everything he was supposed to do. *Please, just let me go outside.*

Jim cracked open his bedroom door and peered down the hall. Dad's arms were wrapped around Mom as she cried onto his shoulder. Jim was pretty sure Dad had won the argument this time, but all the same he stayed put, waiting for the signal it was okay to come out.

Mom looked up at Dad, her eyes shiny. "Go over *all* the rules again, and make him a sandwich or he won't eat, and he *has* to be back before dark. We can't risk them finding out."

"He will be," Dad said. "I'll make sure of it." He kissed Mom on the cheek.

She patted him on the chest, then pressed her fingers to her temples. "I'm going to go lie down."

Jim held his breath.

Dad turned, a faint smile on his face, and gave Jim a quick wink. "Alright kiddo, get dressed and meet me in the kitchen in five."

Jim's cheeks puffed out as he exhaled. Finally! His tummy rumbled with excitement — and something else. Was he nervous? Dad and Governor Gill had both said the town was clean. That meant there wasn't anything left to be scared of anymore. Right?

JIM PATTED HIS POCKETS, CHECKING his supplies. Jacks? Check. His best bounce ball? Check. He pulled on the strap of the canteen slung across his chest and shook his lunch sack. Water, food? Check and check. He was ready to go — out the front door at full speed, headed toward the cluster of old pine trees that stood at the end of the block.

"Back before dark, Jim!" Dad yelled after him.

Jim waved a hand, but he was already thinking — hoping, really — that he would find Flynn waiting for him at their super secret hideout spot.

Previous explorations of this patch of woods guided Jim's movements with confidence as he headed in. He wound his way between sweet-smelling cedars and bristly Douglas firs until the neighborhood houses were no longer visible. He was glad to hear the occasional car passing by — a reminder that home wasn't too far away.

Flynn had found their super secret hideout spot during a game of hide-and-go-seek and they'd met there ever since. Jim slipped between the ring of thick tree trunks, his Chucks crunching on the pine needles that blanketed a small square clearing, and flung his sack lunch on the fallen log wedged between two of the trees.

A branch cracked behind him. His heart stuttered in his chest and he crouched behind the log.

Flynn stepped into the small clearing. He was the same age as Jim, but taller and thinner, with candleflame red hair. He chewed on a stalk of switchgrass. His mouth moved around the obstruction, stretching his words, when he spoke. "What took you so long, kid?" Flynn grinned through his freckles, showing off the gap in his teeth left by the sudden exit of his last baby tooth. He pulled his most prized possession from out a belt loop and pointed it at Jim: a six-shot Cowboy cap gun, made from cast metal so it had the heft of realism. Although the shine of it had long worn away and neither of them had any caps for it, Flynn wore it on his hip with unbridled pride. "Nearly got yourself shot there, Pardner," Flynn said. "Thought you mighta been one of them baddies."

Jim grinned back at his best friend. "Please, you couldn't sneak up on my deaf granny."

"Yeah right." Flynn holstered his cap gun back in its belt loop. "Oh, look what I brought." He dropped to his knees, dug beneath the log, and pulled out a crumpled and torn brown paper bag. He opened it for Jim to inspect the contents.

Jim's eyes lit up as he took the bag from Flynn's hands. "Whoa, where'd you get these?"

"My Pops found him on his route." Flynn grabbed the bag from Jim and dumped a tangled mass of small green soldiers on the ground. Each one was about two inches in height, caught in a different battle pose. "Can you believe someone just threw them away?"

"No way."

"Mom was so mad that he got 'em out of the garbage, she washed the little guys before she let me have 'em."

Jim's jaw dropped. "Why would she do that? We're just going to get them dirty again." Flynn shrugged. The boys shared a knowing look; Moms were weird.

Flynn went on, "We can pretend they're the baddies and we can stop 'em from taking the others away." They shared a moment of silence as they stared down at the small, bent, green men.

"I know," Jim said. "We can build some bunkers for them, and a fort, and — "

"Yeah! And grab some rocks and pinecones and stuff, they can be our explosives and grenades." Flynn threw his toughest look at the plastic soldiers lying in the dirt. "We're gonna blow you guys to the next town. See how you like *our* brand of small town hospitality." He clicked his tongue like cocking a gun.

"Heck yeah," Jim said. The boys high-fived.

They spread out in a circle around base camp, moving in silence between towering trees and rummaging through the thick carpet of pine needles until their pockets bulged with battle supplies — all the pinecones, sticks, acorns, and rocks they could find.

"Locked and loaded?" Flynn asked.

Jim turned to respond, but a noise caught his attention. His head tilted. "You hear that?"

A sudden need for silence fell on them. Flynn nodded, eyes wide. They stood still, heads craned in the direction of the unfamiliar noise.

The crunch of fallen pine needles came from behind them. Both boys jumped. Jim spun around in time to catch sight of a figure in green fatigues disappear behind a tree. His forehead creased in concern. "Flynn, we're not alone."

"Back to the hide-out. Now!"

They ran at the same time. Flynn skidded in the dirt on his knees, then threw himself behind the fallen log. The rough bark of the log caught Jim's elbow as he slung himself over and landed next to Flynn. The boys lay in the dirt, breathing heavily, both watching the blood ooze out along the length of Jim's arm — first blood had been drawn.

"What'd you see?" Flynn asked.

"One of the baddies, I think."

The sound of slow-moving footsteps silenced them. Tentatively, Jim poked his head above the log.

There, weaving between the trees, were three men. They walked single-file, all dressed in an unvarying shade of olive-drab green, and each carrying a long weapon of similar color at their side.

Jim lowered his head and nodded ever so slightly. Fear clotted in the back of his throat, thick and slick as the cod-liver oil Mom spooned out to him sometimes. He squeezed his eyes closed against the sick feeling.

Flynn grabbed Jim's shoulder. "It's okay," he whispered. "They're not allowed to touch us if we're clean."

Jim winced. He'd listened to enough arguments between his parents to know that wasn't always the case. Sometimes it seemed the soldiers followed a different set of rules. "My Dad said they had all cleared out. Why are they still here?"

"Maybe they've gone rogue."

"Hell's bells!"

The footfalls stopped. Flynn clamped a hand over Jim's mouth. Jim's heart pounded like a snare drum; his chest trembled as he tried to forcibly still his panicked breathing.

Slowly, Flynn removed his hand from Jim's mouth. He held up a finger, emptied his pockets, and pointed over the log in the direction of the noise. Jim nodded in agreement.

Once, before the badness began, some older boys had invited Flynn and Jim to play a game of baseball. Flynn had been so good at pitching, he'd been invited back. When it became clear they only meant Flynn , he hadn't gone. Flynn had a hell of a throwing arm. He was also a hell of a friend.

Jim emptied his own supplies onto the pile. Flynn selected the largest rock. He rolled it in his hand. Then, with a flick of his elbow, he hurled it over their heads into the woods. The rock hit high on a tree and crashed down through its branches. The footsteps took up again, headed toward the distraction.

Flynn motioned for Jim to follow. They stayed low to the ground, making their way from the small clearing into the thicket of woods. When the boys reached the trees, they got to their feet and jetted. At the edge of the cluster of old pine trees, they stopped to catch their breaths.

"Should we go get my Dad?" Jim asked. He watched something in Flynn's gaze harden as his friend looked out across the plain little houses that lined their plain little street. From here, everything appeared the same as it always had — pleasant and ordinary. What a lie.

It all started a year ago, when Samantha, the cute red-head a grade above Jim's, had started showing symptoms. One day in gym class she'd made three shots in a row without ever touching the basketball.

Some of the people in town said polluted water was to blame for what was happening to their children, others said it was the power lines or the mother's pregnancies. But when the scary men in black suits and the soldiers with guns showed up, everyone stopped talking altogether.

When Flynn spoke again, the hardness in his eyes made its way to his voice. "No," he said. "I'm sick and tired of being scared of them. Of what they did to us. I say we go back in."

Jim stared at his feet as he considered what Flynn was saying. Beads of sweat broke out on his neck and trickled down his back. Flynn had never left him behind, and now he needed Jim to be there for him. Jim nodded solemnly. He wouldn't abandon his best friend now.

JIM AND FLYNN MOVED FROM tree to tree, keeping apart but within sight of each other, as they drifted back into the woods.

"What's the plan?" Jim whispered.

"We find 'em and follow 'em. See what they're up to. Then we can tell some — " Flynn stopped and held a finger to his lips. He motioned to Jim to move ahead.

Jim slipped around the solid trunk of a bristlecone pine tree and nearly fell over the crouched soldier kneeling in the dirt on the other side. Jim screamed. The soldier raised his portable radio to his mouth. Flynn whipped around from the other side of the tree, a heavy branch in his hands. He whopped the soldier on top of his helmeted head. The impact made a dull brack sound. The soldier collapsed face-first in the dirt, out cold. Flynn nudged the soldier with his toe. No movement.

Suddenly the sound of running feet surrounded them. Their position had been compromised. Flynn grabbed Jim and they bolted back the way they'd come.

Not only did Flynn have the better throwing arm, he was faster too. He rushed out front and headed for the tree line with Jim close on his heels. It was time to get out of the woods.

A soldier stepped out from behind a tree directly in Flynn's path. Flynn pulled up so quickly, Jim smacked into his back. Flynn slid his gun out of his belt loop and pushed it into Jim's hands. "Hide this," Flynn murmured.

Good thinking on Flynn's part, Jim thought as he shoved the cap-gun into his pocket. Even a fake gun could be confused as real and get them hurt. His throat clicked as he tried to swallow the thought away.

The expression on the soldier's face never changed. His cheeks and the area around his eyes had been greased in black; his outfit blended into the wooded background like a ghost in green.

The soldiers blended so well, in fact, that Jim didn't see the soldier with the cracked helmet until he stepped out to stand between him and Flynn. Jim staggered back, tripped over his left foot, and fell on his backside.

Cracked Helmet grabbed Flynn's right arm and twisted it up and high. A startled grunt issued from Flynn's throat, strangled by a cry of pain.

The soldier facing Flynn reached into a side pocket on his pants and pulled out a long, thin-wired collar.

Jim had seen one before, only once, when they'd taken away Sandy from next door. That had been nearly eight months ago, during the worst of the purification. While Jim watched from his front picture window, those soldiers had placed a matching collar on Sandy and led him from his house. Dad had pulled him away when Sandy's mother began to scream. Jim remembered the tortured animal sound — a mixture of grief and madness too big to fit in her body — had poured from her in long, howling wails. He could hear the sound now, could feel it painting his insides with panic. His breath quickened into short, shallow dips. Dark spots danced before his eyes.

A single thought brought him back: They were taking his best friend.

Jim's hands scrabbled through the pine needles and forest floor debris for a rock, a stick, anything. His hand closed around a familiar object — smooth, with the heft of realism.

Jim lifted the cap-gun. "Stop!" he yelled, taking them all — including himself — by surprise.

Flynn took advantage of the moment and wrenched his body back and forth in the soldier's grasp. The first soldier tried to stuff the wire collar back into his pocket while Cracked Helmet struggled to get Flynn under control.

Jim shouted louder. "I said stop! I'll shoot you both, I swear I will." Hot tears, born of the injustice wrought upon his town and his heart, dropped onto his cheeks.

Both soldiers stopped moving.

Jim swung the gun barrel back and forth between them. "Let him go!"

Cracked Helmet let go. Flynn, who had been pulled onto his tiptoes, fell to his knees. He scuttled over behind Jim and stood up.

Jim stood on rubber legs, his breath locked in his chest, and held the cap-gun as steady as possible in two hands. "Now you get the hell out of here, and don't ever come back."

"You heard him," Flynn said. He picked up a pinecone and hurled it at Cracked Helmet. Jim couldn't say he'd seen it, but later Flynn swore the first soldier smirked at him in respect.

"Let's see less of those ugly mugs and more of your backsides," Flynn yelled.

The breath Jim was holding turned into laughter. "You would never talk to a baddie that way." He snorted, still laughing.

Flynn chuckled as he protested. "Yeah, I would. I'd give 'em a good what-for, I tell you what."

Jim laughed more. "Just like my granny would say."

Flynn turned, laughing, and headed back to their secret hide-out spot. Jim wiped the back of his hand across his face, removing all trace of those hot, angry tears. The boys sat on their log, munching on Jim's sandwich, sharing a bag of salty potato chips, and washing down their well-deserved meal with sips of water from his canteen.

Flynn set the green army men up on the log in a line and flicked them off one by one with a popped finger. "Thought I was a goner back there for a moment. That was quick thinking with the gun."

"Yeah," Jim said, "With your aim, if that pinecone had been a grenade, that guy would have been minced meat."

"That'll learn 'em," Flynn said around a mouthful of peanut butter and white bread.

Jim's head rocked back in laughter and he raised the canteen in a mock victory toast. Their triumph echoed through the still woods as they finished their lunch with the fallen soldiers gathered in a tiny, tangled heap at their feet.

AFTER DINNER, AS JIM CHANGED into his dinosaur pajamas, Dad came to the door of his bedroom. "I didn't want to ask at dinner with your Mom there, but how did it go today?"

Jim could no more have stopped the grin that spread across his face then the sun could be put out with a bucket of gasoline. His voice came in a quiet rush. "It was the best, Dad. There were these baddies that tried to get us, but me and Flynn, see, we chased them off. All on our own." He sighed. "Just like old times."

Dad's gaze flickered toward the silver-framed picture on Jim's dresser. In the picture Jim, blue-eyed and black-haired, stood next to Flynn, with his disheveled candle-flame hair and his gap-toothed grin, their arms draped around each other's shoulders. Forever frozen in that moment, the day after Flynn lost his last baby tooth.

Dad picked up the picture and sat next to Jim on the bed.

"I'm sorry, Dad," Jim said. "I was just playing pretend. I didn't mean to..."

Dad's eyes went red. His Adam's apple bobbed up and down several times, but he didn't say anything.

Jim touched his arm. "Is that okay? That I pretend he's still here to play with me? I miss him."

"I think that's — " Dad's voice broke. He placed a hand on Jim's shoulder and squeezed. "I think that's fine, son. Just fine."

A warm sensation sprang up to press on the backs of Jim's eyes. He leaned over and hugged Dad hard around the middle.

Dad hugged him back, then placed a kiss on the top of his head.

Jim slid into the cool space between his sheets as Dad stood and placed the picture on the nightstand.

"Dad," Jim called. "You think Mom will let me out again soon? I followed all the rules, made it back safe."

"It'll get easier for her, but let's just take it a day at a time for now, eh?"

"Yeah," Jim said. "I was thinking maybe tomorrow I'd stay in anyway, we could play board games or something."

Dad smiled. "I think your Mom would really like that." He clicked off the light switch and pulled the door closed.

About the Author

ALICIA CAY IS A WRITER of Speculative and Mystery stories. Her short fiction has appeared in several anthologies including *Hold Your Fire* and *Unmasked* from WordFire Press, and *The Wild Hunt* from Air and Nothingness Press.

She suffers from wanderlust, crochets, collects quotes, and lives beneath the shadows of the Rocky Mountains with a corgi, a kitty, and a lot of fur. Find her at aliciacay.com

About the Story

THE INSPIRATION FOR THIS STORY came wholly from my Dad — who is the character Jim's namesake. My Dad passed away years ago and one day while missing him terribly, I sat down to write a story for him.

He told me tales about his childhood growing up in the 1950's, and how on special occasions, a birthday maybe, he would be gifted five whole cents to spend on anything he wanted. And how once, he spent that entire nickel on a big bag of little green army men. Every day that summer, he played in the woods behind his house, setting up those green army men and fighting battles that would last until his Mom called him in for dinner.

Years later, one of the greatest gifts my Dad would impart to me was showing me how to use my imagination — he showed me how to play — that a wooden block was not just a wooden block, but part of a castle wall being besieged by dragons, or a meteor hurtling out of the sky to devastate the town of Smurfs and My Little Ponies below.

I think this skill of using my imagination continues to be one of my greatest strengths, and is most likely why I grew up to be a writer. Well, writing is just a grown-up version of setting up characters in mock battles and playing, isn't it?

So, what better way to honor my Dad, than to use my imagination to create an alternate version of the stories he used to tell me, and tell my own story.

The Right Decision

Van Alrik

THIS HAD BETTER BE WORTH it.

The thin plastic chip feels weightless in the palm of my hand – almost cheap. I clutch it tightly to keep it from blowing away in the light breeze outside the outlet store. It definitely wasn't cheap. When Tess finds out about the payday loan I took out to pay for it, she'll be hysterical. I can almost hear her:

"Timothy Alan Dunway, you've ruined us! Absolutely ruined us! And for what? A piece of plastic?"

But she'll be wrong. This chip will rescue us from ruin.

I walk down the street towards the high speed rail platform. As I wait for the train, I look down at the chip. But what if I'm wrong? After all, I've been wrong before. I was wrong about the house, wrong about the cars, wrong about the credit cards. I was wrong about the investment company that disappeared, taking with it what remained of our savings.

But this is different. This chip will make all those wrong decisions right. Instead of having to rely on my own intuitions, I'll be able to rely on the chip. It'll fix things.

The chip is the absolute cutting edge – the latest in tech sophistication. It implants right into your brain behind your ear, where your phone usually goes. Based on sensory inputs, it perpetually runs scenarios to determine which possible outcomes are most likely to be favorable. Every decision I make – caffeinated or decaf? solar or nuclear? should I wear that sweater? should I make that purchase? – I'll have this chip in

my brain, running millions of simulations, and determining, based on real data, which decisions have the greatest probability of success.

It will fix everything.

The train rounds the corner and slows to a stop. I press the button for the door with one hand, the chip still held firmly in the other. I find a secluded seat and open my hand.

I frown. Why haven't I put it in yet? This isn't like those other decisions. This was a good decision! But I can't quite bring myself to do it. Sure, it's not technically on the market yet. And the guy at the shop acted a lot like those guys at the car lots. But that's part of why this is so smart — I got cutting edge technology, and I got it at a fraction of the retail price!

My frown deepens. Well, at least what the retail price will be once it's legal to sell.

The train starts pulling away from the station. I turn the chip over in my hands, and then turn it over again. I take a deep breath and hurriedly insert the chip into the flesh behind my left ear.

I sit there, staring blankly, trying to detect the difference, searching for some evidence of my new reasoning power. But there's nothing. A minute passes, and my eyes flutter, blinking away the developing mist. I try to control my heart rate and breathing, but I can't help it. I bury my face in my hands and sob. I feel the awkwardness in those around me, but I don't care. I think of the money spent, the promises made, and gradually my anguish contorts into rage. I raise my face from my hands, eyes burning, and reach up behind my ear to rip out the sham chip.

And then I stop. That is not the correct course of action. There's no warning bell, no flash of data, just a feeling. An intuition. A certainty that I've never felt before.

I put my hand back down. It works. I know it, deep within me, more confidently than I've known anything in my life. It really works. I grin, sheepishly at first, but then proudly — defiantly. And why not? I was right, wasn't I? I was right! I start asking myself questions. Should I get off the train now and go celebrate? No, of course not, I've got to go home and tell Tess! Should I wait to tell her until tomorrow and make it a big surprise? No, better to tell her right away. Maybe I should have other people on the train ask me questions. I could bet them money.

Should I go to a casino?

My thoughts are interrupted by the overhead speakers announcing that my stop is next. I'm still smiling. I stand and get ready to disembark. I reach for the orangutan bar.

I freeze. I reached for the what? The train starts to slow. I look out the window as the talk show homogenizes. I shake my head again. What was that? The telekinesis canned headstone appurtenance blurs past the analgesia emus brain. Something curtain crying wrong with gullet brain phlebitis chip? Peppery larval dessert stops usher. Door thick muslin opens inaugural walk vole down coltish steps. Can't sporty think miserable doorbell stumbling spyglass flashy out despotism onto train gastronomic tracks. Respite conductive lights storefront oncoming librarian train graduate oh —

I open my eyes and see the sky. I turn my head a little to the right and feel the chip, knocked loose, drop from behind my ear. I see my train. I see people from the train coming towards me. They speak to me, but I can't hear them. I look down at my crumpled body. I look past it to the other train, looming above me. People are coming from it as well. I feel my organs struggling.

I was wrong. About the chip; about everything. I'm always wrong. I think about Tess. She'll be hysterical. She'll blame me for everything, for leaving her penniless. Ruined. For leaving her widowed. She'll be angry, and bitter. She'll be lonely.

But at least she'll be right.

About the Author

VAN ALRIK LIVES IN THE Rocky Mountains with his family and a small army of robot novelists. His short stories and poems have been published in *Helios Quarterly Magazine*, *Perihelion*, *Star*Line*, and elsewhere. A data scientist, Van is a strong STEM proponent and enjoys incorporating programming and analytics into his writing as much as possible. His computer-assisted novels *The Trivial Thing* and *Character for Veracity* are available on Amazon, his blog is at vanalrik.blogspot.com, and he occasionally tweets from @vjalrik on Twitter.

About the Story

I'M BIASED, BUT I LOVE *The Right Decision*. It actually came about as an attempt to develop an interactive fiction story, where choices by the reader affect the outcome of the story or there is some other digital effect incorporated into the reading experience. My big idea was to have a story that simulated a character's computer-enhanced brain malfunctioning, and the reader experience would include large blocks of randomly generated prose text at the peak when the malfunction occurs. With that in mind, the need for the story to be written in present tense was readily apparent, which was actually listed as a "harder sell" than past tense in *The Colored Lens'* guidelines. (Fortunately, the story ended up adequately making the case.) I did randomly generate text for the climax, but I still think it would have been a lot more fun to see the text generated in real-time. In the end, this story is about trying too hard and about the futility of looking to the external "things" of life for fulfillment.

Whose Waters Never Fail

Rebecca E. Treasure

I STOOD IN THE DIM LIGHT of swinging propane lamps while the 'fugees beat Susanna to death.

I swayed with the light when a rock split her lips, and tried to forget how soft they'd been. If I let the memory show on my lips, the Elders would suspect I knew Susanna, too.

Biblically.

Of course, they'd say it was more Leviticus and the abomination of lying with a woman than the one flesh of Genesis. Then it would be me pelted by hate-propelled rocks.

Heather had been Cleansed the day before. Now it was Susanna's turn.

Sinners, they called them. *Deviants.* Wasting their precious uteruses on perverted sex. They were dirty, and they must be Cleansed.

Susanna didn't even cry. The dust on her face mixed with the seeping blood and turned to mush on her cheeks. The wounds drove her to her knees, but still, she just looked at the ground. She didn't seem to see the blood pool in her lap, or the bone exposed on her forearm where someone had scored a lucky hit with a chunk of concrete. Then she wilted sideways and I lost sight of her as the 'fugees moved in.

I wouldn't be missed now, so I headed down to the shore to throw a few rocks of my own.

Sounds morbid, but when you hit water with a rock, the result is predictable. Cohesive circles ripple out from impact, each ridge a little

lower until it disappears into the glass surface. Even waves have rhythm.

Hit a person with a rock, and you never know what they'll do.

My brother Shem was already there, skipping stones across the waves. When we were kids we had a pond, round and full of fish. Now the pond was gone, and the black and brown dog, and our parents. Yellowstone and the Ring of Fire took care of the rest of the world. Everything was gone except the dying planet and the barely living camps, the ash-clogged water and the ice, the Elders and the 'fugees.

Shem nodded at me when I sank onto the rocky shore next to him. He waited while I threw up. When I'd finished, he patted me on the shoulder.

"Looking forward to your Service?" He skipped a rock. "Seems like I just got back and you're leaving."

He'd been home a month, back from the long trip to Alaska to wrangle icebergs. Just long enough to drag the 'bergs onto shore where they'd melt into water fit for drinking. I should have asked about the ice, snow, and storms. About being away from camp and the Elders.

Anything but Susanna. So I said, "Susanna wanted to stay on the trawler, do permanent service."

The slapping of waves on the rocks filled my ears, sucking a bit of the shore and my puke out to the bay. Finally, Shem sighed. "She and Heather shouldn't have gotten caught." He reached out and tried to squeeze my hand.

I slid away. "She was doing her marital duty by Ted. You heard them, night after night." Couldn't avoid hearing, with their tent right next to ours. "She'd have had a baby soon enough."

"You know that doesn't matter to the Elders." He intoned like a sermon. "She sinned and must therefore be Cleansed."

I picked up a flat rock and heaved it into black water. A satisfying splash peaked over the other sounds, reminding me of the last time I had met Susanna at the shoreline for a little sinning. "They weren't hurting anyone."

Shem grabbed at my hand. I couldn't jerk away this time. His voice dropped, too soft to carry. "Don't think about it, Bethy. You've got the whole year ahead on your Service to do whatever you want. Nobody cares, on the boat."

"Why should I listen to you?" I snorted. "Just 'cause you finished your service? You couldn't even get a wife."

Shem let go of my hand. "I'll get one from your batch, next year."

I shuddered, thinking of the leftover boys from Shem's Service. They'd have first pick for wives in the Choosing next year. I wasn't pretty, but my teeth were straight and I had a good figure. I'd get picked early. Made me want to puke again. "Got anyone in mind?"

I knew he didn't, but I really didn't want to think about Susanna, about her blonde hair over her face, downturned toward the dirt, and how by the end it dripped red.

Shem shifted on the rocks and picked through them, looking for a good skipper. When he found one, he cocked his arm back and sent it sliding over the waves, skimming the top without getting dragged under. "Nah," he replied. "I'm not picky."

"Yeah," I said. "Me neither." I sent a rock chasing the path his had taken, but in the moonlight mine sank after a few feet. "Me neither."

NEXT MORNING, I PULLED MY Service jumpsuit over my regular clothes. It was warmer once I zipped the front up, even if the bright orange stood out a mile.

Shem, curled under threadbare grey blankets, spoke around slurps of watery porridge. "They'll have good coats on the ship," he said, almost jealous. "Thick gloves. Boots and hats, too."

"You told me."

"I've never been so cold, and I've been cold since Yellowstone."

It wasn't like Shem to repeat himself. "I'll be okay." I sat on the foot of his cot. "I'll volunteer for the latrines, like you said, and I'll keep my head down."

Shem nodded. "Captain Lamech likes volunteers. She gets sick of forcing servicers to do the hard jobs. Ice wrangling is deadly, freezing work. Latrines are — "

"I know, Shem."

He frowned. "Let me get dressed and I'll walk you down."

Crossing over the main path to get to the dock, I stumbled over the wide stream of red in the dirt and fought my heaving stomach. The Elders were watching. I didn't want them to send me to the infirmary. There was no coming back from there, not since the epidemics wiped out most of the doctors and medicines. So I stood, staring at Susanna's blood, and swallowed the rancid fear trying to escape.

"Got what she deserved, eh?" The raw voice shocked me into movement. I glanced behind me, to the Elder sitting on a camp stool rubbing her arthritic knuckles.

I nodded, not daring to open my mouth for fear of what might come out. Shem pulled on my orange sleeve.

"Thank you for your service," the old lady said. She smirked, showing a mouth devoid of teeth. "Enjoy your trip."

Shem led me through the mess in the path. I trudged along, too scared and sick to pick my feet up. I didn't want to end up like Susanna, but I couldn't see a way to avoid it any more than I could avoid memories of Susanna or her blood in the path.

Unless...

Unless I got myself attached to a boy right away on the ship and stayed with him the whole time. When we got back, the Captain would tell the Elders — it was true love — and they'd excuse us from the Choosing. It had happened before. I'd have some choice, some control. And they couldn't Cleanse me, not if I behaved even on Service.

So when we got to the docks, I scanned the boys.

I didn't know what I was looking for. Someone like Shem, maybe. Shem wouldn't beat his wife, when he got one, or force himself on her. He'd take care of her.

I met sharp eyes peering up from under a mop of curly black hair, eyes that reminded me of the way Shem was always watching. I smiled into them. The boy blinked, then smiled back.

I forced my way into line next to him. "Hi," I said, forcing my voice into higher registers. "I'm Bethany."

He glanced, looking me over. Not much to see. Couldn't even see my so-so figure under the thick layers. Just dirty blond hair and a too-red complexion.

He seemed to like what he saw because he straightened and said,

"My name's Jordan. Been here long?" He jerked his head at the camp.

I kept my eyes on his. They sparkled like lamplight on dark water. "Sure. Since about a year after."

He pursed his lips. I tried to like the way they rounded into a perfect circle, but black stubble made it hard. "Long time. I just got here. You've been here the whole time?"

I nodded. "When they set up a camp here, my brother and I got bussed in. There was still gasoline, then."

He glanced down the pier. "Your parents?"

I shook my head and Jordan heaved a great sigh. He didn't say anything, though. I decided he'd do. Most people said something stupid about God or fate, or worse, asked questions. I had a collection of lies I told when they asked.

"Oh," I'd say to their pitying, pitiful faces, "a group of cannibals caught us just outside a camp. The Elders just watched while they ate my parents."

Or my favorite, "We were camping in Yellowstone when it happened. Shem and I made it out, but lava got mom and dad." Their faces paled, thinking about being anywhere near the start.

The truth was so much worse, and so much more tedious. Starvation and sacrifice. Noble, but boring. So I lied.

Jordan shook himself. "Yeah, mine too. You looking forward to this?" He jerked his head at the ship.

I looked at the ice trawler. It was long, low in the water, with a tower in the middle that had once been painted green. Now it looked like a stout bronze lizard in the middle of a particularly itchy molt. The gray water slapped and churned against it. The ship crawled with railings and round windows; steam and wood smoke rose from the stack at the top.

"Sure," I said. "My brother Shem went last year. Said the food was good." I tried for a girlish grin. "And no Elders."

Jordan smiled. "All the way to Alaska and back. They say the whole ocean is frozen over once you get past Cali, and the polar bears can climb right into the boat."

I nodded. "I think that's just supposed to scare us." Jordan looked scared, so I continued. "Shem said, volunteer for latrine duty. It's gross, but it keeps you inside."

Jordan nodded, blinking. "Bethany, right?"

I started to answer but saw *her* and trailed off. She was short, close-cut hair so dark it glistened in the frosty air. And chubby. Only gruel and potatoes to eat, and the occasional military meal or canned fruit or vegetable from the aid boxes. She worked hard at that body. She met my eyes and arched a sparkle-black eyebrow. A hot pulse spread into my hips from deep in my abdomen. How had I missed her in the camp?

Jordan cleared his throat and I remembered I was trying to stay alive. I pulled my eyes from the girl. "Yeah, Bethany. My brother calls me Bethy."

Jordan smiled. "Bethy. I like that." He gave me a lingering kind of look. I forced myself to hold his gaze. *This is good. Safe.* So, instead of glancing at the girl with dark hair, at her body straining at the seams of the orange jumpsuit, I returned his look.

I stuck with Jordan as we filed into the ship, got a tour of the tower section. His hand shot up moments after mine when Captain Lamech asked for latrine volunteers, and it looked like I'd done it. A match made in a metal privy, done up with a toilet paper bow.

Then my eyes found her, drawn like water down a drain, at the end of the row.

Her hand was up.

So instead of my safe romance, I found myself playing eyeball tug-of-war between what I needed to save my stupid skin and what I wanted, knowing full well that what I wanted would get me killed.

And what I wanted was Martha. The name suited her, a chewy mouthful. Martha didn't say much. I liked that, too. She slept in the bunk over mine and smelled like sweat and salt. I leaned into her when she spoke to catch a taste. She was a pool of deep crystal water I longed to dive into.

Jordan liked her, too, and we fell into a routine, with me in the middle like a magnet in a manic spin. After the camps with their blue boxes of vile slop and the Elders who seemed to take on the smell of not-quite-sterilized feces like an odorous perfume, we got used to the smell. In between scrubbings, I worked hard at seducing Jordan. I sat next to him at meals, asked him about his before and after, lingered with him in the passageways.

But I thought about Martha. She ate with focused energy, tearing into the rich food with her wide, uneven teeth. Her before had been a lot like mine, a suburb and a family. After Yellowstone, she'd gotten to an army base. She'd missed out on a lot of the worst stuff, when the Pacific volcanoes all went at once and the sun went out. Her parents were still around, even. They moved from camp to camp, drifting south, trying to find someplace warm, a place they could call home.

"I don't believe in home," she said one night. The wind hissed outside the windows, pushing us north. We were at dinner, reveling in the sinful meatloaf and tomatoes with actual breading, and pudding for dessert. Freezer-burned and shared, it still beat out boiled potatoes.

"Why not?" I spilled some chocolate pudding on my chin watching her mouth move.

She smiled, watching me try to lick it off. "Home is what was. Home is safe. Predictable." She looked out to the white sky and black sea. "We'll never have that again."

I nodded, entranced.

Jordan sniffed. "You missed some, Bethy." He handed me a napkin. "Things will get better. They're trying to negotiate with Mexico, other nations with land that survived the Ring of Fire, to let us come south."

I shook my head. "We didn't want them, why would they want us?"

He shrugged and took a bite of pudding. Around it, he said, "Who wouldn't want me?"

Martha and I laughed, her giggle sounding as forced as mine felt.

That night Jordan and I had our first kiss. It was scratchy and made my stomach twist. I leaned into it, my hands gripping bony shoulders.

After a few moist moments, he pulled back. "What's wrong?"

A flash of panic chilled my face. "Nothing." I leaned in, but he shook his head.

"You're like a robot."

I tried to play it off. "I've never kissed anyone before."

He shook his head. "No, that's not it." He tilted his head. "It's Martha, isn't it?"

I froze like the ice we'd been sent to collect. "No."

He looked me over, sadness splashing into his eyes. "I understand why, but I can't pretend like that. Even with the world," he half-smiled,

"I want the real thing."

So do I. But they'll kill me. "Don't — "

"I won't." He patted me on the shoulder. "Promise." He walked away.

I leaned against the bulkhead, hands clasped over my head, fighting waves of nausea. Instead of the cold hallway, I saw Susanna — in the dark in my tent, laughing on the beach in the moonlight, bleeding at the Cleansing. What would I do now?

I shuffled back to my bunk, shivering. Martha propped her head up. "What's wrong, Bethy?"

I shook my head. "Doesn't matter."

"You and Jordan have a fight?"

A fight. So normal. Safe. Predictable. "Yes."

"He likes you, it'll be okay." She sounded sad, in the dark. All I could see was her head, rocking back and forth with the steady progress of the ship, and the black outline of the bunk against the distant passageway light.

"I don't think so." I pulled my jumpsuit off. "It's cold tonight."

"Do you want to climb in with me? It'll be warmer." I could barely hear her.

The back of my mind buzzed in warning, but I flipped my blankets back into place and nodded in the dark.

She was as soft as she looked, and the waves of heat coming from her washed away my fears and doubts, and before I knew it, we were kissing, but it wasn't like with Jordan — it was fast and smooth and when I fell asleep I wasn't worried about anything except not disturbing her perfect head on my arm.

The next day I went to Captain Lamech to volunteer for ice wrangling.

Martha would get me killed if I stayed on latrines. Worse, I'd get her killed. I'd never be able to stay away from her if I didn't start now.

The captain offered me a cup of coffee before settling behind her desk. Her eyes seemed warm, which was weird considering she spent most of her life in Arctic waters chasing icebergs. "You want to volunteer?" She peered at me over her enormous oak desk, bolted to the floor and scattered with maps.

I held her gaze. "I'm tired of toilets. And ice wrangling is important. Fresh water."

She nodded, but her gaze didn't waver and little lines appeared over her eyebrows. "Sure. But why volunteer?"

I looked into the coffee, watching it slosh up and down the side of the blue and white metal cup. *Be predictable.* "Like I said, I'm sick of cleaning latrines."

She frowned and the lines on her forehead deepened. "I'm not sure you're up to it, frankly."

I couldn't shake the feeling that she knew, somehow, and wanted me to admit it. Well, I wouldn't. "I can handle it."

She raised an eyebrow, disrupting the level lines. "Wrangling is dangerous work. No guarantee. You fall in the water, you're dead."

"I know. My brother Shem told me."

"You're Shem's sister?" Somehow, that convinced her. She nodded. "Alright. Gretchen has been wailing about the weather nonstop. You can take her place."

I drained my coffee in one gulp and thanked the Captain.

She shook her head, not quite laughing. "You'll regret it soon enough."

I did. I lost feeling in my face and hands, and probably my feet, but I couldn't tell inside the three pairs of socks and huge steel-toed boots with nails on the bottom. The numbness crept up my arms and legs, reaching my hips and shoulders, stabbing at my body with icy fingertips. I thought of Susanna, of Shem losing me on top of everything else, and of Martha, and bent to the work.

Hammering pylons into the ice, fighting slushy water to get the heavy tarp around the 'berg, wrenching the ropes against the waves and the ice and the other boat. It took about four hours to harness one of the boulder-sized chunks of ice. When we'd get it into line with the others, we earned two hours downtime before going out and doing it all over again. Twice a day, every day.

The downtime was worse. Martha gave up trying to talk to me after the first day. I just walked away as fast as I could. Didn't she understand I was saving our lives? Instead, she just hovered nearby, staring at me. Jordan and my replacement, Gretchen, had no problems kissing. I was glad. Gretchen would make lots of red-blooded babies.

Then one day Martha showed up on my crew.

"What are you doing here?"

She shrugged and shivered. "Volunteered. If you could, I figured I could talk Captain Lamech into it." Martha glared at me. "You can't avoid me out here, Bethy."

I turned away, collecting pylons. The helmsman steered parallel with the other boat toward a little 'berg bobbing in the grey water. Martha slid next to me on the bench and picked up a coiled rope. I tried to ignore her. Might as well have tried to ignore the wind cutting into my exposed eyelids or the daggers of salt spray hitting my jacket.

"I just want to be with you. Before it's impossible."

"You should have stayed on latrines."

I think she nodded, but it might have been the boat rocking. Then we went to work with our mallets and pylons, the ropes and the tarps. Martha couldn't grip the pylons through the gloves, and kept dropping them when the waves shifted. The tarps flapped in the wind, the crinkling blue material slapping her in the face. Watching Martha struggling with the knots and the folds in the tarps, I had the unfamiliar thought that wrangling was something I was good at.

Then Martha held onto a pylon for too long, determined to drive it into the 'berg. The ice rolled and dragged her into the water.

I dove before her legs left the boat, reaching out. My fingers met the nails on the bottoms of her boots instead of her ankles. The steel tips sliced through my gloves. I ignored the pain, plunging my hands into the water.

One of the other servicers pushed in beside me, shouting.

I couldn't understand where she'd gone, how she could have sunk so fast. The helmsman yanked me back, hollering something and shaking me. It took a few moments for his voice to cut through my panic and the wind. I fought him, trying to get to Martha.

"She's dead! Let her go."

Her hand appeared, clutching at the pylon as the ice bobbed back up out of the water. I shoved him so hard he almost fell in and threw myself toward Martha's hand. I grasped it, clamping down. The other servicer helped me drag her into the boat. She shook like an earthquake when the caldera blew, and her breath came in stuttering jumps.

The helmsman scowled, but signaled the ship. After we got Martha up in a sling, the helmsman insisted I go up to the infirmary because of my hand. It didn't hurt, but it meant I could go with Martha, so I went.

I hesitated at the infirmary door. The white lights and smell of bleach reminded me of stiff bodies and empty cries. The doctor stripped Martha out of her coat and boots with precise hands. It looked like he might actually know how to save her.

I helped him cover her with cool towels, then warm ones. He rested her swollen hands and feet in heated water — only servicers warranted such luxury. When she fell asleep, I let him look at my hand. The cuts weren't deep and the ice water had stopped the bleeding.

"You can go."

"Can I stay with her? Our shift is done. We're friends."

He shrugged and turned away.

Some time later, she stirred and whimpered. She wasn't really awake, so I snuggled closer, smoothing her hair. I told her about way back, about how I'd wanted to be a DJ because my mom listened to pop music while she cleaned. I told her about Shem, how he'd been good at soccer. I even told her about after, when the dog had to be killed because he wouldn't stop barking, and how mom and dad just got thinner and thinner but Shem and I had food to eat, and then mom and dad...

I woke up the next day and Martha was alive. Color tinted her cheeks and a faint waft of sweat surrounded her.

That's as good as love gets, sometimes.

I pulled on my boots and gloves, and went back to wrangling. Between shifts I'd sit with Martha, all through the long winter and the slow crawl back down the coast. Our icebergs trailed behind us in the water like tarp-covered ducklings.

When we were a day or so out from camp, I went to see Captain Lamech again.

"I'd like to do permanent service," I said.

She steepled her fingers. "Tell me why."

This time, she wouldn't accept any dancing around the 'bergs. "There's nothing for me in the camps. I'd get Cleansed before your next service batch got on board anyway. I did the work."

Captain Lamech nodded. "You did. Move your things to the

permanent crew bunks when we dock." She pointed at me. "Leave Martha out of it, though. That's over."

Martha was sitting up when I stepped into the infirmary. Her gauze bandages had come off a few days before. She'd lost good control of her hands, and her face bore angry scars, but she could walk and she would live. She smiled when I came in. I forced the deep pulse aside.

I spilled my guts before I could talk myself out of it. "I'm staying on the ship, doing permanent service."

Martha smiled, but her eyes were sad. "I'm glad for you, Bethy."

I settled on the bed next to her and squeezed her hand. We sat like that for a long time, just holding hands. The Choosing would happen the night we got back. Martha would be lost forever to the future the Elders imagined. Rebuilding the great dream, trying to regain a sense of predictability and safety in a chaotic, dangerous world.

SHEM STOOD AT THE FOOT of the gangplank, waving with a wide overhead sweep like a flag of truce. Or maybe, "Charge!" Other families pressed up to the edge of the dock over the black acid water. They formed a wave of their own, surging against one another in human unpredictability.

Martha walked past him. So did Jordan and Gretchen, clinging to one another in a way that left no doubt in anyone's mind as to their intentions. Shem peered at each orange-clad servicer as they passed, and from the sheltered place on deck I watched fear rise in his face.

When all the servicers were off, his shoulders slammed down with the weight of loss and familiar, new, grief. Another family stood behind him. A girl named Sara had gotten sick in Alaska and never recovered. They turned away but Shem stayed, watching the water.

He was still there when the permanent crew disembarked. I stopped next to him, wearing my grey jumpsuit and fur-lined coat. I counted three surges of waves slapping against the dock before his eyes met mine.

"Oh," Shem gasped. His face rebuilt itself from the chin up. "I should have known."

"I didn't mind the cold so much." I grinned. "And like you said, the food is good."

We fell against each other, hugging and slapping to share feelings we had no words for.

When we pulled apart, I patted his shoulder. "Follow me."

Martha had paused at the end of the dock, facing the assembled Elders and 'fugees cheering the return of life-giving water and servicers. She didn't want to take that last step from the unsteady dock to the still ground beyond. I stopped Shem and stepped around her, turning to look at her soft, scarred face.

Tears blossomed and dripped down her cheeks. I swallowed the lump in my throat. After all, if I couldn't have her, knowing she would marry the best man I knew would be better than nothing. Good, even. He'd understand. They'd have each other, and I'd have the water.

I looked into her eyes, smiling. "I'd like you to meet my brother."

About the Author

REBECCA E. TREASURE GREW UP reading science fiction in the foothills of the Rocky Mountains. She received a degree in history from the University of Arkansas and a Masters degree from the University of Denver. After graduate school, she began writing fiction. Her favorite authors are Raymond E. Feist, Robert A. Heinlein, Larry Niven, Jerry Pournelle, Mercedes Lackey, and dozens more. Rebecca has lived many places, including the Gulf Coast of Mississippi and Tokyo, Japan.

She currently resides in Texas Hill Country with her husband, where she juggles two children, a corgi, a violin studio, and writing. She only drops the children occasionally. Find more of her work at www. rebeccaetreasure.com.

About the Story

LIKE MOST STORIES, "WHOSE WATERS Never Fail" came from a collision of ideas. The first was two paragraphs of prose inspired by a sunset over a reservoir, about a person who found solace in the liquid predictability of water. I wanted to find a setting for this person where everything around them was so unpredictable they would turn to ripples in water as a means of comfort.

Separately, I read an article discussing the danger of global warming to volcanic activity and earthquakes — as the weight on the crust decreases from the release of frozen water into the oceans, there's a potential risk of more volcanic eruptions. From there, I had my setting — a post-apocalyptic world where fresh water was tainted by volcanic ash, and people had to trap icebergs to get drinking water.

To create my characters, I asked the question I often ask to create characters — who has the most to lose in this world? Any gay person in a culture obsessed with procreation is under enormous pressure. Add the risk of stoning, and an intense love, and Bethany's story came to life. I think of this story as a romance, despite the bittersweet nature of the ending.

I rewrote this story numerous times, cutting scenes that showed the depths of that horror without adding anything to the plot or the characters. It was my first professional sale, and I'm delighted to share it again, here, in *4th and Starlight*.

Cold Logic

John D. Payne

MANNY VASQUES CHECKED HIS PHONE. Midnight. The witching hour. It was time. He opened the door to his garage, finally ready to confront whatever it was that was haunting his food truck.

As the door opened, he was hit by a wave of faintly gasoline-scented Texas heat that reminded him of his days in the Sandbox. Not that the rest of the house was exactly cool, even at this hour. He could barely afford the rent, much less run the A/C all day. But however hot the house was, the garage was always hotter. He found the light switch in the dark and stepped in, securing the door behind him with a quiet click. Got to keep that heat contained.

He glanced over at the neat stacks of boxes on the far side of the garage, doing a quick mental inventory. Low on napkins. Again. He burned through those so fast. Well, not Manny — greedy customers who took twenty napkins and threw them all away. Come on, people!

The near side of the garage was occupied by his gorgeous new food truck, which barely fit. It was clean, classy platinum, with a sharp, black silhouette running along the side: a man seen from behind, reclining lazily in a chair, one arm stretched out with the fingers elegantly cradling a bright green pickle. Above, *MAD MAN* in large, block capital letters. Underneath, *meatloaf and more.*

On any other night, he would have stopped to admire the wrap. It had cost five grand, but it was worth it. People came up to the truck to talk about it, or to take selfies with the logo. They remembered it, and came back. It really was the best wrap in town. But tonight he had other things on his mind.

Manny squeezed around the front of the truck, between the hood and the shelves of canned goods. He opened the passenger side door and retrieved his Beretta M9A1 from the glove compartment gunsafe. He checked the chamber and the magazine, tucked it into his pocket, and then made his way around to the back.

He unlocked the rear door, stepped into the galley, and switched on the lights and the A/C. Heat didn't bother him, but for this conversation he needed to be cold as ice, not constantly wiping the sweat of his forehead.

He pulled the weapon from his pocket and sat down on a barstool in the narrow aisle between the cabinets and appliances. He disengaged the safety and cleared his throat.

"We need to talk."

No sound but the hum of the air conditioner.

With a sigh, Manny reached over to the counter and turned the thirteen-inch Big Boy collectible figurine around so it was facing him. A handwritten sign taped to the base declared: *Big Boys Give Big Tips.*

"No use playing dumb." Manny kept the Beretta flat against his thigh. "I know it's you haunting my truck."

Still no answer.

"Why do you think I swapped out the sandwich press, the oven, the fridge?" He slapped the door of the new refrigerator. Well, not new. And not as good as the old one. But for now, it was perfect. "That was the last thing I hadn't checked. I've eliminated every other possibility. Cold logic, *amigo.* Game over."

Silence.

Manny shrugged. "Okay, *güey.*" He lifted the pistol and aimed it at the figurine. "Don't know what this is going to do to you, but... let's find out."

"Put that disgusting thing away," the Big Boy said. "Gun violence is destroying this country."

The voice that came out of the chubby-cheeked tip jar was definitely male, but that didn't mean he was talking to a man. There was a lot he didn't know. Like whether the figurine in the red-checked overalls was really haunted. Like, by a ghost.

His uncle Beto, a big-time *brujo* back in Dallas, said there were three major possibilities for a possessed object. Restless ghost, demon, or human sorcerer playing ventriloquist — each of which had to be handled differently. Manny was prepared for all three but needed to know who he was talking to first, so he did what they taught him in HUMINT training at Fort Huachuca. He started a conversation.

"Do guns make you nervous?" He lifted the Beretta. "Is that why you want me to put it away?"

"Please." The Big Boy waved one hand dismissively. The other held up a platter with a huge burger.

That gave Manny ideas about haunted hamburgers for Halloween, but he shoved them aside for the moment. Ninety percent of interrogation, he knew, was just paying attention.

"I'm so far beyond your reach," the tip jar snorted, "it isn't even funny. What worries me is collateral damage. Do you know how many walls a stray round from an automatic weapon can punch through?"

Manny did. He hadn't fought in Second Fallujah, but he'd seen urban combat. Of course, in a successful interrogation, information flowed only one way. So he kept his face neutral. Blank.

From the conversation so far, Manny guessed it was a sorcerer doing the haunting. Uncle Beto said demons and dead people were easy to pick out — weeping and wailing, ranting about boiling blood. So this was a man. Good. But what kind of man? Time to push some buttons and find out.

Manny held up his pistol. "This isn't an automatic. It's a semiauto." Completely irrelevant to the point about how far a stray round would travel. But the Big Boy struck him as the kind of person who couldn't pass up a pointless argument.

"I know that," the Big Boy said testily. "I can see it's not a rifle."

"It's not." Manny put the pistol down flat against his thigh again. "But most rifles aren't capable of fully automatic fire, either."

"Whatever." The fat little figurine shook its head. "Slap a bump stock on it and you got yourself a frickin' machine gun. Thirty seconds."

Manny leaned back and stroked his chin. "You've done your homework." Without a partner here to be the good cop, he had to play both parts himself. Easy enough. A little needling, a little flattery. Some threatening, an olive branch. Kid stuff.

"Yeah." The Big Boy rolled its eyes and snorted. "Not that you need a doctorate to weigh in on this debate."

Doctorate. Interesting. The only person Manny knew who used that word was his cousin Sofia, who taught at UTEP.

"What do you mean?"

The chubby little collectible heaved a sanctimonious sigh. "You gun nuts are so obsessive about the stupid little technical details. Like it matters if you call it a magazine or a clip. It kills people, that's the point."

Manny's drill sergeant and his firearms instructor would have had a few things to say in response, but it was time for a new subject.

"You care a lot," Manny ventured. "Other people just let stuff happen. Whatever. It's not their business. But you can't let it go, can you?"

The figurine gave him a squinty, suspicious glare. "What are you getting at?"

Time to get a little more direct. Manny leaned forward. "When ketchup and pickles started flying around my truck and all the meat spoiled, I thought it must be a poltergeist."

The Big Boy chuckled, his huge burger bouncing on the upraised tray.

Manny lifted a finger. "But they're *malditos*. Cursed. Malicious. That's not you. You're doing this for a reason. You're an altruist."

It was what every terrorist and insurgent told himself. They cared. It's what separated them from bank robbers, warlords, and drug dealers — even if they ended up also robbing banks, shaking down villagers, and trafficking drugs. Sure they killed, raped, and tortured — but only because they *cared. So. Much.*

"So," Manny asked, "why are you haunting my truck?"

He was not surprised to see the same self-righteous, knowing smirk on the fat plastic figurine that he had seen in countless interrogation rooms. That smug, silent smile that said, 'I know what you want, but you're not going to get it from me.'

But getting that information usually didn't take anything like that S&M circus at Abu Ghraib. All it took was understanding what makes people talk. In this case, his subject loved correcting people. So Manny tossed out something stupid.

"Is it because I have a gun? Is that why you put your curse on me?" The Big Boy blew out a derisive snort.

"I think it is. I think you're fed up with all these mass shootings. All these guns, killing. And politicians doing nothing. You want to do something."

Manny could read it on those plastic lips, screwed up so tight to keep the words from spilling out. The Big Boy had something to say. He was desperate to get it out. Just barely holding it in.

A flash of inspiration hit him. "And the worst are all these school shootings. Those kids, man. Their lives are worth more than that. You know? And here I am, taking my truck — and my gun — onto campus. Into what ought to be a gun free zone."

He leaned back and gave the little plastic figurine a hard stare. It stared back. And still said nothing. But it was a different kind of silence. Not so smug, now. He had scored a point. Figured something out that he wasn't supposed to.

It wasn't the gun thing. That was nonsense. Oh, the Big Boy might have haunted him for it. But he probably never knew there was a gun in the glove compartment in the first place.

No, it was something about the school. His truck was being targeted because he parked it at the school. Why? If the Big Boy had wanted to do something nasty to UT students, he could have done a lot worse than making a mess of the food truck. Like poisoning the food.

So maybe his truck was just a target of opportunity. Which would mean that the Big Boy was somewhere close by. UT faculty? A student? One of the other food trucks? Or maybe just someone who worked across the street.

Too many options. He needed to narrow things down. Which meant he needed more information. Needed the Big Boy to start talking again.

Needed, not wanted. Because what he *wanted* was to kill this conversation already, to go straight to end game and shut this haunted hunk of plastic down. Which he could do. And it would be so satisfying. But it wouldn't stop the man behind the Big Boy from coming right back after him. So he had to keep talking, keep listening, keep learning.

Manny took a deep breath and leaned back, nodding his head. "When someone says 'gun free zone,' you know what I hear? *Ese*? White privilege, mang. *Privilegio blanco*."

"Well, actually — "

Manny ignored the Big Boy's interjection and pushed on. "When my family first came to this country — " Four hundred years ago. As conquistadors. " — we came with nothing. Nothing but a dream."

Not true. But what would be the point in sharing his actual life story (or his real opinions) with some anonymous jerk haunting his truck? Manny just wanted him gone.

"A dream of freedom," he continued, "and justice. But you know what we found? Not opportunity, but oppression."

Again, a lie. Nobody pushed his family around. His dad had been a hard-driving Shell Oil exec, and his mom had ruled the neighborhood ladies' garden club with an iron fist. They were the ones who did the oppressing, as Manny knew from firsthand experience. But this lie was a little easier to sell, because it was all about righteous anger. And Manny was actually angry.

"So, tell me, *güero*," he growled, "why you keeping this brown man down? Huh? Out of all the food trucks parked on Guadalupe, why you haunting mine?"

"This is not about race," the Big Boy hurried to say, waving the hand that wasn't holding up a giant hamburger on a tray.

Manny shook his head, pursing his lips in disgust. He made sure to fold his arms across this chest, a barrier to keep out this white figurine's racist lies. "Must be nice," he sighed, leaning back on his stool, "to be able to tell yourself it's not about race."

All just play acting, of course. In truth, he didn't think this was about race any more than it was about guns. But it was hard for Americans to keep their lips buttoned when someone accused them of prejudice — especially 'woke' Americans. And this possessed piggy bank was woke as hell.

"I'm not trying to tell you what you feel," the Big Boy said, lifting one hand defensively. "Nor will I try to claim I know what it's like. I acknowledge and accept the validity of your unique experience — your truth, as you live it."

Definitely talked like a professor. Or a grad student, maybe? Damn. "My truth," he said out loud, "is this truck pays my rent. Alimony. Child support. My *abuela*'s doctor bills. It's a game for you, but this is real life for me."

This part was actually about half true, which was dangerous. He reminded himself what Captain Bradley had taught him in Army Intelligence. Make it sound like a conversation. Let them feel like it's a conversation. But it's not. It can't be. Information is power. Get it, don't give it.

The Big Boy nodded sympathetically. "I'm not going to pretend I know your pain, but I hope you can recognize me as your ally in this struggle. I marched for fifteen-dollar minimum wage. For rent relief. Better pay and benefits for adjuncts."

This caught Manny's attention. He knew from his cousin Sofia that there was a real divide in colleges between the kind of full-time faculty who could get cushy tenured jobs and the glorified temps who actually did most of the teaching. So now the question was, did mentioning adjuncts mean that the Big Boy was one himself?

Unlikely. Even back to his first comments about collateral damage, he seemed to think of himself as unselfish. He reached down to help the little people beneath him. So, not an adjunct. Someone tenured, then? Or just on the tenure track? The Big Boy liked to play it safe. He was tenured, Manny was sure of it.

He fought back a grin. If his guess was right, he had just narrowed his pool down considerably. Even a big school like UT only had, what? A thousand tenured professors? And more than half of those he could rule out if Big Boy was a white man. He was getting closer. But still not close enough to make his move. Not yet.

"Fifteen-dollar minimum," Manny scoffed. "I own my own business. That doesn't help me, man."

The Big Boy raised his painted eyebrows. "This isn't just about you, or about me."

"Easy for you to say." He pointed at the sign taped to the figurine's fat stomach, and then hooked his finger around to indicate the coin slot on the Big Boy's back. "You are literally full of money. That's some symbolism there, home boy. You could have possessed anything in this truck, and you're occupying my tip jar. Where is your head?"

A flush of red came to the Big Boy's cheeks, which... How was that even possible? Then the chubby little collectible spluttered out, "We have to think bigger. This is about the greater good."

Now we're getting somewhere. Manny leaned in close. "How?" he asked. "What greater good?"

"Not just greater. The *greatest* good," said the Big Boy.

Manny narrowed his eyes. "Is this...?" He took a deep breath and kept his finger off the trigger. "Is this a Jesus thing?"

The Big Boy shook his little plastic head. "I knew you wouldn't understand."

"I can't understand if you won't talk to me."

"You're not ready."

"Try me."

The fat little figurine stared off into space, saying nothing, rubbing its chubby chin with the hand that wasn't holding up a giant burger on a platter. The silence was maddening, but like any interrogator worth his salt, Manny knew that it was his ally. People hate silence, Captain Bradley had taught them. Wait long enough, and your respondent will fill it.

"Have you ever seen," the Big Boy began, "a blue sunset?"

Manny shook his head, slowly.

"You won't see one in Austin," said the Big Boy. "Too much air pollution. The particulates are what gives you all the orange and pink. They give us sunsets that look beautiful, but what we're really seeing are the poisons that are killing us."

Manny nodded. This all sounded like total bullshit to him, but it didn't matter. The Big Boy was building to something. So Manny just let him talk.

"You get out away from the cities," the Big Boy continued. "And you see what sunsets used to look like, when the world was new. Before we came, and wrecked this planet." He let an angry snort out his plastic nose.

"I was driving one summer, in the highlands of New Mexico. It was probably," the Big Boy waggled his upturned fingers as if searching for words. "Nine o'clock in the evening. The sun was sinking low. There were big fluffy clouds everywhere. And nothing on the horizon to interrupt the view. Just... sky."

The Big Boy leaned back with a reverent sigh and tucked his thumb into the strap of his checkered overalls. "I was expecting a spectacular sunset. Intense. The kind you get out in the desert sometimes. Like some celestial cow kicked over a lantern, and now all of heaven is on fire."

The Big Boy looked at him, with that kind of smug smile that said he thought he was being funny, or clever. He wasn't. But Manny smiled back anyway and gave him a little half-chuckle.

"You know what I saw instead?" The Big Boy raised his painted eyebrows. "Blue. Blue clouds, blue sky, blue shadows on the mountains and the trees. Not that light, bright sky blue. A deep, dark, midnight blue. Almost indigo. You can see it in some old paintings, from the 17- and 1800s. But I'd never seen it before. A blue sunset. And it changed me."

Manny cocked his head slightly to one side, drew his eyebrows together and grunted.

"It was like God, whoever or wherever she is — "

With iron determination, Manny successfully fought his eyes' instinctive roll and kept his face neutral and attentive.

" — was speaking to me." The Big Boy looked reverentially upward, the glisten of tears in his plastic eyes. Was that possible? Why not? The thing had already blushed.

"What was she saying?" Manny asked.

"I love you," the Big Boy said. "And I realized in that moment that I loved her. Mother Earth and all her children. Do you understand?"

"I think," Manny lied, "I'm beginning to catch the vision."

The Big Boy sighed in relief. "So now you see why, if we are ever to return this gorgeous green planet to its unspoiled, divine magnificence we must do everything we can to end the barbaric cruelty of eating our fellow animals."

Manny blinked, once. This was beyond his wildest guesses as to where all this hippie-dippy new age nonsense might be leading. Meat? This stupid sorcerer was haunting his beautiful food truck because of *meat?*

Showing surprise now could ruin all the time he had invested in this interrogation. So he mustered all the discipline of his training, all the skill developed in his years in the field, and did what he could to keep the shock and anger off his face.

"So that's why you picked my truck?" Neutral. Calm. "Because I sell meat?"

"Yes."

And there it was. The at once disappointing and reassuring truth that most victims of terrorism are chosen essentially at random. Ninety percent of the food trucks on the street sold meat. Any of them would have worked as a target for the Big Boy. Manny hadn't been special. He'd just been unlucky. The revelation was... infuriating.

"That's why you spoiled all the beef in my refrigerator?"

"Yes."

"Three times."

"Yes."

"And why you..." Manny took a deep breath. "Why you sabotaged my deep freeze." There had been more than three hundred and fifty pounds of beef in there when it had gone. Three hundred. And fifty. Pounds.

The Big Boy smiled, looking all sad and compassionate, which meant he was about to launch into the speech every violent nutjob gave when he thought he had a sympathetic ear. Oh, I'm so sorry. Oh, I had to do it. Oh, I didn't have a choice. Oh, it's not my fault I blew up that school bus.

"I'm so sorry," the Big Boy said. "For what I had to do to you. But I had no choice. You see that now, don't you?"

Pinche cabrón, you always have a choice, Manny was very careful not to say. Then with his mouth he painstakingly formed the necessary words: "It wasn't about me. It wasn't about you. It was this system. The system makes victims of us all."

The Big Boy bit his lower lip and nodded, tapping his fat plastic chest with his fat plastic fist. Right over his non-existent heart. Then he stuck that fist out for perhaps the most patronizing bump Manny had ever received.

"Gracias, mi hermano," said the collectible in badly accented Spanish. "Thank you for understanding."

"De nada."

At this point in a real interrogation, Manny would probably have stopped for a break. Maybe even for the rest of the day. It was getting increasingly difficult to keep his cool — not a good thing in an interrogation. Better to return your respondent to the boredom and isolation of the cell. A little wait and he'll be grateful to see you again, not just ready but positively anxious to talk.

But this was different. The Big Boy — or rather, the sorcerer who was using the figurine to do the haunting — wasn't being detained, cut off from his support network. He was at home, taking it easy. Probably some nice place close to campus, instead of a forty-minute commute away.

So Manny had to take this shot while he had it. But how to approach things at this point? He'd already tried playing tough guy, pushing buttons, guilt tripping, the silent treatment and getting on the bandwagon. He didn't have a lot of cards left in his hand.

But it was time for end game. Time for risks. So he played the riskiest card he had left. Straight talk.

Manny took a deep breath. "So here's my problem."

"Problem?" the Big Boy asked.

"Yeah. I get what you're saying about animal cruelty and saving the planet and all that. But before I think about the saving the planet, I need to pay my rent. And I've sunk my life savings into a business that sells high-end nostalgia food. Pretty hard to do meatloaf without meat."

"Then you haven't tried — "

Manny held up a hand. "Please. You think I wouldn't look into vegetarian and vegan options in Austin? Give me a little credit. That part of the market is pretty overserved right now. So I went a different way."

"That's... disappointing to hear."

"Tell it to the customers lining up around the block for my bacon-wrapped tenderloin loaf with honey glaze."

"Oh," the Big Boy snarled, "I will."

Manny spread his hands. "Right. Well, we can go back to you making the meat scream whenever someone takes a bite. I'll be the first to admit, that was a pretty good trick."

"Spare me your flattery."

"No, man." Manny shook his head. "I'm serious. You're a big bad *brujo*. You've got talent — and more importantly, you know stuff. You're read in." He pulled his stool up close to the countertop so and got nose to nose with the tip jar. "But so am I."

The Big Boy snorted and rolled its plastic eyes, unimpressed.

Manny stood up, towering over the little plastic figurine. "I did six tours, man. Iraq, Afghanistan, the DMZ. I was with one of the units experimenting with the TTR and the Empath. So I have seen some spooky shit."

"You think so?" The Big Boy laughed menacingly and the lights

dimmed to complete blackness. The only things visible inside the food truck were the tip jar's eyes, which were now glowing an ugly red. "Just wait. You haven't seen anything yet."

As the lights flickered back to life, the Big Boy jumped when he saw that the business end of Manny's drawn pistol was mere inches from his plastic face.

Not that Manny was really going to pull the trigger. For starters, he believed the sorcerer when he said shooting the Big Boy wouldn't hurt him. But even if they were face to face, what was he going to do? Murder this idiot? Okay, then what? Everybody in Indian Country bitched about the Rules of Engagement and how they tied your hands. But sometimes tying your hands kept you from doing something stupid. Protected you from blowback. You know, like life in prison. Or a date with the needle.

He put the Beretta back in his pocket and spread his arms. "You trying to scare me, *brujo*? Because I've seen worse possessions at my little cousin's *quinceañera*."

The figurine howled with incoherent rage.

Manny folded his arms and shook his head. "Try harder, *pendejo*. This is 2019. The whole world is a horror show. I turn on the Saw movies to put me to sleep. I've seen Rosie O'Donnell's sex tape, man. My president is Donald Trump. You got to up your game."

With a terrible roar, the Big Boy rose up off the counter and levitated in the air, head spinning around and vomiting blood. Ectoplasm erupted from the sink, and every drawer and cabinet door in the food truck slammed open and closed over and over, producing a deafening clatter.

But Manny stood his ground. He had already removed everything from the drawers and cabinets. There were no cans to pelt him, or knives to cut him. The only dangerous thing in the food truck was...

The Beretta flew out of his pocket and hovered in the air, inches away from his face. The Big Boy, now back on the counter, gave him a smug, nasty smile. "Hands on your head, if you please. Nice and slow."

"Respect." Manny slowly lifted his hands and placed them on his head. "Turning my own weapon me. That's a baller move."

The plastic figurine's smile turned even uglier. A menacing sneer, now. "Kneel."

Manny knelt, grimacing. "Trust me, you don't want to do this."

"You don't know what I want."

"I've been where you are. On that side of the gun. Thinking to myself, what now? Do I really have to do this? Isn't there some other way out of this situation?"

"You're the one who needs a way out." The Big Boy shook his head. "And I offered you one. But you wouldn't take it. You've got no one to blame for this but yourself."

Manny laughed. "Yeah, you tell yourself that."

"Shut up."

"Look," Manny shrugged, "you're putting the blame on me because you know you don't want to do this."

"Shut up."

"And I get that. Taking a life is..." He shrugged his shoulders like he was trying to get dislodge something squirmy. "It changes you, *amigo*. That feeling, that memory, that guilt — it never goes away. Believe me, you don't want it."

"You don't know me," said the Big Boy.

Manny took a deep breath. He had a hand full of cards. Time to see what they were worth. "You're a white middle-aged male," he began. Most domestic terrorists were. "You live alone." Terrorists usually did. Especially those who weren't part of a larger organization.

The Big Boy laughed. "Total crap. You don't know anything."

"You're not from Texas, and even in Austin you're not sure you fit in. You care about politics. You go to protests, you sign petitions, you're active on social media."

The little painted eyebrows drew together, and a frown appeared on the fat little plastic face. Time to push it a little harder.

"Even though you're a tenured professor at UT — "

The Big Boy started.

" — you still read your student reviews. Because you care about your students, you really want them to learn." This last was a freebie. Every professor thought this about himself. "But, yeah, I don't know you."

"Random guesses."

Manny gave him a cold smile and said nothing.

"And even if you did know something," the Big Boy blurted out, "what are you going to do — call the cops and tell them you want their help to track down the man who's haunting your food truck?" He laughed.

Manny laughed, too. "I know, man, cops are useless! That's why I would take care of this myself. In person."

The Big Boy wasn't laughing any more.

"Walk away right now, *brujo*," Manny said quietly. "And we're good. Otherwise, next time you see me, it's going to be too late. And that's not a threat. That's a promise."

The figurine stared, incredulous. "I just wanted to scare you. But you ... " His little plastic nostrils flared in anger, and the Beretta got even closer, hovering maybe an inch in front of the bridge of Manny's nose. "You pushed me to this. This is all you."

Manny watched the trigger slowly depress and then there was a metallic click, loud in the silence of the food truck's galley. He stood up. The trigger kept pulling, producing click after click after click.

"What kind of idiot would bring a loaded gun to a haunting?" Manny said, shaking his head. He picked up the Big Boy figurine, which squirmed in his hands and hit him with its giant plastic hamburger.

"This isn't over!" shouted the collectible. "I'll be back!"

Possible. But unlikely. The cold, brutal logic of terrorism isn't about particular people. It's about soft targets. Manny wasn't soft.

So he said nothing and threw the Big Boy into the refrigerator his Uncle Beto had prepared with spells that would cut a possessed object off from a remote sorcerer. If it had been a real ghost, it would have gone in the oven, prepared with spells of binding and soothing. A demon would have been exorcised with the sandwich press.

He got out his phone and texted his cousins from Dallas to come pick up the refrigerator. Uncle Beto would take care of the figurine. Manny wasn't looking forward to paying off this favor, but that was a problem for some future day.

Today? He checked his phone. It was only 12:30. Handing off the fridge would take some time, and then he still had a lot of prep to do for tomorrow. But he could still get three hours of sleep in if all went well. Not too bad.

So he turned off the lights and the A/C and stepped down out of the of the truck. He made his way over to his new (used) deep freeze, and pulled out two big boxes of ground beef. The frozen beef felt pleasantly cool against his chest as he squeezed past the front of the truck. Then, he turned off the light with his elbow and pulled the garage door closed behind him with his foot. Time to get to work.

About the Author

JOHN D. PAYNE GREW UP watching prairie lightning flash in the deep blue night, imagining himself as everything from a leaf on the wind to the god of thunder. Today, he lives with his wife and family at the foot of the Organ Mountains in New Mexico, where he focuses his weather-god powers on rustling up enough cloud cover for a little shade.

John's debut novel, *The Crown and the Dragon*, is an epic fantasy published by WordFire Press. You can find his stories on podcasts like *The Overcast*, magazines like *StoryHack*, and books like *Horizons – An Anthology of Epic Journeys*. Tabletop RPG fans may also wish to read his *Micronomicon: A Compendium of Magic*.

Stalk John on Twitter @jdp_writes. Patronize him at https://www. patreon.com/johndpayne.

About the Story

WRITE WHAT YOU KNOW, RIGHT? And while I've never seen operated a food truck, interrogated a prisoner, or encountered anything possessed by evil spirits, I did manage to fit a lot of my own experience into this story.

The hero, Manny, is made of pieces of three different Mexican-American men I have known over the years, including my good friend Roger, the best neighbor I've ever had. The villain behind the Big Boy is a little bit me, and a little bit of lots of people I met in my academic career — although as far as I know none of them are nefarious sorcerers. The blue sunset is something I experienced myself driving through the highlands of New Mexico one evening. I took a million pictures, but none of them do it justice. Pictures of sunsets never do.

Usually, I write more about swords and horses than guns and trucks, but I really enjoyed getting to know Manny and exploring his world a bit in this story. Hopefully we'll be able to go back there some day and see what other kinds of trouble might come his way.

Departure Gate 34B

by Kary English

I'VE NEVER LIKED THIS AIRPORT. The endless corridors of white on white remind me of a hospital, but this is the only place I can talk to Stewart after the heart attack. He's not always here, but I come every day to look for him.

Today he's sitting in his favorite spot in the departure gate, a corner seat connected to a low table. I tried sitting on the table once, but we can't talk unless I sit on his right, where I was for the trip to Hawaii.

I sit down beside him. Travelers flow like a river behind us, boarding passes clutched in their hands, cell phones pressed to their ears. Their suitcase wheels hum and click on the tiles like tiny freight trains charting a course between Starbucks and Cinnabon.

"Did you remember to stop the paper?" I ask. His sigh is like wind soughing through the doorways of an abandoned farmhouse. He looks at the floor for a moment before he answers.

"The kids are doing well," he says. "Aaron finished his residency. Anna made the Dean's List again. She'll be starting an internship in June."

I want to hold his hand, but that doesn't work anymore so I lean in close instead. "I got us a suite with a hot tub. Think you're up to that, old man?" He folds his hands together in his lap, twisting his wedding ring with the thumb and forefinger of his right hand.

"It's been two years, Marian." His voice is soft, but the flirtatious whisper I long to hear sounds like patience instead.

269

"Two years? We've been married for thirty, Stu. What's two years compared to that?"

"It's time, Marian. Time to move on."

He's been moody since the heart attack, and I hate it when he gets this way. I get up to leave but he reaches into his pocket and then it's my wedding ring he's holding. He opens his hand to show it to me.

My chest tightens. I look up at the ceiling. The white tiles won't stay in their squares, and their gray flecks go blurry. I remember that day two years ago. Paramedics. Stewart's agonized gasp. How I nearly lost him.

"But you're fine, now," I tell him. "We're fine."

"Yes, I'm fine. But we're not." At first I think it's only me who has to blink back tears, but then I see it's him, too. People around us begin to stare and look away, uncomfortable in their politeness.

"You're making a scene, Stu. People are staring at us."

"Not us, Marian. They're staring at me. They can't see you."

"What do you mean they can't see me? I'm right here."

He tells me to look at my boarding pass, so I look. *Gate 34B.*

"It's 34B, isn't it? Always 34B. Our gate for Hawaii, two years ago. We never went."

"Because of your heart attack."

"No, Marian. Because of yours. Because you died."

The door across the gate stands open, the jetway dark beyond. I close my eyes.

"Don't do this, Stu. Can't we have Hawaii? We waited so long." The stretcher feels stiff and cold beneath me. Mask on my face. Straps tight across my chest. Wheels clicking like train cars over the hospital's white tile.

"I wanted it, too, Marian." His voice breaks, but he holds it together. "I wanted it, too."

A gate agent turns on the light in the jetway. She pastes on a smile and tells us that boarding will begin soon. I look down the carpeted tunnel. Posters of beaches and palm trees line the collapsible walls.

Stu looks, too. He takes a long breath before he turns back to me. "It's time to board, Marian. They're holding the gate for you."

I've got my carry-on on my shoulder, a gift from the kids now that retirement meant we could travel. I grip the handles tighter and shake my head no. "Not alone, Stu. Not without you."

"I can't keep doing this, Marian. It hurts too much. It's time to let go."

"What about Aaron and Anna? What about you?"

"They're fine. We'll all be fine."

Through the gate, I hear the soft strum of a ukulele, the susurrus of waves on sand. A low, sweet voice begins crooning *Aloha, 'Oe.*

Stewart stands, and suddenly I'm standing, too. He reaches for me, and finally I can feel his hand take mine as he swirls me into one last waltz. Three steps later, we're standing at the gate. Plumeria blossoms fill the air with nectar-sweet fragrance. I take a last look at Stewart's face.

"Do you think they'll let me have a window seat?" I adjust the carry-on strap on my shoulder and brush back my hair. "I took the middle so I could sit next to you."

"I'm sure they will," he says. "One fond embrace, Marian. Until we meet again." Stewart steps back to stand alone on the airport's white tile.

The ukulele beckons. I step onto the jetway, and the scent of plumeria carries me down the tunnel.

About the Author

KARY ENGLISH GREW UP IN the snowy Midwest where she avoided siblings and frostbite by reading book after book in a warm corner behind a recliner chair. She blames her one and only high school detention on Douglas Adams, whose The Hitchhiker's Guide to the Galaxy made her laugh out loud while reading it behind her geometry book.

Today, Kary still spends most of her time with her head in the clouds and her nose in a book. To the great relief of her parents, she seems to be making a living at it. Her greatest aspiration is to make her own work detention-worthy.

Kary is a Hugo and Campbell finalist whose work has appeared in Grantville Gazette's Universe Annex, Writers of the Future, Vol. 31 and Galaxy's Edge.

About the Story

DEPARTURE GATE HAPPENED BECAUSE I sat down in a gate area in the Edinburgh Airport and my writer brain said "What if someone could see all of the feelings/memories of whoever sat in the seat right before them?"

As Sunlight Grabs Me

by Rachelle Harp

VOICES FROM THE LINK CEASED transmission right before the crash.

The constant buzz of speech and electronic messages pulsing through my cochlear implant is now static. Unnerving at best. I stand on the beach, sink into wet sand. A sharp breeze cuts across the skin of my face — the part not covered by carbon fiber plating.

Smoke rises from the hull of the *Dragonfly*. Flames devour the cockpit. Even if I could put out the fire, I would have no way to repair the damage. The last reading I took with my sensors showed no inhabitants detected: only settlement remains, mostly charred.

My circuitry energy supply unit blinks in and out, leaving me dependent on the unreliable human components of my system — ones I have not utilized in twelve years, four months, seven days. I upload a distress signal through my Link processor:

```
@Taren5: Requesting assistance.
 Location unknown, unidentified planet.
 Response requested.
```

Feedback.

I wait ten seconds, then resend.

```
@Taren5: Requesting assistance.
 Location unknown, unidentified planet.
 Response requested.
```

More feedback.

Most likely, my transmitter cannot break through the atmosphere from my current elevation. A retinal scan verifies the best location — eight miles, forty-nine feet inland. Atop the tallest peak. The mountain seems to straddle half the island, its rocky point piercing the pale blue sky. Perhaps my signal will breech the atmospheric barrier and make it to the Link. If not...

A strange ripple sensation vibrates at the base of my spine and crawls up to my neck. Survival depends on connection. Survival is connection. Survival is the Link.

Though I am a female unit of twenty-seven standard years, I march with rigid steps toward the tree line, prosthetic knee stiff like an old woman. More damage from when the *Dragonfly* hit the beach. I input a search command to discover the cause, but an error code comes up on my viewport. The manual reset also fails, leaving the white numbers emblazoned across my visual scan area. A swift triple tap to the manual override finally clears the message.

Another step and an odd energy wrenches up my leg, like a fire burst, swift and sharp. Wincing, I grab my knee. Seven seconds later, my breath catches up to my lungs, and I straighten my shoulders. It has been a while since I have felt such a strong impulse. Limping, I cross into the forest. As soon as I am past the border, I listen for the Link.

Silence this time.

The feedback is gone.

Vines wrap the trunks of an unknown tree species. The lattice bark looks similar to a palm tree, but the leaves are a hands-breadth wide and tangled in the canopy, forming a sea of purple and brown. A pale yellow, almost white, fruit hangs from the branches. The breeze picks up and swishes the leaves so they sound like faint clapping.

My circuits flicker. The gridlines on my retinal scanner viewer disappear. I blink four times, focusing. The last time I viewed the world through human eyes was the day of my transformation. These jungle colors are vivid, not filtered through a green haze. No grid lines intersecting. Zoom function has gone offline as well. Half a dozen birds hop on branches, but I cannot identify their fine details — only their bright red and orange feathers.

I tap the side of my temple where the carbon fiber plate attaches to my skin. The scanner does not reboot, meaning I will have to find the safest path without help.

Birdsongs twitter at a steady pulse as I swish through the overgrowth. Twisted fronds reach out from the trees, waving at me with an eerie, slow, up and down movement. A growl erupts from the brush curtain before a creature bursts through. My blaster arm flies into ready position. No scanner, so I cannot get a targeting lock. I fire, but the shot only grazes the creature's hind quarters. The wolf-like beast is nearly the size of a bear, with a snout narrow like a crocodile. He yelps, then homes in his glare.

I run, but the fire sensation flickers hotter in my knee. The creature is faster. In only a few seconds, he will overtake me. My plating may provide some protection, but I cannot trust it entirely. The wolf-beast springs ahead, then flips around. His snarl rivals the Beast of Kandrol Nine that made a meal of my former commander, Arlan7, the one who sent me out.

The wolf-thing snaps at my leg. I jerk back, aim my blaster — this time less than an arm's length away — and fire. The shot hits him in the chest. He collapses.

No heartbeat. No breaths.

Dead.

A surge of energy rushes through my veins. Odd it is not through my sensors. When I look at my hands, they shake, steady like membrane vibrations. Then I realize I am panting, uncontrolled. Fast. Swift. A quick check for wounds verifies I'm intact. No blood soaking. No flesh torn. Only shredded circuits in my firing arm and a small tear in the carbon plating. As I gape at my flesh-covered hand, trembling, I conclude the rest of my circuits must be compromised.

To the east, the mountain peak pierces the horizon.

Approximately 5.3 hours were left in my energy unit. Now, I cannot calculate the balance. Is it empty? What else could explain the shakes? Even if I do make it to the top, there may not be enough power to send another signal, so I leave the unit off to preserve what is left.

With no central decision-making boost from my neuro-sensors, I am uncertain of the best course of action. Staying here will attract more predators. Energy reserves minimal. Connection to the Link is imperative. Yet one thing seems logical.

Brush the dirt off. Face the mountain. March toward it.

Exactly as Arlan7 would have wished.

Strange that thought came to me. I remember him as he was before the attack, before the end. A strong leader. A strong companion. The strongest voice of them all.

I'm not sure how much time passes, but the sun drifts toward the west. Emptiness speaks out from my auditory sensor, not even feedback. The voices are gone, lost until connection can be re-established. Yet, I hear the commander's voice clear in my mind. *Run*, he said. *Run, do not look back*. Melancholy and desperate. Arlan7's voice ceased communication the day he was severed from the Link.

I do not want to remember, so I march on. Palm leaves sweep against each other, rustling, waving. The call of unidentifiable birds, singing. Are they mating songs? Or simply happy songs? There's no way to analyze their purpose. No way to analyze my progress. No way to stop the dance of spiders across the floor of my stomach.

A strange sensation of a weight sinks into my chest, heavier and heavier. Like bricks slowly added. Reminds me of the times I used to get frustrated, even angry, before my transformation. The feeling is so foreign, I cannot quite pinpoint it. And there is gnawing, a growl in my stomach, to the point of nausea. Hunger most likely.

During the past ten days, I've had only rations to survive on. Standard military. With my energy stores waning, I will need to locate a food source. A patch of berries sits along the trail. They are not poisonous, that much I remember from survival training. The first bite is sweet, moist, like a kiss of honey. I pull another handful from the branch and devour them. At first, one at a time. Then two. Maybe more. After the long trek, the moisture cools my tongue and the emptiness in my stomach subsides, but the nausea lingers.

There are sounds of running water, bubbling, soothing. Off the trail, behind the brush, I find a creek with a shallow fall. At first, I stand on the edge, hesitant. The water might short out the circuits the beast exposed when he tore into my arm plating, but the gentle song of ripples on rocks is too inviting.

I dip my toes in, unable to feel the movement of water since my sensors flicker in and out. I wade in deeper until water flows across my thighs, cool on my flesh. I plunge my hands in, splash water on my face. Refreshing. Like the days I swam in the summer heat on Earth. Was I only twelve? Maybe thirteen? The laughter, the feeling of freedom. They rush back to me. Running barefoot back to the house and Mother scolding me for treading muddy water all over her clean floor.

Another smile as I splash the water on my face again.

She hugged me tight the day I was taken away for my transformation. I never saw her after that, though part of me wished I could.

The sun dips in the sky. Not much time left, so I take a final drink of water, say good-bye to the creek. I climb toward the mouth of the fall — the best way to find a clear route up the mountain. Either that or I don't want to be that far away from the only reminder of home since I crashed here.

Arlan7's face grows in my mind. Kind eyes. The way he held me the night before the attack. Warm and tight. Romantic thoughts or deep emotions are normally filtered out by the neural-sensors. This flood of sensation, a fond embrace. My male counterpart... I told him not to go into the forest. Kandrols were ruthless. The war has been long. He did not listen. And now I am alone, missing his voice.

The mission must be completed, do my duty.

If I send the signal, the others will find me, bring me back.

The war must end.

I climb higher. Grass morphs into rock. My calves bear the brunt of the upward slope with each step. As I trek, the trees thin. The birdsongs disappeared over an hour ago. Maybe two. An eagle squawks above.

Do not look back.

I grab a branch and pull my body higher. There's no worn path up the mountainside, no road spiraling through a clear road — only rocks

and roots, sparse trees. My muscles tighten with each push upward. Sweat invaded the crevices of my carbon fiber plating hours ago. I wipe my brow, clench my teeth with the next shove. The swell in my stomach is too great; I must release the pressure. I lean my head over and retch on the rocks. Without looking down, I clench my fingers, keep climbing.

A flat rock blocks the path. I crawl on top. My body aches. Every muscle is tight. There's a scratch on my forearm. A slight stinging sensation meanders across my skin. Blood creeps through the flesh, wet and warm. I don't wipe it away as I stand up tall. Another catch in my lungs. Another sharp twist in my back, yet I smile. Hardly the reaction I would have guessed when I left the beach this morning.

Sunlight grabs me from all sides. I am atop the peak, lost in the landscape, shielding my eyes from the bright light. My carbon fiber hand feels no wind, no heat, no pulsation of life.

To the north, firelight dances through the trees. Not a forest fire. More like the soft glow of hearths or camps. My ship reading was negative for human habitation, but perhaps sensors were faulty. Seems like there's life on this planet after all.

I lift my wrist and press a small power-up button – the backup transmitter. Only to be used if all others fail. A faint wave of feedback rushes through my Link processor. A hollow series of voices calls back, but Arlan7's is not among them. How could it be? The spider dance in my stomach returns as I remember his lifeless body, circuits without flickers, emptiness. He wanted me to live. That's why he ordered me to run. My finger hovers over the call signal. One push and the distress signal will be sent. They will take me back and make me look. At the war. All the ruin.

Do not look back.

The pain in my stomach jolts me, another sensation of nausea. I cannot go back. I cannot stand to be without his voice. I turn off the transmitter. Not like this.

I reach down and press my hand against the lower part of my belly. The emotion sensors always filtered strong feelings away. Without power, the sensors are useless. Now that Arlan7 is gone and his child is within me, there is nothing to keep strong feelings at bay. Tears slide down my cheeks, but I don't wipe them away. If the others come for me, they will take the child when it is time. Arlan7 must have known I was carrying it, though I never had a chance to tell him the truth.

In the distance, a sliver of beach pops out against the ocean waves. Smoke rises.

Charred rubble of the *Dragonfly* smolders. I tear the transmitter from my wrist. As soon as the last circuits are powerless, the device goes black. I hurl it at the *Dragonfly*.

No, I won't go back. I close my eyes, swaying, hands pressed to my belly.

The kiss of wind caresses my skin.

Do not look back.

About the Author

Rachelle Harp grew up in a small Texas town, often wishing she could be Princess Leia or Wonder Woman (either would be awesome). When that didn't happen of course, she did the next best thing and started writing. Her short fiction has found homes in *Galaxy's Edge Magazine, Perihelion SF Magazine,* and *StarShipSofa.* Over the years, she's taught English, music, history, and at writing conferences. She's a band director's wife and mom to two amazing kids. When she's not writing, Rachelle is drinking coffee and trying to keep the cats off her computer while writing her next adventure. Her debut YA dystopian novel, *The Breakout,* is now available from 48fourteen Publishing.

About the Story

I FIRST WROTE THIS STORY as I was sitting in my local coffee shop one day, pondering the complex question of what I should write my next short story about. I kept thinking about a lot of interesting what ifs — like what would happen if a future cyborg became isolated from all the technology they'd ever known? — and this story was born. The story flowed pretty easily and quickly. In fact, it's probably the only story I've ever sat down to write that came beginning to end in about an hour or so. I revised and edited it a few times, of course, before finally feeling it was done. I submitted to the Writers of the Future Contest and was surprised to learn a few weeks later that it had become a finalist. Although it didn't ultimately win, it did become my first professionally published science fiction short story about a year later when Mike Resnick purchased it for *Galaxy's Edge Magazine*. This story is truly one of my favorites I've ever written, and I hope my readers enjoy it!

Laila Tov: Good Night

Robert B Finegold, MD

From the Sefer haYehudim b'Galut

WHEN THE WORLD WAS YOUNGER and the moon still inspired wonder, there was a lamia so low among the lilin that she had no name. In service to Samael, the demon king, she shepherded all living creatures within the beylik of east Eretna, which crafty Mutaherten once ruled. She loyally performed her duties: collecting the seed from men who lusted in their sleep; snatching the breath from infants swaddled in their cribs; drying up the milk within mothers' breasts be they of beast or daughter of Eve. She freed each — seed, breath, and milk — from their mortal constraints.

One evening in the waning of the year when the chill winds blew down from the Armenian Highlands and the moon's Cyclopean eye cast glints from the snows of distant Mt Ararat, the lamia was drawn to the cot of Bilchek the cripple, a tailor of some skill though near blind.

Near the west bank of the sluggish Ahern, his small broken-fenced yard was a lake of frozen mud strewn with tiny islands of brittle grass, nibbled short and capped with the first snow. His hut held only a simple plank table and chair, a cold stone hearth and equally cold tin bedpan, and an empty hope chest of boot-scuffed pine with dull and dented brass hinges. To one side an overturned bucket huddled near a strawmat bed,

283

its mattress crushed so flat that even the fleas rubbed elbows. A fat goat slept at the foot of the bed chewing on the edge of a patchwork blanket that covered the crumpled form of the sleeping tailor. In spite of all, the hut was a pauper's castle, for there was nothing poor or dull about Bilchek's dreams.

He dreamed of his youth, long-passed, and of young women, grossly and inaccurately imagined, for he'd never stood under the wedding huppa, nor dallied in the autumn fields at harvest when the grain was high and the elders could not see, nor had he any sisters as a child to share the family bath barrel. What lay beneath kaftan or hirka, when his few lady clients permitted him to measure, was unknown to Bilchek; thus, the lamia who wove her cloak of desire from the vivid lust-laced imaginings of dreaming men, found naught but vague visions of cotton softness and felt-covered curves, and of warmth; warmth to be shared under a patchwork blanket during the long nights as the year neared its frigid end.

It was the latter that gave her pause. This man's longings were not as those of other men, of struggle and moist release, but of pairings and sharings. However, his urgent need drew her as strongly as that of any man rutting in his sleep, and she never shirked her duties.

Bilchek was a challenge, for the fire was more in his heart than in his beytsim. Yet Bilchek's God had empowered the urge to engender even among the ignorant; and the lamia caressed him in his dreams, successfully raising the pride and embarrassment of men, and coaxed his seed from him as he slept. Unlike the innumerable others who upon attaining their release turned and ran back to sleep's depths, Bilchek awoke. He rested his hand upon her waist as she moved off of him.

"By *Hashem*, please don't go."

She turned to rake him with her claws, but there is power in the Holy Name said in love and need. His words were like a prayer, and they were answered.

"Why should I not go? Why should you not wish to be rid of me? Why don't you cower in horror and shame?"

"I am familiar with all these things. I see them in others' eyes at the sight of me."

"You're blind!" she declared.

"And crippled," he replied.

"You're a fool."

"And poor."

The lamia had no answer. She longed to strike him and flee. Yet she stood by the bed, the man's hand at her waist. The few of her herd who'd seen her... they were the ones who fled. Not her. And not Bilchek.

"Help me, please," he said. "My spectacles. Pass them to me."

She looked and saw them upon the floor. They had fallen from the overturned bucket he used for a nightstand. She hooked them with the claw of one finger and passed them to him. They were of frail bent wire and small mismatched circles of thick glass.

He hooked the stems around his ears, the wires nearly encircling them to help support the weight of the lenses that over the years had left a permanent furrow upon his nose. Then he looked at the lamia. Her skin from her waist down was of fine iridescent scales like a mountain viper's, her feet were owls' talons, and her wings... from the bony spines of her shoulders rose nearly translucent wings of soft leather on long bony fingers. They curved forward over her thin muscular arms and thick-fingered claws like a long black cloak. Her eyes were large and contained no white. Instead, a deep black filled them, like mountain tarns on winter nights when the moon was hidden. She had ebon hair that fell in waves to below her breasts, two small pale cones crowned with tightened nipples the color of amethysts. Her chin was delicately pointed; her lips thin, drawn inward with ire; and her nose was as subtle as an infant's. Her skin from forehead to navel was so pale that she seemed to float upon the ripples of her black hair and enfolding wings like moonlight on dark water.

He did not scream. He did not flinch in fear. He did not flee.

Instead he begged, "Stay."

"Stay?" The word, the suggestion, so strange to hear.

"Yes. Please stay."

She blinked and pulled away from his hand. It had merely rested upon her and had never grasped her in possession. She spread her wings.

"I am a demon!"

"Is that your fault?"

"You are a mere mortal!"

"Is that mine?"

She leaned toward him and opened her mouth to display delicate fangs like small scythes.

"You are prey!"

"To every mocking word and pitying stare," he said in calm reply.

Her fangs retracted. She stared at the crippled tailor in confusion. He stared at her with longing and... something else. "You would forswear a mate of your own kind?" she asked in a whisper.

He spread his hands wide, displaying his shallow chest and protuberant belly, and how the curvature of his spine made him seem stuck in mid-dance, belly over right hip, shoulders over left. Extending his arms to either side he bared his breast and the soul rhythm of what beat beneath. "What woman would have Bilchek?" he said. "They love my skills but loathe my looks and know not I have a heart that loves."

And with this she relented. She sat on the strawmat cot and tentatively took his sure hands within her claws, careful not to wound him.

When Bilchek asked, "Be my wife," she did not strike, she did not mock, she did not flee.

"If you will have me, then let us wed," she said.

As it was the Sabbath eve, and they consented to one another, it was so.

Bilchek broke no wine glass, but instead filled it with the wine saved for the Sabbath and shared it with her.

"What is your name?" he asked.

"I have no name. I am a daughter of the Night."

"Then I will call you Laila." And he smiled. "My Laila Tov, my Good Night."

ב

Snow as fine as confectionary sugar was falling upon the frozen village lane outside the shop of Melis, the baker's wife, when she first heard the suppressed laughter and whispers that Bilchek the cripple had a woman. The widow Tansu scolded her nieces. "Ansa, Trelip, stop tittering like dormice." The two girls, heads bent together with hands covering their mouths, tried to stifle their laughter.

"What's this?" asked Melis, placing hot braided loaves of bread upon the counter. She pressed her hands firmly upon them. "Bilchek has a wife?" The widow's nieces giggled.

"Tshah," said Tansu, tugging at the loaves. "Who said anything about a wife?" She leaned forward and whispered, "We were out for a stroll..."

To pass the home of the widower Nathan the moneylender, Melis knew.

"... and we took the Farmer's Way by the river..."

To avoid being seen by good folk.

"... when we heard a woman's voice, sweet as a spring lark, coming from the shack of Bilchek!"

Melis shrugged. "Some low-born wife seeking a new entari or feraçe to please her husband. Bilchek is as gifted with cloth and thread as he is ugly."

"No. No," Tansu said. "I know every voice of our village. It was no voice ever heard before in Kirkatel."

"A traveler. A stranger, then. Where was her husband or escort?"

"Exactly what I thought. 'A stranger is danger, ' no? I crept to Bilchek's window, a single filmy pane like ice with bubbles. Even so, I could see the crooked form of Bilchek... dancing! I imagine only the demons in Gehinnom cavort so grotesquely. And he was dancing with a woman!"

Melis leaned forward, nose to nose with the old gossip. She said, "What did she look like?"

"Like a Musselman's woman," Tansu whispered.

"No!" Melis straightened, releasing the loaves.

"Yes!" Tansu snatched the bread and a sweet roll as well, passing them behind her back to her nieces. "She was tall. Well, taller than Bilchek, and covered head to toe in black, hiding her shape as they do. Formless, sexless, except for that voice. A woman's voice, strangely accented, but young and sweet." She leaned forward again and slid another sweet roll off the counter as she kept her eyes on Melis' face. "And she called him 'husband'!"

Melis dropped onto the stool behind the counter. "God forfend. If the Musselmen discover one of their women with a Jew! The village could be burned!"

The widow Tansu chewed a sweet roll wearing a satisfied smirk, sugar paling her upper lip like a cat that had got into the cream. She turned and left, her giggling nieces trailing her like ducklings.

The door to the shop closed, and Melis looked through her window of pristine glass. Flakes of snow landed upon the panes, a myriad of tiny stars, melting, running together, and blurring the world without.

ג

BILCHEK RELEASED LAILA, AND THEY fell to the floor with laughter. The floorboards creaked, unused to such gay tread.

Laila had sought to cover herself, to conceal her form that caused aurochs to tremble, wolves to howl, and babes to shriek. She'd taken a sheaf of black drape, the one thrown out by the rich widow Liat at the end of her year of mourning (on the same day she announced her engagement to Tilc, who was half her age and half her weight and as poor as a flea on a hairless cur). The drape was black as night and Laila found comfort within its folds, hidden from the glaring beam of sunlight that thrust through the melted glass eye of Bilchek's window and determinedly sought her, gazing accusingly from one side of the hut to the other as the day passed from dawn to dusk.

She found haven for her shame under the dark cloth, hiding her owl's feet, scaled pale flesh, long taloned fingers, bat's wings, and gaunt vulpine face and fangs. She found herself ugly compared to the swayback slant-toothed balding Bilchek, who was radiant in his love for her. And this love was both foreign and enticing, like a strange new fruit from a distant land, one both sweet and tart and odd of texture yet delightful upon the tongue, even hers which was forked.

Love. She had yet to understand it or know how to accept it or reciprocate. But she desired it. She who was mistress of desire in others had never herself felt its ache. Perhaps she sought to hide from this as well within the comforting dark under the mourning drape.

When Bilchek had come back from his goings about the village, a hem to fix here, a feraçe to mend there, he had found Laila sitting under her drape, the eye of the sun winking with the passing of clouds and worrying a knot of wood on the floorboards in front of her. He laughed.

"Excuse me, Drape, have you seen my lovely Laila?"

From the concealment of the cloth, the demoness replied, "Your Laila is a hideous creature of the Night. She is not as human women. She need hide her ugliness from the day, unless she be discovered and forced to leave her husband."

"You don't know my Laila then, Drape. She is lovely, my greatest delight of both night and day. And though other women pale to her, she is not unlike them in this needless fear."

The black mound of drapery shivered. "How so?"

"Do not all women, at some time, mistake their treasures for ugliness? Cover them in the day only to reveal them to their loving husbands under the concealment of night?"

"Perhaps. But one man's treasure is another's offal. And I would not be so seen and thereby disgrace you or, worse, bring man's hatred and fear of me upon you. Other women have clothing, I have nothing."

"You are clothed in my love."

"For the night, and for when we are alone. But for the day..."

Bilchek placed one long finger upon the side of his bulbous nose. "You shall have all you desire, day or night, or I'm not Bilchek the Tailor." But looking at the hill of black drapery on the floor before him, he could not but laugh again.

"My wife has become a tent, like that for the Purim festival dance."

He ran his long thin fingers, almost needles themselves, down her drape-covered shoulders until he grasped her hands through the cloth and raised her to her feet.

"Though I have longed to dance under the festival tent, I never thought to dance *with* the tent."

And with that he turned with her and capered upon the hut floor that squeaked and drummed under his wood-soled shoes. Her feet made no noise except the scratch of her talons upon the wood, like the scrape of a chair pulled across the floor.

Laila knew not what to say or do. She did not protest, nor resist, nor assert, but let him lead her in turns around the small hut as he bobbed and weaved and spun with her, making two become one in a way new

and different yet not unlike the binding of lovers she knew far better and had perverted for her Lord Samael these many centuries of Men.

His eyes held hers even through the veil of cloth, and as they brightened with his smile, with his joy of her, she felt herself smiling in return, and not in the delight of anticipated or conquered prey. From shuffling her feet as he turned her, she first raised one clawed foot and put it down, and then the other, first in an awkward stumble, then more and more in harmony with the rhythm of his own.

He laughed and urged her on. She bumped the table with a cloaked wing and a tin cup clattered to the floor. The goat, who'd been watching the antics of his master and mistress with patient disdain, bleated, scampered around them, and burrowed under the bed. Laila laughed.

It was a laugh unlike any she had ever voiced. It was a laugh not at the wail of a mother who found her child pale and cold in its crib, or a man who woke with dreams of guilt and his nightshirt soiled. No. She laughed because *she felt joy in another who found joy in her.*

Bilchek stuck his large head through a cleft in the drape, joining her in her shadow, seeing her as she was. "My lovely wife," he said.

Her joy made her laugh again, a songbird's trill as sweet as a cool gurgling highlands stream. "My loving husband," she said.

And they laughed and danced more wildly until the black drape slipped from her shoulders and tangled their feet. Hands still clasped, they fell to the floor, their breath mingling in mirth. The floorboards boomed like the staccato of a drum, the rumble slowly fading like echoing thunder.

Bilchek held her hands. She noted thin scratches where her nails had cut his flesh, a few welling with blood, and she jerked her hands from him. She grabbed the black drape in her claws and clutched it to her chest, drawing her wings around her, hiding her face.

"Ah, no, my Laila Tov." He reached again for her hands, gently placing his upon hers. "There is nothing to hide from. There is nothing for which to feel shame."

She let one wing slide back just enough that her left eye, dark and shiny as obsidian, looked at him from beneath feathers of raven hair. "I... I hurt you."

He shook his head. "Love always leaves marks. Man bleeds for love, as does woman, but when love is returned there is only joy, my rose of Sharon."

He kissed her, and she leaned forward, encompassed him in the shield of her wings and returned his kiss, dropping the black cloth drape and letting it flow like Night to puddle upon the now silent and sated floor.

7

THE FIRST CRYSTALLINE SNOW CAME and passed, leaving the eaves and lintels and roofs and lanes of Kirkatel to sparkle like gems in the late autumn sun. A second snow soon followed, leaving a half-foot of powder as fine and dry as flour. When winds came, light for the season, ribbons of snow flowed down the narrow ways and wider lanes, buffeting the villagers as they walked like waders in a swift-moving stream. The last of the traveling merchants and tinkers passed through Kirkatel, their horse-drawn carts like small houses that clanged and drummed as pots banged and barrels rolled. The tinkers remarked at how the village had been blessedly spared from the ice and snow now deepening to the west, the north, and particularly among the eastern highlands.

Melis stormed the lanes of Kirkatel, the village women in her wake. Snow scattered away from the hem of her kaftan like hens from the butcher's wife. While the women of Kirkatel remarked on the strangeness of the unusually mild weather, Melis worried at the knowledge of the ugly cripple's Muslim wife like a cur with too large a bone, unable to get to the marrow.

Melis had seen her.

For three restless nights, like Jonah tossed within the belly of the whale, she lay abed next to the bulk of her snoring husband. Then, on the following morning, she stole from the shop, leaving her husband to serve any late breakfasting customers. She cloaked herself in an old tattered wool kaftan and a plain brown yasmak that veiled her nose and mouth. No one called to her in her disguise as she slipped along the narrow ways down the hill to the farmer's track. She stopped in the shadow of Pilpul the tanner's shed, wrinkling her nose at the foul smell, and waited. When Bilchek hobbled past, his large multicolored pack of fabrics and rags upon his back, she'd scuttled to his small yard.

For a moment she stood amazed. While snow lightly rested upon the packed earth and small islets of twisted winter grass, small violets and peonies like tiny amethysts and sapphires poked their heads above the canopy of snow. Not a single icicle hung from the edge of the thatched roof, and swathes of grass, green as spring, huddled against the walls of the hovel. She scuttled to the ramshackle of a window where she felt the warmth of the hut radiating through her mittens. The heat caressed her face as if she had raised it to the summer sun. Bilchek and his foreign woman must be burning all his winter's store of firewood. Was the stranger from the Arab or African sands to require such warmth? Was she one of the black-skinned Muslims? She heard they were the fiercest. She shivered and noticed, despite the warmth, her breath still steamed the air and frosted the single melted pane of the window. She wiped it and peered in as the widow Tansu claimed to have done.

And Melis saw what Tansu claimed to have seen.

She could not tell her bear of a husband. He abhorred gossip. After the death of Joseph, their infant son, he became fiercely religious, spending evenings at studies with the rabbi and his students. Every Sabbath eve he was atop her, doing his duty as she did hers. For all the good it did them. The only thing that rose in the ovens of Melis and Reuven the baker was his breads.

Melis gave Tupi the beggar half a loaf of day-old bread to fetch Bilchek to her. The tailor came, bowing and smiling, his large bag of rags lifted high over the curve of his spine like a turtle shell.

She gave him a robe. "The fur lining is parting at the hem, Bilchek. And winter deepens."

"I can mend this, Dame Melis."

"And I require a fur muffler. My hands are fair."

"Truly fair. You shall have it."

She offered him the other half of the loaf of bread that she'd given Tupi.

He thanked her, but he placed it in his pack rather than wolf it down as had the beggar. He took out his needle, sat upon the bench by the window where the light was best, and began mending the hem.

"You are well, Bilchek?"

He nodded, kissing needle to thread, joining them.

"You are keeping warm?"

He nodded again, his head bobbing in rhythm with his hands that pierced and pulled, pierced and pulled, drawing the edges of the fur-lining and the woolen robe together seamlessly.

"I often wonder how you and your little goat can survive in the winter in your hut by the river. The winds from the highlands blow unhindered there, and the snows drift like ocean waves. How do you keep warm on winter's nights? How do you light your fires, care for your animals, cook and wash and clean, and tailor? Who watches over you when you are ill? Who warms you in your bed when the nights are long and the days are cold? Surely not your goat?"

Without looking up, Bilchek answered, "God provides. Baruch HaShem."

"Baruch HaShem," her husband repeated as he entered from the back room, his face red and beaded with sweat from the heat of the ovens.

Bilchek stood and displayed the repaired lining. It looked as good as new, even better than when she had taken a knife to it and pulled the hem loose an hour before. Her husband admired it as well.

"Good hands, good heart, Bilchek," he said, and gave him a few copper manghirs and a fresh loaf of bread still warm from the ovens.

Melis said nothing.

Three weeks passed, and winter remained mild, at least for the village of Kirkatel. No further travelers came and none were expected until spring, when the town would be full of people passing to the Highlands with their flocks, or taking the old Roman roads upon oxen-drawn wains carrying winter-made goods to the tiled cities of the west and south. The Sultan's tax collector would come to collect the jizya, lightly slapping each man of the eyil of Kirkatel upon the face as he collected the Sultan's due from the Jews of Anatolia.

And he would come with his soldiers, Melis told Tansu and her nieces. If he discovered a Jew had taken a Muslim to wife, he would burn the village. To discover the Jew was the ugly cripple Bilchek... he could burn them all *with* the village.

Melis' words sparked fear in the gossip Tansu and, like a smoldering fire, soon ignited small flames that whispered among the other women of Kirkatel.

Fat Esther crossed her arms over her breasts and rested her chins upon them. "Why would a Musselman woman marry Bilchek?"

"Why would *any* woman marry Bilchek?" asked Miri.

"He's got good hands," said Huddle and tittered.

This evoked outrage and exclamations of disgust.

Huddle shrugged. "Just saying."

They squawked at one another, all but Melis. They're as flighty as hens, she thought; someone needed to be the fox. "I saw her as well. She will be the *death* of us all!"

The women quieted.

"She could just be a girl from another village, possibly betrothed long ago."

"Poor thing."

"Could you imagine lifting one's veil to kiss... that?"

The hens clucked and squawked until Melis stated, "We must know!"

A cool wind, tinged with the scent of snow, gusted and sent the hems of their kaftans flapping.

"We should visit her."

"Yes," said Tansu. "We have a duty to welcome her to Kirkatel."

"We should leave well enough alone," Esther said.

"We should be a comfort to her," said Melis. She smiled, and it was a smile as cold as the wind that gusted and made them shiver.

Gathering together, they walked down the hill. When they reached the farm track that led to the tailor's hovel, Huddle asked, "I wonder if Bilchek's pitzel is as nimble as his hands?"

The hens squawked.

ה

LAILA WAS COMBING BURS OUT of the goat's pelt with her fingers. It lay on its side upon the slatted wooden floor and raised its head with a look of disdain when a knock came at the door. Laila rose, and the folds of her black robe flowed over her like night. The silver veil that covered her face, barely visible beneath the dark hood, rose and fluttered before settling. The robe hid both her hands and feet, and silver moons and stars were embroidered along its hem.

She stood a moment, indecisive. Except for her husband, none before had knocked upon the door in the weeks since her marriage, but his knock was a respectful tap followed by a cheerful "Shalom!" She had asked him why he knocked to enter his own home, and he had answered it was her home now.

The knock repeated, more insistent. She suddenly feared for Bilchek, and the little goat nudged the back of her knee.

Opening the door, Laila saw five women in rich kaftans of green, blue, maroon, magenta, and purple. One said, "Shalom aleichem."

"Aleichem shalom," said Laila.

They seemed to study her words as they stood looking at her. The one in blue shuffled her feet. Suddenly remembering human customs, she invited them to come in. They all did, except the fat one in purple who merely asked for a chair so she could sit outside the door. The woman in magenta and the old one in green had already taken the hut's only two chairs, including the new one Bilchek had made for her from scraps of old wood purchased from Isaac the carpenter. The two young women sat on the cot bed, the moon-eyed one locking eyes with the goat. Laila took the bucket and placed it upside-down outside the door. The fat woman looked at it distrustfully but settled her weight upon it. The bucket gave a muffled creak.

Introductions were made. "Laila?" said the old woman Tansu. "What sort of name is that?"

"One my husband gave me."

"What's your true name?" asked Melis.

"Any which my husband calls me under God."

"Some names my husband calls me at night he wouldn't speak before God," said Huddle. That set the two on the couch tittering. Melis and Tansu frowned.

"May... may I offer you tea?" Laila asked, and in the chorus of first nays and then, "If it would not be too much trouble," she poured water in the kettle and placed it upon the nail within the hearth, then looked for cups. She saw only the two tin cups she and Bilchek used, but also four clay bowls. When Miri added, "A slice of bread to dip would be lovely," Laila felt dismay at what little she had to offer, of bringing dishonor to her husband, but took the single loaf of bread she had saved for the Sabbath and placed it upon the table along with a knife and small pad of butter.

"Where are you from, dear?" asked Melis, slicing the bread.

"From over the hills and under them. East Eretna is my home."

"Were you promised to Bilchek?" Esther asked from the doorway.

"He holds my promise."

Huddle shuddered.

Laila poured tea, grasping the handle of the kettle through the hem of her robe. Melis held a tin cup, gazed sourly at it, and put it down to watch Laila serve the other women. She had not an inch of skin exposed. "Why don't you loosen your veil, Laila? We are all women here. Even among you Musselmen, women may gaze upon one another."

The crackling of the hearth flames filled the hut. The goat snorted.

"I am not a Muslim," Laila said and continued passing cups of tea to Tansu, Miri, Huddle, and Esther.

"But are you a Jew?" blurted Esther.

Laila lifted her head and gazed at her through her veil. "'*I am my beloved's and my beloved is mine.*'"

Esther nodded.

"You have a wonderful voice," said Miri, "like a nightingale."

"Perhaps that is where she got her name," said Esther at the door.

Laila took up the wooden plate of sliced bread and offered it first to Melis, who waved her away, and then to the widow Tansu.

"When God gives one gift, it is in balance for another," said Tansu, worrying a slice of bread between her gums.

Miri leaned forward and whispered, "Do you cover yourself because you are scarred or ugly?"

Laila straightened and stood still even as Esther barked at her to save her the heel of the bread. "Come on, girl. Bring it here before I starve."

"Is that it then?" Melis said. Her voice was accusatory and held no compassion. "An ugly bride for an ugly tailor?"

"Bilchek is not ugly!" said Laila.

"And I'm not fat," said Esther. The women laughed.

"He has a heart of gold!" Laila felt herself flushing.

"It's the only gold you'll ever have from him," said Tansu and sipped her tea. That set the others laughing again.

Laila turned to face the hearth. The flames therein began to roil and snap.

"His hands have never been raised against me in anger nor left bruises upon my flesh, Tansu. Only caresses. I will never feel the need to place belladonna in his wine to win free of him."

Tansu choked, tea spluttering from her lips.

"He never calls me names nor looks at me with disgust, nor seeks the embrace of other women, Esther. Isn't that right, Miri?"

The fat woman howled and Miri's eyes widened until she looked more frog-faced than moon-faced.

"He has strength in his flesh and joy of me. I need not find solace rutting with strangers, nor recall their different visages each day upon the faces of my children, Huddle. Nor lie each Sabbath under a man I abhor with a penis as small as his belly is huge and find pleasure only in my hand while he snores, Melis."

"*Lies!*"

Melis leapt from her chair. Her face was as red as the fire and her eyes matched its sparks. "Ugly words from an ugly whore! Let's see if you are uglier than Bilchek!" She grabbed Laila's robe and pulled. The cloth tore, and Melis flung it toward the door. The robe floated and rippled as it fell, silver stars and moons fluttering on fabric black as midnight until it pooled upon the floorboards like a shadow in the morning sun.

And Laila was revealed. A slender woman, pale of skin, with long black hair, and gowned in white muslin. Her slender hands and slippered feet were like a dancer's; her face was oval and flawless: full lipped, peg-nosed and hazel-eyed — human eyes, large and piercing beneath long dark lashes.

"Lies," Melis repeated as if to reassure herself, but her words were a whisper. "Disgusting lies."

"Ugly truths," Laila said. "We all possess them. Yet they are past. While I am here, you'll never need fear their repetition."

ר

THE LAMIA PAROSH, FLEA (a name she detested), sat upon a gnarled branch of a leafless oak on a hill overlooking the village of Kirkatel. The village was silent beneath the stars. Wisps of smoke rose from chimneys and made the stars dance. Snow climbed the trunk of the tree and piled in tall sway-backed hillocks that ringed Kirkatel like fortifications. But Parosh sensed the snow was not a barrier but instead barred from the stone and mud brick homes and packed earth lanes. There was a power in Kirkatel that forbid winter's harsh incursion.

Something was not quite wrong. Not as it should be.

Much of east Eretna seemed the same. There was a tense yet content susurration across the beylik. An anticipatory quiet. No mothers wailed, no children screeched in tantrums. The old fostered the young with memories of pleasant times. There was still gossip, there would be as long as there were men, but it was like dry snow that failed to cling and was dispersed by the lightest breath of wind. Men still cursed, but more out of habit than rancor. A patina of snow and ice coated village lanes like melted sugar and crunched like the crusts of crisp breads and sweet crackers beneath the tread of boots as neighbor visited neighbor and taverns stayed alight and echoed laughter until the winter moon passed its zenith. Contrarily, there were too few footprints cracking the lace of ice on the paths to mosque, church, and synagogue; and fewer still marring the snow that blanketed the cemeteries.

She spread her wings and leaned forward. A passing breeze lifted her from the branch and into the night air. The wind currents were unseasonably warm and gentle, cool caresses rather than bitter bites, kinder than the wintry gusts that ruled her own beylik leagues to the south. She drifted over Kirkatel, gliding low across the rooftops. She let her talons scrape and mar snowy parapets and roof ridges, grasping and releasing, as she propelled herself in a tightening circle toward the center of the perturbation.

She alighted on a ramshackle hovel, small and odd in its haphazard construction of mud brick, raw stone, and broken wood. She readied herself to spring up again in fear the roof would collapse under her weight; but despite its decrepit appearance, it was sturdy, firm and unyielding. The roof was bare of snow, as was the yard from doorway to crooked fence. Grass ringed the home and small flowers grew like a scattering of rubies, sapphires, and agates. A garden in winter? The lamia sidled across the roof. Grasping the eaves with her feet, she swung her body over the edge to hang face down and peered into the hut through the mottled single glass eye of its window.

There was darkness within, tinged only by the glow of coals slumbering in the hearth. Wan red light and still shadows bathed two intertwined forms asleep under a patchwork blanket. A goat lay at the foot of the bed chewing on the blanket's tattered edge as it slept. It twitched an ear then opened one eye. Parosh bent her knees, lifting her face from the window. She waited until starred Kesel the Hunter nodded his head toward the horizon before lowering herself again. The goat was asleep but had pulled the blanket off the foot of one of its bedmates. The foot was that of a young woman, slender and smooth, and yet... The lamia blinked and nictitating membranes slid over her eyes. Through them, she could see the ghostly outline of iridescent scales and hooked talons surrounding the human foot. She pulled herself back up to the roof and crouched.

Her sister was not dead as had been feared. She had lain with the sleeping man. The smell of sex was evident. But why did her sister stay? She gazed again at the strange town, held in spring rather than mid-winter. She started. Was her sister held as well? Was the hovel's occupant a mage who had bound her? The thought of being so constrained ignited her anger, as sudden and fierce as lightning. She leapt into the air, claws extending, her wings spreading wide.

She would kill the man.

A hand grabbed her ankle and pulled her to the roof. She gave a stifled cry and fell onto her back as a black shadow with eyes scarlet as the hearth's coals fell over her.

"You overstep your border, sister," Laila said.

The lamia snarled and made to rise, but to her surprise found she could not. That delicate semblance of a human foot rested on her chest, and it was as if it held the weight of all Creation. How? Parosh was larger, stronger, higher in the cloud of lilin who served their Lord Samael. But she let not this wonder defeat her. It was a lilin's nature to use craft and wiles where strength and power alone did not serve. She lay back, displaying her throat and palms in a gesture of submission.

"The cloud grew concerned, sister," she said. "For a moon, no Eretnan seed, breath, nor milk has been brought before Lord Samael; and neither wing nor claw nor fang seen of you."

"Was I missed, or just my tithes?"

"I... don't understand." Parosh gasped as the weight of the foot increased, pinning her to the roof. Her wings fluttered like a trapped moth's against the tiles of interwoven broken pottery, adobe, and thatch.

Then the weight eased and her strange sister spoke, "No. You wouldn't."

Hazel eyes now met obsidian. Parosh rose to a crouch but found she still could not stand; her bindings had been loosened but not released.

Laila turned and gazed skyward. The moon was near full and ringed with ghostly light, a necklace of ice crystals trapped high above Kirkatel.

"What do you know of love, sister?" Laila asked.

"Love?" The lamia smiled and moonlight glistened off her fangs. "Love is taking pleasure from others."

Laila shook her head. "Love is giving of oneself to please others."

"Giving is lessening. We are gatherers. We take, we collect."

"And then?"

"We bring all to Lord Samael."

"And he takes everything from us. How does this make you feel?"

"Feel?" Parosh frowned. "I am emptied. I need get more!"

"And yet what you take does not last. Love... love is stronger than lust. It persists when lust abates." Their eyes met again. "With love, the more you *give*, the more you have. You always feel full."

The lamia crouched in Laila's shadow, a shadow cast by the moon that silvered the outline of this strange sister who had assumed the form of their prey, who mouthed such odd words with the certainty of Lord Samael himself. Again Parosh made to rise and spread her wings, but found she could not. From where did this least among her sisters acquire such power? She spoke in the tongue they shared, but Parosh did not understand her.

"There is a wonder in love," Laila said, looking over her shoulder at the moon. Her eyes once onyx, then hazel, now glowed bright with reflected moonlight. "A wonder which Samael has taught us to deny and ridicule without ever tasting. He fears if we did, we'd be free. We'd know joy. We'd have lovers' names." She looked back at the crouching lamia and said with a rush, "Seek it, sister!"

The words struck Parosh with the force of Command, but they also seemed a plea. Words with power that did not pierce her flesh, but bathed it, then passed behind her into the night. The lamia blinked, flicking her nictitating membranes over her eyes. She narrowed them and asked, "What power does love have over our own that I should seek it?"

"Mercy," Laila answered in a whisper.

Parosh felt the weight upon her dissipate. She rose. "I will consider all you have said," she lied. Stretching her wings, she launched herself into the night.

She flew south almost to the border of her beylik of Dulkadir before arcing westward, flying faster than the wind toward Mount Ericyes and Samael.

She joined a murder of crows as they winged toward Karamano ollan, but when she smiled, they fled from her with panicked squawks and cries.

As a reward, perhaps Samael would grant her a new name.

ז

MELIS DREAMED.

Egg yolks slid between her fingers like tadpoles as she strove to mash them into the flour. She grabbed a wooden spoon and fiercely beat the inside of the bowl, raising a cloud of white dust. She stopped, breathing heavily as the cloud settled. Intact yolks slid like golden galleons over waves of flour. They came to rest, staring up at her with accusing eyes.

Reuven sat on the floor in front of an oven that was cold and bare. He sobbed quietly, his face buried in his hands.

The door to the shop banged open, so startling Melis that she dropped her spoon. A parade of customers entered, Tansu at their head, a bloom of nightshade in her hair.

Her nieces rolled Reuven onto his back. Taking their hands, Tansu stepped onto Reuven's belly before the open maw of the oven, now red-mouthed and exhaling a fierce heat. She cast one disapproving look at Melis then lowered her head and walked into the flames. Her screams were stifled by the oven's roar. Her nieces followed and were consumed with two small squeaks. The oven belched a cloud of gray ash.

Huddle urged her children forward. They sprung nimbly into the oven laughing, bouncing off Reuven's belly, thinking it a game, their laughter bursting into brief cries of pain cut short. Long tongues of flame lapped them up.

Melis coughed, covering her nose at the sickly smell of burning flesh, too reminiscent of caramelized butter. The heat in the shop was stifling. Melis' sweat-drenched hirka clung to her body, binding her.

The oven became a living thing, growing muscled arms of baked adobe. Large-knuckled stone hands grappled Esther. She fell forward, filling its throat that stretched to accommodate her like a serpent swallowing a rat.

Each villager was swallowed in turn with bursts of flame and ash until only the rabbi remained. He regarded Melis accusingly; then he lowered his head, shaking it once side-to-side, and followed the rest of his congregation into the flames.

Smoke and ash stung Melis' eyes. She blinked away black tears and... the oven was just an oven, and the room was cold and empty save for wisps of snow curling through the open shop door.

"You could have stopped this," said a familiar voice.

Reuven stood by the washbasin in his nightshift preparing for bed. With a cloth, he wiped flour and soot from his face. "You could have said something."

"I wanted to!"

"But you didn't."

He turned and looked at her. Melis stepped back, catching her breath.

Reuven's eyes were black, deep black orbs, cold wells of utter darkness save for motes of tiny flames floating like sparks above an evening fire.

"They're all gone," Samael said. "Friends, neighbors..." He paused, "... our son Joseph. All dead. All your fault."

"It's *not* my fault!"

His eyes held hers. She feared she'd fall into them as Tansu, Huddle, and fat Esther had fallen into the maw of the oven.

"Then whose fault, is it?"

His words were a sibilant purr. She shuddered and recalled the face of Bilchek's woman, her pale alabaster skin, so young and smooth, unmarred by time, eyelashes long as a fawn's, and hair as black as the dark between the stars. It was an abomination to imagine her beauty with the ugly tailor when Melis' own beauty had faded; an abomination for Laila to find joy in such a poor uncomely husband and he in her when she and Reuven now shared naught but cool acceptance.

It had been so different once.

"And could be again," Reuven-Samael said and placed his hand upon her breast.

Melis started. Reuven's hair had lost its gray, his beard was now close-cropped and neat, his belly flat and firm, his chest and arms muscled as they were in his youth.

Where had his shift gone?

Where had hers!

"Who is this Laila, this cripple's wife? Where did she come from?" he asked.

"No one knows. She's not of the village. Tansu says she's a Musselman woman." She groaned as Reuven's hands began to wander upon her. His hands were warm, feverishly hot.

"And if she is discovered by the sultan's tax-collector?"

Melis gasped, though she was uncertain if it was from the image of the villagers consumed by the holocaust of the oven or from the trembling aroused by Reuven's hands. "We'll all burn! All because of that woman."

"Woman?" He leaned forward and his breath curled around the soft hairs of her ear, caressing it before entering. "She's no daughter of Eve."

And Melis again recalled the slender form of Laila standing in slippered feet upon the uneven plank floor of Bilchek's hut. The figure shimmered, blurred, then twisted into a creature of horror: talons, claws, fangs, and bat's wings black as midnight draping her from her fox-like face to owl's feet.

"A demon!"

"A lilin," Reuven said. "The very one who took our child Joseph from us." He pushed her back upon the bed.

Melis cried even as she opened herself to receive him. "That sorceress," she sobbed as tears flowed down her cheeks. "That witch!"

"And what does the Lord command concerning witches?" Reuven asked, lowering himself upon her, filling her unlike ever before.

"*Thou shalt not suffer a witch to live!*" She cried and shuddered against him as pleasure took her.

But she was uncertain if this pleasure was from the ending of their long unshared intimacy or from anticipation of the revenge she would bring upon the disgusting cripple and his demon bride.

ח

So IT WAS THAT WHEN Bilchek opened his door one morning, he saw his neighbors gathered at his broken gate, old Rabbi Pinchas at their head looking distressed, as if he had yet to complete his morning ablutions. The crowd muttered, some pointing to the garden of violets and peonies and belled snowdrops, others to the rich growth of grass that flowed across the yard like a sultan's carpet.

The tailor smiled. "Yom tov! How may I be of service?"

Did he seem taller? Was his back straighter? Rabbi Pinchas raised a hand to hush the whisperers.

"We hear you have taken a wife, Bilchek," he said.

"This is true, Rabbi. HaShem has so blessed me."

"But you have not stood under the huppa before the community and declared her your wife." The rabbi shook his finger. "It is not good for a man to be with an unwed woman."

"'*It is not good for a man to be alone,*'" Bilchek replied. "Like Adam and Eve, my Laila and I have wed under the canopy of Heaven and declared ourselves for one another. As this sufficed for God for His first children, shall it not suffice for us all? But come, rabbi, for my neighbors and friends, I would have you marry us for *shalom*."

The rabbi looked relieved and nodded, turning to the crowd. Frowns greeted him, none deeper than that of Melis the baker's wife.

Someone called out, "*Is* she a Jew, Bilchek?"

Another added, "What have you brought upon us?"

The rabbi felt the bony finger of the widow Tansu prod his back. Discomfited, he shrugged, turned his palms upward and asked the tailor, "Is she a Jew, Bilchek?"

At that, the door to the tailor's hut opened and out stepped Laila. Gone was the ebon drape of mourning. She was gowned in a feraçe of many colors, lovingly crafted by her husband, and embroidered with birds aflight and beasts afield. A ring of goats capered along its hem, some beneath trees and others upon hills. Her yasmak veiled the lower half of her face like spider silk affixed with small stars. The crowd gaped, some in wonder, some making the sign to ward off the evil eye.

"'*Thy people shall be my people, and thy God shall be my God,* '" she said. She stood respectfully a step behind Bilchek.

Some slowly nodded, their frowns fading, but someone murmured loud enough for her neighbors to hear, "'*where thou diest will I die, and there shall I be buried.*'"

"There is concern that your woman is a Musselman's daughter, Bilchek," the rabbi said. "It would not go well with us if this be true. The Muslims forbid our marrying their women."

A voice called out, "Is she a Saracen, Bilchek? Will her people seek revenge upon us?"

Another said, "Things are finally good! Will you bring war and death upon us?"

And a third shouted, "Bilchek, she must go!"

Many nodded assent.

Bilchek took Laila's hand. "'*Her ways are ways of pleasantness, and all her paths are peace.*'"

The crowd's voices rose like squabbling crows until the rabbi raised a veined hand and they quieted. "That may be, Bilchek," he said, "but the world turns as it will, not as we desire. *Is* she a daughter of Ishmael?"

But again someone muttered just loud enough to be heard, "... or of Samael!"

"Look at the yard!" said Huddle.

"Unnatural," said Miri.

"Sorcery," said Esther, and the villagers again began to talk and argue in a cacophony of noise.

The rabbi raised his arms to quiet them, but it was like holding back a flood with an unfurled Torah scroll. People began to shout at one another.

"She's a witch! A demon!"

"Superstitious nonsense! She's just a girl!"

Laila stepped in front of Bilchek and lowered her veil.

The crowd fell silent.

Thereafter, none could agree on what they saw. Those who looked upon her with malice said she was hideous, those who viewed her with wonder said she was angelic.

Laila met the eyes of each in turn.

They had been the herd she had shepherded for Samael. Now they were her neighbors. Meeting her eyes, many felt lost, confused, recalling her visage from some past night, some past dream. The rabbi (whom she also had known as Lilith had known Adam) averted his gaze as did most of the men, but the women (her flawed competition) grew stern, feeling inexplicable rage mixed with loss, and it was one among them who cast the first stone.

Bilchek swept Laila behind him, and the stone struck him upon the brow with a crack as sharp and loud as a tree snapped by winter ice. He fell to his knees.

The rabbi cried, "Tah'ana! Stop!" and others, "Hold!" and still others, "Kill them!"

And Laila changed.

With a mournful cry, she spread her wings around Bilchek. They were like Joseph's rainbow coat to some (eliciting shame), angel's wings to others (inspiring awe), and devil's wings in the eyes of the rest who bent to raise stones of their own.

Laila flowed around Bilchek like the Ahern in summer flood, pressing her body against his, enfolding him between her arms and the shield of her wings. He collapsed inward, limbs curling fetal-like. Her lips touched his, soft, warm, and sweet. The stones fell upon them like hail.

And winter returned to Kirkatel.

ט

THE SMALL SWARD OF EARTH and patchwork hut where the crippled tailor and his demon bride once lived was shunned for its evil, or so the villagers would claim; but whether it was for the evil that once dwelt there or the evil that was inflicted upon it none would say. It was not fear but some other emotion they displayed, averting their eyes and hurrying past, when they need take the farmer's path.

The Sultan's soldiers arrived in the spring and the jizya was collected, each man of Kirkatel receiving the light slap on his cheek in token acknowledgment of the Prophet's words, yet the humiliation they felt did not abate. No war came to Kirkatel; but slowly, as is the way with all things from empires to eyils, more left the village than were there born. With them like scattered seed went the story, first told in whispers, of Bilchek and Laila. In time, only the heat and rain and snow swept the lanes and broached the shadowed doorways and open windows of Kirkatel.

At the foot of the village near where the slow Ahern curled, a swath of green grass covered the splintered wood and cracked brick of a fallen hut, and upon the grass a single cloudy eyelet of glass winked in turn at the passing sun and moon. There among the violets, peonies, and snowbells grew a juniper tree.

And people began to return to Kirkatel.

The young mostly, but also old soldiers and widows cherishing memories more than new trials. But not one stayed, for one does not take residence near, for fear of soiling, the places where wonder has touched the earth.

The juniper tree and the small swath of grass by the river became a place lovers met to make secret betrothals and pray for a love strong and lasting. And while the village is long gone, and its people dust or scattered among the Gentile Nations or, Baruch Hashem, in Eretz Yisrael, the moon still shines, the mountains still stand, the wind still blows, and the tree grows there still.

AFTERWORD: OF THE THREE KNOWN copies of the *Sefer ha-Yehudim min ha-Galut,* two end here, but one (rescued from the Nazi burning of the Rashi synagogue in Worms) contains the following hand-written script in the margins:

27 Marchesvan. I came at night upon the place the Turkamen claimed had been Kirkatel, and rested there. Snow glistened atop far Mount Ararat under the full moon, a reminder of this day and G-d's Promise. "*The earth had dried.*" Rubble was strewn in patterns hinting at the foundations of homes that once were. Betwixt moonlight and shadows I could imagine their walls and roofs, and the people who had lived within them, greeting friends, comforting children, and raising their voices in Psalms. All gone, except for the memories in stone.

At the foot of the village, I found the tree as promised. Tall, thrusting upward as if to ward against the Night, standing as a sentinel, or a memorial. The ground was uncannily warm and there was grass, soft and full for so late in the season. Perhaps a hot spring lies beneath, though the nearby stream was cool to drink. I sat to take my rest and recalled the tales of the cripple and his demon bride until I fell asleep.

Past midnight I awoke to a rustle in the tree above me, as if some night creature had alighted and stirred restlessly. Looking up, I was shocked to see a woman crouched upon a high branch, her skin pale and glowing in the moonlight. She whispered to herself, but her words carried in the still air.

"What was it like, sister? What was it like?"

She stood with a cry, unfolding leathery wings that blocked the moonlight as she leapt into the sky.

Then I fled.

About the Author

ROBERT B. FINEGOLD, MD, IS a retired radiologist residing in Maine and a multiple Writers of the Future contest Finalist. His stories of science fiction, fantasy, and Yiddishkeit have appeared in a farsheydnkayt of anthologies, magazines, and ezines since 2011.

His most recent tales recount, if with a shtickle of... okay, okay... heaping spoonfuls of embellishment, the adventures of the historical Jewish 'Pirate of the Caribbean' Moses Cohen Henriques. ("Yes, Virginia, there were Jewish pirates.")

He serves as consulting editor for the ezine *Cosmic Roots and Eldritch Shores* and assistant editor for *Future SF Digest,* and the editor of *3rd and Starlight* [Future Finalists Publishing, Nov 2017].

Links to his works and ramblings can be found at his website robertbfinegold.com and, on occasion, on Twitter (@DocHistory) and Facebook at Robert B. Finegold's Kvells and Kvetching (www.facebook. com/robertbfinegold/).

About the Story

WHY DID I WRITE THIS tale? How did it spring to life in my mind? The wellspring of my creative muse is as much a mystery to me as it is to you. Although I suspect a therapist could deconstruct the tale and shine a Klieg light into the dark recesses of my psyche if we truly wished to know, but I am not one to pry too deep and thereby deny myself the joy and experience of what is best described as "wonder." It is what I love most as a reader, and I fear to dissect it or part the veil and thereby deny myself this pleasure. I will only say that, though clinical medical scientist by training, I am also and always have been a romantic. Because I love so deeply, perhaps, and have been blessed with many years of life (and hope for many healthy more), in my experience, romance and tragedy are the two sides of the same coin. I am not alone in this observation, as the great Bard of Avon can attest. I am also, by profession as well as by curiosity, an observer of people and cultures and a lover of history — what has been recorded and, in my imagination, what has not; an explorer of the lands we know and, wistfully, of those just beyond the edges of the map. It is at the urging of my fickle muse that I, at times, set quill to paper and tell the histories that were missed by the scribes or that never were but should have been. This is not dissembling. I truly do not know, quite exactly, how this story came to my mind. However, there is a bit of Jewish folklore that perhaps explains this.

It is said that "when a student studies Torah, he is confronted with something... familiar, because he has already studied it and the knowledge was stored up in the recesses of his memory." This is because, as Rabbi Elimelekh of Lizhensk declared, "If we hadn't learned Torah before we are born, it would be impossible to grasp it now."

So why do we lose this knowledge, and who takes it from us? Up until the point of birth, all we know is in the spiritual dimension. When we are born, we must relearn it to apply it, as is our purpose, to the physical world — for the betterment of our fellows, our world, and all of Creation. Thus, an angel comes to us at the moment of birth and places a gentle fingertip on our upper lip, as if to say, "Shh!" This is why we have an indentation between the base of our nose and the border of our upper lip, the philtrum.

Mine is rather shallow, perhaps that of many writers, artists, and dreamers are.

Oh. And the name of this angel per the ancient Hebrew texts?
"Laila."